PACHINKO

ALSO BY MIN JIN LEE:

Free Food for Millionaires

PACHINKO

Min Jin Lee

GRAND CENTRAL
PUBLISHING

NEW YORK   BOSTON

Copyright © 2017 by Min Jin Lee
Cover design by Anne Twomey
Cover image by Tom Hallman
Cover copyright © 2017 by Hachette Book Group, Inc.

Grand Central Publishing
Hachette Book Group
1290 Avenue of the Americas
New York, NY 10104
grandcentralpublishing.com
twitter.com/grandcentralpub

First Edition: February 2017

Grand Central Publishing is a division of Hachette Book Group, Inc.
The Grand Central Publishing name and logo is a trademark of Hachette Book Group, Inc.

The publisher is not responsible for websites (or their content) that are not owned by the publisher.

The Hachette Speakers Bureau provides a wide range of authors for speaking events. To find out more, go to www.hachettespeakersbureau.com or call (866) 376-6591.

Library of Congress Cataloging-in-Publication Data
Names: Lee, Min Jin, author.
Title: Pachinko / Min Jin Lee.
Description: First edition. | New York : Grand Central Publishing, 2017.
Identifiers: LCCN 2016023353| ISBN 9781455563937 (hardcover) | ISBN
  9781455569496 (large print) | ISBN 9781478907121 (audio download) | ISBN
  9781478967439 (audio book) | ISBN 9781455563913 (ebook)
Subjects: LCSH: Families—Korea—Fiction. | Domestic fiction. | BISAC:
  FICTION / Literary. | FICTION / Cultural Heritage. | FICTION / Family
  Life. | FICTION / Historical.
Classification: LCC PS3612.E346 P33 2017 | DDC 813/.6—dc23 LC record available at
https://lccn.loc.gov/2016023353

ISBN: 978-1-4555-6393-7 (hardcover); 978-1-4555-6391-3 (ebook); 978-1-4789-7088-0 (signed edition); 978-1-4555-6949-6 (large print)

LSC-C

10 9 8 7 6 5 4 3 2 1

For Christopher and Sam

BOOK I

Gohyang/Hometown

1910–1933

Home is a name, a word, it is a strong one; stronger than magician ever spoke, or spirit answered to, in strongest conjuration.

—Charles Dickens

I

Yeongdo, Busan, Korea

History has failed us, but no matter.

At the turn of the century, an aging fisherman and his wife decided to take in lodgers for extra money. Both were born and raised in the fishing village of Yeongdo—a five-mile-wide islet beside the port city of Busan. In their long marriage, the wife gave birth to three sons, but only Hoonie, the eldest and the weakest one, survived. Hoonie was born with a cleft palate and a twisted foot; he was, however, endowed with hefty shoulders, a squat build, and a golden complexion. Even as a young man, he retained the mild, thoughtful temperament he'd had as a child. When Hoonie covered his misshapen mouth with his hands, something he did out of habit meeting strangers, he resembled his nice-looking father, both having the same large, smiling eyes. Inky eyebrows graced his broad forehead, perpetually tanned from outdoor work. Like his parents, Hoonie was not a nimble talker, and some made the mistake of thinking that because he could not speak quickly there was something wrong with his mind, but that was not true.

In 1910, when Hoonie was twenty-seven years old, Japan annexed Korea. The fisherman and his wife, thrifty and hardy peasants, refused to be distracted by the country's incompetent aristocrats and corrupt rulers, who had lost their nation to thieves. When the rent for their house was raised again, the couple moved out of their bedroom and slept in the anteroom near the kitchen to increase the number of lodgers.

The wooden house they had rented for over three decades was not large, just shy of five hundred square feet. Sliding paper doors divided the interior into three snug rooms, and the fisherman himself had replaced its leaky grass roof with reddish clay tiles to the benefit of his landlord, who lived in splendor in a mansion in Busan. Eventually, the kitchen was pushed out to the vegetable garden to make way for the larger cooking pots and the growing number of portable dining tables that hung on pegs along the mortared stone wall.

At his father's insistence, Hoonie learned to read and write Korean and Japanese from the village schoolmaster well enough to keep a boarding-house ledger and to do sums in his head so he couldn't be cheated at the market. When he knew how to do this, his parents pulled him out of school. As an adolescent, Hoonie worked nearly as well as a strong man twice his age with two well-shaped legs; he was dexterous with his hands and could carry heavy loads, but he could not run or walk quickly. Both Hoonie and his father were known in the village for never picking up a cup of wine. The fisherman and his wife raised their surviving son, the neighborhood cripple, to be clever and diligent, because they did not know who would care for him after they died.

If it were possible for a man and his wife to share one heart, Hoonie was this steady, beating organ. They had lost their other sons—the youngest to measles and the middle, good-for-nothing one to a goring bull in a pointless accident. Except for school and the market, the old couple kept young Hoonie close by the house, and eventually, as a young man, Hoonie needed to stay home to help his parents. They could not bear to disappoint him; yet they loved him enough not to dote on him. The peasants knew that a spoiled son did more harm to a family than a dead one, and they kept themselves from indulging him too much.

Other families in the land were not so fortunate as to have two such sensible parents, and as happens in countries being pillaged by rivals or nature, the weak—the elderly, widows and orphans—were as desperate as ever on the colonized peninsula. For any household that could feed one more, there were multitudes willing to work a full day for a bowl of barley rice.

In the spring of 1911, two weeks after Hoonie turned twenty-eight, the red-cheeked matchmaker from town called on his mother.

Hoonie's mother led the matchmaker to the kitchen; they had to speak in low tones since the boarders were sleeping in the front rooms. It was late morning, and the lodgers who'd fished through the evening had finished their hot suppers, washed up, and gone to bed. Hoonie's mother poured the matchmaker a cup of cold barley tea but didn't break from her own work.

Naturally, the mother guessed what the matchmaker wanted, but she couldn't fathom what to say. Hoonie had never asked his parents for a bride. It was unthinkable that a decent family would let their daughter marry someone with deformities, since such things were inevitable in the next generation. She had never seen her son talk to a girl; most village girls avoided the sight of him, and Hoonie would have known enough not to want something he could not have—this forbearance was something that any normal peasant would have accepted about his life and what he was allowed to desire.

The matchmaker's funny little face was puffy and pink; black flinty eyes darted intelligently, and she was careful to say only nice things. The woman licked her lips as if she was thirsty; Hoonie's mother felt the woman observing her and every detail of the house, measuring the size of the kitchen with her exacting eyes.

The matchmaker, however, would have had great difficulty in reading Hoonie's mother, a quiet woman who worked from waking until bed, doing what was needed for that day and the next. She rarely went to the market, because there was no time for distracting chatter; she sent Hoonie for the shopping. While the matchmaker talked, Hoonie's mother's mouth remained unmoving and steady, much like the heavy pine table she was cutting her radishes on.

The matchmaker brought it up first. So there was that unfortunate matter of his foot and broken lip, but Hoonie was clearly a good boy—educated and strong as a pair of oxen! She was blessed to have such a fine son, the matchmaker said. She deprecated her own children: Neither of her boys was dedicated to books or commerce, but they were not terrible boys. Her daughter married too early and lived too far away. All good marriages, the matchmaker supposed, but her sons were lazy. Not like Hoonie. After her speech, the matchmaker stared at the olive-skinned woman whose face was immobile, casting about for any sign of interest.

Hoonie's mother kept her head down, handling her sharp knife confidently—each cube of radish was square and certain. When a large mound of white radish cubes formed on the cutting board, she transferred the load in a clean swipe into a mixing bowl. She was paying such careful attention to the matchmaker's talking that privately, Hoonie's mother feared she would begin to shake from nerves.

Before stepping into the house, the matchmaker had walked around its perimeter to assess the financial condition of the household. From all appearances, the neighborhood talk of their stable situation could be confirmed. In the kitchen garden, ponytail radishes, grown fat and heavy from the early spring rain, were ready to be pulled from the brown earth. Pollack and squid strung neatly across a long clothesline dried in the lacy spring sun. Beside the outhouse, three black pigs were kept in a clean pen built from local stone and mortar. The matchmaker counted seven chickens and a rooster in the backyard. Their prosperity was more evident inside the house.

In the kitchen, stacks of rice and soup bowls rested on well-built shelves, and braids of white garlic and red chilies hung from the low kitchen rafters. In the corner, near the washbasin, there was an enormous woven basket heaped with freshly dug potatoes. The comforting aroma of barley and millet steaming in the black rice pot wafted through the small house.

Satisfied with the boardinghouse's comfortable situation in a country growing steadily poorer, the matchmaker was certain that even Hoonie could have a healthy bride, so she plowed ahead.

The girl was from the other side of the island, beyond the dense woods. Her father, a tenant farmer, was one of the many who'd lost his lease as a result of the colonial government's recent land surveys. The widower, cursed with four girls and no sons, had nothing to eat except for what was gathered from the woods, fish he couldn't sell, or the occasional charity from equally impoverished neighbors. The decent father had begged the matchmaker to find grooms for his unmarried daughters, since it was better for virgins to marry anyone than to scrounge for food when men and women were hungry, and virtue was expensive. The girl, Yangjin, was the last of the four girls and the easiest to unload because she was too young to complain, and she'd had the least to eat.

Yangjin was fifteen and mild and tender as a newborn calf, the matchmaker said. "No dowry, of course, and surely, the father could not expect much in the way of gifts. Perhaps a few laying hens, cotton cloth for Yangjin's sisters, six or seven sacks of millet to get them through the winter." Hearing no protest at the tally of gifts, the matchmaker grew bolder, "Maybe a goat. Or a small pig. The family has so little, and bride prices have come down so much. The girl wouldn't need any jewelry." The matchmaker laughed a little.

With a flick of her thick wrist, Hoonie's mother showered the radish with sea salt. The matchmaker could not have known how hard Hoonie's mother was concentrating and thinking about what the woman wanted. The mother would have given up anything to raise the bride price demanded; Hoonie's mother found herself surprised at the imaginings and hopes rising within her breast, but her face remained collected and private; nevertheless, the matchmaker was no fool.

"What I wouldn't give to have a grandson of my own one day," the matchmaker said, making her closing gambit while peering hard at the boardinghouse keeper's creased, brown face. "I have a granddaughter but no grandsons, and the girl cries too much."

The matchmaker continued. "I remember holding my first son when he was a baby. How happy I was! He was as white as a basket of fresh rice cakes on New Year's—soft and juicy as warm dough. Tasty enough to take a bite. Well, now he's just a big dolt," feeling the need to add a complaint to her bragging.

Hoonie's mother smiled, finally, because the image was almost too vivid for her. What old woman didn't yearn to hold her grandson when such a thought had been inconceivable before this visit? She clenched her teeth to calm herself and picked up the mixing bowl. She shook it to even out the salt.

"The girl has a nice face. No pockmarks. She's well mannered and obeys her father and sisters. And not too dark. She's a little thing, but she has strong hands and arms. She'll need to gain some weight, but you understand that. It's been a difficult time for the family." The matchmaker smiled at the basket of potatoes in the corner as if to suggest that here, the girl would be able to eat as much as she wanted.

Hoonie's mother rested the bowl on the counter and turned to her guest.

"I'll speak to my husband and son. There's no money for a goat or a pig. We may be able to send some cotton wool with the other things for the winter. I'll have to ask."

The bride and groom met on their wedding day, and Yangjin had not been scared by his face. Three people in her village had been born that way. She'd seen cattle and pigs with the same thing. A girl who lived near her had a strawberry-like growth between her nose and split lip, and the other children called her Strawberry, a name the girl did not mind. When Yangjin's father had told her that her husband would be like Strawberry but also with a crooked leg, she had not cried. He told her that she was a good girl.

Hoonie and Yangjin were married so quietly that if the family had not sent out mugwort cakes to the neighbors, they would have been accused of stinginess. Even the boarders were astonished when the bride appeared to serve the morning meal the day following the wedding.

When Yangjin became pregnant, she worried that her child would have Hoonie's deformities. Her first child was born with a cleft palate but had good legs. Hoonie and his parents were not upset when the midwife showed him to them. "Do you mind it?" Hoonie asked her, and she said no, because she did not. When Yangjin was alone with her firstborn, she traced her index finger around the infant's mouth and kissed it; she had never loved anyone as much as her baby. At seven weeks, he died of a fever. Her second baby had a perfect face and good legs, but he, too, died before his *baek-il* celebration from diarrhea and fever. Her sisters, still unmarried, blamed her weak milk flow and advised her to see a shaman.

Hoonie and his parents did not approve of the shaman, but she went without telling them when she was pregnant for the third time. Yet in the midst of her third pregnancy, she felt odd, and Yangjin resigned herself to the possibility that this one, too, may die. She lost her third to smallpox.

Her mother-in-law went to the herbalist and brewed her healing teas. Yangjin drank every brown drop in the cup and apologized for the great expense. After each birth, Hoonie went to the market to buy his wife choice seaweed for soup to heal her womb; after each death, he brought her sweet rice cakes still warm from the market and gave them to her: "You have to eat. You must get your strength."

Three years after the marriage, Hoonie's father died, then months after, his wife followed. Yangjin's in-laws had never denied her meals or clothing. No one had hit her or criticized her even as she failed to give them a surviving heir.

At last, Yangjin gave birth to Sunja, her fourth child and the only girl, and the child thrived; after she turned three, the parents were able to sleep through the night without checking the pallet repeatedly to see if the small form lying beside them was still breathing. Hoonie made his daughter dollies out of corn husks and forsook his tobacco to buy her sweets; the three ate each meal together even though the lodgers wanted Hoonie to eat with them. He loved his child the way his parents had loved him, but he found that he could not deny her anything. Sunja was a normal-looking girl with a quick laugh and bright, but to her father, she was a beauty, and he marveled at her perfection. Few fathers in the world treasured their daughters as much as Hoonie, who seemed to live to make his child smile.

In the winter when Sunja was thirteen years old, Hoonie died quietly from tuberculosis. At his burial, Yangjin and her daughter were inconsolable. The next morning, the young widow rose from her pallet and returned to work.

2

November 1932

The winter following Japan's invasion of Manchuria was a difficult one. Biting winds sheared through the small boardinghouse, and the women stuffed cotton in between the fabric layers of their garments. This thing called the Depression was found everywhere in the world, the lodgers said frequently during meals, repeating what they'd overheard from the men at the market who could read newspapers. Poor Americans were as hungry as the poor Russians and the poor Chinese. In the name of the Emperor, even ordinary Japanese went without. No doubt, the canny and the hardy survived that winter, but the shameful reports—of children going to bed and not waking up, girls selling their innocence for a bowl of wheat noodles, and the elderly stealing away quietly to die so the young could eat— were far too plentiful.

That said, the boarders expected their meals regularly, and an old house needed repairs. The rent had to be paid each month to the landlord's agent, who was persistent. In time, Yangjin had learned how to handle money, deal with her suppliers, and say no to terms she did not want. She hired two orphaned sisters and became an employer. She was a thirty-seven-year-old widow who ran a boardinghouse and no longer the shoeless teenager who'd arrived on its doorstep clutching a set of clean undergarments wrapped in a square bit of fabric.

Yangjin had to take care of Sunja and earn money; they were fortunate to have this business even though they didn't own the house. On the first of every month, each lodger paid twenty-three yen for room and board, and increasingly, this was not enough to buy grain at the market or coal for heat. The lodging fees couldn't go up, because the men were not making any more money, but she still had to feed them the same amount. So from shinbones, she made thick, milky broths and seasoned the garden vegetables for tasty side dishes; she stretched meals from millet and barley and the meager things they had in the larder when there was little money left at the end of the month. When there wasn't much in the grain sack, she made savory pancakes from bean flour and water. The lodgers brought her fish they couldn't sell in the market, so when there was an extra pail of crabs or mackerel, she preserved them with spices to supplement the scantier meals that were sure to come.

For the previous two seasons, six guests took turns sleeping in the one guest room: The three Chung brothers from Jeollado fished at night and slept during the day shift, and two young fellows from Daegu and a widower from Busan worked at the seaside fish market and went to sleep in the early evening. In the small room, the men slept beside each other, but none complained, because this boardinghouse was better than what they were used to back at their respective homes. The bedding was clean, and the food was filling. The girls laundered their clothing well, and the boardinghouse keeper patched up the lodgers' worn work clothes with scraps to make them last another season. None of these men could afford a wife, so for them, this setup was not half bad. A wife could have given some physical comfort to a workingman, but a marriage could beget children who would need food, clothing, and a home; a poor man's wife was prone to nagging and crying, and these men understood their limits.

The rise in prices accompanied by the shortage of money was distressing, but the lodgers were almost never late with the rent. The men who worked at the market were occasionally paid in unsold goods, and Yangjin would take a jar of cooking oil in place of a few yen on rent day. Her mother-in-law had explained that you had to be very good to the lodgers: There were always other places for workingmen to stay. She explained, "Men have choices that women don't." At the end of each season, if there were any coins left over, Yangjin dropped them into a dark earthenware crock and stowed it behind a panel in the closet where her husband had put away the two gold rings that had belonged to his mother.

At meals, Yangjin and her daughter served the food noiselessly while the lodgers talked brashly about politics. The Chung brothers were illiterate, but they followed the news carefully at the docks and liked to analyze the fate of the country at the boardinghouse dining table.

It was the middle of November, and the fishing had been better than expected for the month. The Chung brothers had just woken up. The evening-shift lodgers would soon be heading home to sleep. The fishermen brothers would eat their main meal before going out to sea. Well rested and feisty, the brothers were convinced that Japan couldn't conquer China.

"Yes, the bastards can take a nibble, but China will not be eaten whole. Impossible!" exclaimed the middle Chung brother.

"Those dwarves can't take over such a great kingdom. China is our elder brother! Japan is just a bad seed," Fatso, the youngest brother, cried, slapping down his cup of warm tea. "China will get those sons of bitches! You watch!"

The poor men mocked their powerful colonizer within the shabby walls of the boardinghouse, feeling secure from the colonial police, who wouldn't bother with fishermen with grandiose ideas. The brothers boasted of China's strengths—their hearts yearning for another nation to be strong since their own rulers had failed them. Korea had been colonized for twenty-two years already. The younger two had never lived in a Korea that wasn't ruled by Japan.

"*Ajumoni*," Fatso shouted genially. "*Ajumoni*."

"Yes?" Yangjin knew he wanted more to eat. He was a puny young man who ate more than both his brothers combined.

"Another bowl of your delicious soup?"

"Yes, yes, of course."

Yangjin retrieved it from the kitchen. Fatso slurped it down, and the men left the house for work.

The evening-shift lodgers came home soon after, washed up, and ate their suppers quickly. They smoked their pipes, then went to sleep. The women cleared the tables and ate their simple dinner quietly because the men were sleeping. The servant girls and Sunja tidied the kitchen and cleaned the dirty washbasins. Yangjin checked the coal before she prepared for bed. The brothers' talk of China lingered in her mind. Hoonie used to listen carefully to all the men who brought him news, and he would nod, exhale resolutely, and then get up to take care of the chores. "No matter," he would say, "no matter." Whether China capitulated or avenged itself, the weeds would have to be pulled from the vegetable garden, rope sandals would need to be woven if they were to have shoes, and the thieves who tried often to steal their few chickens had to be kept away.

The dampened hem of Baek Isak's woolen coat had frozen stiff, but at last Isak found the boardinghouse. The long trip from Pyongyang had exhausted him. In contrast to the snowy North, the cold in Busan was deceptive. Winter in the South appeared milder, but the frosty wind from the sea seeped into his weakened lungs and chilled him to the marrow. When he'd left home, Isak had been feeling strong enough to make the train journey, but now he felt depleted again, and he knew he had to rest. From the train station in Busan, he had found his way to the small boat that ferried him across to Yeongdo, and once off the boat, the coal man from the area had brought him to the door of the boardinghouse. Isak exhaled and knocked, ready to collapse, believing that if he could sleep well for the night, he would be better in the morning.

Yangjin had just settled onto her cotton-covered pallet when the younger servant girl tapped on the doorframe of the alcove room where all the women slept together.

"*Ajumoni*, there's a gentleman here. He wants to speak to the master of the house. Something about his brother who was here years ago. The gentleman wants to stay. Tonight," the servant girl said, breathless.

Yangjin frowned. Who would ask for Hoonie? she wondered. Next month would mark three years since his death.

On the heated floor, her daughter, Sunja, was asleep already, snoring lightly, her loose hair crimped by the braids she'd worn during the day and spread across her pillow like a shimmering rectangle of black silk. Beside her remained just enough space for the maids to turn in when they finished their work for the evening.

"Didn't you tell him that the master passed away?"

"Yes. He seemed surprised. The gentleman said his brother had written to the master but hadn't heard back."

Yangjin sat up and reached for the muslin *hanbok* that she'd just removed, which was folded in a neat pile by her pillow. She put on the quilted vest over her skirt and jacket. With a few deft movements, Yangjin put her hair into a bun.

At the sight of him, it made sense that the maid hadn't turned him away. He was formed like a young pine, straight and elegant, and he was unusually handsome: slender smiling eyes, a strong nose, and long neck. The man had a pale, unlined brow, and he looked nothing like the grizzled lodgers who yelled for their food or teased the maids for being unmarried. The young man wore a Western-style suit and a thick winter coat. The imported leather shoes, leather suitcase, and trilby were all out of place in the small entryway. From the looks of him, the man had enough money for a room downtown in a larger inn for merchants or tradespeople. Nearly all the inns of Busan where Koreans could stay were full, but for good money, it was possible to get something. He could have passed for a rich Japanese in the way he dressed. The maid stared at the gentleman with her mouth slightly agape, hoping he would be allowed to stay.

Yangjin bowed, not knowing what to say to him. No doubt, the brother had sent a letter, but she did not know how to read. Once every few months, she asked the schoolmaster in town to read her mail, but she hadn't done so this winter for lack of time.

"*Ajumoni*"—he bowed—"I hope I didn't wake you. It was dark when I got off the ferry. I didn't know about your husband until today. I am sorry to hear the sad news. I am Baek Isak. I come from Pyongyang. My brother Baek Yoseb stayed here many years ago."

His northern accent was mild, and his speech was learned.

"I'd hoped to stay here for a few weeks before going to Osaka."

Yangjin looked down at her bare feet. The guestroom was already full, and a man like this would expect his own sleeping quarters. At this time of night, to find a boatman to take him back to the mainland would be hard.

Isak withdrew a white handkerchief from his trousers and covered his mouth to cough.

"My brother was here almost ten years ago. I wonder if you remember him. He had admired your husband very much."

Yangjin nodded. The older Baek stood out in her memory because he wasn't a fisherman or someone who worked in the market. His first name was Yoseb; he'd been named after a person in the Bible. His parents were Christians and founders of a church up north.

"But your brother—that gentleman didn't look like you very much. He was short, with round metal spectacles. He was headed to Japan; he stayed for several weeks before going."

"Yes, yes." Isak's face brightened. He hadn't seen Yoseb in over a decade. "He lives in Osaka with his wife. He's the one who wrote to your husband. He insisted that I stay here. He wrote about your stewed codfish. 'Better than home,' he said."

Yangjin smiled. How could she not?

"Brother said your husband worked very hard." Isak didn't bring up the club foot or the cleft palate, though of course, Yoseb had mentioned these things in his letters. Isak had been curious to meet this man who'd overcome such difficulties.

"Have you had dinner?" Yangjin asked.

"I'm all right. Thank you."

"We could get you something to eat."

"Do you think I could rest here? I realize you were not expecting me, but I've been traveling now for two days."

"We don't have an empty room, sir. This is not a big place, you see...."

Isak sighed, then smiled at the widow. This was his burden, not hers, and he did not want her to feel bad. He looked about for his suitcase. It was near the door.

"Of course. Then I should return to Busan to find a place to stay. Before I head back, would you know of a boardinghouse around here that might have a spare room for me?" He straightened his posture, not wanting to appear discouraged.

"There's nothing around here, and we don't have an empty room," Yangjin said. If she put him with the others, he might be upset about the smell of the men. No amount of washing could remove the fish odors from their clothes.

Isak closed his eyes and nodded. He turned to leave.

"There's some extra space where all the lodgers sleep. There's only one room, you see. Three guests sleep during the day and three at night, depending on their work schedule. There's just enough space for an extra man, but it wouldn't be comfortable. You could look in if you like."

"It will be fine," Isak said, relieved. "I would be very grateful to you. I can pay you for the month."

"It might be more crowded than you are used to. There weren't as many men here when your brother stayed with us. It was not so busy then. I don't know if—"

"No, no. I would just like a corner to lie down."

"It's late, and the wind is very strong tonight." Yangjin felt embarrassed suddenly by the condition of her boardinghouse, when she had never felt this way before. If he wanted to leave the next morning, she would give him back his money, she thought.

She told him the monthly rate that had to be paid up front. If he left before the end of the month, she'd return the remainder. She charged him twenty-three yen, the same as a fisherman. Isak counted out the yen and handed them to her with both hands.

The maid put down his bag in front of the room and went to fetch a clean bedroll from the storage cabinet. He would need hot water from the kitchen to wash. The servant girl lowered her eyes but she was curious about him.

Yangjin went with the servant girl to make up the pallet, and Isak watched them quietly. Afterward, the maid brought him a water basin filled with warm water and a clean towel. The boys from Daegu slept side by side neatly, and the widower slept with his arms raised over his head. Isak's pallet was parallel to the widower's.

In the morning, the men would fuss a little about having to share the space with another lodger, but it wasn't as if Yangjin could have turned him out.

3

At dawn, the Chung brothers returned from their boat. Right away, Fatso noticed the new lodger, who remained asleep in the room.

He grinned at Yangjin. "I'm glad to see that a hardworking lady like you is so successful. The news of your great cooking has reached the rich. Next, you'll be taking in Japanese guests! I hope you charged him triple what we poor fellows pay."

Sunja shook her head at him, but he didn't notice. Fatso fingered the necktie hanging by Isak's suit.

"So is this what *yangban* wear around their necks to look important? Looks like a noose. I've never seen such a thing up close! *Waaaah*— smooth!" The youngest brother rubbed the tie against his whiskers. "Maybe this is silk. A real silk noose!" He laughed out loud, but Isak did not stir.

"Fatso-ya, don't touch that," said Gombo sternly. The eldest brother's face was covered in pockmarks, and when he was angry, his pitted skin turned red. Ever since their father had died, he had watched over his two brothers by himself.

Fatso let go of the tie and looked sheepish. He hated upsetting Gombo. The brothers bathed, ate, then all three fell asleep. The new guest continued to sleep beside them, his slumber punctuated now and then by a muffled cough.

Yangjin went to the kitchen to tell the maids to look out for the new lodger in case he woke up. They were to have a hot meal ready for him. Sunja was crouched in the corner scrubbing sweet potatoes, not looking up when her mother entered the room or when she left it. For the past week, they had been speaking only when necessary. The servant girls couldn't figure out what had happened to make Sunja so quiet.

In the late afternoon, the Chung brothers woke up, ate again, and went to the village to buy tobacco before getting on the boat. The evening lodgers had not yet returned from work, so the house was still for a couple of hours. The sea wind seeped through the porous walls and around the window edges, causing a considerable draft in the short hallway connecting the rooms.

Yangjin was seated cross-legged nearby one of the hot spots on the heated floor of the alcove room where the women slept. She was mending a pair of trousers, one of the half dozen in the pile of the guests' well-worn garments. The men's clothes were not washed often enough, since the men owned so little and didn't like to bother.

"They'll only get dirty again," Fatso would complain, though his older brothers preferred them clean. After laundering, Yangjin patched up whatever she could, and at least once a year, she'd change the collars of shirts and jackets that could no longer be repaired or cleaned. Every time the new lodger coughed, her head bobbed up. She tried to focus on her neat stitches rather than on her daughter, who was cleaning the floors of the house. Twice a day, the yellow wax-papered floors were swept with a short broom, then mopped by hand with a clean rag.

The front door of the house opened slowly, and both mother and daughter looked up from their work. Jun, the coal man, had come for his money.

Yangjin rose from the floor to meet him. Sunja bowed perfunctorily, then returned to her work.

"How is your wife?" Yangjin asked. The coal man's wife had a nervous stomach and was occasionally bedridden.

"She got up early this morning and went to the market. Can't stop that woman from making money. You know how she is," Jun said with pride.

"You're a fortunate man." Yangjin pulled out her purse to pay him for the week's coal.

"*Ajumoni*, if all my customers were like you, I'd never go hungry. You always pay when the bill is due!" He chuckled with pleasure.

Yangjin smiled at him. Every week, he complained that no one paid on time, but most people went with less food to pay him, since it was too cold this winter not to have coal. The coal man was also a portly gentleman who took a cup of tea and accepted a snack at every house on his route; he would never starve even in such lean years. His wife was the best seaweed hawker in the market and made a tidy sum of her own.

"Down the street, that dirty dog Lee-seki won't cough up what he owes—"

"Things are not easy. Everyone's having troubles."

"No, things are not easy at all, but your house is full of paying guests because you are the best cook in Kyungsangdo. The minister is staying with you now? Did you find him a bed? I told him your sea bream is the finest in Busan." Jun sniffed the air, wondering if he could grab a bite of something before his next house, but he didn't smell anything savory.

Yangjin glanced at her daughter, and Sunja stopped cleaning the floor to go to the kitchen to fix the coal man something to eat.

"But did you know, the young man had already heard of your cooking from his brother who stayed ten years ago? Ah, the belly has a better memory than the heart!"

"The minister?" Yangjin looked puzzled.

"The young fellow from the North. I met him last night, wandering around the streets looking for your house. Baek Isak. Sort of a fancy-looking fellow. I showed him your place and would have stopped in, but I had a late delivery for Cho-seki, who finally found the money to pay me after a month of dodging—"

"Oh—"

"Anyway, I told the minister about my wife's stomach troubles and how hard she works at the stall, and you know, he said he would pray for her right then and there. He just dropped his head and closed his eyes! I don't know if I believe in that mumbling that people do, but I can't see how it can hurt anyone. Very nice-looking young man, don't you think? Has he left for the day? I should say hello."

Sunja brought him a wooden tray holding a cup of hot barley tea, a teapot, and a bowl of steamed sweet potatoes and set it before him. The coal man plopped down on the floor cushion and devoured the hot potatoes. He chewed carefully, then started to speak again.

"So this morning, I asked the wife how she felt, and she said things were not so bad and went to work! Maybe there's something to that praying after all. Ha!—"

"Is he a Cath-o-lic?" Yangjin didn't mean to interrupt him so frequently, but there was no other way to speak with Jun, who could have talked for hours. For a man, her husband used to say, Jun had too many words. "A priest?"

"No, no. He's not a priest. Those fellows are different. Baek is a Protes-tant. The kind that marries. He's going to Osaka, where his brother lives. I don't remember meeting him." He continued to chew quietly and took small sips from his teacup.

Before Yangjin had a chance to say anything, Jun said, "That Hirohito-seki took over our country, stole the best land, rice, fish, and now our young people." He sighed and ate another bite of potato. "Well, I don't blame the young people for going to Japan. There's no money to be made here. It's too late for me, but if I had a son"—Jun paused, for he had no children, and it made him sad to think of it—"I'd send him to Hawaii. My wife has a smart nephew who works on a sugar plantation there. The work is hard, but so what? He doesn't work for these bastards. The other day when I went to the docks, the sons of bitches tried to tell me that I couldn't—"

Yangjin frowned at him for cursing. The house being so small, the girls in the kitchen and Sunja, who was now mopping the alcove room, could hear everything, and they were no doubt paying attention.

"May I get you more tea?"

Jun smiled and pushed his empty cup toward her with both hands.

"It's our own damn fault for losing the country. I know that," he continued. "Those goddamn aristocrat sons of bitches sold us out. Not a single *yangban* bastard has a full set of balls."

Both Yangjin and Sunja knew the girls in the kitchen were giggling at the coal man's tirade, which didn't vary from week to week.

"I may be a peasant, but I'm an honest workingman, and I wouldn't have let some Japanese take over." He pulled out a clean, white handkerchief from his coal dust–covered coat and wiped his runny nose. "Bastards. I better get on with my next delivery."

The widow asked him to wait while she went to the kitchen. At the front door, Yangjin handed Jun a fabric-tied bundle of freshly dug potatoes. One slipped out of the bundle and rolled onto the floor. He pounced on it and dropped it into his deep coat pockets. "Never lose what's valuable."

"For your wife," Yangjin said. "Please say hello."

"Thank you." Jun slipped on his shoes in haste and left the house.

Yangjin remained by the door watching him walk away, not going back inside until he stepped into the house next door.

The house felt emptier without the blustering man's lofty speeches. Sunja was crawling on her knees finishing up the hallway connecting the front room with the rest of the house. The girl had a firm body like a pale block of wood—much in the shape of her mother—with great strength in her dexterous hands, well-muscled arms, and powerful legs. Her short, wide frame was thick, built for hard work, with little delicacy in her face or limbs, but she was quite appealing physically—more handsome than pretty. In any setting, Sunja was noticed right away for her quick energy and bright manner. The lodgers never ceased trying to woo Sunja, but none had succeeded. Her dark eyes glittered like shiny river stones set in a polished white surface, and when she laughed, you couldn't help but join her. Her father, Hoonie, had doted on her from birth, and even as a small child, Sunja had seen it as her first duty to make him happy. As soon as she learned to walk, she'd tagged behind him like a loyal pet, and though she admired her mother, when her father died, Sunja changed from a joyful girl to a thoughtful young woman.

None of the Chung brothers could afford to marry, but Gombo, the eldest, had said on more than one occasion that a girl like Sunja would have made a fine wife for a man who wanted to go up in the world. Fatso admired her, but prepared himself to adore her as an elder sister-in-law, though she was only sixteen years old, the same age as he. If any of the brothers could marry, Gombo, the firstborn, would take a wife before the others. None of this mattered anymore, since recently Sunja had lost all of her prospects. She was pregnant, and the baby's father was unable to marry her. A week ago, Sunja had confessed this to her mother, but, of course, no one else knew.

"*Ajumoni, ajumoni!*" the older servant girl shrieked from the front of the house, where the lodgers slept, and Yangjin rushed to the room. Sunja dropped her rag to follow her.

"There's blood! On the pillow! And he's soaked with sweat!"

Bokhee, the older sister of the two servant girls, breathed deeply to calm herself. It wasn't like her to raise her voice, and she hadn't meant to frighten the others, but she didn't know if the lodger was dead or dying, and she was too afraid to approach him.

No one spoke for a moment, then Yangjin told the maid to leave the room and wait by the front door.

"It's tuberculosis, I think," Sunja said.

Yangjin nodded. The lodger's appearance reminded her of Hoonie's last few weeks.

"Get the pharmacist," Yangjin told Bokhee, then changed her mind. "No, no, wait. I might need you."

Isak lay asleep on the pillow, perspiring and flushed, unaware of the women staring down at him. Dokhee, the younger girl, had just come from the kitchen, and she gasped loudly, only to be hushed by her sister. When the lodger had arrived the night before, his ashen pallor was noticeable, but in the light of day, his handsome face was gray—the color of dirty rainwater collecting in a jar. His pillow was wet with numerous red pindots where he had coughed.

"*Uh-muh—*" Yangjin uttered, startled and anxious. "We have to move him immediately. The others could get sick. Dokhee-ya, take everything out of the storage room now. Hurry." She would put him in the storage room, where her husband had slept when he was ill, but it would have been far easier if he could have walked to the back part of the house rather than her attempting to move him by herself.

Yangjin pulled on the corner of the pallet in an attempt to jostle him awake.

"Pastor Baek, sir, sir!" Yangjin touched his upper arm. "Sir!"

Finally, Isak opened his eyes. He couldn't remember where he was. In his dream, he had been home, resting near the apple orchard; the trees were a riot of white blooms. When he came to, he recognized the boardinghouse keeper.

"Is everything all right?"

"Do you have tuberculosis?" Yangjin asked him. Surely, he must have known.

He shook his head.

"No, I had it two years ago. I've been well since." Isak touched his brow and felt the sweat along his hairline. He raised his head and found it heavy.

"Oh, I see," he said, seeing the red stains on the pillow. "I'm so sorry. I would not have come here if I had known that I could harm you. I should leave. I don't want to endanger you." Isak closed his eyes because he felt so tired. Throughout his life, Isak had been sickly, his most recent tuberculosis infection being just one of the many illnesses he'd suffered. His parents and his doctors had not wanted him to go to Osaka; only his brother Yoseb had felt it would be better for him, since Osaka was warmer than Pyongyang and because Yoseb knew how much Isak didn't want to be seen as an invalid, the way he had been treated for most of his life.

"I should return home," Isak said, his eyes still closed.

"You'll die on the train. You'll get worse before getting better. Can you sit up?" Yangjin asked him.

Isak pulled himself up and leaned against the cold wall. He had felt tired on the journey, but now it felt as if a bear was pushing against him. He caught his breath and turned to the wall to cough. Blood spots marked the wall.

"You will stay here. Until you get well," Yangjin said.

She and Sunja looked at each other. They had not gotten sick when Hoonie had this, but the girls, who weren't there then, and the lodgers would have to be protected somehow.

Yangjin looked at his face. "Can you walk a little to the back room? We would have to separate you from the others."

Isak tried to get up but couldn't. Yangjin nodded. She told Dokhee to fetch the pharmacist and Bokhee to return to the kitchen to get the supper ready for the lodgers.

Yangjin made him lie down on his bedroll, and she dragged the pallet slowly, sliding it toward the storage room, the same way she had moved her husband three years before.

Isak mumbled, "I didn't mean to bring you harm."

The young man cursed himself privately for his wish to see the world outside of his birthplace and for lying to himself that he was well enough to go to Osaka when he had sensed that he could never be cured of being so sickly. If he infected any of the people he had come into contact with, their death would be on his head. If he was supposed to die, he hoped to die swiftly to spare the innocent.

4

June 1932

At the very beginning of summer, less than six months before the young pastor arrived at the boardinghouse and fell ill, Sunja met the new fish broker, Koh Hansu.

There was a cool edge to the marine air on the morning Sunja went to the market to shop for the boardinghouse. Ever since she was an infant strapped to her mother's back, she had gone to the open-air market in Nampo-dong; then later, as a little girl, she'd held her father's hand as he shuffled there, taking almost an hour each way because of his crooked foot. The errand was more enjoyable with him than with her mother, because everyone in the village greeted her father along the way so warmly. Hoonie's misshapen mouth and awkward steps seemingly vanished in the presence of the neighbors' kind inquiries about the family, the boardinghouse, and the lodgers. Hoonie never said much, but it was obvious to his daughter, even then, that many sought his quiet approval—the thoughtful gaze from his honest eyes.

After Hoonie died, Sunja was put in charge of shopping for the boardinghouse. Her shopping route didn't vary from what she had been taught by her mother and father: first, the fresh produce, next, the soup bones from the butcher, then a few items from the market *ajumma*s squatting beside spice-filled basins, deep rows of glittering cutlass fish, or plump sea bream caught hours earlier—their wares arrayed attractively on turquoise and red waxed cloths spread on the ground. The vast market for seafood—one of the largest of its kind in Korea—stretched across the rocky beach carpeted with pebbles and broken bits of stone, and the *ajumma*s hawked as loudly as they could, each from her square patch of tarp.

Sunja was buying seaweed from the coal man's wife, who sold the best quality. The *ajumma* noticed that the new fish broker was staring at the boardinghouse girl.

"Shameless man. How he stares! He's almost old enough to be your father!" The seaweed *ajumma* rolled her eyes. "Just because a man's rich doesn't give him the right to be so brazen with a nice girl from a good family."

Sunja looked up and saw the new man in the light-colored Western suit and white leather shoes. He was standing by the corrugated-tin and wood offices with all the other seafood brokers. Wearing an off-white Panama hat like the actors in the movie posters, Koh Hansu stood out like an elegant bird with milky-white plumage among the other men, who were wearing dark clothes. He was looking hard at her, barely paying attention to the men speaking around him. The brokers at the market controlled the wholesale purchases of all the fish that went through there. Not only did they have the power to set the prices, they could punish any boat captain or fisherman by refusing to buy his catch; they also dealt with the Japanese officials who controlled the docks. Everyone deferred to the brokers, and few felt comfortable around them. The brokers rarely mixed socially outside their group. The lodgers at the boardinghouse spoke of them as arrogant interlopers who made all the profits from fishing but kept the fish smell off their smooth white hands. Regardless, the fishermen had to stay on good terms with these men who had ready cash for purchases and the needed advance when the catch wasn't any good.

"A girl like you is bound to be noticed by some fancy man, but this one seems too sharp. He's a Jeju native but lives in Osaka. I hear he can speak perfect Japanese. My husband said he was smarter than all of them put together, but crafty. *Uh-muh*! He's still looking at you!" The seaweed *ajumma* flushed red straight down to her collarbone.

Sunja shook her head, not wanting to check. When the lodgers flirted with her, she ignored them and did her work, and she would behave no differently now. The *ajumma*s at the market tended to exaggerate, anyway.

"May I have the seaweed that my mother likes?" Sunja feigned interest in the oblong piles of dried seaweed, folded like fabric, separated in rows of varying quality and price.

Remembering herself, the *ajumma* blinked, then wrapped a large portion of seaweed for Sunja. The girl counted out the coins, then accepted the parcel with two hands.

"Your mother is taking care of how many lodgers now?"

"Six." From the corner of her eye, Sunja could see that the man was now talking to another broker, but still looking in her direction. "She's very busy."

"Of course she is! Sunja-ya, a woman's life is endless work and suffering. There is suffering and then more suffering. It's better to expect it, you know. You're becoming a woman now, so you should be told this. For a woman, the man you marry will determine the quality of your life completely. A good man is a decent life, and a bad man is a cursed life—but no matter what, always expect suffering, and just keep working hard. No one will take care of a poor woman—just ourselves."

Mrs. Jun patted her perpetually bloated stomach and turned to the new customer, allowing Sunja to return home.

At dinner, the Chung brothers mentioned Koh Hansu, who had just bought their entire catch.

"For a broker, he's okay," Gombo said. "I prefer a smart one like him who doesn't suffer fools. Koh doesn't haggle. It's one price, and he's fair enough. I don't think he's trying to screw you like the others, but you can't refuse him."

Fatso then added that the ice broker had told him that the fish broker from Jeju was supposed to be unimaginably rich. He came into Busan only three nights a week and lived in Osaka and Seoul. Everyone called him Boss.

Koh Hansu seemed to be everywhere. Whenever she was in the market, he would turn up, not concealing his interest. Although she tried to overlook his stares and go about her errands, her face felt hot in his presence.

A week later, he spoke to her. Sunja had just finished her shopping and was walking alone on the road toward the ferry.

"Young miss, what are you cooking for dinner at the boardinghouse tonight?"

They were alone, but not far from the bustle of the market.

She looked up, then walked away briskly without answering. Her heart was pounding in fear, and she hoped he wasn't following her. On the ferry ride, she tried to recall what his voice had sounded like; it was the voice of a strong person who was trying to sound gentle. There was also the slightest Jeju lilt to his speech, a lengthening of certain vowels; it was different from how Busan people talked. He pronounced the word "dinner" in a funny way, and it had taken her a moment to figure out what he was saying.

The next day, Hansu caught up with her as she headed home.

"Why aren't you married? You're old enough."

Sunja quickened her steps and left him again. He did not follow.

Though she had not replied, Hansu didn't stop trying to talk to her. It was one question always, never more than that and never repeated, but when he saw her, and if Sunja was within hearing distance, he'd say something, and she'd hurry away without saying a word.

Hansu wasn't put off by her lack of replies; if she had tried to keep up a banter, he would have thought her common. He liked the look of her—glossy braided hair, a full bosom bound beneath her white, starched blouse, its long sash tied neatly, and her quick, sure-footed steps. Her young hands showed work; they were not the soft, knowing hands of a teahouse girl or the thin, pale hands of a highborn one. Her pleasant body was compact and rounded—her upper arms sheathed in her long white sleeves appeared pillowy and comforting. The hidden privacy of her body stirred him; he craved to see her skin. Neither a rich man's daughter nor a poor man's, the girl had something distinct in her bearing, a kind of purposefulness. Hansu had learned who she was and where she lived. Her shopping habits were the same each day. In the morning, she came to the market and left immediately afterward without dawdling. He knew that in time, they would meet.

It was the second week of June. Sunja had finished her shopping for the day and was going home carrying a loaded basket on the crook of each arm. Three Japanese high school students with their uniform jackets unbuttoned were heading to the harbor to go fishing. Too hot to sit still, the boys were skipping school. When they noticed Sunja, who was going in the direction of the Yeongdo ferry, the giggling boys surrounded her, and a skinny, pale student, the tallest of the three, plucked one of the long yellow melons out of her basket. He tossed it over Sunja's head to his friends.

"Give that back," Sunja said in Korean calmly, hoping they weren't getting on the ferry. These sorts of incidents happened often on the mainland, but there were fewer Japanese in Yeongdo. Sunja knew that it was important to get away from trouble quickly. Japanese students teased Korean kids, and occasionally, vice versa. Small Korean children were warned never to walk alone, but Sunja was sixteen and a strong girl. She assumed that the Japanese boys must have mistaken her for someone younger, and she tried to sound more authoritative.

"What? What did she say?" they snickered in Japanese. "We don't understand you, you smelly slut."

Sunja looked around, but no one seemed to be watching them. The boatman by the ferry was busy talking to two other men, and the *ajummas* near the outer perimeter of the market were occupied with work.

"Give it back now," she said in a steady voice, and stretched out her right hand. Her basket was lodged in the crook of her elbow, and it was getting harder to keep her balance. She looked directly at the skinny boy, who stood a head taller than her.

They laughed and continued to mutter in Japanese, and Sunja couldn't understand them. Two of the boys tossed the yellow melon back and forth while the third rummaged through the basket on her left arm, which she was now afraid to put down.

The boys were about her age or younger, but they were fit and full of unpredictable energy.

The third boy, the shortest, pulled out the oxtails from the bottom of the basket.

"*Yobo*s eat dogs and now they're stealing the food of dogs! Do girls like you eat bones? You stupid bitch."

Sunja swiped at the air, trying to get the soup bones back. The only word she understood for certain was *yobo*, which normally meant "dear" but was also a derogatory epithet used by the Japanese to describe Koreans.

The short boy held up a bone, then sniffed it. He made a face.

"Disgusting! How do these *yobo*s eat this shit?"

"Hey, that's expensive! Put that back!" Sunja shouted, unable to keep from crying.

"What? I don't understand you, you stupid Korean. Why can't you speak Japanese? All of the Emperor's loyal subjects are supposed to know how to speak Japanese! Aren't you a loyal subject?"

The tall one ignored the others. He was gauging the size of Sunja's breasts.

"The *yobo* has really big tits. Japanese girls are delicate, not like these breeders."

Afraid, Sunja decided to forget the groceries and start walking, but the boys crowded her and wouldn't let her pass.

"Let's squeeze her melons." The tall one grabbed her left breast with his right hand. "Very nice and full of juice. You want a bite?" He opened his mouth wide close to her breasts.

The short one held on to her light basket firmly so she couldn't move, then twisted her right nipple using his index finger and thumb.

The third boy suggested, "Let's take her somewhere and see what's beneath this long skirt. Forget fishing! She can be our catch."

The tall one thrust his pelvis in her direction. "How much do you want to have a taste of my eel?"

"Let me go. I'm going to scream," she said, but it felt like her throat was closing up. Then she saw the man standing behind the tallest boy.

Hansu grabbed the short hairs on the back of the boy's head with one hand and clamped the boy's mouth with his free hand. "Come closer," he hissed at the others, and to their credit, they did not abandon their friend, whose eyes were wide open in terror.

"You sons of bitches should die," he said in perfect Japanese slang. "If you ever bother this lady again or ever show your ugly faces near this area, I will have you killed. I will have you and your families murdered by the finest Japanese killers I know, and no one will ever know how you died. Your parents were losers in Japan, and that's why you had to settle here. Don't get any dumb ideas about how much better you are than these people." Hansu was smiling as he was saying this. "I can kill you now, and no one would do a thing, but that's too easy. When I decide, I can have you caught, tortured, then killed. Today, I am giving you a warning because I'm gracious, and we are in front of a young lady."

The two boys remained silent, watching their friend's eyes bulge. The man in the ivory-colored suit and white leather shoes pulled the boy's hair harder and harder. The boy didn't even try to scream, because he could feel the terrifying power of the man's unyielding force.

The man spoke exactly like a Japanese, but the boys figured that he had to be Korean from his actions. They didn't know who he was, but they didn't doubt his threats.

"Apologize, you pieces of shit," Hansu said to the boys.

"We're very sorry." They bowed formally to her.

She stared at them, not knowing what to do.

They bowed again, and Hansu released his grip on the boy's hair just slightly.

Hansu turned to Sunja and smiled.

"They said they are sorry. In Japanese, of course. Would you like them to apologize also in Korean? I can have them do that. I can have them write you a letter if you like."

Sunja shook her head. The tall boy was now crying.

"Would you like me to throw them into the sea?"

He was joking, but she couldn't smile. Sunja managed to shake her head again. The boys could have dragged her somewhere, and no one would have seen them go. Why wasn't Koh Hansu afraid of the boys' parents? A Japanese student could get a grown Korean man in trouble for certain, she thought. Why wasn't he worried? Sunja started to cry.

"It's all right," Hansu said to her in a low voice and let the tall boy go.

The boys put the melon and the bones back in the baskets.

"We are very sorry," they said, bowing deeply.

"Never ever come around here again. Do you understand, you shit-for-brains?" Hansu said in Japanese, smiling genially to make sure that Sunja did not understand his meaning.

The boys bowed again. The tall one had peed a little in his uniform. They walked in the direction of the town.

Sunja put the baskets down on the ground and sobbed. Her forearms felt like they were going to fall off. Hansu patted her shoulder gently.

"You live in Yeongdo."

She nodded.

"Your mother owns the boardinghouse."

"Yes, sir."

"I'm going to take you home."

She shook her head.

"I've troubled you enough. I can go home by myself." Sunja couldn't raise her head.

"Listen, you have to be careful not to travel alone or ever be out at night. If you go to the market by yourself, you must stay on the main paths. Always in public view. They are looking for girls now."

She didn't understand.

"The colonial government. To take to China for the soldiers. Don't follow anyone. It will likely be some Korean person, a woman or a man, who'll tell you there's a good job in China or Japan. It may be someone you know. Be careful, and I don't mean just those stupid boys. They're just bad kids. But even those boys could hurt you if you are not cautious. Do you understand?"

Sunja wasn't looking for a job, and she didn't understand why he was telling her any of this. No one had ever approached her about working away from home. She would never leave her mother, anyway, but he was right. It was always possible for a woman to be disgraced. Noblewomen supposedly hid silver knives in their blouses to protect themselves or to commit suicide if they were dishonored.

Hansu gave her a handkerchief, and she wiped her face.

"You should go home. Your mother will worry."

Hansu walked her to the ferry. Sunja rested her baskets on the floor of the ferryboat and sat down. There were only two other passengers.

Sunja bowed. Koh Hansu was watching her again, but this time his face was different from before; he looked concerned. As the boat moved away from the dock, she realized that she had not thanked him.

5

As Koh Hansu was putting her on the ferry, Sunja had the opportunity to observe him up close without distractions. She could even smell the mentholated pomade in his neatly combed black hair. Hansu had the broad shoulders and the thick, strong torso of a larger man; his legs were not very long, but he was not short, either. Hansu was perhaps the same age as her mother, who was thirty-six. His tawny brow was creased lightly, and faded brown spots and freckles had settled on his sharp cheekbones. His nose—narrow, with a bump below a high bridge—made him look somewhat Japanese, and small, broken capillaries lay beneath the skin around his nostrils. More black than brown, his dark eyes absorbed light like a long tunnel, and when he looked at her, she felt an uncomfortable sensation in her stomach. Hansu's Western-style suit was elegant and well cared for; unlike the lodgers, he didn't give off an odor from his labors or the sea.

On the following market day, she spotted him standing in front of the brokers' offices with a crowd of businessmen and waited until he could see her. She bowed to him. Hansu nodded ever so slightly, then returned to his work. Sunja went to finish her shopping, and as she walked to the ferry, he caught up with her.

"Do you have some time?" he asked.

She widened her eyes. What did he mean?

"To talk."

Sunja had been around men all her life. She had never been afraid of them or awkward in their presence, but around him, she didn't have the words she needed. It was difficult for her to stand near him even. Sunja swallowed and decided that she would speak to him no differently than to the lodgers; she was sixteen years old, not a scared child.

"Thank you for your help the other day."

"It's nothing."

"I should have said this earlier. Thank you."

"I want to talk to you. Not here."

"Where?" She should have asked why, she realized.

"I'll come to the beach behind your house. Near the large black rocks where the tide is low. You do the wash there by the cove." He wanted her to know that he knew a little about her life. "Can you come alone?"

Sunja looked down at her shopping baskets. She didn't know what to tell him, but she wanted to speak with him some more. Her mother would never allow it, however.

"Can you get away tomorrow morning? Around this time?"

"I don't know."

"Is afternoon better?"

"After the men leave for the day, I think," she found herself saying, her voice trailing off.

He was waiting for her by the black rocks, reading a newspaper. The sea was bluer than she had remembered, and the long, thin clouds seemed paler—everything seemed more vibrant with him here. The corners of his newspaper fluttered with the breeze, and he grasped them firmly, but when he saw her approaching, he folded the paper and put it under his arm. He didn't move toward her, but let her come to him. She continued to walk steadily, a large wrapped bundle of dirty clothes balanced on her head.

"Sir," she said, trying not to sound afraid. She couldn't bow, so she put her hands around the bundle to remove it, but Hansu quickly reached over to lift the load from her head, and she straightened her back as he laid the wash on the dry rocks.

"Sir, thank you."

"You should call me *Oppa*. You don't have a brother, and I don't have a sister. You can be mine."

Sunja said nothing.

"This is nice." Hansu's eyes searched the cluster of low waves in the middle of the sea and settled on the horizon. "It's not as beautiful as Jeju, but it has a similar feeling. You and I are from islands. One day, you'll understand that people from islands are different. We have more freedom."

She liked his voice—it was a masculine, knowing voice with a trace of melancholy.

"You'll probably spend your entire life here."

"Yes," she said. "This is my home."

"Home," he said thoughtfully. "My father was an orange farmer in Jeju. My father and I moved to Osaka when I was twelve; I don't think of Jeju as my home. My mother died when I was very young." He didn't tell her then that she looked like someone on his mother's side of the family. It was the eyes and the open brow.

"That's a great deal of laundry. I used to do laundry for my father and me. I hated it. One of the greatest things about being rich is having someone else wash your clothes and cook your meals."

Sunja had washed clothes almost since she could walk. She didn't mind doing laundry at all. Ironing was more difficult.

"What do you think about when you do the laundry?"

Hansu already knew what there was to know about the girl, but that was different from knowing her thoughts. It was his way to ask many questions when he wanted to know someone's mind. Most people told you their thoughts in words and later confirmed them in actions. There were more people who told the truth than those who lied. Very few people lied well. What was most disappointing to him was when a person turned out to be no different than the next. He preferred clever women over dumb ones and hardworking women over lazy ones who knew only how to lie on their backs.

"When I was a boy, my father and I each owned only one suit of clothes, so when I washed our things, we would try to have them dry overnight and wore them still damp in the morning. Once—I think I was ten or eleven—I put the wet clothes near the stove to speed up the drying, and I went to cook our supper. We were having barley gruel, and I had to stir it in this cheap pot, otherwise the bottom would burn right away, and as I was stirring, I smelled something awful, and it turned out that I had burned a large hole in my father's jacket sleeve. I was scolded for that severely." Hansu laughed at the memory of the thrashing he got from his father. "A head like an empty gourd! A worthless idiot for a son!" His father, who had drunk all his earnings, had never blamed himself for being unable to support them and had been hard on his son, who was keeping them alive through foraging, hunting, and petty theft.

Sunja had not imagined that a person like Koh Hansu could do his own laundry. His clothes were so fine and beautifully tailored. She had already seen him wear several different white suits and white shoes. No one dressed like he did.

She had something to say.

"When I wash clothes, I think about doing it well. It's one of the chores I like because I can make something better than it was. It isn't like a broken pot that you have to throw away."

He smiled at her. "I have wanted to be with you for a long time."

Again, she wanted to ask why, but it didn't matter in a way.

"You have a good face," he said. "You look honest."

The market women had told her this before. Sunja could not haggle well and didn't try. However, this morning she hadn't told her mother that she was meeting Koh Hansu. She had not even told her about the Japanese students picking on her. The night before, she told Dokhee, who did the laundry with her, that she'd do the wash herself, and Dokhee had been overjoyed to get out of the task.

"Do you have a sweetheart?" he asked.

Her cheeks flushed. "No."

Hansu smiled. "You are almost seventeen. I'm thirty-four. I am exactly twice your age. I am going to be your elder brother and your friend. Hansu-oppa. Would you like that?"

Sunja stared at his black eyes, thinking that she had never wanted anything more except for the time she'd wanted her father to recover from his illness. There wasn't a day when she didn't think of her father or hear his voice in her head.

"When do you do your wash?"

"Every third day."

"This time?"

She nodded. Sunja breathed deeply, her lungs and heart filling with anticipation and wonder. She had always loved this beach—the unending expanse of pale green and blue water, the tiny white pebbles framing the black rocks between the water and the rocky soil. The silence here made her safe and content. Almost no one ever came here, but now she would never see this place the same way again.

Hansu picked up a smooth, flat stone by her foot—black with thin gray striations. From his pocket, he took out a piece of white chalk that he used to mark the wholesale containers of fish, and he made an X on the bottom of the stone. He crouched and felt about the enormous rocks that surrounded them and found a dry crevice in a medium-sized rock, the height of a bench.

"If I come here and you're not here yet, but I have to go back to work, I'll leave this stone in the hollow of this rock so you'll know that I came. If you're here and I'm not, I want you to leave this stone in the same spot, so I can know that you came to see me."

He patted her arm and smiled at her.

"Sunja-ya, I better go now. Let's see each other later, okay?"

She watched him walk away, and as soon as he was gone, she squatted and opened the bundle to begin the wash. She took a dirty shirt and soaked it in the cool water. Everything had changed.

Three days later, she saw him. It took nothing to convince the sisters to let her do the wash by herself. Again, he was waiting by the rocks, reading the paper. He wore a light-colored hat with a black hatband. He looked elegant. He acted as if meeting her by the rocks was normal, though Sunja was terrified that they might be discovered. She felt guilty that she had not told her mother, or Bokhee and Dokhee, about him. Seated on the black

rocks, Hansu and Sunja spoke for half an hour or so, and he asked her
odd questions: "What do you think about when it's quiet and you're not
doing much?"

There was never a time when she wasn't doing anything. The
boardinghouse required so much work; Sunja could hardly remember her
mother ever being idle. After she told him she was always busy, she realized she was wrong. There were times when she was working when it
felt like the work was nothing at all, because it was something she knew
how to do without paying much attention. She could peel potatoes or
wipe down the floors without thinking, and when she had this quiet in her
mind, lately, she had been thinking of him, but how could she say this?
Right before he had to go, he asked her what she thought a good friend
was, and she answered he was, because he had helped her when she was
in trouble. He had smiled at that answer and stroked her hair. Every few
days, they saw each other at the cove, and Sunja grew more efficient with
the wash and housework, so that no one at home noticed how she spent
her time at the beach or at the market.

Before Sunja crossed the threshold of the kitchen door to leave the
house for the market or the beach, she would check her reflection on the
polished metal pot lid, primping the tight braid she'd made that morning.
Sunja had no idea how to make herself lovely or appealing to any man,
and certainly not a man as important as Koh Hansu, so she endeavored to
be clean and tidy at the least.

The more she saw him, the more vivid he grew in her mind. His stories
filled her head with people and places she had never imagined before. He
lived in Osaka—a large port city in Japan where he said you could get anything you wanted if you had money and where almost every house had
electric lights and plug-in heaters to keep you warm in the winter. He said
Tokyo was far busier than Seoul—with more people, shops, restaurants,
and theaters. He had been to Manchuria and Pyongyang. He described
each place to her and told her that one day she would go with him to these
places, but she couldn't understand how that would ever happen. She
didn't protest, because she liked the idea of traveling with him, the idea of
being with him longer than the few minutes they had at the cove. From his

travels, he brought her beautifully colored candies and sweet biscuits. He would unwrap the candies and put one in her mouth like a mother feeding a child. She had never tasted such lovely and delicious treats—pink hard candies imported from America, butter biscuits from England. Sunja was careful to throw away the wrappers outside the house, because she didn't want her mother to know about them.

She was enraptured by his talk and his experiences, which were far more unique than the adventures of fishermen or workers who had come from far-flung places, but there was something even more new and powerful in her relationship with Hansu that she had never expected. Until she met him, Sunja had never had someone to tell about her life—the funny habits of the lodgers, her exchanges with the sisters who worked for her mother, memories of her father, and her private questions. She had someone to ask about how things worked outside of Yeongdo and Busan. Hansu was eager to hear about what went on in her day; he wanted to know what she dreamed about even. Occasionally, when she didn't know how to handle something or someone, he told her what she could do; he had excellent ideas on how to solve problems. They never spoke of Sunja's mother.

At the market, it was strange to see him doing business, for he was this other person when he was with her—he was her friend, her elder brother, the one who'd lift the bundle of laundry from her head when she came to him. "How gracefully you do that," he would remark, admiring how straight and strong her neck was. Once, he touched the nape of her neck lightly with both his thick, square hands, and she sprang from his touch, shocked by the sensation she felt.

She wanted to see him all the time. Who else did he talk to or ask questions of? What did he do in the evening when she was at home serving the lodgers, polishing the low dining tables, or sleeping beside her mother? It felt impossible to ask him, so she kept those questions to herself.

For three months, they met in the same way, growing easier in each other's company. When fall arrived, it was brisk and cold by the sea, but Sunja hardly felt the chilly air.

Early September, it rained for five days straight, and when it finally cleared, Yangjin asked Sunja to gather mushrooms at Taejongdae Forest the following morning. Sunja liked mushroom picking, and as she was about to meet Hansu at the beach, she felt giddy that she could tell him she was going to do something different from her regular chores. He traveled and saw new things often; this was the first time she was doing something out of her normal routine.

In her excitement, she blurted out her plans to pick mushrooms right after breakfast the next day, and Hansu said nothing for a few moments and stared at her pensively.

"Your Hansu-*oppa* is good at finding mushrooms and wild roots. I know a lot about the ones you can eat and the ones you can't. When I was a boy, I spent hours searching for roots and mushrooms. In the spring, I'd look for fernbrake and dry them. I used to catch rabbits for our dinner with a slingshot. Once, I caught a pair of pheasants before dusk—it was the first time we had meat in a long time. My father was so delighted!" His face softened.

"We can go together. How much time do you have to get the mushrooms?" he asked.

"You want to go?"

It was one thing to talk to him twice a week for half an hour, but she couldn't imagine spending a day with him. What would happen if someone saw them together? Sunja's face felt hot. What was she supposed to do? She had told him, and she couldn't keep him from going.

"I'll meet you here. I better go back to the market." Hansu smiled at her differently this time, like he was a boy, excitement beaming from his face. "We'll find a huge bundle of mushrooms. I know it."

They walked along the outer perimeter of the island, where no one would see them together. The coastline seemed more glorious than it had ever been. As they approached the forest located on the opposite side of the island, the enormous pines, maples, and firs seemed to greet them, decked in golds and reds as if they were wearing their holiday clothes. Hansu told her about living in Osaka. The Japanese were not to be vilified, he said. At this moment in time, they were beating the Koreans, and of course, no one liked losing. He believed that if the Koreans could stop quarreling with each other, they could probably take over Japan and do much worse things to the Japanese instead.

"People are rotten everywhere you go. They're no good. You want to see a very bad man? Make an ordinary man successful beyond his imagination. Let's see how good he is when he can do whatever he wants."

Sunja nodded as he spoke, trying to remember his every word, to hold on to his every image, and to grasp whatever he was trying to tell her. She treasured his stories like the beach glass and rose-colored stones she used to collect as a girl—his words astonished her because he was taking her by the hand and showing her new, unforgettable things.

Of course, there were many subjects and ideas she didn't understand, and sometimes just trying to learn it all without experiencing it was difficult. Yet she crammed her mind the way she might have overfilled a pig intestine with blood sausage stuffing. She tried hard to figure things out because she didn't want him to think she was ignorant. Sunja didn't know her letters in either Korean or Japanese. Her father had taught her some addition and subtraction so she could count money, but that was all. Both she and her mother could not even write their names.

Hansu had brought a large kerchief so he could gather mushrooms as well. His obvious delight at their excursion made her feel better, but Sunja was still worried that someone would see them. No one knew they were friends. Men and women were not supposed to be that, and they were not sweethearts, either. He had never mentioned marriage, and if he wanted to marry her, he would have to speak to her mother, but he had not. In fact, after he asked her if she had a sweetheart three months before, he'd never raised the subject again. She tried not to think about what his life was like with women. It would not have been difficult for him to find a girl to be with, and his interest in her did not always make sense.

The long walk to the forest felt brief, and when they entered the woods, it felt even more isolated than the cove, but unlike the openness of the low rocks and the expanse of blue-green water, immense trees stood high above them, and it was like entering the dark, leafy house of a giant. She could hear birds, and she looked up and about to see what kind they were. She noticed Hansu's face: There were tears in his eyes.

"*Oppa*, are you all right?"

He nodded. He had talked for the entire length of the walk about traveling and work, yet at the sight of the colored leaves and bumpy tree trunks, Hansu fell silent. He placed his right hand on her back and touched the end of her hair braid. He stroked her back, then removed his hand carefully.

Hansu had not been in a forest since he was a boy—that time before he became a tough teenager who could hustle and steal with the wisest street kids of Osaka. Before he moved to Japan, the wooded mountains of Jeju had been his sanctuary; he had known every tree on the volcano Halla-san. He recalled the small deer with their slender legs and mincing, flirtatious steps. The heavy scent of orange blossoms came back to him, though there were no such things in the woods of Yeongdo.

"Let's go," he said, walking ahead, and Sunja followed him. Less than a dozen paces in, he stopped to pluck a mushroom gently from the ground. "That's our first," he said, no longer crying.

He had not lied to her. Hansu was an expert at finding mushrooms, and he found numerous edible weeds for her, even explaining how to cook them.

"When you're hungry, you'll learn what you can eat and what you cannot." He laughed. "I don't like being hungry. So, where's your spot? Which way?"

"A few minutes from here—it's where my mother used to pick them after a heavy rain when she was a girl. She's from this side of the island."

"Your basket is not large enough. You could have brought two and had plenty to dry for the winter! You might have to return tomorrow!"

Sunja smiled at him. "But, *Oppa*, you haven't even seen the spot!"

When they reached her mother's mushroom spot, it was carpeted with the brown mushrooms that her father had adored.

He laughed, as pleased as he could be. "Didn't I tell you? We should have brought something to make supper with. Next time, let's plan to have lunch here. This is too easy!" Immediately, he began to gather mushrooms by the handful and threw them into the basket on the ground between them. When it grew full, he put more into his handkerchief, and when that was heaping, she untied the apron around her waist and gathered more.

"I don't know how I will carry them all," she said. "I'm being greedy."

"You are not greedy enough."

Hansu moved toward her. She could smell his soap and the wintergreen of his hair wax. He was cleanly shaven and handsome. She loved how white his clothes were. Why did such a thing matter? The men at the boardinghouse could not help being filthy. Their work dirtied all their things, and no amount of scrubbing would get the fish smell off their shirts and pants. Her father had taught her not to judge people on such shallow points: What a man wore or owned had nothing to do with his heart and character. She inhaled deeply, his scent mingled with the cleansing air of the forest.

Hansu slid his hands beneath her short traditional blouse, and she did not stop him. He untied the long sash that held her blouse together and opened it. Sunja started to cry quietly, and he pulled her toward him and held her, making low, soothing sounds, and she allowed him to comfort her as he did what he wanted. He lowered her on the ground tenderly.

"*Oppa* is here. It's all right. It's all right."

He had his hands firmly under her buttocks the entire time, and though he had tried to shield her from the twigs and leaves, bits of the forest had made red welts on the backs of her legs. When they separated, he used his handkerchief to clean the blood.

"Your body is pretty. Full of juice like a ripened fruit."

Sunja couldn't say anything. She had suckled him like an infant. While he was moving inside her, doing this thing that she had witnessed pigs and horses doing, she was stunned by how sharp and bright the pain was and was grateful that the ache subsided.

When they rose from the carpet of yellow and red leaves, he helped to straighten her undergarments, and he dressed her.

"You are my dear girl."

This was what he told her when they did this again.

6

Hansu had gone to Japan for business. He promised there would be a surprise for her when he returned. Sunja thought it would only be a matter of time before he would speak to her of marriage. She belonged to him, and she wanted to be his wife. She didn't want to leave her mother, but if she had to move to Osaka to be with him, she would go. Throughout the day, she wondered what he was doing at that moment. When she imagined his life away from her, she felt like she was part of something else, something outside of Yeongdo, outside of Busan, and now outside of Korea even. How was it possible that she had lived without knowing anything else beyond her father and mother? Yet that was all she had known. It was right for a girl to marry and bear children, and when she didn't menstruate, Sunja was pleased that she would give him a child.

She counted the days until his return, and if there had been a clock in the house, she would have measured the hours and minutes. On the morning of his return, Sunja hurried to the market. She walked by the brokers' offices until he spotted her, and in his discreet way, he set a meeting time at the cove for the following morning.

As soon as the lodgers left for work, Sunja gathered the laundry and ran to the beach, unable to wait any longer. When she saw her sweetheart waiting beside the rocks, wearing a handsome overcoat over his suit, she felt proud that a man like this had chosen her.

Unlike the other times, when she would approach him in careful, lady-like steps, today she rushed to him impatiently with the bundle of laundry clutched in her arms.

"*Oppa*! You're back!"

"I told you—I always return." He embraced her tightly.

"I'm so happy to see you."

"How is my girl?"

She beamed in his presence.

"I hope you won't go away again too soon."

"Close your eyes," he said, and she obeyed him.

He opened her right hand and placed a thick disc in her palm. The metal felt cool in her hand.

"It's just like yours," she said, opening her eyes. Hansu had a heavy gold pocket watch from England. Similarly sized, hers was made of silver with a gold wash, he said. A while back, he'd taught her the difference between the long hand and the short and how to tell time. His watch hung from a solid gold chain with a T-bar that went through his vest buttonhole.

"You press this." Hansu pushed the crown and the pocket watch opened to reveal an elegant white face with curved numerals.

"This is the most beautiful thing I have ever seen. *Oppa*, thank you. Thank you so much. Where did you get it?" She could not imagine a store where they'd sell such things.

"If you have money, there's nothing you can't have. I had it ordered for you from London. Now we can know exactly when we will meet."

She couldn't imagine being happier than she was at that moment.

Hansu stroked her face and pulled her toward him.

"I want to see you."

She lowered her gaze and opened her blouse. The night before, she had bathed in hot water, scrubbing every pore of her body until her skin was red.

He took the watch from her hand and looped the thin sash of her slip through its hook.

"I'll order a proper chain and pin the next time I am in Osaka."

He pushed down her inner slip to expose her breasts and put his mouth over her. He opened her long skirt.

Her shock at the urgency of his needs had diminished somewhat since the first time they made love. They had been together many times, and by now, the pain was not as great as it had been for her initially. What Sunja liked about lovemaking was the gentle touching as well as the powerful desires of his body. She liked how his face changed from grave to innocent in those moments.

When it ended, she closed her blouse. In a few moments, he would have to return to work and she would wash the boardinghouse linens.

"I am carrying your child."

He opened his eyes and paused.

"Are you certain?"

"Yes, I think so."

"Well." He smiled.

She smiled in return, feeling proud of what they had done together.

"Sunja—"

"*Oppa*?" She studied his serious face.

"I have a wife and three children. In Osaka."

Sunja opened her mouth, then closed it. She could not imagine him being with someone else.

"I will take good care of you, but I cannot marry you. My marriage is already registered in Japan. There are work implications," he said, frowning. "I will do whatever I can to make sure we are together. I had been planning on finding a good house for you."

"A house?"

"Near your mother. Or if you want, it can be in Busan. It'll be winter soon, and we can't keep meeting outside." He laughed. He rubbed her upper arms, and she flinched.

"Is that why you went to Osaka? To see your—"

"I have been married since I was a boy nearly. I have three daughters," Hansu said. His girls were neither terribly clever nor interested in much of anything, but they were sweet and simple. One was pretty enough to marry, and the others were too skinny like their nervous mother, who looked fragile and perpetually bothered.

"Maybe it's a son you're carrying!" He couldn't help but smile at the thought. "How do you feel? Is there anything you feel like eating?" He pulled out his wallet and withdrew a stack of yen bills. "You should buy whatever you want to eat. Also, you'll need more fabric for clothing for yourself and for the child."

She stared at the money but didn't reach for it. Her hands hung by her side. He sounded increasingly excited.

"Do you feel different?" He put his hands on her stomach and laughed with delight.

Hansu's wife, who was two years older than he was, hadn't been pregnant in years; they rarely made love. As recently as a year ago, when he had a string of mistresses, none had even missed a period, so he hadn't given much thought to Sunja having a child. Hansu had planned on getting Sunja a small house before winter, but now he'd find something much larger. The girl was young and obviously fertile, so he realized they could have more children. He felt happy at the prospect of having a woman and children in Korea. He was no longer a young man, but his desires for lovemaking had not declined with age. While he'd been away, he'd masturbated thinking about her. Hansu did not believe that man was designed to have sex with only one woman; marriage was unnatural to him, but he would never abandon a woman who had borne him children. He thought a man may need a number of women, but he found that he preferred this one girl. He loved the sturdiness of Sunja's body, the fullness of her bosom and hips. Her soft face comforted him, and he had come to depend on her innocence and adoration. After being with her, Hansu felt like there was little he couldn't do. It was true after all: Being with a young girl made a man feel like a boy again. He pressed the money into Sunja's hand, but she let the bills drop and scatter on the beach. Hansu bent down to pick them up.

"What are you doing?" He raised his voice a little.

Sunja looked away from him. He was saying something, but she couldn't hear what it was. It was as if her mind would no longer interpret his words with meaning. His talk was just sounds, beats of noise. Nothing made sense. He had a wife and three daughters in Japan? Since she had met him, he had been straightforward, she supposed. Every promise he'd ever made had been kept. He said there would be a surprise, and he had brought a watch for her, but the surprise she had for him, she no longer wanted him to know. Nothing about him had ever made her suspect that he was a *jebi*—a kind of man who could flit from one woman to another. Did he make love to his wife, too? What did she know about men, anyway?

What was the wife like? Sunja wanted to know. Was she beautiful? Was she kind? Sunja could not look at his face anymore. She glanced at her white muslin skirt, its tattered hem remaining gray no matter how much she tried to clean it.

"Sunja, when can I go to speak to your mother? Should we go speak to her now? Does she know about the baby?"

It felt like a slap when he mentioned her mother.

"My mother?"

"Yes, have you told her?"

"No. No, I have not told her." Sunja tried not to think of her mother.

"I will buy that boardinghouse for you, and your mother and you won't have to keep lodgers anymore. You could just take care of the child. We could have more children. You could get a much bigger house if you like."

The bundle of laundry by her foot seemed to glow in the sun. There was work to do for the day. She was a foolish peasant girl who'd let a man take her on the grounds of a forest. When he had wanted her in the open air of the beach, she had let him have her body as much as he liked. But she had believed that he loved her as she loved him. If he did not marry her, she was a common slut who would be disgraced forever. The child would be another no-name bastard. Her mother's boardinghouse would be contaminated by her shame. There was a baby inside her belly, and this child would not have a real father like the one she'd had.

"I will never see you again," she said.

"What?" Hansu smiled in disbelief. He put his arms on her shoulders, and she shrugged him off.

"If you ever come near me again, I will kill myself. I may have behaved like a whore—" Sunja couldn't speak anymore. She could see her father so clearly: his beautiful eyes, broken lip, his hunched and delayed gait.

When he finished his long day's work, he would carve her dolls out of dried corncobs and branches. If there was a brass coin left in his pocket, he'd buy her a piece of taffy. It was better that he was dead so he would not see what a filthy creature she had become. He had taught her to respect herself, and she had not. She had betrayed her mother and father, who had done nothing but work hard and take care of her like a jewel.

"Sunja, my dear child. What is upsetting you? Nothing has changed." Hansu was confused. "I will take excellent care of you and the baby. There is money and time for another family. I will honor my obligations. My love for you is very strong; it is stronger than I had ever expected. I don't say this lightly, but if I could, I would marry you. You are someone I would marry. You and I, we are alike. Our child will be deeply loved, but I cannot forget my wife and three girls—"

"You never told me about them. You made me think—"

Hansu shook his head. The girl had never opposed him before; he had never heard a contrary word from her lips.

"I will not see you again," she said

He tried to hold her, and Sunja shouted, "Get away from me, you son of a bitch! I want to have nothing to do with you."

Hansu stopped and looked at her, needing to reevaluate the girl standing in front of him. The fire in her body had never been expressed in words, and now he knew she could be different.

"You don't care about me. Not really." Sunja felt clear suddenly. She expected him to treat her the way her own parents had treated her. She felt certain her father and mother would have preferred her to have any honest job than to be a rich man's mistress. "And what will you do if the child is a girl? Or what if she is born like my father? With a mangled foot and no upper lip?"

"Is that why you have not married?" Hansu furrowed his brow.

Sunja's mother had never pushed the idea of marriage when many girls in her village had married well before her. No one had come to her mother with proposals, and the lodgers who flirted with her were not serious prospects. Perhaps this was why, Sunja wondered. Now that she was pregnant, it dawned on her that she could give birth to a child who had her father's deformities. Every year, she cleaned the graves of her siblings; her mother had told her that several had been born with cleft palates. He was expecting a healthy son, but how about if she couldn't produce one? Would he discard them?

"Were you trying to get me to marry you? Because you couldn't marry a normal fellow?"

Even Hansu realized the cruelty of his own words.

Sunja grabbed her bundle and ran home.

7

Pharmacist Chu had grown fond of the pastor from Pyongyang and was pleased to see his recovery. He visited Isak only once a week now, and the young man seemed completely well.

"You're too healthy to be in bed," the pharmacist said. "But don't get up just yet." Chu was seated beside Isak, who was lying flat on a bedroll in the storage closet. The draft from the gaps around the windowsill lifted Chu's white forelocks slightly. He placed the thick quilt over Isak's shoulders. "You're warm enough?"

"Yes. I'm indebted to you and *ajumoni*."

"You still look too thin." Chu frowned. "I want to see you stout. There's no curve to your face. Don't you like the food here?"

The boardinghouse keeper looked as if she'd been scolded.

"The meals have been wonderful," Isak protested. "I'm eating far more than what I pay in board. The food here is better than at home." Isak smiled at Yangjin and Sunja, who were standing in the hallway.

Chu leaned in to Isak's chest, where he had placed the bell of his stethoscope. The breathing sounded strong and even, similar to the week before. The pastor seemed very fit.

"Make a coughing sound."

Chu listened thoughtfully to the timbre of the pastor's chest. "You've improved for certain, but you've been ill most of your life. And you had tuberculosis before. We need to be vigilant."

"Yes, but I feel strong now. Sir, I'd like to write to my church in Osaka to let them know my travel dates. That is, if you think I can travel. My brother made me promise that I'd get your permission first." Isak closed his eyes as if in prayer.

"Before you left Pyongyang, did your doctor think you could travel all the way to Osaka by yourself?"

"I was told that I could travel, but the doctor and my mother didn't encourage my leaving home. But I was the strongest I'd ever been when I left. But of course, since being here like this—no doubt, I should've listened to them. It's just that the church in Osaka wanted me to come."

"Your doctor told you not to go, but you went anyway." Chu laughed. "Young men can't be locked up, I suppose. So now you want to head out again, and this time you want my permission. How would it look if something happened to you on the way, or if you got sick when you got there?" Chu shook his head and sighed. "What can I say? I cannot stop you, but I think you should wait."

"How long?"

"At least two more weeks. Maybe three."

Isak glanced up at Yangjin and Sunja. He was embarrassed.

"I feel terrible that I've burdened you and put you at risk. Thank God no one has gotten sick. I'm so sorry. For everything."

Yangjin shook her head. The pastor had been a model guest; if anything, the other lodgers had improved their behavior in the proximity of such a well-mannered person. He had paid his bills on time. She was relieved that his health had improved so dramatically.

Chu put away his stethoscope.

"I'm in no rush for you to return home, however. The weather here is better for your lungs compared to the North, and the weather in Osaka will be similar to the weather here. The winters are not as severe in Japan," Chu said.

Isak nodded. The climate had been a major consideration for his parents' consent for Isak to go to Osaka.

"Then, may I write the church in Osaka? And my brother?"

"You'll take the boat to Shimonoseki and then the train?" Chu asked, making a face. The journey would take a day, two at the most with delays.

Isak nodded, relieved that the pharmacist was signaling that he could leave.

"Have you been going out?"

"Not beyond the yard. You'd said that it wasn't a good idea."

"Well, you can now. You should take a good walk or two every day— each one longer than the one before it. You need to strengthen your legs. You're young, but you've been in bed and in the house for almost three months." The pharmacist turned to Yangjin. "See if he can make it as far as the market. He shouldn't go alone obviously. He could fall." Chu patted Isak on the shoulder before going and promised to return the following week.

The next morning, Isak finished his Bible study and prayers, then ate his breakfast in the front room by himself. The lodgers had already gone out for the day. He felt strong enough to go to Osaka, and he wanted to make preparations to leave. Before heading out to Japan, he had wanted to visit the pastor of a church in Busan, but there had been no chance for that. He hadn't contacted him for fear that he'd stop by and get sick. Isak's legs felt okay, not wobbly as before. In his room, he had been doing light cal- isthenics that his eldest brother, Samoel, had taught him when he was a boy. Having spent most of his life indoors, he'd had to learn how to keep fit in less obvious ways.

Yangjin came to clear his breakfast tray. She brought him barley tea, and he thanked her.

"I think I'd like to take a walk. I can go by myself," he said, smiling. "It wouldn't be for long. I feel very well this morning. I won't go far."

Yangjin couldn't keep her face blank. She couldn't keep him cooped up like a prized rooster in her henhouse, but what would happen if he fell? The area near her house was desolate. If he walked by the beach and had an accident, no one would see him.

"I don't think you should go by yourself, sir." The lodgers were at work or in town doing things she didn't want to know about. There was no one to ask to accompany him at the moment.

Isak bit his lip. If he didn't strengthen his legs, the journey would be delayed.

"It would be a big imposition." He paused. "You have a great deal of work, but perhaps you can take me for just a short while." It was outrageous to ask a woman to walk with him on the beach, but Isak felt he'd go insane if he didn't walk outside today. "If you cannot go, I understand. I will take a very short walk near the water. For a few minutes."

As a boy, he had lived the life of a privileged invalid. Tutors and servants had been his primary companions. When it was good weather and he wasn't well enough to walk, the servants or his elder brothers used to carry him on their backs. If the doctor wanted him to get air, the blade-thin gardener would put Isak in an A-frame and stroll through the orchard, letting the child pull off the apples from the lower branches. Isak could almost smell the heady perfume of the apples, feel the weight of the red fruit in his hands and taste the sweet crunch of the first bite, its pale juice running down his wrist. He missed home, and he felt like a sick child again, stuck in his room, begging for permission to see the sunlight.

Yangjin was seated on her knees with her small, coarse hands folded in her lap, not knowing what to say. It was not appropriate for a woman to walk with a man who wasn't a member of her family. She was older than he was, so she didn't fear any gossip, but Yangjin had never walked alongside a man who wasn't her father or husband.

He peered into her troubled face. He felt awful for making another imposition.

"You've already done so much, and I'm asking for more."

Yangjin straightened her back. She'd never gone on a leisurely walk on the beach with her husband. Hoonie's legs and back had given him profound pain throughout his brief life—he had not complained of it, but he would conserve his energies for the work he had to get done. How much he must have wanted to run as a normal boy, swallow lungfuls of salty air and chase the seagulls—things nearly every child in Yeongdo had done growing up.

"There is something very selfish in me," he said. "I'm sorry." Isak decided to wait until one of the lodgers could take him out.

Yangjin got up. "You'll need your coat," she said. "I'll get it."

The heavy scent of seaweed, the foamy lather of the waves along the rocky beach, and the emptiness of the blue-and-gray landscape but for the white circling birds above them—the sensations were almost too much to bear after being in that tiny room for so long. The morning sun warmed Isak's uncovered head. He had never been drunk on wine, but he imagined that this was how the farmers must have felt dancing during *Chuseok* after too many cups.

On the beach, Isak carried his leather shoes in his hands. He walked steadily, not feeling any trace of illness within his tall, gaunt frame. He didn't feel strong, but he felt better than he'd been.

"Thank you," he said, without looking in her direction. His pale face shone in the morning light. He closed his eyes and inhaled deeply.

Yangjin glanced at the smiling young man. He possessed an innocence, she supposed, a kind of childlike wholeness that couldn't be hidden. She wanted to protect him.

"You have been so kind."

She dismissed this with a wave, not knowing what to do with his gratitude. Yangjin was miserable. She had no time for this walk, and being outside made the dull weight in her heart take a definable shape; it pressed against her from the inside.

"May I ask you something?"

"Hmm?"

"Is your daughter all right?"

Yangjin didn't answer. As they were walking toward the other end of the beach, she'd been feeling as if she were somewhere else, though she couldn't say where exactly. This place didn't feel like the beach behind her house, just a few paces from her backyard. Being with the young pastor was disorienting, yet his unexpected question broke the gauzy spell. What had he noticed for him to ask about Sunja? Soon, her rising belly would be obvious, but she didn't look very different now. What would the pastor think of this? Did it matter?

"She's pregnant." She said this, and she knew it would be okay to tell him.

"It must be difficult for her with her husband being away."

"She doesn't have a husband."

It wouldn't have been unusual for him to think that the child's father worked in Japan in a mine or a factory.

"Is the man...?"

"She won't say anything." Sunja had told her that the man was already married and had children. Yangjin didn't know anything else. She couldn't tell the pastor, however; it was too shameful.

The woman looked hopeless. The lodgers brought Isak newspapers to read aloud for them, and lately, every story was a sad one. He felt an overwhelming sense of brokenness in the people. The country had been under the colonial government for over two decades, and no one could see an end in sight. It felt like everyone had given up.

"These things happen in all families."

"I don't know what will happen to her. Her life is ruined. It would have been difficult for her to marry before, but now..."

He didn't understand.

"My husband's condition. People don't want that in the bloodline."

"I see."

"It's a difficult thing to be an unmarried woman, but to bear a child without a husband— The neighbors will never approve. And what will happen to this baby who has no name? He cannot be registered under our family name." She had never talked so freely to a stranger. Yangjin continued to walk, but her pace slowed.

Since learning the news, she had tried to think of any possible way to make this easier, but could not come up with anything. Her unmarried sisters couldn't help her, and their father had died long ago. She had no brothers.

Isak was surprised, but not so much. He had seen this before at his home church. You saw all sorts of things in a church where forgiveness was expected.

"The father of the child—he's nowhere to be found?"

"I don't know. She won't speak of him. I haven't told anyone except for you. I know it's your job to counsel people, but we aren't Christians. I'm sorry."

"You saved my life. I would have died if you had not taken me in and nursed me. You've gone far beyond what an innkeeper does for his guest."

"My husband died of this thing. You're a young man. You should live a long life."

They continued to walk, and Yangjin did not seem interested in turning around. She stared at the light green–colored water. She felt like sitting down; she was so tired suddenly.

"Can she know that I know? May I speak with her?"

"You're not shocked?"

"Of course not. Sunja seems like a very responsible young woman; there must be some reason for this. *Ajumoni*, this must feel very terrible now, but a child is a gift from God."

There was no change in Yangjin's sad expression.

"*Ajumoni*, do you believe in God?"

She shook her head no. "My husband said Christians were not bad people. Some were patriots who fought for independence. Right?"

"Yes, my teachers at the seminary in Pyongyang fought for independence. My oldest brother died in 1919."

"Are you political, too?" She looked concerned; Hoonie had told her that they should avoid housing activists because it would be dangerous. "Like your brother?"

"My brother Samoel was a pastor. He led me to Christ. My brother was a brilliant man. Fearless and kind."

Yangjin nodded. Hoonie had wanted independence for Korea, but he believed that a man had to care for his family first.

"My husband didn't want us to follow anyone—not Jesus, not Buddha, not an emperor or even a Korean leader."

"I understand. I do."

"So many terrible things are happening here."

"God controls all things, but we don't understand his reasons. Sometimes, I don't like his actions, either. It's frustrating."

Yangjin shrugged.

"And we know that God causes all things to work together for good to those who love God, to those who are called according to his purpose," Isak said, reciting a favorite verse, but he could see that Yangjin was unmoved, and it occurred to him that she and her daughter could not love God if they did not know him.

"I am sorry that you are suffering. I'm not a parent, but I think parents hurt with their children."

The boardinghouse keeper was lost in her sadness.

"I'm glad you had a chance to walk a little today," she said.

"If you don't believe, I understand," he said.

"Does your family observe *jesa*?"

"No." Isak smiled. No one in his family observed the rituals for the dead. The Protestants he knew didn't, either.

"My husband thought it was unnecessary. He told me so, but I still make his favorite foods and prepare a shrine for him. I do it for his parents and my own. His parents thought it was important. They were very good to me. I clean their graves and the ones for all my dead babies. I talk to the dead although I don't believe in ghosts. But it makes me feel good to speak with them. Maybe that is what God is. A good God wouldn't have let my babies die. I can't believe in that. My babies did nothing wrong."

"I agree. They did nothing wrong." He looked at her thoughtfully. "But a God that did everything we thought was right and good wouldn't be the creator of the universe. He would be our puppet. He wouldn't be God. There's more to everything than we can know."

Yangjin said nothing but felt strangely calmer.

"If Sunja will talk to you, perhaps it can help. I don't know how, but maybe it might."

"I will ask her to walk with me tomorrow."

Yangjin turned back, and Isak walked beside her.

8

After Isak finished the letter to his brother, he rose from the low table and opened the narrow window in the front room. Isak pulled the crisp air deep into his lungs. His chest didn't hurt. Throughout his life, everyone around him had talked about his early death as a certainty. He had been sick as an infant and throughout his youth with serious ailments in his chest, heart, and stomach. Consequently, little had been expected of his future. When Isak graduated from seminary, even he had been surprised that he was alive to see such a day. Oddly enough, all the talk of his inevitable death hadn't discouraged him. He had become almost inured to death; his frailty had reinforced his conviction that he must do something of consequence while he had the time.

His brother Samoel, the eldest son, was never ill, but he had died young. He had been beaten badly by the colonial police after a protest and did not survive the arrest. Isak decided then that he would live a braver life. He had spent his youth indoors with his family and tutors, and the healthiest he had ever been was when he attended seminary while working as a lay pastor for his church back home. While alive, Samoel had been a shining light at the seminary and their home church, and Isak believed that his deceased brother was carrying him now, no different than how he had done so physically when Isak was a boy.

The middle Baek brother, Yoseb, wasn't religious like Samoel or Isak. He had never liked school, and at the first opportunity, he had struck out for Japan in search of a different life. He had taught himself to be a machinist and now worked as a foreman of a factory in Osaka. He had sent for Kyunghee, the beloved daughter of a family friend, and they were married in Japan. They didn't have any children. It had been Yoseb's idea for Isak to come to Osaka, and he had found him the job at the church. Isak felt certain that Yoseb would understand his decision to ask Sunja to marry him. Yoseb was an open-minded person with a generous nature. Isak addressed the envelope and put on his coat.

He picked up his tea tray and brought it to the threshold of the kitchen. He had been reminded numerous times that there was no need for him to bring his tray to the kitchen, where men were not supposed to enter, but Isak wanted to do something for the women, who were always working. Near the stove, Sunja was peeling radishes. She was wearing her white muslin *hanbok* beneath a dark quilted vest. She looked even younger than her age, and he thought she looked lovely as she focused on her task. He couldn't tell if she was pregnant in her full-bodied *chima*. It was hard to imagine a woman's body changing. He had never been with a woman.

Sunja rushed to get his tray.

"Here, please let me take that."

He handed the tray to her and opened his mouth to say something but wasn't sure how.

She looked at him. "Do you need something, sir?"

"I was hoping to go into town today. To see someone."

Sunja nodded like she understood.

"Mr. Jun, the coal man, is down the street and will be headed to town. Do you want me to ask him to take you?"

Isak smiled. He had been planning on asking her to accompany him, but he lost his courage suddenly. "Yes. If Mr. Jun's schedule permits it. Thank you."

Sunja rushed outside to get him.

The church building had been repurposed from an abandoned wood-frame schoolhouse. It was located behind the post office. The coal man pointed it out to him and promised to take him back to the boardinghouse later.

"I have to run some errands. And I'll mail your letter."

"Do you know Pastor Shin? Would you like to meet him?"

Jun laughed. "I've been to a church once. That was plenty."

Jun didn't like going to places that asked for money. He didn't like monks who collected alms, either. As far as he was concerned, the whole religion thing was a racket for overeducated men who didn't want to do real work. The young pastor from Pyongyang didn't seem lazy, and he had never asked Jun for anything, so he was fine enough. That said, Jun liked the idea of having someone pray for him.

"Thank you for bringing me here."

"It's nothing. Don't be mad because I don't want to be a Christian. You see, Pastor Baek, I'm not a good man, but I'm not a bad one, either."

"Mr. Jun, you're a very good man. It was you who led me to the boardinghouse on the night when I was lost. I was so dizzy that evening, I could barely say my own name. You've done nothing but help me."

The coal man grinned. He wasn't used to being complimented.

"Well, if you say so." He laughed again. "When you're done, I'll be waiting for you across the street at the dumpling stand by the post office. I'll meet you over there after I finish with my errands."

The servant of the church was wearing a patched men's overcoat that was far too large for her tiny body. She was a deaf-mute, and she swayed gently while sweeping the chapel floor. At the vibration of Isak's step, she stopped what she was doing with a jolt and turned. Her worn-down broom grazed her stocking feet, and she clutched on to its handle in surprise. She said something, but Isak couldn't make out what she was saying.

"Hello, I'm here to see Pastor Shin." He smiled at her.

The servant scampered to the rear of the church, and Pastor Shin came out of his office at once. He was in his early fifties. Thick glasses covered his deep-set brown eyes. His hair was still black and he kept it short. His white shirt and gray trousers were well pressed. Everything about him seemed controlled and restrained.

"Welcome." Pastor Shin smiled at the nice-looking young man in the Western-style suit. "What may I do for you?"

"My name is Baek Isak. My teachers at the seminary have written to you, I think."

"Pastor Baek! You're finally here! I thought you'd be here months ago. I'm so pleased to see you. Come, my study is in the back. It's a bit warmer there." He asked the servant to bring them tea.

"How long have you been in Busan? We've been wondering when you'd stop by. You're headed to our sister church in Osaka?"

There was hardly any chance to reply to all his questions. The elder pastor spoke rapidly without pausing to hear Isak's reply. Pastor Shin had attended the seminary in Pyongyang near the time of its founding, and he was delighted to see a recent graduate. Friends who had been at the seminary with him had been Isak's professors.

"Do you have a place to stay? We could fix a room for you here. Where are your things?" Shin felt gleeful. It had been a long time since they'd had a new pastor stop by. Many of the Western missionaries had left the country due to the colonial government's crackdown, and fewer young men were joining the ministry. Lately, Shin had been feeling lonesome. "I hope you will stay awhile."

Isak smiled.

"I apologize for not calling on you sooner. I'd intended to come by, but I was very ill, and I've been recuperating at a boardinghouse in Yeongdo. The widow of Kim Hoonie and her daughter have been taking care of me. The boardinghouse is closer to the beach than the ferry. Do you know them?"

Pastor Shin cocked his head.

"No, I don't know many people on Yeongdo Island. I shall come see you there soon. You look well. A bit thin, but everyone is not eating enough lately, it seems. Have you eaten? We have food to share."

"I've eaten already, sir. Thank you."

When the tea was brought in, the men held hands and prayed, giving thanks for Isak's safe arrival.

"You're preparing to go to Osaka soon?"

"Yes."

"Good, good."

The elder pastor spoke at length about the troubles the churches had been facing. More people were afraid to attend services here and in Japan because the government didn't approve. The Canadian missionaries had already left.

Although Isak knew of these sad developments, he felt ready to face the trials. His professors had discussed the government's opposition with him. Isak grew quiet.

"Are you all right?" Shin asked.

"Sir, I was wondering if we could talk. Talk about the Book of Hosea."

"Oh? Of course." Pastor Shin looked puzzled.

"God makes the prophet Hosea marry a harlot and raise children he didn't father. I suppose the Lord does this to teach the prophet what it feels like to be wedded to a people who continually betray him. Isn't that right?" Isak asked.

"Well, yes, among other things. And the prophet Hosea obeys the Lord's request," Pastor Shin said in his sonorous voice. This was a story he had preached on before.

"The Lord continues to be committed to us even when we sin. He continues to love us. In some ways, the nature of his love for us resembles an enduring marriage, or how a father or mother may love a misbegotten child. Hosea was being called to be like God when he had to love a person who would have been difficult to love. We are difficult to love when we sin; a sin is always a transgression against the Lord." Shin looked carefully at Isak's face to see if he had reached him.

Isak nodded gravely. "Do you think it's important for us to feel what God feels?"

"Yes, of course. If you love anyone, you cannot help but share his suffering. If we love our Lord, not just admire him or fear him or want things from him, we must recognize his feelings; he must be in anguish over our sins. We must understand this anguish. The Lord suffers with us. He suffers like us. It is a consolation to know this. To know that we are not in fact alone in our suffering."

"Sir, the boardinghouse widow and her daughter saved my life. I reached their doorstep with tuberculosis, and they cared for me for three months."

Pastor Shin nodded with recognition.

"That is a wonderful thing they did. A noble and kind work."

"Sir, the daughter is pregnant, and she has been abandoned by the father of the child. She is unmarried and the child will not have a name."

Shin looked concerned.

"I think I should ask her to marry me, and if she says yes, I will take her to Japan as my wife. If she says yes, I would ask you to marry us before we go. I would be honored if—"

Pastor Shin covered his own mouth with his right hand. Christians did such things—sacrificed possessions and their own lives even—but such choices had to be made for good reason and soberly. St. Paul and St. John had said, "Test everything."

"Have you written to your parents about this?"

"No. But I think they would understand. I've refused to marry before, and they had not expected me to do so. Perhaps they will be pleased."

"Why have you refused to marry before?"

"I've been an invalid since I was born. I have been improving the past few years, but I got sick again on the journey here. No one in my family expected me to live past twenty-five. I am twenty-six now." Isak smiled. "If I'd married and had children, I would have made a woman a young widow and perhaps left orphans behind me."

"Yes, I see."

"I should have been dead by now, but I am alive, sir."

"I'm very glad of it. Praise God." Shin smiled at the young man, not knowing how to protect him from his wish to make such a grand sacrifice. More than anything, he was incredulous. If it hadn't been for the warm letters from his friends in Pyongyang attesting to Isak's intelligence and competence, Shin would have thought that Isak was a religious lunatic.

"What does the young woman think of this idea?"

"I don't know. I have yet to speak with her. The widow told me about her daughter only yesterday. And last night before my evening prayers, it occurred to me that this is what I can do for them: Give the woman and child my name. What is my name to me? It's only a matter of grace that I was born a male who could enter my descendants in a family registry.

If the young woman was abandoned by a scoundrel, it's hardly her fault, and certainly, even if the man is not a bad person, the unborn child is innocent. Why should he suffer so? He would be ostracized."

Shin was unable to disagree.

"If the Lord allows me to live, I shall try to be a good husband to Sunja and a good father to this child."

"Sunja?"

"Yes. She's the boardinghouse keeper's daughter."

"Your faith is good, son, and your intentions are right, but—"

"Every child should be wanted; the women and men in the Bible prayed patiently for children. To be barren was to be an outcast, isn't that right? If I do not marry and have children, I would be a kind of barren man." Isak had never articulated this thought before, and this surge of wanting a wife and family felt strange and good to him.

Shin smiled weakly at the young minister. After losing four of his children and his wife to cholera five years ago, Shin found that he could not speak much about loss. Everything a person said sounded glib and foolish. He had never understood suffering in this way, not really, until he had lost them. What he had learned about God and theology had become more graphic and personal after his family had died so gruesomely. His faith had not wavered, but his temperament had altered seemingly forever. It was as if a warm room had gotten cooler, but it was still the same room. Shin admired this idealist seated before him, his young eyes shining with faith, but as his elder, he wanted Isak to take care.

"Yesterday morning, I had begun the study of Hosea, and then a few hours later, the boardinghouse *ajumoni* told me about her pregnant daughter. By evening, I knew. The Lord was speaking to me. This has never happened to me before. I've never felt that kind of clarity." Isak felt it was safe to admit this here. "Has that ever happened to you?" He checked for doubt in the elder pastor's eyes.

"Yes, it has happened to me, but not always so vividly. I hear the voice of God when I read the Bible, so yes, I suppose I understand what you felt, but there are coincidences, too. We have to be open to that. It's dangerous to think that everything is a sign from God. Perhaps God is always talking to us, but we don't know how to listen," Shin stated. It felt awkward to confess this uncertainty, but he thought it was important.

"When I was growing up, I can remember at least three unmarried girls who were abandoned after becoming pregnant. One was a maid in our house. Two of the girls killed themselves. The maid in our house returned to her family in Wonsan and told everyone that her husband had died. My mother, a woman who never lies, had told her to say this," Isak said.

"This sort of thing happens with greater frequency these days," Shin said. "Especially in difficult times."

"The boardinghouse *ajumoni* saved my life. Maybe my life can matter to this family. I had always wanted to do something important before I died. Like my brother Samoel."

Shin nodded. He had heard from his seminary friends that Samoel Baek had been a leader in the independence movement.

"Maybe my life can be significant—not on a grand scale like my brother, but to a few people. Maybe I can help this young woman and her child. And they will be helping me, because I will have a family of my own—a great blessing no matter how you look at it."

The young pastor was beyond dissuading. Shin took a breath.

"Before you do anything, I would like to meet her. And her mother."

"I'll ask them to come. That is if Sunja agrees to marry me. She doesn't know me really."

"That hardly matters." Shin shrugged. "I didn't see my wife until the wedding day. I understand your impulse to help, but marriage is a serious covenant made before God. You know that. Please bring them when you can."

The elder pastor put his hands on Isak's shoulders and prayed over him before he left.

When Isak returned to the boardinghouse, the Chung brothers were sprawled out on the heated floor. They had eaten their supper, and the women were clearing away the last of the dishes.

"Ah, has the pastor been walking around town? You must be well enough now to have a drink with us?" Gombo, the eldest brother, winked.

Getting Isak to have a drink with them was a joke the brothers had kept up for months.

"How was the catch?" Isak asked.

"No mermaids," Fatso, the youngest brother, answered with disappointment.

"That's a shame," Isak said.

"Pastor, would you like your dinner now?" Yangjin asked.

"Yes, thank you." Being outdoors had made him hungry, and it felt wonderful to want food in his stomach again.

The Chung brothers had no intention of sitting up properly, but they made room for him. Gombo patted Isak on the back like an old friend.

Around the lodgers, especially the good-natured Chung brothers, Isak felt more like a man, not a sickly student who'd spent most of his life indoors with books.

Sunja carried in a low dinner table for him, its small surface covered with side dishes, a piping hotpot brimming with stew, and a generously rounded portion of steamed millet and barley rice.

Isak bowed his head in prayer, and everyone else remained silent, feeling awkward, until he raised his head again.

"So, the good-looking pastor gets far more rice than I do," complained Fatso. "Why should I be surprised?" He tried to make an angry face at Sunja, but she didn't pay him any mind.

"Have you eaten?" Isak lifted his bowl to Fatso. "There's plenty here—"

The middle Chung brother, the sensible one, pulled back the pastor's outstretched arm.

"Fatso ate three bowls of millet and two bowls of soup. This one has never missed a meal. If we don't make sure that he's well fed, he'd chew off my arm! He's a pig."

Fatso poked his brother in the ribs.

"A strong man has a strong appetite. You're just jealous because mermaids prefer me to you. One day, I'm going to marry a beautiful market girl and have her work for me the rest of my days. You can repair the fishing nets by yourself."

Gombo and the middle brother laughed, but Fatso ignored them.

"Maybe I should have another bowl of rice. Is there any left in the kitchen?" he asked Sunja.

"Don't you want to leave some for the women?" Gombo interjected.

"Is there enough food for the women?" Isak put down his spoon.

"Yes, yes, there's plenty of food for us. Please don't worry. If Fatso wants more food, we can bring him some," Yangjin assured him.

Fatso looked sheepish.

"I'm not hungry. We should smoke a pipe." He rooted in his pockets for his tobacco.

"So, Pastor Isak, will you be leaving us soon for Osaka? Or will you join us on the boat and look for mermaids? You look strong enough to pull in the nets now," Fatso said. He lit the pipe and handed it to his eldest brother before smoking it himself. "Why would you leave this beautiful island for a cold city?"

Isak laughed. "I'm waiting for a reply from my brother. And as soon as I feel well enough to travel, I'll go to my church in Osaka."

"Think of the mermaids of Yeongdo." Fatso waved at Sunja, who was heading to the kitchen. "They will not be the same in Japan."

"Your offer is tempting. Perhaps I should find a mermaid to go with me to Osaka."

Isak raised his eyebrows.

"Is the pastor making a joke?" Fatso slapped the floor with delight.

Isak took a sip of his tea.

"It might be better if I had a wife for my new life in Osaka."

"Put down your tea. Let's pour this groom a real drink!" Gombo shouted.

The brothers laughed out loud and the pastor laughed, too.

In the small house, the women overheard everything the men said. At the thought of the pastor marrying, Dokhee's neck flushed scarlet with desire, and her sister shot her a look like she was crazy. In the kitchen, Sunja unloaded the dinner trays; she crouched down before the large brass basin and began to wash the dishes.

9

After she finished cleaning up in the kitchen, Sunja said good night to her mother and retreated to the makeshift bedroom they shared with the servant girls. Normally, Sunja went to bed at the same time as the others, but in the past month, she'd been more tired than she'd ever been; it was no longer possible to wait for them to finish their work. Waking up was no less difficult; in the morning, strong hands seemed to clamp down on her shoulders to keep her from rising. Sunja undressed quickly in the cold room and slipped under the thick quilt. The floor was warm; Sunja rested her heavy head on the lozenge-shaped pillow. Her first thought was of him.

Hansu was no longer in Busan. The morning after she'd left him at the beach, she'd asked her mother to go to the market in her place, claiming that she was nauseous and couldn't be far from the outhouse. For a week, she didn't go to the market. When Sunja finally returned to her usual routine of food shopping for the house, Hansu was no longer there. Each morning that she went to the market, she had looked for him, but he was not there.

The heat from the *ondol* floor warmed the pallet beneath her; all day she had been feeling chilled. Her eyes finally closed, Sunja rested her hands over the slight swell of her stomach. She could not yet feel the child, but her body was changing. Her keener sense of smell was the most noticeable change and hard to bear: Walking through the fish stalls made

72

her feel sick; the worst was the smell of crabs and shrimp. Her limbs felt puffier, almost spongy. She knew nothing about having a baby. What she was growing inside her was a secret—mysterious even to herself. What would the child be like? she wondered. Sunja wanted to talk about these things with him.

Since Sunja's confession to her mother, neither of them talked again about the pregnancy. Anguish had deepened the lines along her mother's mouth like a frown setting in for good. During the day, Sunja went about her work faithfully, but at night, before she went to bed, she wondered if he thought about her and their child.

If she had agreed to remain his mistress and waited for him to visit her, she would have been able to keep him. He could've gone to see his wife and daughters in Japan whenever he wanted. Yet this arrangement had felt impossible to her, and even in her present weakness, it felt untenable. She missed him, but she couldn't imagine sharing him with another woman he also loved.

Sunja had been foolish. Why had she supposed that a man of his age and position wouldn't have a wife and children? That he could want to marry some ignorant peasant girl was absurd indeed. Wealthy men had wives and mistresses, sometimes even in the same household. She couldn't be his mistress, however. Her crippled father had loved her mother, who had grown up even poorer than most; he had treasured her. When he was alive, after the boardinghouse guests were served their meals, the three would eat together as a family at the same low dinner table. Her father could've eaten before the women, but he'd never wanted that. At the table, he'd make sure that her mother had as much meat and fish on her plate as he did. In the summer, after finishing a long day, he'd tend to the watermelon patch because it was his wife's favorite fruit. Each winter, he'd procure fresh cotton wool to pad their jackets, and if there wasn't enough, he'd claim his own jacket didn't need new filling.

"You have the kindest father in the land," her mother would often remark, and Sunja had been proud of his love for them, the way a child from a rich family might have been proud of her father's numerous bags of rice and piles of gold rings.

Nevertheless, she couldn't stop thinking of Hansu. Whenever she'd met him at the cove, the cloudless sky and jade-colored water would recede from her sight, leaving only the images of him, and she used to wonder how their time together could vanish so quickly. What amusing story would he tell her? What could she do to make him stay even a few minutes longer?

So when he would tuck her in between two sheltering boulders and untie the long sash of her blouse, she let him do what he wanted even though the cold air cut her. She'd dissolve herself into his warm mouth and skin. When he slid his hands below her long skirt and lifted her bottom to him, she understood that this was what a man wanted from his woman. Lovemaking would make her feel alert; her body seemed to want this touch; and her lower parts accommodated the pressure of him. Sunja had believed that he would do what was good for her.

Sometimes, she imagined that if she carried the load of wash on her head and walked to the beach, he'd be waiting for her on that steep rock by the clear water, his open newspaper flapping noisily in the breeze. He'd lift the bundle from her head, tug at her braid gently, and say, "My girl, where were you? Do you know I would have waited for you until the morning." Last week, she'd felt the call of him so strongly that she made an excuse one afternoon and ran to the cove, and of course, it had been in vain. The chalk-marked rock they used to leave behind like a message was no longer in its crevice, and she was bereft because she would have liked to have drawn an X and left it in the hollow of the rocks to show him that she had come back and waited for him.

He had cared for her; those feelings were true. He had not been lying, she thought, but it was little consolation. Sunja opened her eyes suddenly when she heard the servant girls laughing in the kitchen, then quieting down. There was no sound of her mother. Sunja shifted her body away from the door to face the interior wall and placed her hand on her cheek to imitate his caress. Whenever he saw her, he would touch her constantly, like he could not help from doing so; after making love, his finger traced the curve of her face from her small, round chin to the bend of her ears to the expanse of her pale brow. Why had she never touched him that way? She'd never touched him first; it was he who'd reached for her. She wanted to touch his face now—to memorize the continuous line of his bones.

In the morning, Isak put on his navy woolen sweater over his warmest undershirt and dress shirt and sat on the floor of the front room using a low dining table as his desk. The lodgers had left already, and the house was quiet except for the sounds of the women working. Isak's Bible lay open on the table; Isak had not begun his morning studies, because he couldn't concentrate. In the small foyer by the front room, Yangjin tended to the brazier filled with hot coals. He wanted to speak to her, yet feeling shy, Isak waited. Yangjin stirred the coals using a crude poker, observing the glowing embers.

"Are you warm enough? I'll put this by you." Yangjin got on her knees and pushed the brazier to where he was seated.

"Let me help you," Isak said, getting up.

"No, stay where you are. You just slide it." This was how her husband, Hoonie, used to move the brazier.

As she moved closer, he looked around to see if the others could hear.

"*Ajumoni*," Isak whispered, "do you think she would have me as a husband? If I asked her?"

Yangjin's crinkled eyes widened, and she dropped the poker, making a clanging sound. She picked up the metal stick quickly and laid it down with care as if to correct her earlier movement. She slumped beside him, closer than she'd ever sat next to another man except for her husband and father.

"Are you all right?" he asked.

"Why? Why would you do this?"

"If I had a wife, my life would be better in Osaka, I think. I've written my brother already. I know he and his wife would welcome her."

"And your parents?"

"They've wanted me to marry for years. I've always said no."

"Why?"

"Because I've always been ill. I feel well now, but it's not possible to know how and when I might die. Sunja knows this already. None of this would be a surprise."

"But, you know that she is—"

"Yes. And it is also likely that I'll make her a young widow. And you know that's not easy, but I would be the father. Until I die."

Yangjin said nothing; she was a young widow herself. Her husband was an honest man who had made the best of a difficult birth. When he died, she knew that he had been a very special man. She wished he were here to tell her what to do.

"I didn't mean to trouble you," Isak said, seeing the shock in her face. "I thought it might be something she could want. For the child's future. Do you think she'd agree? Perhaps she intends to stay here with you. Would that be better for her and the child?"

"No, no. Of course it would be far better for them if she went away," Yangjin replied, knowing the hard truth. "The child would have a terrible life here. You'd be saving my daughter's life as well. If you would take care of my daughter, I'd gladly pay you with my life, sir. I'd pay twice if I could." She bowed low, her head almost touching the yellow floor, and wiped her eyes.

"No, you mustn't say that. You and your daughter have been angels."

"I'll speak to her right away, sir. She'll be grateful."

Isak got quiet. He wanted to know how to say this next thing properly.

"I don't want that," he said, feeling embarrassed. "I'd like to ask her, to ask her about her heart. I'd like to know if she could love me one day." Isak felt embarrassed, because it had occurred to him that, like an ordinary man, he wanted a wife who'd love him, not just feel indebted to him.

"What do you think?"

"You should speak to her." How could Sunja not care for a man like this?

Isak whispered, "She's not getting a good bargain. I may fall ill again soon. But I'd try to be a decent husband. And I would love the child. He would be mine, too." Isak felt happy thinking of living long enough to raise a child.

"Please walk with her tomorrow. You can speak to her about all these things."

Her mother told her Baek Isak's intentions, and Sunja prepared herself to be his wife. If Baek Isak married her, a painful sentence would be lifted from her mother, the boardinghouse, herself, and the child. An honorable man from a good family would give the child his name. Sunja couldn't comprehend his reasons. Her mother had tried to explain, but neither thought what they'd done for him was so unusual. They would have done it for any lodger, and he had even paid his fees on time. "No normal man would want to raise another man's child unless he was an angel or a fool," her mother said.

He didn't seem like a fool. Perhaps he needed a housekeeper, yet that didn't seem like him. As soon as the pastor had been feeling better, and even when he wasn't entirely well, he'd carried his finished meal trays to the threshold of the kitchen. In the mornings, he shook out his own bedding and put away the pallet. He did more to care for himself than any of the lodgers. She'd never imagined an educated man from an upper-class family who'd grown up in a household with servants would ever do these things.

Sunja put on her thick coat. She wore straw sandals over two pairs of white cotton socks and waited by the door outside. The air was frigid and misty. In a month or so, it would be spring, but it felt like deep winter still. Her mother had asked the pastor to meet her outside, not wanting the servants to see the two together.

Isak came out momentarily, holding his felt hat.

"Are you well?" Isak stood parallel to her, not knowing where they should go. He'd never been out with a young woman before—not in this way, and never with the intention of asking her to marry him. He tried to pretend that he was counseling a female parishioner—something he had done many times back home.

"Would you like to go into town? We could take the ferry." The suggestion came to him spontaneously.

Sunja nodded and draped her head with a thick muslin scarf to cover her exposed ears. She resembled the women selling fish in the market.

They walked quietly toward the Yeongdo ferry, not knowing what the others who saw them together might think. The boatman accepted their fares.

The wooden boat was mostly empty, so they sat together for the duration of the short trip.

"Your mother spoke to you," Isak said, trying to keep his voice level.

"Yes."

He tried to read her feelings in her young, pretty face. She looked terrified.

"Thank you," she said.

"What do you think of it?"

"I'm very grateful. It's a heavy burden that you've taken off our shoulders. We don't know how to thank you."

"My life is nothing. It wouldn't have any meaning without putting it to good use. Don't you think?"

Sunja played with the side edge of her *chima*.

"I have a question," Isak said.

Sunja kept her eyes lowered.

"Do you think you can love God?" He inhaled. "If you could love God, then I know everything will be all right. It's a lot, I think, to ask of you. It might not make sense now. It will take time. I do understand that."

This morning, it had occurred to Sunja that he'd ask her something like this, and she'd given thought to this God that the pastor believed in. Spirits existed in the world—she believed this even though her father had not. After he died, she felt that he was with her. When they went to his grave for the *jesa*, it was easy to feel his comforting presence. If there were many gods and dead spirits, then she felt that she could love his god, especially if his god could encourage Baek Isak to be such a kind and thoughtful person.

"Yes," she said. "I can."

The boat docked, and Isak helped her off. The mainland was very cold, and Sunja tucked her hands into her jacket sleeves to warm them.

The sharp winds cut through their bodies. She worried that the bitter weather would be bad for the pastor.

Neither knew where they should go next, so she pointed to the main shopping street not far from the ferry. It was the only place she'd ever gone with her parents on the mainland. She walked in that direction, not wanting to take the lead, but he did not seem to care about that. He followed her steps.

"I'm glad you'll try—try to love God. It means a great deal. I think we can have a good marriage if we share this faith."

She nodded again, not entirely understanding what he meant, but she trusted that he had a sound reason for his request.

"Our lives will be strange at first, but we'll ask God for his blessing—on us and the child."

Sunja imagined that his prayer would act like a thick cloak to shield them.

Gulls hovered, shrieking loudly, then flew away. She realized that the marriage had a condition, but it was easy to accept it; there was no way for him to test her devotion. How do you prove that you love God? How do you prove that you love your husband? She would never betray him; she would work hard to care for him—this she could do.

Isak paused in front of a tidy Japanese restaurant that served noodles.

"Have you ever had udon?" He raised his eyebrows.

She shook her head no.

He led her inside. The customers there were Japanese, and she was the only female. The owner, a Japanese man in a spotless apron, greeted them in Japanese. The couple bowed.

Isak asked for a table for two in Japanese, and the owner relaxed upon hearing his language spoken so well. They chatted amiably, and the owner offered them seats at the edge of the communal table near the door with no one beside them. Isak and Sunja sat opposite each other, making it impossible to avoid each other's faces.

Sunja couldn't read the hand-painted menus on the plywood walls but recognized some of the Japanese numbers. Office workers and shopkeepers sat on three long tables covered in wax cloths and slurped from their steaming bowls of soupy noodles. A Japanese boy with a shaved head went around pouring brown tea from a heavy brass kettle. He tipped his head to her slightly.

"I've never been to a restaurant before," she found herself saying, more out of surprise than from a wish to talk.

"I haven't been to many myself. This place looks clean, though. My father said that's important when you eat outside your home." Isak smiled, wanting Sunja to feel more comfortable. The warmth of being inside had brought color to her face. "Are you hungry?"

Sunja nodded. She hadn't eaten anything that morning.

Isak ordered two bowls of udon for them.

"It's like *kalguksu*, but the broth is different. I thought maybe you might like it. I'm sure it's sold everywhere in Osaka. Everything there will be new for us." More and more, Isak liked the idea of having her go with him.

Sunja had heard many stories about Japan from Hansu already, but she couldn't tell Isak this. Hansu had said that Osaka was an enormous place where you'd hardly ever see the same person twice.

As he talked, Isak observed her. Sunja was a private person. Even at the house, she did not talk much to the girls who worked there or even to her mother. Was she always this way? he wondered. It was hard to imagine that she'd had a lover.

Isak spoke to her quietly, not wishing to be heard by the others.

"Sunja, do you think you could care for me? As your husband?" Isak clasped his hands as if in prayer.

"Yes." The answer came quickly because this felt true to her. She cared for him now, and she didn't want him to think otherwise.

Isak felt light and clean inside, as if his diseased lungs had been scoured back to health. He took a breath.

"I expect it will be difficult, but would you try to forget him?" There, he said it. They would not have secret thoughts.

Sunja winced, not having expected him to speak of this.

"I'm not different from other men. I have my pride, which I know is probably wrong." He frowned. "But I'll love this child, and I will love you and honor you."

"I'll do my best to be a good wife."

"Thank you," he said. He hoped he and Sunja would be close, the way his parents were.

When the noodles arrived, he bowed to say grace, and Sunja laced her fingers together, copying his movements.

IO

A week later, Yangjin, Sunja, and Isak took the morning ferry to Busan. The women wore freshly laundered *hanbok* made of white hemp beneath padded winter jackets; Isak's suit and coat had been brushed clean and his shoes polished bright. Pastor Shin was expecting them after breakfast.

Upon their arrival, the church servant recognized Isak and led them to Pastor Shin's office.

"You're here," the elder pastor said, rising from his seat on the floor. He spoke with a northern accent. "Come in, come in." Yangjin and Sunja bowed deeply. They'd never been inside a church before. Pastor Shin was a thin man whose clothes were too big for him. The sleeve hems on his aging black suit were frayed, but the white collar at his throat was clean and well starched. His unwrinkled dark clothes appeared to flatten the bent C-curve of his shoulders.

The servant girl brought three floor cushions for the guests and laid them near the brazier in the center of the poorly heated room.

The three guests stood awkwardly until Pastor Shin took his seat. Isak was seated beside Pastor Shin, and Yangjin and Sunja opposite the elder minister.

Once they were seated, no one spoke, waiting for Pastor Shin to lead the meeting with a prayer. After he finished, the elder pastor took his time to assess the young woman whom Isak planned to marry. He'd been thinking a great deal about her since the young pastor's last visit. In preparation for the interview, Shin had even reread the Book of Hosea. The elegant young man in his charcoal woolen suit contrasted dramatically with the stocky girl—Sunja's face was round and plain, and her eyes were lowered either in modesty or shame. Nothing in her prosaic appearance conjured up the harlot the prophet Hosea had been forced to marry. She was, in fact, unremarkable in her manner. Pastor Shin didn't believe in reading faces to determine a person's fate as his own father had, but if he were to filter her destiny through his father's eyes, it didn't look as if her life would be easy, but neither was it cursed. He glanced at her stomach, but he couldn't tell her condition under the full *chima* and her coat.

"How do you feel about going to Japan with Isak?" the elder pastor asked Sunja.

Sunja looked up, then looked down. She wasn't sure what it was that ministers did exactly or how they exercised their powers. Pastor Shin and Pastor Isak weren't likely to fall into spells like male shamans or chant like monks.

"I'd like to hear what you think," Shin said, his body leaning in toward her. "Please say something. I wouldn't want you to leave my office without my having heard your voice."

Isak smiled at the women, not knowing what to make of the elder pastor's stern tone of voice. He wanted to assure them that the pastor was well-meaning.

Yangjin placed her hand gently on her daughter's knee. She'd expected some sort of questioning but she hadn't realized until now that Pastor Shin thought badly of them.

"Sunja-ya, tell Pastor Shin what you think about marrying Baek Isak," Yangjin said.

Sunja opened her mouth, then closed it. She opened it again, her voice tremulous.

"I'm very grateful. To Pastor Baek for his painful sacrifice. I will work very hard to serve him. I will do whatever I can to make his life in Japan better."

Isak frowned; he could see why she'd say this, but all the same, Sunja's sentiment saddened him.

"Yes." The elder pastor clasped his hands together. "This is indeed a painful sacrifice. Isak is a fine young man from a good family, and it cannot be easy for him to undertake this marriage, given your situation."

Isak lifted his right hand slightly in a weak protest, but he kept quiet in deference to his elder. If Pastor Shin refused to marry them, his parents and teachers would be troubled.

Pastor Shin said to Sunja, "You've brought this condition upon yourself; is this not true?"

Isak couldn't bear to look at her hurt expression and wanted to take the women back to the boardinghouse.

"I made a serious mistake. I'm very sorry for what I have done to my mother and for the burden I made for the good pastor." Tears filled Sunja's dark eyes. She looked even younger than she normally did.

Yangjin took her daughter's hand and held it, not knowing if it was right or wrong; she broke into sobs herself.

"Pastor Shin, she is suffering so much already," Isak blurted out.

"She must recognize her sin and wish to be forgiven. If she asks, our Lord will forgive her." Shin said each word thoughtfully.

"I suppose she would want that." Isak had not wanted Sunja to turn to God in this way. Love for God, he'd thought, should come naturally and not out of fear of punishment.

Pastor Shin looked hard at Sunja.

"Do you, Sunja? Do you want to be forgiven for your sin?" Pastor Shin didn't know if the girl knew what sin was. In the young man's exuberance to be a kind of martyr or prophet, had Isak explained any of this to her? How could he marry a sinful woman who would not turn from sin? And yet this was precisely what God had asked the prophet Hosea to do. Did Isak understand this?

"To have been with a man without marrying is a sin in the eyes of God. Where is this man? Why must Isak pay for your sin?" Shin asked.

Sunja tried to mop up the tears on her flushed cheeks using her jacket sleeve.

In the corner, the deaf servant girl could make out some of what was being said by reading their lips. She withdrew a clean cloth from her overcoat pocket and gave it to Sunja. She gestured to Sunja to wipe her face, and Sunja smiled at her.

Pastor Shin sighed. Although he didn't want to upset the girl any further, he felt compelled to protect the earnest young minister.

"Where is the father of your child, Sunja?" Pastor Shin asked.

"She does not know, Pastor Shin," Yangjin replied, though she was curious to know the answer herself. "She's very sorry for this." Yangjin turned to her daughter: "Tell the pastor—tell him that you want forgiveness from the Lord."

Neither Yangjin nor Sunja knew what that would mean. Would there be a ritual like when you gave the shaman a sow and money to make the crops grow? Baek Isak had never once mentioned this thing about forgiveness.

"Could you? Could you forgive me?" Sunja asked the older minister.

Pastor Shin felt pity for the child.

"Sunja, it's not up to me to forgive you," he replied.

"I don't understand," she said, finally looking directly at Pastor Shin's face, unable to keep her eyes lowered. Her nose was running.

"Sunja, all you have to do is ask the Lord to forgive you. Jesus has paid our debts, but you still have to ask for forgiveness. Promise that you'll turn from sin. Repent, child, and sin no more." Pastor Shin could sense that she wanted to learn. He felt something inside, and he was reminded of the infant within her who had done nothing wrong. Then Shin recalled Gomer, Hosea's harlot wife, who remained unrepentant and later cheated on him again. He frowned.

"I'm very sorry," Sunja repeated. "I won't do it again. I will never be with another man."

"It makes sense that you'd want to marry this young man. Yes, he wants to marry you and to take care of the child, but I don't know if this is prudent. I worry that he is perhaps too idealistic. His family isn't here, and I need to make sure that he will be all right."

Sunja nodded in agreement, her sobs subsiding.

Yangjin gulped, having feared this ever since Baek Isak had mentioned that they'd need to speak with Pastor Shin.

"Pastor Shin, I believe Sunja will be a good wife," Isak pleaded. "Please marry us, sir. I'd like your blessing. You speak from deep and wise concern, but I believe this is the Lord's wish. I believe this marriage will benefit me as much as it will benefit Sunja and the child."

Pastor Shin exhaled.

"Do you know how difficult it is to be a pastor's wife?" he asked Sunja.

Sunja shook her head no. Her breathing was more normal now.

"Have you told her?" he asked Isak.

"I'll be the associate pastor. I don't expect that much will be expected of her. The congregation isn't large. Sunja is a hard worker and learns quickly," Isak said. He had not thought much about this, however. The pastor's wife at his home church in Pyongyang had been a great lady, a tireless woman who'd borne eight children, worked alongside her husband to care for orphans and to serve the poor. When she died, the parishioners had wailed as if they'd lost their own mother.

Isak, Sunja, and Yangjin sat quietly, not knowing what else to do.

"You must swear that you'll be faithful to this man. If you're not, you'll bring far greater shame on your mother and your dead father than what you've already done. You must ask the Lord for forgiveness, child, and ask Him for faith and courage as you make your new home in Japan. Be perfect, child. Every Korean must be on his best behavior over there. They think so little of us already. You cannot give them any room to think worse of us. One bad Korean ruins it for thousands of others. And one bad Christian hurts tens of thousands of Christians everywhere, especially in a nation of unbelievers. Do you understand my meaning?"

"I want to," she said. "And I want to be forgiven, sir."

Pastor Shin got on bended knees and placed his right hand on her shoulder. He prayed at length for her and Isak. When he finished, he got up and made the couple rise and married them. The ceremony was over in minutes.

While Pastor Shin went with Isak and Sunja to the municipal offices and the local police station to register their marriage, Yangjin made her way to the shopping street, her steps rapid and deliberate. She felt like running. At the wedding ceremony, there were many words she had not understood. It was preposterous and ungrateful for her to have wished for a better outcome under the circumstances, but Yangjin, no matter how practical her nature, had hoped for something nicer for her only child. Although it made sense to marry at once, she hadn't known that the wedding would take place today. Her own perfunctory wedding had taken minutes, also. Perhaps it didn't matter, she told herself.

When Yangjin reached the sliding door of the rice shop, she knocked on the wide frame of the entrance prior to entering. The store was empty of customers. A striped cat was slinking about the rice seller's straw shoes and purring happily.

"*Ajumoni*, it's been a long time," Cho greeted her. The rice seller smiled at Hoonie's widow. There was more gray in her bun than he remembered.

"*Ajeossi*, hello. I hope your wife and girls are well."

He nodded.

"Could you sell me some white rice?"

"*Waaaaah*, you must have an important guest staying with you. I'm sorry, but I don't have any to sell. You know where it all goes," he said.

"I have money to pay," she said, putting down the drawstring purse on the counter between them. It was Sunja who had embroidered the yellow butterflies on the blue canvas fabric of the purse—a birthday present from two years back. The blue purse was half full, and Yangjin hoped it was enough.

Cho grimaced. He didn't want to sell her the rice, because he had no choice but to charge her the same price he would charge a Japanese.

"I have so little stock, and when the Japanese customers come in and there isn't any, I get into very hot water. You understand. Believe me, it's not that I don't want to sell it to you."

"*Ajeossi*, my daughter married today," Yangjin said, trying not to cry.

"Sunja? Who? Who did she marry?" He could picture the little girl holding her crippled father's hand. "I didn't know she was betrothed! Today?"

"The guest from the North."

"The one with tuberculosis? That's crazy! Why would you let your daughter marry a man who has such a thing. He's going to drop dead any minute."

"He'll take her to Osaka. Her life will be less difficult for her than living at a boardinghouse with so many men," she said, hoping this would be the end of it.

She wasn't telling him the truth, and Cho knew it. The girl must have been sixteen or seventeen. Sunja was a few years younger than his second daughter; it was a good time for a girl to marry, but why would he marry her? Jun, the coal man, had said he was a fancy sort from a rich family. She also had diseases in her blood. Who wanted that? Though there weren't as many girls in Osaka, he supposed.

"Did he make a good offer?" Cho asked, frowning at the little purse. Kim Yangjin couldn't have given a man like that any kind of decent dowry; the boardinghouse woman would barely have a few brass coins left after she fed those hungry fishermen and the two poor sisters she shouldn't have taken in.

His own daughters had married years ago. Last year, the younger one's husband had run away to Manchuria because the police were after him for organizing demonstrations, so now Cho fed this great patriot's children by selling his finest inventory to rich Japanese customers whom his son-in-law had been so passionate about expelling from the nation. If his Japanese customers refused to patronize him, Cho's shop would shut down tomorrow and his family would starve.

"Do you need enough rice for a wedding party?" he asked, unable to fathom how the woman would pay for such a thing.

"No. Just enough for the two of them."

Cho nodded at the small, tired woman standing in front of him who wouldn't meet his eyes.

"I don't have much to sell," he repeated.

"I want only enough for the bride and groom's dinner—for them to taste white rice again before they leave home." Yangjin's eyes welled up in tears, and the rice seller looked away. Cho hated seeing women cry. His grandmother, mother, wife, and daughters—all of them cried endlessly. Women cried too much, he thought.

His older daughter lived on the other side of town with a man who worked as a printer, and his younger one and her three children lived at home with him and his wife. As much as the rice seller complained about the expense of upkeep of his daughter and grandchildren, he worked hard and did the bidding of any Japanese customer who'd pay the top price because he could not imagine not providing for his family; he could not imagine having his girls live far away—in a nation where Koreans were treated no better than barn animals. He couldn't imagine losing his flesh and blood to the sons of bitches.

Yangjin counted out the yen notes and placed them on the wooden tray on the counter beside the abacus.

"A small bag if you have it. I want them to eat their fill. Whatever's left over, I'll make them some sweet cake."

Yangjin pushed the tray of money toward him. If he still said no, then she would march into every rice shop in Busan so her daughter could have white rice for her wedding dinner.

"Cakes?" Cho crossed his arms and laughed out loud; how long had it been since he heard women talking of cakes made of white rice? Such days felt so distant. "I suppose you'll bring me a piece."

She wiped her eyes as the rice seller went to the storeroom to find the bit he'd squirreled away for occasions such as these.

II

At last, the lodgers had relented and allowed their work clothes to be washed. The smell was no longer bearable even to themselves. Carrying four enormous bundles, Bokhee, Dokhee, and Sunja went to the cove. Their long skirts gathered up and tied, the women crouched by the stream and set up their washboards. The icy water froze their small hands, the skin on them thickened and rough from years of work. With all her might, Bokhee scrubbed the wet shirts on the ridged wooden board while her younger sister, Dokhee, sorted the remainder of the filthy clothing beside her. Sunja was tackling a pair of dark trousers belonging to one of the Chung brothers, stained with fish blood and guts.

"Do you feel different being married?" Dokhee asked. The girls had been the first to be told the news immediately after the marriage was registered. They'd been even more astonished than the lodgers. "Has he called you *yobo*?"

Bokhee looked up from her work for Sunja's reaction. She would've chided her sister's impertinence, but she was curious herself.

"Not yet," Sunja said. The marriage had taken place three days ago, but for lack of space, Sunja still slept in the same room with her mother and the servant girls.

"I'd like to be married," Dokhee said.

Bokhee laughed. "Who'd marry girls like us?"

"I would like to marry a man like Pastor Isak," Dokhee said without blinking. "He's so handsome and nice. He looks at you with such kindness when he talks to you. Even the lodgers respect him, even though he doesn't know anything about the sea. Have you noticed that?"

This was true. Routinely, the lodgers made fun of upper-class people who went to schools, but they liked Isak. It was still difficult for Sunja to think of him as her husband.

Bokhee slapped her sister's forearm. "You're crazy. A man like that would never marry you. Get these stupid ideas out of your head."

"But he married Sunja—"

"She's different. You and I are servants," Bokhee said.

Dokhee rolled her eyes.

"What does he call you, then?"

"He calls me Sunja," she said, feeling freer to talk. Before Hansu, Sunja had chatted more often with the sisters.

"Are you excited about going to Japan?" Bokhee asked. She was more interested in living in a city than being married, which seemed like a horrible thing. Her grandmother and mother had been more or less worked to death. She had never once heard her mother laugh.

"The men said that Osaka is a busier place than Busan or Seoul. Where will you live?" Bokhee asked.

"I don't know. At Pastor Isak's brother's house, I guess." Sunja was still thinking about Hansu and how he might be nearby. More than anything, she was afraid of running into him. Yet it would be worse, she thought, never to see him at all.

Bokhee peered into Sunja's face.

"Are you afraid of going? You mustn't be. I think you're going to have a wonderful life there. The men said there are electric lights everywhere—on trains, cars, streets, and in all the houses. They said Osaka has all the things you could possibly want to buy in stores. Maybe you'll become rich and you can send for us. We can keep a boardinghouse there!" Bokhee was amazed at such a prospect that she had just invented for them. "They must need boardinghouses, too. Your mother can cook, and we can clean and wash—"

"You think I have crazy thoughts in my head?" Dokhee slapped her sister's shoulder, leaving a wet handprint on her sister's jacket sleeve.

Sunja had difficulty wringing out the wet trousers because they were so heavy.

"Can a minister's wife be rich?" Sunja asked.

"Maybe the minister will make lots of money!" Dokhee said. "And his parents are rich, right?"

"How do you know that?" Sunja asked. Her mother had said that Isak's parents owned some land, but many of the landowners had been selling off their plots to the Japanese to pay the new taxes. "I don't know if we'll have much money. It doesn't matter."

"His clothes are so nice, and he's educated," Dokhee said, not clear as to how people had money.

Sunja started to wash another pair of trousers.

Dokhee glanced at her sister. "Can we give it to her now?"

Bokhee nodded, wanting to take Sunja's mind off leaving. The girl looked anxious and sad, nothing like a happy bride.

"You're like a little sister to us, but you've always felt older because you're smart and patient," Bokhee said, smiling.

"When you're gone, who'll defend me when I get a scolding from your mother? You know my sister won't do anything," Dokhee added.

Sunja laid aside the pants she was washing by the rocks. The sisters had been with her ever since her father had died; she couldn't imagine not living with them.

"We wanted to give you something." Dokhee held out a pair of ducks carved out of acacia wood hanging from a red silk cord. They were the size of a baby's hand.

"The *ajeossi* at the market said ducks mate for life," Bokhee said. "Maybe you can come back home in a few years and bring home your children to show us. I'm good at taking care of babies. I raised Dokhee almost by myself. Although she can be naughty."

Dokhee pushed up her nostrils with her index finger to make a piggy face.

"Lately, you've been looking so unhappy. We know why," Dokhee said.

Sunja was holding the ducks in her hand, and she looked up.

"You miss your father," Bokhee said. The sisters had lost their parents as little girls.

Bokhee's broad face broke into a sad smile. Her tiny, gracious eyes, which resembled tadpoles, pulled downward to meet her knobby cheek-bones. The sisters had almost identical faces; the younger one was shorter and slightly plump.

Sunja wept and Dokhee folded her into her strong arms.

"*Abuji*, my *abuji*," Sunja said quietly.

"It's all right, it's all right," Bokhee said, patting Sunja on the back. "You have a kind husband now."

Yangjin packed her daughter's things herself. Every article of clothing was folded with care, then stacked in a broad square of fabric to form a manageable bundle. The fabric corners were tied neatly into a loop handle. In the days before the couple left, Yangjin kept thinking that she'd forgotten something, forcing her to unpack one of the four bundles and repeat the process. She wanted to send more pantry items like dried jujubes, chili flakes, chili paste, large dried anchovies, and fermented soybean paste to give to Isak's sister-in-law, but Isak told her that they could not carry too much on the ferry. "We can purchase things there," he assured her.

Bokhee and Dokhee remained at the house on the morning Yangjin, Sunja, and Isak went to the Busan ferry terminal. The good-byes with the sisters were difficult; Dokhee cried inconsolably, afraid that Yangjin might leave for Osaka and abandon the sisters in Yeongdo.

The Busan ferry terminal was a utilitarian brick and wooden structure that had been built hastily. Passengers, family members who'd come to see them off, and hawkers milled around noisily in the crowded terminal. Immense lines of passengers waited to show their papers to the police and immigration officials before embarking on the Busan ferry to Shimonoseki. While Isak stood in line to speak to the police, the women sat on a bench nearby, ready to spring up in case he needed anything. The large ferry was already docked and waiting for the passengers' inspections to be completed. The algae scent of the sea mingled with the fuel smells of the ferry; Sunja had been queasy since morning, and she looked sallow and exhausted. She had vomited earlier and had nothing left in her stomach.

Yangjin held the smallest bundle close to her chest. When would she see her daughter again? she wondered. The whole world felt broken. What was better for Sunja and the child no longer seemed to matter. Why did they have to go? Yangjin would not be able to hold her grandchild. Why couldn't she go with them? There must be work for her in Osaka, she reasoned. But Yangjin knew she had to stay. It was her responsibility to care for her in-laws' graves and her husband's. She couldn't leave Hoonie. Besides, where would she stay in Osaka?

Sunja doubled over slightly, emitting a little cry of pain.

"Are you okay?"

Sunja nodded.

"I saw the gold watch," Yangjin said.

Sunja folded her arms and hugged herself.

"Was it from that man?"

"Yes," Sunja said, not looking at her mother.

"What kind of man can afford something like that?"

Sunja didn't reply. There were only a few men left in front of Isak in the line.

"Where is the man who gave you the watch?"

"He lives in Osaka."

"What? Is that where he's from?"

"He's from Jeju, but he lives in Osaka. I don't know if that's where he is now."

"Are you planning on seeing him?"

"No."

"You cannot see this man, Sunja. He abandoned you. He's not good."

"He's married."

Yangjin took a breath.

Sunja could hear herself talking to her mother, yet it felt like she was another person.

"I didn't know he was married. He didn't tell me."

Yangjin sat still with her mouth opened slightly.

"At the market, some Japanese boys were bothering me, and he told them off. Then we became friends."

It felt natural to speak of him finally; she was always thinking of him but there had been no one to talk about him with.

"He wanted to take care of me and the baby, but he couldn't marry me. He said he had a wife and three children in Japan."

Yangjin took her daughter's hand.

"You cannot see him. That man"—Yangjin pointed at Isak—"that man saved your life. He saved your child. You're a member of his family. I've no right to ever see you again. Do you know what that's like for a mother? Soon, you'll be a mother. I hope that you'll have a son who won't have to leave you when he marries."

Sunja nodded.

"The watch. What will you do with it?"

"I'll sell it when I get to Osaka."

Yangjin was satisfied with this answer.

"Save it for an emergency. If your husband asks where you got it, tell him that I gave it to you."

Yangjin fumbled with the purse tucked beneath her blouse.

"This belonged to your father's mother." Yangjin gave her the two gold rings her mother-in-law had given her before she died.

"Try not to sell these unless you have to. You should have something in case you need money. You're a thrifty girl, but raising a child requires money. There will be things you can't expect, like doctor's visits. If it's a boy, you'll need fees for school. If the pastor doesn't give you money for the household, earn something and put aside savings for emergencies. Spend what you need but just throw even a few coins into a tin and forget that you have it. A woman should always have something put by. Take good care of your husband. Otherwise, another woman will. Treat your husband's family with reverence. Obey them. If you make mistakes, they'll curse our family. Think of your kind father, who always did his best for us." Yangjin tried to think of anything else she was supposed to tell her. It was hard to focus.

Sunja slipped the rings into the fabric bag beneath her blouse where she kept her watch and money.

"*Omoni*, I'm sorry."

"I know, I know." Yangjin closed her mouth and stroked Sunja's hair. "You're all I have. Now, I have nothing."

"I will ask Pastor Isak to write to you when we arrive."

"Yes, yes. And if you need anything, ask Isak to write me a letter in plain Korean, and I'll ask someone in town to read it for me." Yangjin sighed. "I wish we knew our letters."

"We know our numbers, and we can do sums. Father taught us."

Yangjin smiled. "Yes. Your father taught us.

"Your home is with your husband," Yangjin said. This was what her father had told her when she married Hoonie. "Never come home again," he'd said to her, but Yangjin couldn't say this to her own child. "Make a good home for him and your child. That's your job. They must not suffer."

Isak returned, looking calm. Dozens of people had been turned away for lack of papers or fees, but Sunja and he were fine. Every item required had been satisfied. The officers could not trouble him. He and his wife could go.

12

Osaka, April 1933

When Yoseb Baek tired of shifting his weight from one foot to the other, he paced about the Osaka train station like a man in a cell. If he'd come with a friend, he would've been able to keep still just by shooting the breeze, but he was alone. Yoseb was an easy talker by nature, and though his Japanese was better than proficient, his accent never failed to give him away. From appearances alone, he could approach any Japanese and receive a polite smile, but he'd lose the welcome as soon as he said anything. He was a Korean, after all, and no matter how appealing his personality, unfortunately he belonged to a cunning and wily tribe. There were many Japanese who were fair-minded and principled, but around foreigners they tended to be guarded. *The smart ones, especially, you have to watch out for those—Koreans are natural troublemakers.* After living in Japan for over a decade, Yoseb had heard it all. He didn't dwell on these things; that seemed pathetic to him. The sentry patrolling Osaka Station had noticed Yoseb's restlessness, but waiting anxiously for a train to arrive was not a crime.

The police didn't know he was a Korean, because Yoseb's manner and dress wouldn't have given him away. Most Japanese claimed they could distinguish between a Japanese and a Korean, but every Korean knew that was rubbish. You could ape anyone. Yoseb wore the street clothes of a modest workingman in Osaka—plain trousers, a Western-style dress shirt, and a heavy woolen coat that didn't show its wear. Long ago, he'd put aside the finery that he'd brought from Pyongyang—expensive suits his parents had ordered from a tailor who made clothes for the Canadian missionaries and their families. For the past six years, Yoseb had been working as the foreman at a biscuit factory, overseeing thirty girls and two men. For his employment, he needed to be neat—that was all. He didn't need to dress better than his boss, Shimamura-san, who'd made it plain that he could replace Yoseb by morning. Every day, trains from Shimonoseki and boats from Jeju brought more hungry Koreans to Osaka, and Shimamura-san could have the pick of the litter.

Yoseb was grateful that his younger brother was arriving on a Sunday, his only day off. Back home, Kyunghee was preparing a feast. Otherwise, she'd have tagged along. They were both terribly curious about the girl Isak had married. Her circumstances were shocking, but what Isak had decided to do was not at all surprising. No one in the family would have ever been taken aback by Isak's acts of selflessness. As a child, he'd been the kind who'd have sacrificed all his meals and possessions to the poor if allowed. The boy had spent his childhood in his sickbed reading. His abundant meals were sent to his room on a lacquered jujube tray. Yet he remained as slender as a chopstick, though every grain of rice would have been picked off its metal bowl when his tray was returned to the kitchen. Naturally, the servants had never gone without a sizable portion of his meals, which Isak had given away deliberately. Your rice and fish were one thing, Yoseb thought, but this marriage seemed excessive. To agree to father another man's child! His wife, Kyunghee, had made him promise to reserve judgment until they had a chance to get to know her. She, much like Isak, was tenderhearted to a fault.

When the Shimonoseki train arrived at the station, the awaiting crowd dispersed with a kind of organized precision. Porters dashed to help first-class passengers; everyone else seemed to know where to go. A head taller than the others, Isak stood out from the mob. A gray trilby was cocked on his beautiful head, and his tortoiseshell glasses were set low on his straight nose. Isak scanned the crowd and, spotting Yoseb, he waved his bony right hand high in the air.

Yoseb rushed to him. The boy had become an adult. Isak was even thinner than he last remembered; his pale skin was more olive, and radial lines had surfaced around his gentle, smiling eyes. Isak had their brother Samoel's face; it was uncanny. The Western suit, handmade by the family tailor, hung slack on his drawn frame. The shy, sickly boy Yoseb had left eleven years ago had grown into a tall gentleman, his gaunt body depleted further by his recent illness. How could his parents have let him come to Osaka? Why had Yoseb insisted?

Yoseb wrapped his arms around his brother and pulled him close. Here, the only other person Yoseb ever touched was his wife, and it was gratifying to have his kin so near—to be able to feel the stubble of his brother's face brush against his own ears. His little brother had facial hair, Yoseb marveled.

"You grew a lot!"

They both laughed because it was true and because it had been far too long since they had last seen each other.

"Brother," Isak said. "My brother."

"Isak, you're here. I'm so glad."

Isak beamed, his eyes fixed to his elder brother's face.

"But you've grown much bigger than me. That's disrespectful!"

Isak bowed waist-deep in mock apology.

Sunja stood there holding her bundles. She was comforted by the brothers' ease and warmth. Isak's brother Yoseb was funny. His joking reminded her a little of Fatso, the boardinghouse guest. When Fatso first learned that she'd married Isak, he had pretended to faint, making a *splat* sound on the floor of the front room. Moments later, he took out his wallet and gave her two yen—over two days of a workman's wages—telling her to buy something tasty to eat with her husband when she got to Osaka. "When you're munching on sweet rice cakes in Japan, remember me, lonely and sad in Yeongdo, missing you; imagine Fatso's heart torn out like the mouth of a sea bass hooked too young." He had pretended to cry, rubbing his meaty fists into his eyes and making loud *boo-hoo* noises. His brothers had told him to shut up, and each of them had also given her two yen as a wedding present.

"And you're married!" Yoseb said, looking carefully at the small girl beside Isak.

Sunja bowed to her brother-in-law.

"It's good to meet you again," Yoseb said. "You were just a little thing, though; you used to follow your father around. Maybe you were five or six? I don't think you can remember me."

Sunja shook her head because she had tried but couldn't.

"I remember your father very well. I was sorry to hear about his death; he was a very wise man. I enjoyed talking with him. He didn't have extra words, but everything he said was well considered. And your mother made the most outstanding meals."

Sunja lowered her eyes.

"Thank you for letting me come here, Elder Brother. My mother sends her deepest thanks for your generosity."

"You and your mother saved Isak's life. I'm grateful to you, Sunja. Our family is grateful to your family."

Yoseb took the heavy suitcases from Isak, and Isak took Sunja's lighter bundles. Yoseb noticed that her stomach protruded, but her pregnancy was not entirely obvious. He looked away in the direction of the station exits. The girl didn't look or talk like some village harlot. She seemed so modest and plain that Yoseb wondered if she could have been raped by someone she knew. That sort of thing happened, and the girl might have been blamed for having misled a fellow.

"Where's Sister?" Isak asked, looking around for Kyunghee.

"At home, cooking your dinner. You better be hungry. The neighbors must be dying of jealousy from the smells coming from the kitchen!"

Isak smiled; he adored his sister-in-law.

Sunja pulled her jacket closer to her body, aware of the passersby staring at her traditional dress. No one else in the station was wearing a *hanbok*.

"My sister-in-law's a wonderful cook," Isak said to Sunja, happy at the thought of seeing Kyunghee again.

Yoseb noticed the people staring at the girl. She'd need clothes, he realized.

"Let's go home!" Yoseb guided them out of the station in no time.

The road opposite the Osaka station was teeming with streetcars;

hordes of pedestrians streamed in and out of the main entrances. Sunja walked behind the brothers, who darted carefully through the crowd. As they walked toward the trolley, she turned back for a moment and caught sight of the train station. The Western-style building was like nothing she had ever seen before—a stone and concrete behemoth. The Shimonoseki station, which she'd thought was big, was puny compared to this immense structure.

The men walked quickly, and she tried to keep up. The trolley car was approaching. In her mind, she had been to Osaka before. In her mind, she had ridden the Shimonoseki ferry, the Osaka train, and even the trolley that could outpace a boy running or cycling. As cars drove past them, she marveled that they did look like metal bulls on wheels, which was what Hansu had called them. She was a country girl, but she had heard of all these things. Yet she could not let on that she knew of uniformed ticket collectors, immigration officers, porters, and of trolleys, electric lamps, kerosene stoves, and telephones, so at the trolley stop, Sunja remained quiet and still like a seedling sprouting from new soil, upright and open to collect the light. She would have uprooted herself to have seen the world with him, and now she was seeing it without him.

Yoseb directed Sunja to the only empty seat at the back of the trolley and deposited her there. She took back the bundles from Isak and held them in her lap. The brothers stood close to each other and caught each other up on family news. Sunja didn't pay any mind to the men's conversation. As before, she held her bundles close to her heart and belly to inhale the lingering scent of home on the fabric covering their possessions.

The wide streets of downtown Osaka were lined with rows of low brick buildings and smart-looking shops. The Japanese who had settled in Busan resembled the ones here, but there were many more kinds of them. At the station, there were young men in fancy Western suits that made Isak's clothing look dated and fusty, and beautiful women wearing glorious kimonos that would have made Dokhee swoon with pleasure at their exceptional colors and embroidery. There were also very poor-looking people who must have been Japanese—that was something she had never seen in Busan. Men spat in the streets casually. The trolley ride felt brief to her.

They got off at Ikaino, the ghetto where the Koreans lived. When they reached Yoseb's home, it looked vastly different from the nice houses she'd passed by on the trolley ride from the station. The animal stench was stronger than the smell of food cooking or even the odors of the outhouses. Sunja wanted to cover her nose and mouth, but kept from doing so.

Ikaino was a misbegotten village of sorts, comprised of mismatched, shabby houses. The shacks were uniform in their poorly built manner and flimsy materials. Here and there, a stoop had been washed or a pair of windows polished, but the majority of the facades were in disrepair. Matted newspapers and tar paper covered the windows from inside, and wooden shims were used to seal up the cracks. The metal used on the roof was often rusted through. The houses appeared to have been put up by the residents themselves using cheap or found materials—not much sturdier than huts or tents. Smoke vented from makeshift steel chimneys. It was warm for a spring evening; children, half-dressed in rags, played tag, ignoring the drunken man asleep in the alley. A small boy defecated by a stoop not far from Yoseb's house.

Yoseb and Kyunghee lived in a boxlike shack with a slightly pitched roof. Its wooden frame was covered with corrugated steel. A plywood panel with a metal covering served as the front door.

"This place is fit for only pigs and Koreans," Yoseb said, laughing. "It's not quite like home, is it?"

"No, but it'll do very well for us," Isak said, smiling. "I'm sorry for the inconvenience we'll be causing."

Sunja couldn't believe how poorly Yoseb and his wife lived. It could not be possible that a foreman of a factory could live in such impoverished quarters.

"The Japanese won't rent decent properties to us. We bought this house eight years ago. I think we're the only Koreans who own a house on this row, but no one can know that."

"Why?" Isak asked.

"It's not good to let on that you're an owner. The landlords here are bastards; that's all everyone complains about. I bought this with the money Father gave me when I moved out here. I couldn't afford to buy it now."

Pig squeals came from the house next door with the tar-papered windows.

"Yes, our neighbor raises pigs. They live with her and her children."

"How many children?"

"Four children and three pigs."

"All in there?" Isak whispered.

Yoseb nodded, raising his eyebrows.

"It can't be that expensive to live here," Isak said. He had planned on renting a house for Sunja, himself, and the baby.

"Tenants pay more than half their earnings on rent. The food prices are much higher than back home."

Hansu owned many properties in Osaka. How did he do that? she wondered.

The side door that led to the kitchen opened, and Kyunghee looked out. She put down the pail she was carrying by the doorstep.

"What! What are you doing standing outside? Come in, come in! *Uh-muh!*" Kyunghee cried out loud. She rushed over to Isak and held his face in her hands. "*Uh-muh*, I'm so happy. You're here! Praise God!"

"Amen," Isak said, letting himself be petted over by Kyunghee, who'd known him since he was an infant.

"The last time I saw you was right before I left home! Go inside the house now!" she ordered Isak playfully, then turned to Sunja.

"You don't know how long I've wanted a sister. I've been so lonely here wanting to talk to a girl!" Kyunghee said. "I was worried that you didn't make your train. How are you? Are you tired? You must be hungry."

Kyunghee took Sunja's hand in hers, and the men followed the women.

Sunja hadn't expected this warmth. Kyunghee had a remarkably pretty face—eyes shaped and colored like persimmon seeds and a beautiful mouth. She had the complexion of white peonies. She appeared far more appealing and vibrant than Sunja, who was more than a dozen years younger. Her dark, smooth hair was rolled up with a wooden hairpin, and Kyunghee wore a cotton apron over her plain blue Western-style dress. She looked like a wispy schoolgirl more than a thirty-one-year-old house-wife.

Kyunghee reached for the brass teakettle resting above the kerosene heater. "Did you get them something to drink or eat at the station?" she asked her husband. She poured tea into four terra-cotta cups.

He laughed. "You said to come home as fast as possible!"

"What a brother you are! Never mind. I'm too happy to nag. You brought them home." Kyunghee stood close by Sunja and stroked her hair.

The girl had an ordinary, flat face and thin eyes. Her features were small. Sunja was not ugly, but not attractive in any obvious way. Her face and neck were puffy and her ankles heavily swollen. Sunja looked nervous, and Kyunghee felt sorry for her and wanted her to know that she needn't be anxious. Two long braids hanging down Sunja's back were bound with thin strips of ordinary hemp. Her stomach was high; and Kyunghee guessed that the child might be a boy.

Kyunghee passed her the tea, and Sunja bowed as she accepted the cup with two shaky hands.

"Are you cold? You're not wearing much." Kyunghee put down a floor cushion near the low dining table and made the girl sit there. She wrapped a quilt the color of green apples over Sunja's lap. Sunja sipped her hot barley tea.

The exterior of the house belied its comfortable interior. Kyunghee, who'd grown up in a household with many servants, had taught herself to keep a clean and inviting house for her and her husband. They owned a six-mat house with three rooms for just the two of them, which was unheard-of in this crowded Korean enclave where ten could sleep in a two-mat room; nevertheless, compared to the grand houses where she and her husband had grown up, their house was absurdly small, not fit for an aging servant. The couple had bought the house from a very poor Japanese widow who had moved to Seoul with her son when Kyunghee arrived to join Yoseb in Osaka. There were many different kinds of Koreans who lived in Ikaino, and they had learned to be wary of the deceitfulness and criminality among them.

"Never lend anyone money," Yoseb said, looking straight at Isak, who appeared puzzled by this order.

"Can't we discuss these things after they've eaten? They just got here," Kyunghee pleaded.

"If you have extra money or valuables, let me know. We'll put it aside. I have a bank account. Everyone who lives here needs money, clothes, rent, and food; there's very little you can do to fix all of their problems. We'll give to the church—no different than how we were raised—but the church has to hand things out. You don't understand what it's like here. Try to avoid talking to the neighbors, and never ever let anyone in the house," Yoseb said soberly to Isak and Sunja.

"I expect you to respect these rules, Isak. You're a generous person, but it can be dangerous for us. If people think we have extra, our house will be robbed. We don't have a lot, Isak. We have to be very careful, too. Once you start giving, it will never stop. Some people here drink and gamble; the mothers are desperate when the money runs out. I don't blame them, but we must take care of our parents and Kyunghee's parents first."

"He's saying all this because I got us in trouble," Kyunghee said.

"What do you mean?" Isak asked.

"I gave food to the neighbors when I first got here, and soon they were asking us every day, and I was giving away our dinners, and they didn't understand when I had to keep back some food for your brother's lunch the next day; then one day, they broke into our house and took our last bag of potatoes. They said it wasn't them, someone they knew—"

"They were hungry," Isak said, trying to understand.

Yoseb looked angry.

"We're all hungry. They were stealing. You have to be careful. Just because they're Korean doesn't mean they're our friends. Be extra careful around other Koreans; the bad ones know that the police won't listen to our complaints. Our house has been broken into twice. Kyunghee has lost her jewelry." Yoseb stared at Isak again with warning in his eyes.

"And the women are home all day. I never keep money or other valuable things in the house."

Kyunghee said nothing else. It had never occurred to her that giving up a few meals would lead to her wedding ring and her mother's jade hairpin and bracelets being stolen. After the house was broken into the second time, Yoseb was angry with her for days.

"I'll fry the fish now. Why don't we talk as we eat?" she said, smiling, heading to the tiny kitchen by the back door.

"Sister, may I please help you?" Sunja asked.

Kyunghee nodded and patted her back.

She whispered, "Don't be afraid of the neighbors. They're good people. My husband—I mean, your brother-in-law—is right to be cautious. He knows more about these things. He doesn't want us to mingle with the people who live here, so I don't. I've been so alone. I'm so glad you're here. And there will be a baby!" Kyunghee's eyes lit up. "There will be a child in this house, and I'll be an aunt. What a blessing this is."

The heartbreak in Kyunghee's beautiful face was obvious, but her suffering and privation had made her finer in a way. In all these years, there had been no child for them, and Isak had told Sunja that this was all Kyunghee and Yoseb had ever wanted.

The kitchen was no more than a stove, a pair of washtubs, and a workbench that doubled as a cutting board—the space was a fraction of the size of the kitchen in Yeongdo. There was just enough room for the two of them to stand side by side, but they could not move about much. Sunja rolled up her sleeves and washed her hands with the hose in the makeshift sink by the floor. The boiled vegetables had to be dressed, and the fish had to be fried.

"Sunja-ya—" Kyunghee touched her forearm lightly. "We'll always be sisters."

The young woman nodded gratefully, devotion already taking root in her heart. The sight of the prepared dishes made her hungry for the first time in days.

Kyunghee picked up a pot lid—white rice.

"Just for today. For your first night. This is your home now."

13

After dinner, the two couples walked to the public bathhouse, where the men and women bathed separately. The bathers were Japanese mostly, and they refused to acknowledge Kyunghee and Sunja. This had been expected. After scrubbing away the dirt of the long journey and having a long soak, Sunja felt elated. They put on clean undergarments beneath their street clothes and walked home, clean and ready to sleep. Yoseb sounded hopeful—yes, life in Osaka would be difficult, but things would change for the better. They'd make a tasty broth from stones and bitterness. The Japanese could think what they wanted about them, but none of it would matter if they survived and succeeded. There were four of them now, Kyunghee said, and soon five—they were stronger because they were together. "Right?" she said.

Kyunghee linked arms with Sunja. They walked closely behind the men.

Yoseb warned his brother: "Don't get mixed up in the politics, labor organizing, or any such nonsense. Keep your head down and work. Don't pick up or accept any of the independence-movement or socialist tracts. If the police find that stuff on you, you'll get picked up and put in jail. I've seen it all."

Isak had been too young and ill to participate in the March 1 Independence Movement, but many of its founding fathers had been graduates of his seminary in Pyongyang. Many of the seminary teachers had marched in 1919.

"Are there many activists here?" Isak whispered, though no one on the road was nearby.

"Yeah, I think so. More in Tokyo and some hiding out in Manchuria. Anyway, when those guys get caught, they die. If you're lucky, you get deported, but that's rare. You better not do any of that stuff under my roof. That's not why I invited you to Osaka. You have a job at the church."

Isak stared at Yoseb, who was raising his voice.

"You won't give the activists a minute. Right?" Yoseb said sternly. "It's not just you now. You have to think of your wife and child."

Back home in Pyongyang, when Isak had been feeling strong enough to make the journey to Osaka, he had considered reaching out to the patriots fighting against colonization. Things were getting worse at home; even his parents had been selling parcels of their property to pay taxes from the new land surveys. Yoseb was sending them money now. Isak believed that it was Christlike to resist oppression. But in a few months, everything had changed for Isak. These ideals seemed secondary to his job and Sunja. He had to think of the safety of others.

Isak's silence worried Yoseb.

"The military police will harass you until you give up or die," Yoseb said. "And your health, Isak. You have to be careful not to get sick again. I've seen men arrested here. It's not like back home. The judges here are Japanese. The police are Japanese. The laws aren't clear. And you can't always trust the Koreans in these independence groups. There are spies who work both sides. The poetry discussion groups have spies, and there are spies in churches, too. Eventually, each activist is picked off like ripe fruit from the same stupid tree. They'll force you to sign a confession. Do you understand?" Yoseb slowed down his walking.

From behind, Kyunghee touched her husband's sleeve.

"*Yobo*, you worry too much. Isak's not going to get mixed up in such things. Let's not spoil their first night."

Yoseb nodded, but the anxiety in his body felt out of control, and warning his brother—even if it meant sounding hysterical—felt necessary to dissipate some of that worry. Yoseb remembered how good it was before the Japanese came—he was ten years old when the country was colonized;

and yet he couldn't do what their elder brother, Samoel, had done so bravely—fight and end up as a martyr. Protesting was for young men without families.

"Mother and Father will kill me if you get sick again or get into trouble. That will be on your conscience. You want me dead?"

Isak swung his left arm around his elder brother's shoulder and embraced him.

"I think you've gotten shorter," Isak said, smiling.

"Are you listening to me?" Yoseb said quietly.

"I promise to be good. I promise to listen to you. You mustn't worry so much. Your hair will gray, or you will lose what's left of it."

Yoseb laughed. This was what he had needed—to have his younger brother near him. It was good to have someone who knew him this way and to be teased even. His wife was a treasure, but it was different to have this person who'd known you almost from birth. The thought of losing Isak to the murky world of politics had scared him into lecturing his younger brother on his first night in Osaka.

"A real Japanese bath. It's wonderful," Isak said. "It's a great thing about this country. Isn't it?"

Yoseb nodded, praying inside that Isak would never come to any harm. His unqualified pleasure at his brother's arrival was short-lived; he hadn't realized what it would mean to worry about another person in this way.

On their walk home, Kyunghee told Isak and Sunja about the famous noodle shops near the train station and promised to take them. Once they returned to the house, Kyunghee turned on the lights, and Sunja remembered that this was now where she lived. The street outside was quiet and dark, and the tiny shack was lit with a clean, bright warmth. Isak and Sunja went to their room, and Kyunghee said good night, closing the panel door behind them.

Their windowless room was just big enough for a futon and a steamer trunk converted into a dresser. Fresh paper covered the low walls; the tatami mats had been brushed and wiped down by hand; and Kyunghee had plumped up the quilts with new cotton padding. The room had its own kerosene heater, a midpriced model that was nicer than the one in the main room, where Kyunghee and Yoseb slept, and it emitted a steady, calming hum.

Isak and Sunja would sleep on the same pallet. Before Sunja left home, her mother had spoken to her about sex as if everything was new to her; she explained what a husband expected; and she said that relations were allowed when pregnant. *Do what you can to please your husband. Men need to have sex.*

A single electric bulb hung from the ceiling and cast a pale glow about the room. Sunja glanced at it, and Isak looked up, too.

"You must be tired," he said.

"I'm fine."

Sunja crouched down to open up the folded pallet and quilt on the floor. What would it be like to sleep beside Isak, who was now her husband? The bed was made up quickly, but they were still wearing street clothes. Sunja pulled out her nightclothes from her clothing bundle—a white muslin nightgown her mother had fashioned from two old slips. How would she change? She knelt by the pallet, the gown in her hands.

"Would you like me to turn out the light?" he asked.

"Yes."

Isak pulled the chain cord, and the switch made a loud clicking sound. The room was still suffused with the dim glow from the adjoining room, separated by a paper screen door. On the other side of the thin wall was the street; pedestrians talked loudly; the pigs next door squealed now and then. It felt like the street was inside rather than out. Isak removed his clothes, keeping on his underwear to sleep in—intimate garments Sunja had already seen, since she'd been doing his wash for months. She had already seen him vomit, have diarrhea, and cough up blood—aspects of illness that no young wife should have had to witness so early on in a relationship. In a way, they'd been living together longer and more intimately than most people who got married, and each had seen the other in deeply compromised situations. They shouldn't feel nervous around the other, he told himself. And yet Isak was uncomfortable. He had never slept next to a woman, and though he knew what should happen, he was not entirely sure of how it should begin.

Sunja removed her day clothes. At the bathhouse under the electric lights, she had been alarmed by the darkening vertical stripe reaching from her pubis to the base of her round, sloping breasts. She put on her nightgown.

Like children fresh from their baths, Isak and Sunja slipped quickly beneath the blue-and-white quilt, carrying with them the scent of soap.

Sunja wanted to say something to him, but she didn't know what. They'd started off with him being ill, her having done something shameful, and him saving her. Perhaps here in their new home, they could each begin again. Lying in this room that Kyunghee had made for them, Sunja felt hopeful. It occurred to her that she'd been trying to bring Hansu back by remembering him, but that didn't make sense. She wanted to devote herself to Isak and her child. To do that, she would have to forget Hansu.

"Your family is very kind."

"I wish you could meet my parents, too. Father is like my brother—good-natured and honest. My mother is wise; she seems reserved, but she'd protect you with her life. She thinks Kyunghee is right about everything and always takes her side." He laughed quietly.

Sunja nodded, wondering how her mother was.

Isak leaned his head closer to her pillow, and she held her breath.

Could he have desire for her? she wondered. How was that possible?

Isak noticed that when Sunja worried, she furrowed her brow like she was trying to see better. He liked being with her; she was capable and level-headed. She was not helpless, and that was appealing because, although he wasn't helpless himself, Isak knew that he was not always sensible. Her competence would be good for what his father had once termed Isak's "impractical nature." Their journey from Busan would have been difficult for anyone, let alone a pregnant woman, but she hadn't whimpered a complaint or spoken a cross word. Whenever he forgot to eat or drink, or to put on his coat, she reminded him with no trace of rebuke. Isak knew how to talk with people, to ask questions, and to hear the concerns in a person's voice; she seemed to understand how to survive, and this was something he did not always know how to do. He needed her; a man needed a wife.

"I feel well today. My chest doesn't have that pulling feeling," he said.

"Maybe it was the bath. And that good dinner. I don't remember having eaten so well. We had white rice twice this month. I feel like a rich person."

Isak laughed. "I wish I could get white rice for you every day." In the service of the Lord, Isak wasn't supposed to care about what to eat, where to sleep, or what to wear, but now that he was married, he thought he ought to care about her needs.

"No, no. I didn't mean that. I was just surprised by it. It's not necessary for us to eat such luxurious things." Sunja berated herself privately, not wanting him to think that she was spoiled.

"I like white rice, too," he said, though he rarely gave much thought to what he ate. He wanted to touch her shoulder to comfort her and wouldn't have hesitated if they were dressed, but lying so close and wearing so little, he kept his hands by his sides.

She wanted to keep talking. It felt easier to whisper to him in the dark; it had felt awkward to talk on the ferry or train when all they had was time for longer conversations.

"Your brother is very interesting; my mother had mentioned that he told funny stories and made Father laugh—"

"I shouldn't have favorites, but he's always been my closer sibling. When we were growing up, he was scolded a lot because he hated going to school. Brother had trouble with reading and writing, but he's good with people and has a remarkable memory. He never forgets anything he hears and can pick up most languages after just a little while of hearing it. He knows some Chinese, English, and Russian, too. He's always been good at fixing machines. Everyone in our town loved him, and no one wanted him to go to Japan. My father wanted him to be a doctor, but of course that wasn't possible if he wasn't good at sitting still and studying. The schoolmasters chastised him all the time for not trying hard enough. He used to wish that he was the one who was sick and had to stay home. Schoolmasters came to the house to teach me my lessons, and sometimes he'd get me to do his work for him when he'd skip school to go fishing or swimming with his buddies. I think he left for Osaka to avoid fighting with Father. He wanted to make a fortune, and he knew he'd never be a doctor. He couldn't see how he'd ever make any money in Korea when honest Koreans were losing property every day."

Neither of them spoke, and they listened to the street noises—a woman yelling at her children to come inside, a group of tipsy men singing off-key, "*Arirang, arirang, arariyo—*" Soon, they could hear Yoseb's snoring and Kyunghee's light, steady breathing as if they were lying beside them.

Isak put his right hand on her belly but felt no movement. She never spoke about the baby, but Isak often wondered what must be happening to the growing child.

"A child is a gift from the Lord," he said.

"It must be, I think."

"Your stomach feels warm," he said.

The skin on the palms of her hands was rough with calluses, but the skin on her belly was smooth and taut like fine fabric. He was with his wife, and he should have been more sure of himself, but he wasn't. Between his legs, his cock had grown to its full measure—this thing that had happened to him each morning since he was a boy felt different now that he was lying beside a woman. Of course, he had imagined what this might be like, but what he hadn't anticipated was the warmth, the nearness of her breath, and the fear that she might dislike him. His hand covered her breast—its shape plush and heavy. Her breath changed.

Sunja tried to relax; Hansu had never touched her like this with such care and gentleness. When she'd met him at the cove, sex was initiated in haste, with her not knowing what it was supposed to mean—the awkward thrusting, his face changing with relief and gratitude, then the need to wash her legs in cold seawater. He used to stroke her jawline and neck with his hands. He had liked to touch her hair. Once, he wanted her to take her hair out of her braids and she did so, but it had made her late in returning home. Within her body, his child was resting and growing, and he could not feel this because he was gone.

Sunja opened her eyes; Isak's eyes were open, too, and he was smiling at her, his hand rubbing her nipple; she quickened at his touch.

"*Yobo,*" he said.

He was her husband, and she would love him.

14

Early next morning, using the map his brother Yoseb had drawn for him on a scrap of butcher paper, Isak found the Hanguk Presbyterian Church—a slanted wooden frame house in the back streets of Ikaino, a few steps away from the main *shotengai*—its only distinguishing mark a humble white cross painted on its brown wooden door.

Sexton Hu, a young Chinese man raised by Pastor Yoo, led Isak to the church office. Pastor Yoo was counseling a brother and sister. Hu and Isak waited by the office door. The young woman was speaking in low tones, and Yoo nodded sympathetically.

"Should I return later?" Isak asked Hu quietly.

"No, sir."

Hu, a matter-of-fact sort of person, examined the new minister carefully: Pastor Baek Isak did not look very strong. Hu was impressed by the man's obvious handsomeness, but Hu believed that a man in the prime of his life should have greater physical stature. Pastor Yoo was once a much larger man, able to run long distances and play soccer skillfully. He was older now and diminished in size; he suffered from cataracts and glaucoma.

"Each morning, Pastor Yoo has been asking for any word from you. We didn't know when you'd come. If we'd known that you were arriving yesterday, I would've come to pick you up at the station." Hu was no older than twenty; he spoke Japanese and Korean very well and had the mannerisms of a much older man. Hu wore a shabby white dress shirt with a blown-out collar, tucked into a pair of brown woolen trousers. His dark blue sweater was knit from heavy wool and patched in places. He was wearing the winter remnants of Canadian missionaries who hadn't had much themselves.

Isak turned away to cough.

"My child, who is that with you?" Yoo turned his head to the voices by the door and pushed up his heavy horn-rimmed eyeglasses closer to his face, though doing so hardly helped to sharpen his vision. Behind the milky gray cast clouding his eyes, his expression remained calm and certain. His hearing was acute. He could not make out the shapes by the door, but he knew that one of them was Hu, the Manchurian orphan who'd been left at the church by a Japanese officer, and that the man he was speaking with had an unfamiliar voice.

"It's Pastor Baek," Hu said.

The siblings seated on the floor by the pastor turned around and bowed.

Yoo felt impatient to end the meeting with the brother and sister, who were no closer to a resolution.

"Come to me, Isak. It's not so easy for me to reach you."

Isak obeyed.

"You have come at last. Hallelujah." Yoo put his right hand lightly over Isak's head.

"The Lord bless you, my dear child."

"I'm sorry to have kept you waiting. I arrived in Osaka last night," Isak said. The elder pastor's unfocused pupils were ringed with silver. He wasn't blind, but the condition was severe. Despite his nearly lost vision, the minister appeared vigorous; his seated posture was straight and firm.

"My son, come closer."

Isak drew near, and the older man clasped Isak's hands at first, then cradled his face between his thick palms.

The brother and sister looked on without saying anything. By the transom of the door, Hu sat on bended knees, waiting for Yoo's next instruction.

"You were sent to me, you know," Yoo said.

"Thank you for allowing me to come."

"I'm pleased that you're here at last. Did you bring your wife? Hu read me your letter."

"She's at home today. She will be here on Sunday."

"Yes, yes." The older man nodded. "The congregation will be so pleased to have you here. Ah, you should meet this family!"

The siblings bowed again to Isak. They'd noticed that the pastor looked happier than they'd ever seen him.

"They've come to see us about a family matter," Yoo said to Isak, then turned to the siblings.

The sister did little to hide her irritation. The brother and sister were from a rural village in Jeju, and they were far less formal than young people from cities. The dark-skinned girl with the thick black hair was wholesome looking; she was remarkably pretty while appearing very innocent. She wore a long-sleeved white shirt buttoned to the collar and a pair of indigo-colored *mompei*.

"This is the new associate pastor, Baek Isak. Should we ask for his counsel, too?" From the tone of Yoo's voice, there was no possibility of the siblings' dissent.

Isak smiled at them. The sister was twenty or so; the brother was younger.

The matter was complicated but not out of the ordinary. The brother and sister had been arguing about money. The sister had been accepting gifts of money from a Japanese manager at the textile factory where she worked. Older than their father, the manager was married with five children. He took the sister to restaurants and gave her trinkets and cash. The girl sent the entire sum to their parents living with an indigent uncle back home. The brother felt it was wrong to take anything beyond her salary; the sister disagreed.

"What does he want from her?" the brother asked Isak bluntly. "She should be made to stop. This is a sin."

Yoo craned his head lower, feeling exhausted by their intransigence.

The sister was furious that she had to be here at all, having to listen to her younger brother's accusations. "The Japanese took our uncle's farm.

We can't work at home because there are no jobs; if a Japanese man wants to give me some pocket money to have dinner with him, I don't see the harm," the sister said. "I'd take double what he gives me if I could. He doesn't give that much."

"He expects something, and he's cheap," said the brother, looking disgusted.

"I'd never let Yoshikawa-san touch me. I sit, smile, and listen to him talk about his family and his work." She didn't mention that she poured his drinks and wore the rouge that he bought for her, which she scrubbed off before coming home.

"He pays you to flirt with him. This is how a whore behaves." The brother was shouting now. "Good women don't go to restaurants with married men! While we work in Japan, Father said I'm in charge and must watch out for my sister. What does it matter that she's older? She's a girl and I'm a man; I can't let this continue. I won't allow it!"

The brother was four years younger than his nineteen-year-old sister. They were living with a distant cousin in an overcrowded house in Ikaino. The cousin, an elderly woman, never bothered them as long as they paid their share of the rent; she didn't come to church, so Pastor Yoo didn't know her.

"Father and Mother are starving back home. Uncle can't feed his own wife and children. At this point, I'd sell my hands if I could. God wants me to honor my parents. It's a sin not to care for them. If I have to be disgraced—" The girl started to cry. "Isn't it possible that the Lord is providing Yoshikawa-san as our answer?" She looked at Pastor Yoo, who took the girl's hands into his and bent his head as if in prayer.

It wasn't uncommon to hear rationalizations of this sort—the longing to transform bad deeds into good ones. No one ever wanted to hear that God didn't work that way; the Lord would never want a young woman to trade her body to follow a commandment. Sins couldn't be laundered by good results.

"*Aigoo*," Yoo sighed. "How difficult it must be to bear the weight of this world on your small shoulders. Do your parents know where you're getting this money?"

"They think it's from my wages, but that barely covers our rent and expenses. My brother has to go to school; Mother told me that it's my responsibility for him to finish. He's threatening to quit his studies so he can work, but that's a foolish decision in the long run. Then we'll always be working these terrible jobs. Without knowing how to read and write Japanese."

Isak was astonished by her clarity; she had thought this through. He was half a dozen years older than she was, and he had not thought of such things. He'd never given his parents one sen of his wages, since he'd never earned money before. When he served briefly as a lay pastor at his church back home, he had gone without a salary because the church had so little for the senior clergy and the congregation had such great needs. He wasn't certain what he would earn here. When he received the call to work at this church, the terms hadn't been discussed; he'd assumed that his compensation would be enough to support him—and now, his family. With money always in his pocket and more readily available when he asked his parents or brother, Isak hadn't bothered to figure out his earnings or his expenses. In the presence of these young people, Isak felt like a selfish fool.

"Pastor Yoo, we want you to decide. She won't listen to me. I cannot control where she goes after work. If she keeps meeting with that goat, he'll do something terrible, and no one will care what happens to her. She'll listen to you," the brother said quietly. "She has to."

The sister kept her head down. She did not want Pastor Yoo to think badly of her. Sunday mornings were very special to her; church was the only place she felt good. She wasn't doing anything wrong with Yoshikawa-san, but she was certain that his wife didn't know about these meetings, and often he wanted to hold her hand, and though it didn't seem harmful, it didn't seem innocent, either. Not long ago, he'd mentioned that she should accompany him to a marvelous *onsen* in Kyoto, but she had demurred, saying she had to take care of her brother's meals.

"We must support our family, this is true," Yoo prefaced, and the sister appeared visibly relieved, "but we have to be careful of your virtue—it is more valuable than money. Your body is a sacred temple where the Holy

Spirit dwells. Your brother's concern is legitimate. Apart from our faith and speaking practically, if you are to marry, your purity and reputation are important, too. The world judges girls harshly for improprieties—and even accidents. It's wrong, but it is the way this sinful world works," Yoo said.

"But he can't quit school, sir. I promised Mother—" the sister said.

"He's young. He can go to school at a later time," Yoo countered, though he knew this was not likely.

At this, the brother perked up; he hadn't expected this suggestion. He hated school—the Japanese teachers thought he was stupid and the kids taunted him daily for his clothes and accent; the brother planned on making as much money as possible so his sister could quit or work elsewhere and so he could send money to Jeju.

The young woman sobbed.

Yoo swallowed and said calmly, "You're right, it'd be better if your brother could go to school. Even for a year or two so he could know how to read and write. There's no better choice than education, of course; our country needs a new generation of educated people to lead us."

The sister quieted down, thinking the pastor might take her side. It wasn't that she wanted to continue seeing Yoshikawa, a silly old man who smelled of camphor, but she believed that her being here in Osaka had a noble purpose, that there was a respectable future for them if she worked and her brother went to school.

Isak listened to Yoo in admiration, observing that the senior pastor was an exceptional counselor, at once sympathetic and powerful.

"Yoshikawa-san doesn't want anything but your company for now, but he may wish for other things later, and you'll find yourself in his debt. You'll feel the obligation. You may fear the loss of your job. Then it may be too late. You may think you're using him, but is that who we are? Shall we exploit because we have been exploited, my dear child?"

Isak nodded in agreement, gratified by the pastor's compassion and wisdom. He wouldn't have known what to say.

"Isak, would you bless these children?" Yoo asked, and Isak began to pray for them.

The brother and sister left without argument and, no doubt, would return on Sunday morning to worship.

The sexton, who had disappeared, returned, bringing three large bowls of wheat noodles in a black bean sauce. The three men prayed before eating. They sat on the floor, their legs crossed, their hot lunches on top of the low dining table that Hu had made from abandoned crates. The room was chilly, and it didn't help that there were no floor cushions. Isak was surprised at himself for noticing this; he'd always believed that he was not the kind of person who cared about such niceties, but it was uncomfortable sitting on a concrete floor.

"Eat, son. Hu is a fine cook. I'd go hungry without him," Yoo said, and started to eat.

"Will the sister stop seeing him, do you think?" Hu asked Pastor Yoo.

"If the girl gets pregnant, Yoshikawa will throw her away, and then there would be no school for the brother anyway. The manager is just one of those romantic old fools who wants to be with a young girl and to feel like he's in love. Soon he will need to lie with her, then eventually he will lose interest. Men and women are not very difficult to understand," Yoo said. "She must stop seeing the manager, and the brother must get a job. She should change her workplace immediately. Together they will make enough money to live and to send to their parents."

Isak was surprised by the pastor's change in tone; he sounded cold, almost haughty.

Hu nodded and ate his noodles quietly as if he were ruminating deeply about this.

Yoo turned in Isak's direction. "I've seen this many times. Girls think they'll have the upper hand because these kinds of men seem so pliable, when in fact, the girls are the ones who end up paying bitterly for their mistakes. The Lord forgives, but the world does not forgive."

"Yes," Isak murmured.

"How's your wife settling in? There's enough space at your brother's for you two?"

"Yes. My brother has room. My wife is expecting a baby."

"So fast! How wonderful," Yoo said with pleasure.

"That's wonderful," Hu said excitedly, sounding young for the first time. Seeing all the small children running about in the back of the sanctuary was Hu's favorite part of attending services. Before coming to Japan, he'd lived in a large orphanage, and he liked hearing children's voices.

"Where does your brother live?"

"Only a few minutes from here. I understand that good housing is difficult to find."

Yoo laughed. "No one will rent to the Koreans. As pastor, you'll get a chance to see how the Koreans live here. You can't imagine: a dozen in a room that should be for two, men and families sleeping in shifts. Pigs and chickens inside homes. No running water. No heat. The Japanese think Koreans are filthy, but they have no choice but to live in squalor. I've seen aristocrats from Seoul reduced to nothing, with no money for bathhouses, wearing rags for clothing, shoeless, and unable to get work as porters in the markets. There's nowhere for them to go. Even the ones with work and money can't find a place to live. Some are squatting illegally."

"The men who were brought here by Japanese companies—wouldn't they provide housing?"

"There are camps attached to mines or larger factories in places like Hokkaido, but the camps aren't for families. The camps are no better; the conditions are deplorable," Yoo said without emotion. Again, Yoo's tone sounded unfeeling, and it surprised Isak. When the siblings had been there, Yoo had seemed concerned about their hardship.

"Where do you live?" Isak asked.

"I sleep in the office. In that corner." Yoo pointed to the area beside the stove. "And Hu sleeps in that corner."

"There are no pallets or bedding—"

"They're in the cupboard. Hu makes the beds each night and clears them up in the morning. We could make room for you and your family if you need to stay here. That would be part of your compensation."

"Thank you, sir. But I think we are all right for now."

Hu nodded, though he would've liked to have had a baby living with them; the church building was too drafty for a child.

"And your meals?"

"Hu fixes our meals on the stove at the back of the house. There's a sink with running water; the outhouse is by the back. The missionaries put those in, thankfully."

"You don't have a family?" Isak asked Yoo.

"My wife passed away two years after we arrived. That was fifteen years ago. We never had children." Yoo added, "But Hu is a son to me. He is my blessing, and now you've arrived to bless us both."

Hu blushed, pleased by this mention.

"How are you with money?" Yoo asked.

"I meant to speak with you," Isak said, wondering if he should discuss this in front of Hu, but realizing that Hu had to be present to function as the pastor's eyes.

Yoo lifted his head and spoke firmly, like a hard-nosed merchant:

"Your wages will be fifteen yen per month. It isn't enough for one man to live on. Hu and I don't take a salary. Just living expenses. Also, I can't guarantee fifteen yen per month, either. The Canadian churches send us some support, but it's not steady, and our congregation doesn't give much. Will you be all right?"

Isak didn't know what to say. He'd no idea what his contribution was to be for living at his brother's. He couldn't imagine asking his brother to support him and his wife and child.

"Can your family help?" It had been part of Yoo's calculation in hiring Isak. The boy's family owned land in Pyongyang; his references there had mentioned that the family had money, so Isak's salary would likely not be so important. They told him that he hadn't even asked for a salary when he served as a lay pastor. Isak was sickly and not a strong hire. Yoo had been counting on Isak's family's financial support for the church.

"I...I cannot ask my brother for help, sir."

"Oh? Is that so?"

"And my parents cannot help at this time."

"I see."

Hu felt sorry for the young pastor, who looked both stunned and ashamed.

"Our parents have been selling their land in large parcels to pay taxes, and things are precarious now. My brother has been sending them money so they could get by. I think he may also be supporting my sister-in-law's family."

Yoo nodded. This had not been expected, though it made sense, of course. Isak's family was no different from the others who had been assessed egregiously by the colonial government. He'd been counting on Isak's being able to sustain himself. With his vision so heavily impaired, Yoo needed a bilingual pastor to help him to write sermons as well as to deal with administrative matters with the local officials.

"There isn't enough from the offerings, I suppose . . ." Isak said.

"No." Yoo shook his head vigorously. There were seventy-five to eighty regular attendees on Sunday mornings, but it was really five or six of the better-off congregants who made up the lion's share of the giving. The rest could hardly afford two shabby meals a day.

Hu picked up the empty bowls from the table.

"The Lord has always provided for us, sir," Hu said.

"Yes, my son, you've spoken well." Yoo smiled at the young man, wishing he could've provided him with an education. The boy had such natural intelligence and tremendous aptitude; he would have made a fine scholar, even a pastor.

"We will find a way," Yoo said. "This must be very disappointing to you." His tone of voice sounded the way he had spoken to the sister earlier.

"I'm grateful for this job, sir. I'll speak with my family about the salary. Hu is right, of course; the Lord will provide," Isak said.

"All I have needed Thy hand hath provided; Great is Thy faithfulness, Lord, unto me!" Pastor Yoo sang in his rich tenor voice. "The Lord provided you for our church. Surely, He will care for all of our material needs."

15

The summer had come fast. The Osaka sun felt hotter than the sun back home, and the brutal humidity slowed down Sunja's heavy movements. However, her workdays were easy, and until the baby came, she and Kyunghee had to care only for themselves and their husbands, who didn't come home until late in the evening. Isak spent long days and nights at the church serving the needs of a growing congregation, and Yoseb managed the biscuit factory during the day and repaired machines in factories in Ikaino in the evenings for extra money. The daily tasks of cooking, laundry, and cleaning for four were considerably less onerous than caring for a boardinghouse. Sunja's life felt luxurious in contrast to her old life in Busan.

She loved spending the day with Kyunghee, whom she called Sister. After two brief months, they found themselves enjoying a close friendship—an unexpected gift for two women who'd neither expected nor asked for much happiness. Kyunghee was no longer alone in the house all day, and Yoseb was grateful that Isak had brought the boardinghouse daughter as his wife.

In the minds of Yoseb and Kyunghee, the cause of Sunja's pregnancy had long been settled with a rationalization of their making: The girl had been harmed through no fault of her own, and Isak had rescued her because it was his nature to make sacrifices. No one asked her the particulars, and Sunja did not speak of the matter.

Kyunghee and Yoseb hadn't been able to have children, but Kyunghee was undeterred. Sarah in the Bible had a child in old age, and Kyunghee didn't believe that God had forgotten her. A devout woman, she spent her time helping the poor mothers at the church. She was also a thrifty housewife, able to save every extra sen that her husband entrusted to her. It had been Kyunghee's idea to buy the Ikaino house with the money Yoseb's father had given him combined with her dowry, even when Yoseb had had his doubts. "Why would we pay rent to the landlord and have nothing left when the month is over?" she'd said. Because Kyunghee stuck to a careful budget, they'd been able to send money to Yoseb's parents and her own— both families having lost all of their arable land.

Kyunghee's dream was to own her own business selling kimchi and pickles at the covered market near Tsuruhashi Station, and when Sunja moved in, she finally had a person who'd listen to her plans. Yoseb disapproved of her working for money. He liked coming home to a rested and pretty housewife who had his supper ready—an ideal reason for a man to work hard, he believed. Each day, Kyunghee and Sunja made three meals: a hot, traditional breakfast with soup; a packed lunch for the men to take to work; and a hot dinner. Without refrigeration or the cold Pyongyang climate, Kyunghee had to cook often to avoid waste.

It was unusually warm for the beginning of summer, and the thought of making soup on the stone stove at the back of the house would have been unappealing to any normal housewife, but Kyunghee didn't mind. She enjoyed going to the market and thinking about what to fix for their meals. Unlike most of the Korean women in Ikaino, she spoke decent Japanese and was able to negotiate with the merchants for what she wanted.

When Kyunghee and Sunja entered the butcher shop, Tanaka-san, the tall young proprietor, snapped to attention and shouted "*Irasshai!*" to welcome them.

The butcher and his helper, Koji, were delighted to see the pretty Korean and her pregnant sister-in-law. They weren't big customers; in fact, they spent very little money, but they were steady, and as Tanaka's father and grandfather had taught him—the eighth generation of sons to run the shop—the daily, cumulative payments were more valuable than the infrequent, outsize purchases. Housewives were the backbone of the business, and the Korean women couldn't fuss like the local women, which made them preferable customers. It was also rumored that one of his great-grandfathers may have been Korean or *burakumin*, so the young butcher had been raised by his father and mother to be fair to all the customers. Times might have changed, to be sure, but butchery, which required touching dead animals, was still a shameful occupation—the chief reason given as to why the matchmaker had such difficulty arranging an *omiai* for him—and Tanaka couldn't help but feel a kind of kinship with foreigners.

The men ogled Kyunghee, altogether ignoring Sunja, who had by now grown used to this invisibility whenever the two went anywhere. Kyunghee, who looked smart in her midi skirts and crisp white blouses, easily passing for a schoolteacher or a merchant's modest wife with her fine features, was welcomed in most places. Everyone thought she was Japanese until she spoke; even then, the local men were pleasant to her. For the first time in her life, Sunja felt aware of her unacceptable plainness and inappropriate attire. She felt homely in Osaka. Her well-worn, traditional clothes were an inevitable badge of difference, and though there were enough older and poorer Koreans in the neighborhood who wore them still, she had never been looked upon with scorn with such regularity, when she had never meant to call attention to herself. Within the settled boundaries of Ikaino, one would not be stared at for wearing a white *hanbok*, but outside the neighborhood and farther out from the train station, the chill against identifiable Koreans was obvious. Sunja would have preferred to wear Western clothes or *mompei*, but it would make no sense to spend money on fabric to sew new things now. Kyunghee promised to make her new clothes after the baby was delivered.

Kyunghee bowed politely to the men, and Sunja retreated into the corner of the shop.

"How can we help you today, Boku-san?" Tanaka-san asked.

Even after two months, it still surprised Sunja to hear her husband's family name pronounced in its Japanese form. Due to the colonial government's requirements, it was normal for Koreans to have at least two or three names, but back home she'd had little use for the Japanese *tsumei*—Junko Kaneda—written on her identity papers, because Sunja didn't go to school and had nothing to do with official business. Sunja was born a Kim, yet in Japan, where women went by their husband's family name, she was Sunja Baek, which was translated into Sunja Boku, and on her identity papers, her *tsumei* was now Junko Bando. When the Koreans had to choose a Japanese surname, Isak's father had chosen Bando because it had sounded like the Korean word *ban-deh*, meaning objection, making their compulsory Japanese name a kind of joke. Kyunghee had assured her that all these names would become normal soon enough.

"What will you be cooking today, Boku-san?" the young owner asked.

"May I please have shinbones and a bit of meat? I'm making soup," Kyunghee said in her radio announcer–style Japanese; she regularly listened to Japanese programs to improve her accent.

"Right away." Tanaka grabbed three large hunks of shinbone from the stock of beef bones and oxtails he kept in the ice chest for Korean customers; Japanese did not have any use for bones. He wrapped up a handful of stew meat. "Will that be all?"

She nodded.

"Thirty-six sen, please."

Kyunghee opened her coin purse. Two yen and sixty sen had to last her for eight more days until Yoseb gave her his pay envelope.

"*Sumimasen desu,* how much would it be for just the bones?"

"Ten sen."

"Please pardon my error. Today, I'll take only the bones. Meat another time, I promise."

"Of course." Tanaka returned the meat to the case. It wasn't the first time a customer didn't have enough money to pay for food, but unlike his other customers, the Koreans didn't ask him for credit, not that he would have agreed to it.

"You're making a broth?" Tanaka wondered what it might be like to have such an elegant wife worrying about his meals and being thrifty with her pin money. He was the first son, and although he was eager to be married, he lived with his mother as a bachelor. "What kind?"

"*Seolleongtang*." She looked at him quizzically, wondering if he knew what that was.

"And how do you make this soup?" Tanaka folded his arms leisurely and leaned into the counter, looking carefully into Kyunghee's lovely face. She had beautiful, even teeth, he thought.

"First, you wash the bones very carefully in cold water. Then you boil the bones and throw that first batch of water out because it will have all the blood and dirt that you don't want in your broth. Then you boil it again with clean, cold water, then simmer it for a long, long time until the broth is white like tofu, then you add daikon, chopped scallions, and salt. It's delicious and very good for your health."

"It would be better to have some meat with it, I would imagine."

"And white rice and noodles! Why not?" Kyunghee laughed, her hand raised reflexively to cover her teeth.

Both men laughed with pleasure, understanding her joke, since rice was costly even for them.

"And do you eat kimchi with that?" Tanaka asked, never having had such a long conversation with Kyunghee. It felt safe for him to talk with her with his assistant and her sister-in-law present. "Kimchi is a bit spicy for me, yet I think it's nice with grilled chicken or grilled pork."

"Kimchi is delicious with every meal. I will bring you some from our house next time."

Tanaka reopened the paper packet of bones and put back half of the meat he'd just returned to the case.

"It's not much. Just enough for the baby." Tanaka smiled at Sunja, who was surprised that the butcher had noticed her. "A mother must eat well if she's to raise a strong worker for the Emperor."

"I couldn't take anything for free," Kyunghee said, perplexed. She didn't know what he was doing exactly, but she really couldn't afford the meat today.

Sunja was confused by their conversation. They were saying something about kimchi.

"This is the first sale of the day. Sharing will bring me luck," Tanaka said, feeling puffed up like any man who could give something worthwhile to an attractive woman whenever he pleased.

Kyunghee placed the ten sen on the spotless money dish resting on the counter, smiled, and bowed to both men before she left.

Outside the shop, Sunja asked what happened.

"He didn't charge us for the meat. I didn't know how to make him take it back."

"He likes you. It was a present." Sunja giggled, feeling like Dokhee, the younger servant girl back home, who'd joke about men whenever she had the chance. Though she thought of her mother often, it had been a while since she'd thought about the sisters back home. "I'll call Tanaka-san your boyfriend from now on."

Kyunghee swatted playfully at Sunja, shaking her head.

"He said it's for your baby, so he can grow up to be a good worker for the country." Kyunghee made a face. "And Tanaka-san knows I'm Korean."

"Since when do men care about such things? Mrs. Kim next door told me about the quiet lady who lives at the end of the road who's Japanese and married to the Korean who brews alcohol in his house. Their kids are half Japanese!" This had shocked Sunja when she'd first heard of it, though everything Mrs. Kim, the lady who raised pigs, told her was shocking. Yoseb didn't want Kyunghee and Sunja to speak with Mrs. Kim, who also didn't go to church on Sundays. They weren't allowed to speak to the Japanese wife, either, because her husband was routinely sent to jail for his bootlegging.

"If you run away with the nice butcher, I'll miss you," Sunja said.

"Even if I weren't married, I would not choose that man. He smiles too much." Kyunghee winked at her. "I like my cranky husband who's always telling me what to do and worries about everything.

"Come on, we have to buy vegetables now. That's why I didn't buy the meat. We should try to find some potatoes to roast. Wouldn't that be good for our lunch?"

"Sister—"

"Yes?" Kyunghee said.

"We're not contributing to the house. The groceries, fuel, *sento* fees— I've never seen such prices in my life. Back home, we had a garden, and we never paid for vegetables. And the price of fish! My mother would never eat it again if she knew the cost. Back home, we scrimped, but I didn't realize how easy we had it—we got free fish from the guests, and here, an apple costs more than beef ribs in Busan. Mother was careful with money, the way you are, but even she couldn't have made the kinds of delicious things you make on a budget. Isak and I think you should take the money he makes to help with the food budget at least."

The fact that Sister and Brother wouldn't allow Isak and her to pay for a single thing was difficult to accept, and it wasn't as if they could afford to rent a place separately. Besides, even if they could have afforded to do so, it would have hurt Sister's feelings deeply for Isak and Sunja to move out.

"I'm sure you ate much better and more filling things back home," Kyunghee said, appearing sad.

"No, no. That's not what I meant. We just feel terrible that you won't let us contribute to the enormous expenses."

"Yoseb and I won't allow it. You should be saving money for the baby. We'll have to get clothes for him and diapers, and one day he'll go to school and become a gentleman. Won't that be something? I hope he'll like school like his father and not dodge books like his uncle!" The thought of a baby living with them made Kyunghee smile. This child felt like an answer to her prayers.

"Mother sent me three yen in her last letter. And we have money we brought and Isak's recent earnings to help. You shouldn't have to worry about expenses so much or selling kimchi to support two extra mouths— and soon, three," Sunja said.

"Sunja-ya, you're being disrespectful. I'm your elder. We can manage just fine. Also, if I can't talk about my wish to earn money without you jumping in about wanting to contribute, then I can't talk about my pipe dreams of becoming the kimchi *ajumma* of Tsuruhashi Station."

Kyunghee laughed. "Be a good little sister and let me dream out loud about my business where I'll make so much money that I can buy us a castle and send your son to medical school in Tokyo."

"Do you think housewives would buy another woman's kimchi?"

"Why not! Don't you think I make good kimchi? My family cook made the finest pickles in Pyongyang." Kyunghee lifted her chin, then broke down laughing. She had a joyous laugh. "I'd make a great kimchi *ajumma*. My pickled cabbage would be clean and delicious."

"Why can't you start now? I have enough money to buy cabbage and radish. I can help you make it. If we sell a lot, it would be better for me than working in a factory, because I can watch the baby at home when he's born."

"Yes, we would be really good at it, but Yoseb would kill me. He said he'd never have his wife work. Never. And he wouldn't want you to work, either."

"But I grew up working with my mother and father. He knows that. My mother served the guests and did all the cooking, and I cleaned and washed—"

"Yoseb is old-fashioned." Kyunghee sighed. "I married a very good man. It's my fault. If I had children, I wouldn't feel so restless. I just don't want to be so idle. This isn't Yoseb's fault. No one works harder than he does. Back in the olden days, a man in his situation could've thrown me out for not having a son." Kyunghee nodded to herself, recalling the numerous stories of barren women that she'd heard as a child, never having considered that such a thing could happen to her. "I'll listen to my husband. He has always taken such good care of me."

Sunja could neither agree nor disagree, so she let the statement hang in the air. Her brother-in-law, Yoseb, was in actuality saying that a *yangban* woman like Kyunghee couldn't work outside the house; Sunja was an ordinary peasant's daughter, so working in a market was fine for her. The distinction didn't trouble Sunja, since she agreed that Kyunghee was a superior person in so many ways. Nevertheless, living with Kyunghee and speaking so truthfully with her about everything, Sunja also knew that her sister-in-law was heartbroken about what she could not have and might have been far happier trying her luck as a kimchi *ajumma*.

Regardless, it wasn't her place to say. All this was what her brother-in-law would call "foolish women's talk." For Kyunghee's sake, Sunja brightened up and linked arms with her sister-in-law, who seemed to drag a little. Arm in arm, they went to buy cabbage and daikon.

16

Kyunghee didn't recognize the two men at her door, but they knew her name.

The taller one with the pointy face smiled more frequently, but the shorter one had the kinder expression. They were dressed similarly in workmen's clothing—dark slacks and short-sleeved shirts—but both wore expensive-looking leather shoes. The taller one spoke with a distinct Jeju accent; he dug out a folded sheet of paper from the back pocket of his pants.

"Your husband signed this," he said, flashing her the formal-looking document. Part of it was written in Korean but much of it was in Japanese and Chinese characters. On the upper right-hand corner, Kyunghee recognized Yoseb's name and *hanko*. "He's late on his payments."

"I don't know anything about this. My husband's at work now."

Kyunghee thought she might cry and put her hand on the door, hoping the men would leave. "Please come by later when he's home."

Sunja stood close by her, her hands resting on her abdomen. The men didn't look dangerous to Sunja. Physically, they resembled the lodgers back home, but her sister-in-law appeared flustered.

"He'll be home late tonight. Come back then," Sunja repeated, but much more loudly than Kyunghee had.

"You're the sister-in-law, right?" the shorter one said to her. He had dimples when he smiled.

Sunja said nothing, trying not to appear surprised by the fact that he knew who she was.

The taller one continued grinning at Kyunghee. His teeth were large and square and rooted in pale pink gums.

"We've already spoken to your husband, but he hasn't been responsive so we thought we'd drop by and visit with you." He paused and said her name slowly: "Baek Kyunghee—I had a cousin named Kyunghee. Your *tsumei* is Bando Kimiko, *nee*?" The man placed his wide hand on the door and pressed it in slightly toward her. He glanced at Sunja. "The fact that we're meeting your sister-in-law just doubles our pleasure. Right?" The men laughed heartily together.

Again, Kyunghee attempted to scan the document held before her. "I don't understand it," she said finally.

"This is the important part: Baek Yoseb owes my boss a hundred twenty yen." He pointed to the number 120 written in kanji in the second paragraph. "Your husband has missed the last two payments. We're hoping that you'll get him to make them today."

"How much are the payments?" Kyunghee asked.

"Eight yen plus interest per week," the shorter man said; he had a strong accent from the Kyungsangdo region. "Maybe you keep some money at home and can pay us?" he asked. "It comes out to about twenty yen."

Yoseb had just given her the food money for the next two weeks. She had six yen in her purse. If she gave that to him, they'd have no money for food.

"Is a hundred twenty yen the whole amount?" Sunja asked. The paper didn't make any sense to her, either.

The short man looked a little worried and shook his head.

"By now, it's almost double if you include the interest. Why? Do you have the money?"

"As of today, the total would be two hundred thirteen yen," the taller man said. He'd always been good at doing sums in his head.

"*Uh-muh*," Kyunghee exclaimed. She closed her eyes and leaned her body against the doorframe.

Sunja stepped forward and said calmly, "We'll get you the money." She spoke to them the same way she would've spoken to Fatso, the lodger, as to when he could expect his wash to be ready. She didn't even glance in their direction. "Just come back in three hours. Before it gets dark."

"We'll see you later," the taller one said.

The sisters-in-law walked briskly toward the shopping street near Tsuruhashi Station. They didn't linger in front of the fabric shop window or pause at the *senbei* stall; they didn't greet the friendly vegetable sellers. Rather, their bodies moved in unison toward their destination.

"I don't want you to do this," Kyunghee said.

"Father told me about people like this. If the entire debt isn't paid off immediately, the interest gets higher and higher, and you'll never be able to pay it all back. Father said that you always end up owing a great deal more than you borrow. Think about it—how did a hundred twenty yen become two hundred thirteen?"

Hoonie Kim had witnessed his neighbors lose everything after borrowing a small amount of money to buy seedlings or equipment; when the moneylenders were through with them, his neighbors would end up giving them all their crops on top of their initial loans. Sunja's father had loathed moneylenders and had warned her often about the dangers of debt.

"If I'd known, I would've stopped sending money to our parents," Kyunghee mumbled to herself.

Sunja looked straight ahead, avoiding eye contact with anyone on the busy street who glanced in their direction. She was trying to figure out what she'd say to the broker.

"Sister, you saw his sign in Korean, right?" Sunja said. "That would make him Korean, right?"

"I'm not sure. I don't know anyone who's ever been there."

Following the Korean signs posted on the facade of the low brick building, the women climbed up the wide stairs to the second floor. The pawnbroker's office door had a curtained window, and Sunja opened it gingerly.

It was a warm, breezeless day in June, but the older man behind the desk wore a green silk ascot tucked into his white dress shirt and a brown woolen vest. The three square windows facing the street were open, and two electric fans whirred quietly in the opposite corners of the office. Two younger men with similar chubby faces played cards by the middle window. They glanced up and smiled at the two women.

"Welcome. How can I be of service?" the pawnbroker asked them in Korean. His hometown accent was hard to place. "Would you like to sit down?" He motioned to the chairs, and Sunja told him she'd prefer to stand. Kyunghee stood next to Sunja and refused to look at the men.

Sunja opened the palm of her hand to show him the pocket watch.

"*Ajeossi*, how much could you give us for this?"

The man raised his gray-black eyebrows and pulled out a loupe from his desk drawer.

"Where did you get this?"

"My mother gave it to me. It's solid silver and washed in gold," Sunja said.

"She knows you're selling it?"

"She gave it to me to sell. For the baby."

"Wouldn't you prefer a loan for the watch? Maybe you don't want to let go of it," he asked. Loans were rarely repaid, and he'd be able to keep the collateral.

Sunja spoke slowly: "I want to sell it. If you don't wish to buy it, I won't trouble you any longer."

The broker smiled, wondering if the pregnant girl had already been to his competitors. There were three pawnbrokers just a few streets away. None of the others were Korean, but if she spoke any Japanese, it would have been easy to sell the watch. The pretty woman who accompanied the pregnant one before him looked a little Japanese in the way she dressed; it was hard to tell. It was possible that the pretty one had brought the pregnant girl along to negotiate with him and that the watch belonged to her.

"If you have a need to sell it," the broker said, "I always take pleasure helping a person from home."

Sunja said nothing. In the market, say very little, her father had taught her.

Kyunghee marveled at her sister-in-law appearing calmer than she'd ever seen her.

The pawnbroker examined the watch with care, opening its silver casing to study the mechanical workings visible through its open crystal back. It was an extraordinary pocket watch, and impossible to believe that this pregnant woman's mother could have owned such a thing. The watch was maybe a year old if that and without a scratch. He turned it faceup again and laid it on the green leather blotter on his desk.

"Young men prefer wristwatches these days. I'm not even sure if I can sell this."

Sunja noticed that the broker had blinked hard after saying this, but he hadn't blinked once when he was talking to her before.

"Thank you for looking at it," Sunja said, and turned around. Kyunghee was trying not to appear worried. Sunja picked up the watch and gathered the tail end of her long *chima*, preparing to walk out of the office. "We appreciate your time. Thank you."

"I'd like to help you," the broker said, raising his voice slightly.

Sunja turned around.

"If you need the money right away, perhaps it would be easier for you to sell it here than walking around in this hot day in your condition. I can help you. It looks like you'll have the child soon. I hope it's a boy who'll take good care of his mother," he said.

"Fifty yen," he said.

"Two hundred," she said. "It's worth at least three hundred. It's made in Switzerland and brand-new."

The two men by the window put down their cards and got up from their seats. They'd never seen a girl talk like this.

"If you think it's worth so much, then why don't you sell it for a higher price elsewhere," the broker snapped, irritated by her insolence. He couldn't stand women who talked back.

Sunja bit her inner lower lip. If she sold it to a Japanese pawnbroker, Sunja feared that the broker may alert the police about the watch. Hansu had told her that the police were involved in nearly all the businesses here.

"Thank you. I won't waste any more of your time," Sunja said.

The pawnbroker chuckled.

Kyunghee suddenly felt confident of her sister-in-law, who had been so helpless upon her arrival in Osaka that she had to carry her name and address written in Japanese on a card in case she got lost.

"What did your mother do back home?" the pawnbroker asked. "You sound like you're from Busan."

Sunja paused, wondering if she had to answer the question.

"Did she work in the markets there?"

"She's a boardinghouse keeper."

"She must be a clever businesswoman," he said. The broker had figured that her mother must have been a whore or a merchant of some sort who collaborated with the Japanese government. The watch could also have been stolen. From her speech and dress, the pregnant girl was not from a wealthy family. "Young lady, you're sure that your mother gave this to you to sell. You are aware that I will need your name and address in case there's any trouble."

Sunja nodded.

"Okay, then. A hundred twenty-five yen."

"Two hundred." Sunja didn't know if she'd get this amount, but she felt certain that the broker was greedy, and if he was willing to go to 125 from fifty, then surely the Japanese brokers would think it was valuable, too.

The broker burst out laughing. The young men were now standing by the desk, and they laughed as well. The younger one said, "You should work here."

The broker folded his arms close to his chest. He wanted the watch; he knew exactly who would buy it.

"Father, you should give the little mother her price. If only because she's so persistent!" the young one said, knowing his father didn't like to lose a bargain and would need some coaxing. He felt sorry for the girl with the puffy face. She wasn't the usual kind of girl who came up here to sell gold rings whenever she was in trouble.

"Does your husband know you're here?" the pawnbroker's younger son asked.

"Yes," Sunja replied.

"Is he a drinker or a gambler?" The son had seen desperate women before, and the stories were always the same.

"Neither," she said in a stern voice, as if to warn him not to ask any more questions.

"A hundred seventy-five yen," the broker said.

"Two hundred." Sunja could feel the warm, smooth metal in her palm; Hansu would have held firm to his price.

The broker protested, "How do I know that I can sell it?"

"Father," the older son said, smiling. "You'd be helping a little mother from home."

The broker's desk was made of an unfamiliar wood—a rich dark brown color with teardrop-shaped whorls the size of a child's hand. She counted three teardrop whorls on the surface. When she'd gone to collect mushrooms with Hansu, there had been innumerable types of trees. The musty smell of wet leaves on the forest carpet, the baskets filled to bursting with mushrooms, the sharp pain of lying with him—these memories would not leave her. She had to be rid of him, to stop this endless recollection of the one person she wished to forget.

Sunja took a deep breath. Kyunghee was wringing her hands.

"We understand if you don't wish to buy this," Sunja said quietly, and turned to leave.

The pawnbroker held up his hand, signaling her to wait, and went to the back room, where he kept his cashbox.

When the two men returned to the house for the payments, the women stood by the door and didn't invite them inside.

"If I pay you the money, how do I know that the debt is totally gone?" Sunja asked the taller one.

"We'll get the boss to sign the promissory note to say it's canceled," he said. "How do I know that you have the money?"

"Can your boss come here?" Sunja asked.

"You must be crazy," the taller one said, in shock at her request.

Sunja sensed that she shouldn't give these men the money. She tried to close the door a little so she could speak with Kyunghee, but the man pushed it back with his foot.

"Listen, if you really have the money, you can come with us. We'll take you right now."

"Where?" Kyunghee spoke up, her voice tremulous.

"By the sake shop. It's not far."

The boss was an earnest-looking young Korean, not much older than Kyunghee. He looked like a doctor or a teacher—well-worn suit, gold-wire spectacles, combed-back black hair, and a thoughtful expression. No one would have thought he was a moneylender. His office was about the size of the pawnbroker's, and on the wall opposite the front door, a shelf was lined with books in Japanese and Korean. Electric lamps were lit next to comfortable-looking chairs. A boy brought the women hot *genmaicha* in pottery cups. Kyunghee understood why her husband would borrow money from a man like this.

When Kyunghee handed him all the money, the moneylender said thank you and canceled the note, placing his red seal on the paper.

"If there's anything else I can ever do for you, please let me be of service," he said, looking at Kyunghee. "We must support each other while we're far from home. I am your servant."

"When, when did my husband borrow this money?" Kyunghee asked the moneylender.

"He asked me in February. We're friends, so of course, I obliged."

The women nodded, understanding. Yoseb had borrowed the money for Isak and Sunja's passage.

"Thank you, sir. We shall not bother you again," Kyunghee said.

"Your husband will be very pleased to have the matter settled," he said, wondering how the women had raised the money so quickly.

The women said nothing and returned home to make dinner.

17

W here did you get the money?" Yoseb shouted, clutching the canceled promissory note.

"Sunja sold the watch her mother gave her," Kyunghee replied.

Invariably, each night on their street, someone was yelling or a child was crying, but loud noises had never come from their house. Yoseb, who didn't anger easily, was enraged. Sunja stood wedged in the back corner of the front room, her head lowered—mute as a rock. Tears streamed down her reddened cheeks. Isak wasn't home yet from church.

"You had a pocket watch worth over two hundred yen? Does Isak know about this?" he shouted at Sunja.

Kyunghee raised her hands and put herself between him and Sunja.

"Her mother gave her the watch. To sell for the baby."

Sunja slid down the wall, no longer able to stand. Sharp pains pierced her pelvis and back. She shut her eyes and covered her head with her forearms.

"Where did you sell this watch?"

"At the pawnbroker by the vegetable stand," Kyunghee said.

"Are you out of your mind? What kind of women go to pawnbrokers?" Yoseb stared hard at Sunja. "How can a woman do such a thing?"

From the floor, Sunja looked up at him and pleaded, "It's not Sister's fault—"

"And did you ask your husband if you could go to a pawnbroker?"

"Why are you getting so upset? She was just trying to help us. She's pregnant. Leave her alone." Kyunghee averted her eyes, trying to keep from talking back to him. He knew full well that Sunja hadn't spoken to Isak. Why did Yoseb have to pay for everything? Why did he control all the money? The last time they'd argued was when she'd wanted to get a factory job.

"Sunja was worried about us. I'm sorry that she had to sell that beautiful watch. Try to understand, *yobo*." Kyunghee laid her hand gently on his forearm.

"Stupid women! Every time I walk down the street, how am I supposed to face these men again, knowing that some foolish women paid my debts? My nuts are shriveling."

Yoseb had never spoken in such a vulgar way before, and Kyunghee understood that he was insulting Sunja. He was calling Sunja stupid, Sunja foolish; Kyunghee was also being blamed because she'd allowed it to happen. But it was smarter for them to pay off this debt; if she'd been allowed to get a job before, they would've had savings.

Sunja couldn't stop crying. The agonizing pains around her lower abdomen had returned with greater force, and she didn't know what to say. It wasn't clear what was happening to her body.

"*Yobo*, please, please understand," Kyunghee said.

Yoseb said nothing. Sunja's legs were splayed out like a drunk on the street with her swollen hands holding up her enormous belly. He wondered if he should've let her into his house. How could a gold pocket watch have come from her mother? It had been years, but he'd met both her mother and her father. Hoonie Kim was the crippled son of two peasants who'd operated a boardinghouse on a minuscule rented plot. Where would his wife have gotten such a valuable thing? Their lodgers were mainly fishermen or men who worked at the fish market. He could've accepted that the girl had been given a few gold rings worth thirty or forty yen by her mother. Perhaps a jade ring worth ten. Had she stolen the watch? he wondered. Could Isak have married a thief or a whore? He couldn't bring himself to say these things, so Yoseb opened the corrugated metal door and left.

*   *   *

When he came home, Isak was alarmed at the sight of the sobbing women. He tried to calm them so they could speak more coherently. He listened to their broken explanations.

"So where did he go?" Isak asked.

"I don't know. He doesn't go out normally. I didn't realize he'd be this—" Kyunghee stopped, not wanting to upset Sunja any further.

"He'll be all right," Isak said, and turned to Sunja.

"I didn't know you had such a valuable thing from home. It's from your mother?" Isak asked tentatively.

Sunja was still crying, and Kyunghee nodded in her place.

"Oh?" Isak looked again at Sunja.

"Where did your mother get this, Sunja?" Isak asked.

"I didn't ask. Perhaps someone owed her money."

"I see." Isak nodded, not sure what to make of this.

Kyunghee stroked Sunja's feverish head. "Will you explain this to Yoseb?" she asked her brother-in-law. "You understand why we did this, right?"

"Yes, of course. Brother borrowed the money to help me. Sunja sold the watch to pay that debt, so in fact she sold it to help us get here. The passage here was expensive, and how was he to raise all that money so quickly? I should've thought it through. I was naïve and childish, as usual, and Brother was just taking care of me. It's unfortunate that Sunja had to sell the watch, but it's right for us to pay our debts. I'll say all this to him, Sister. Please don't worry," he said to the women.

Kyunghee nodded, feeling a little better finally.

A spasm flared through Sunja's side, knocking her back almost. "*Uh-muh. Uh-muh!*"

"Is it? Is it—?"

Warm water rushed down Sunja's leg.

"Should I get the midwife?" Isak asked.

"Sister Okja—three houses down on our side of the street," Kyunghee said, and Isak ran out of the house.

"It's okay, it's okay," Kyunghee cooed, holding Sunja's hand. "You're doing mother's work. Women suffer, don't they? Oh, my dear Sunja. I'm so sorry you're in pain." Kyunghee prayed over her, "Lord, dear Lord, please have mercy—"

Sunja took a fistful of her skirt material and put it in her mouth to keep from screaming. It felt as if she was being stabbed repeatedly. She bit down hard on the coarse fabric. "*Umma, umma,*" she cried out.

Sister Okja, the midwife, was a fifty-year-old Korean from Jeju who'd delivered most of the children in the ghetto. Well trained by her aunt, Okja had kept her own children housed and fed through midwifery, nursing, and babysitting. Her husband, the father of their six children, was as good as dead to her, though he was alive and living in her house several days a week in a drunken stupor. When she wasn't delivering babies, Okja minded the children of the neighborhood women who worked in the factories and markets.

This delivery was no trouble at all. The boy was long and well shaped, and the labor, as terrifying as it might have been for the new mother, was brief, and thankfully for the midwife, the baby didn't arrive in the middle of the night but only in time to interrupt her making dinner. Sister Okja hoped her daughter-in-law, who lived with them, hadn't burned the barley rice again.

"Hush, hush. You did well," Okja said to the girl who was still crying for her mother. "The boy's very strong and nice looking. Look at all that black hair! You should rest a little now. The child will need to feed soon," she said, before getting up to leave.

"Damn these knees." Okja rubbed her kneecaps and shins and got up leisurely, making sure that the family had enough time to find her some money.

Kyunghee got her purse and gave Sister Okja three yen.

Okja was unimpressed. "If you have any questions, just get me."

Kyunghee thanked her; she felt like a mother herself. The child was beautiful. Her heart ached at the sight of his small face—the shock of jet hair and his blue-black eyes. She was reminded of the Bible character Samson.

After Kyunghee bathed the child in the dinged-up basin normally used to salt cabbage, she handed the baby, wrapped in a clean towel, to Isak.

"You're a father," Kyunghee said, smiling. "He's handsome, isn't he?"

Isak nodded, feeling more pleased than he'd imagined he'd be.

"*Uh-muh*, I have to make soup for Sunja. She has to have soup right away." Kyunghee went to check on Sunja, who was already fast asleep, leaving Isak with the child in the front room. In the kitchen, as Kyunghee soaked the dried seaweed in cold water, she prayed that her husband would come home soon.

In the morning, the house felt different. Kyunghee hadn't slept. Yoseb hadn't come home the night before. Isak had tried to stay awake, too, but she'd made him go to sleep, because he had to give a sermon the next morning and work at church the whole Sunday. Sunja slept so soundly that she snored and had only gotten up to feed; the child latched on her breast well and fussed very little. Kyunghee had cleaned the kitchen, prepared breakfast, and sewed shirts for the baby while waiting for Yoseb. Every few minutes, she glanced at the window.

While Isak was finishing his breakfast, Yoseb came in the house smelling of cigarettes. His eyeglasses were smudged and his face stubbly. As soon as Kyunghee saw him, she went to the kitchen to get his breakfast.

"Brother." Isak got up. "Are you all right?"

Yoseb nodded.

"The baby was born. It's a boy," Isak said, smiling.

Yoseb sat down on the floor by the low acacia dining table—one of the few things he'd brought from home. He touched the wood and thought of his parents.

Kyunghee placed his food tray in front of him.

"I know you're upset with me, but you should eat something and rest," she said, patting his back.

Isak said, "Brother, I'm sorry about what happened. Sunja's very young, and she was worried for us. The debt's really mine, and—"

"I can take care of this family," Yoseb said.

"That's true, but I put a burden on you that you hadn't anticipated.

I put you in that position. The fault is mine. Sunja thought she was helping."

Yoseb folded his hands. He couldn't disagree with Isak or be upset with him. It was hard to see his brother's sad face. Isak needed to be protected like a fine piece of porcelain. All night, Yoseb had nursed a bottle of *doburoku* at a bar that Koreans frequented not far from the train station, wondering all the while if he should've brought the frail Isak to Osaka. How long would Isak live? What would happen to Isak if Sunja was not a good woman after all? Kyunghee was already so attached to the girl, and once the baby came, Yoseb was responsible for one more. His parents and in-laws were counting on him. At the crowded bar, men were drinking and making jokes, but there hadn't been a soul in that squalid room—smelling of burnt dried squid and alcohol—who wasn't worried about money and facing the terror of how he was supposed to take care of his family in this strange and difficult land.

Yoseb covered his face with his hands.

"Brother, you're a very good man," Isak said. "I know how hard you work."

Yoseb wept.

"Will you forgive Sunja? For not going to you first? Will you forgive me for making you take on a debt? Can you forgive us?"

Yoseb said nothing. The moneylender would see him like all the other men who sponged off their wives toiling in factories or working as domestics. His wife and pregnant sister-in-law had paid his debt with what was likely a stolen watch. What could he do?

"You have to go to work, don't you?" Yoseb asked. "It's Sunday."

"Yes, Sister said she'd stay here with Sunja and the baby."

"Let's go," Yoseb said.

He would forgive. It was too late for anything else.

When the men stepped outside the house, Yoseb held his brother's hand.

"So you're a father now."

"Yes." Isak smiled.

"Good," Yoseb said.

"I want you to name him," Isak said. "It takes a lot of time for us to write to Father and to wait. You're the head of our house here—"

"It shouldn't be me."

"It must be you."

Yoseb took a breath and faced the empty street, and it came to him. "Noa."

"Noa," Isak repeated, smiling. "Yes. That's wonderful."

"Noa—because he obeyed and did what the Lord asked. Noa—because he believed when it was impossible to do so."

"Maybe you should give the sermon today," Isak said, patting his brother on the back.

The brothers walked briskly toward the church, their bodies close, one tall, frail, and purposeful, and the other short, powerful, and quick.

Book II

Motherland

1939–1962

I thought that no matter how many hills and brooks you crossed, the whole world was Korea and everyone in it was Korean.

—Park Wan-suh

I

Osaka, 1939

Yoseb inhaled deeply and planted his feet squarely on the threshold—ready to be tackled by a six-year-old boy who had been waiting all week for his bag of taffy. He slid open the front door, steeling himself for what would come.

But nothing.

There was no one in the front room. Yoseb smiled. Noa must be hiding.

"*Yobo*. I've arrived," he shouted in the direction of the kitchen.

Yoseb closed the door behind him.

Pulling out the packet of candy from his coat pocket, Yoseb said dramatically, "Huh, I wonder where Noa could be. I suppose if he isn't home, then I can eat his share of the candy. Or I can put it aside for his brother. Maybe today would be a good day for baby Mozasu to have his first taste of candy. One can never be too young for a treat! He's already a month old. Before you know it, Mozasu and I'll be wrestling, too, just like Noa and me! He'll need some pumpkin taffy to make him stronger." Not hearing a sound, Yoseb unfolded the crinkly paper with a flourish and pretended to put a chunk of taffy in his mouth.

"*Wah*, this is the best batch of pumpkin taffy that Piggy *ajumma* has ever made! *Yobo*," he shouted, "come out here, you must have some of this! Really tasty!" he said, making chewing noises while checking behind the clothing chest and the screen door—Noa's usual hiding spots.

The mere mention of Noa's infant brother, Mozasu, should have made the boy bolt out from hiding. Normally a well-behaved child, Noa had been in trouble at home lately for pinching his brother, given the chance.

Yoseb checked the kitchen, but there was no one there. The stove was cool to the touch, and the side dishes had been put out on the small table by the door; the rice pot was empty. Dinner was always made by the time he came home. The soup kettle was half-filled with water, cut-up potatoes, and onions, waiting to be put on the fire. Saturday evening meals were Yoseb's favorite, because there was no work on Sundays, and yet nothing had been prepared. After a leisurely Saturday dinner, the family would go to the bathhouse together. He opened the kitchen back door and stuck his head out, only to face the filthy gutters. Next door, Piggy *ajumma*'s oldest girl was fixing supper for her family and didn't even look out from her open window.

They could have gone to the market, he supposed. Yoseb sat down on a floor cushion in the front room and opened up one of his many newspapers. Printed columns of words about the war floated in front of his eyes—Japan would save China by bringing technological advancements to a rural economy; Japan would end poverty in Asia and make it prosper; Japan would protect Asia from the pernicious hands of Western imperialism; and only Germany, Japan's true and fearless ally, was fighting the evils of the West. Yoseb didn't believe any of it, but propaganda was inescapable. Each day, Yoseb read three or four papers to glean some truth from the gaps and overlaps. Tonight, all the papers repeated virtually the same things; the censors must've been working especially hard the night before.

In the quiet of the house, Yoseb felt impatient and wanted his dinner. If Kyunghee had gone to pick up something at the market, there was still no reason why Sunja, Noa, and the baby would've gone, too. No doubt, Isak was busy at church. Yoseb put on his shoes.

On the street, no one knew where his wife was, and when he reached the church, his brother wasn't there. The office in the back was empty, except for the usual group of women seated on the floor, their heads bowed, mumbling their prayers.

He waited for a long time until the women raised their heads.

"I'm sorry to bother you, but have you seen Pastor Baek or Pastor Yoo?"

The women, middle-aged *ajumma*s who came to church nearly every evening to pray, recognized him as Pastor Baek's older brother.

"They've taken him," the eldest one cried, "and Pastor Yoo and the Chinese boy Hu. You have to help them—"

"What?"

"The police arrested them this morning—when everyone went to the Shinto shrine to bow, one of the village leaders noticed Hu mouthing the words of the Lord's Prayer when they were supposed to be pledging allegiance to the Emperor. The police officer who was supervising questioned Hu, and Hu told him that this ceremony was idol worshipping and he wouldn't do it anymore. Pastor Yoo tried to tell the police that the boy was misinformed, and that he didn't mean anything by it, but Hu refused to agree with Pastor Yoo. Pastor Baek tried to explain, too, but Hu said he was willing to walk into the furnace. Just like Shadrach, Meshach, and Abednego! Do you know that story?"

"Yes, yes," Yoseb said, annoyed by their religious excitement. "Are they at the station now?"

The women nodded.

Yoseb ran outside.

Noa was sitting on the steps of the police station, holding his baby brother, who was asleep.

"Uncle," Noa whispered, smiling with relief. "Mo is very heavy."

"You're a very good brother, Noa," Yoseb said. "Where's your aunt?"

"In there." He tilted his head toward the station, unable to use his hands. "Uncle, can you hold Mozasu? My arms hurt."

"Can you wait here just a little longer? I'll be right back, or I'll send your mother outside."

"*Umma* said she'd give me a treat if I didn't pinch Mozasu and kept him still. They won't let babies inside," Noa said soberly. "But I'm hungry now. I've been here forever and ever."

"Uncle will give you a treat, too, Noa. Uncle will be right back," Yoseb said.

"But, Uncle—Mo's—"

"Yes, Noa, but you're very strong."

Noa straightened his shoulders and sat up. He didn't want to disappoint his uncle, who was his favorite person.

Yoseb was about to open the door of the station, but he turned at the sound of Noa's voice.

"Uncle, what do I do if Mozasu cries?"

"You should sing him a song while you walk back and forth. The way I did when you were his age. Maybe you remember?"

"No, I don't remember," he said, looking tearful.

"Uncle will be right out."

The police wouldn't let them see Isak. The women had been waiting inside the station, with Sunja going outside to check on Noa and Mozasu every few minutes. Children weren't allowed in the station, so Kyunghee had remained near the front desk, since she was the one who spoke Japanese. When Yoseb entered the waiting area, Kyunghee gasped, then exhaled. Seated beside her, Sunja was doubled over, weeping.

"Do they have Isak?" Yoseb asked.

Kyunghee nodded.

"You have to talk quietly," she said, continuing to pat Sunja on the back. "I don't know who's listening."

Yoseb whispered, "The ladies at the church told me what happened. Why did that boy make such a fuss about the bowing?" Back home, the colonial government had been rounding up Christians and making them bow at the shrines each morning. Here, the volunteer community leaders made you do this only once or twice a week. "Is there a fine we can pay?"

"I don't think so," Kyunghee said. "The officer told us to go home, but we waited in case they'd let him out—"

"Isak can't be inside a jail," Yoseb said. "He can't."

At the front desk, Yoseb lowered his shoulders and bowed deeply from the waist.

"My brother's in poor health, sir; he has been this way since he was a boy, and it would be difficult for him to be in jail. He just recovered from tuberculosis. Is there any way he can go home and come back to the station tomorrow so he can be questioned?" Yoseb asked, using honorific Japanese.

The officer shook his head politely, indifferent to these appeals. The cells were full of Koreans and Chinese, and according to their family members, nearly all of them had some sort of serious health problem that should preclude them from jail time. Although the officer felt bad for the man pleading for his truant brother, there was nothing he could do. The minister would be held for a very long time—these religious activists always were. In times of war, there had to be crackdowns against troublemakers for the sake of national security. It was pointless to say any of this, however. Koreans caused trouble, then made excuses.

"You and the women should go home. The minister is being questioned, and you will not be able to see him. You're wasting your time."

"You see, sir, my brother isn't against the Emperor or the government in any way. He's never been involved in anything against the government," Yoseb said. "My brother is not interested in politics, and I'm sure he—"

"He's not allowed to have visitors. If he's cleared of all charges, you can be assured that he'll be released and sent home." The officer smiled politely. "No one wants to keep an innocent man here." The officer believed this—the Japanese government was a fair and reasonable one.

"Is there anything I can do?" Yoseb said in a lowered voice, patting his pockets for his wallet.

"There's nothing you or I can do," the officer said, peeved. "And I hope you're not suggesting a bribe. Making such an attempt would only exacerbate your brother's crime. He and his colleagues refused to acknowledge loyalty to the Emperor. This is a serious offense."

"I didn't mean any harm. I beg your pardon for my foolish words— I would never insult your honor, sir." Yoseb would have crawled on his belly across the floor of the station if that would have made Isak free. Their eldest brother, Samoel, had been the brave one, the one who would've confronted the officers with audacity and grace, but Yoseb knew he was no hero. He would have borrowed more money and sold their shack if the police would take a bribe in exchange for Isak; Yoseb didn't see the point of anyone dying for his country or for some greater ideal. He understood survival and family.

The officer adjusted his spectacles and looked past Yoseb's shoulder, though no one else was standing there.

"Perhaps you can take your women home? They have no place here. The boy and the baby are outside. You people are always letting your kids play in the streets even in the evening. They should be at home. If you don't take care of your children, they'll end up in jail one day," the officer said, appearing exhausted. "Your brother will be staying here tonight. Do you understand?"

"Yes, sir. Thank you, sir. I'm sorry to bother you. May I bring him his things tonight?"

The officer replied patiently. "In the morning. You can bring him clothes and food. Religious books are not allowed, however. Also, all reading material must be in Japanese." The officer's tone of voice was calm and thoughtful. "Unfortunately, he cannot have visitors. I'm very sorry about that."

Yoseb wanted to believe that this uniformed man was not all bad—he was just another man who was doing a job he didn't like, and he was tired because it was the end of the week. Perhaps he, too, wanted his dinner and his bath. Yoseb saw himself as a rational person, and it was too simplistic to believe that all Japanese police officers were evil. Also, Yoseb needed to believe that there were decent people watching over his brother; the alternative was unbearable.

"We shall bring his things tomorrow morning, then," Yoseb said, peering into the guarded eyes of the officer. "Thank you, sir."

"Of course."

The man tipped his head slightly.

Noa was allowed to eat all the taffy and to play outside, and while Sunja fixed dinner in the kitchen, Yoseb fielded Kyunghee's questions. She was standing with Mozasu tied to her back with a narrow blanket.

"Can you contact someone?" she asked quietly.

"Who?"

"The Canadian missionaries," she suggested. "We met them a few years ago. Remember? They were so nice, and Isak said they send money regularly to support the church. Maybe they can explain to the police that the pastors weren't doing anything wrong." Kyunghee paced in small circles, and Mozasu burbled contentedly.

"How would I reach them?"

"By letter?"

"Can I write them in Korean? How long would it take for them to get the letter and to reply? How long can Isak survive in—?"

Sunja entered the room and untied Mozasu from Kyunghee's back and took him to the kitchen to nurse. The scent of steaming barley rice filled the small house.

"I don't think the missionaries spoke Korean. Can you get someone to help you write a proper letter in Japanese?" Kyunghee asked.

Yoseb said nothing. He would write a letter to them somehow, but he didn't see why the police would care what a Canadian missionary had to say when there was a war going on. A letter would take at least a month.

Sunja returned with Mozasu.

"I put together some things for him. Can I take them tomorrow morning?" she asked.

"I'll take them," Yoseb said. "Before work."

"Can you ask your boss to help? Maybe they'll listen to a Japanese?" Kyunghee said.

"Shimamura-san would never help anyone in jail. He thinks that Christians are rebels. The people who were in charge of the March 1 *demo* were Christians. All the Japanese know that. I don't even tell him that I go to church. I don't tell him anything. He'd just fire me if he thought I was mixed up in any kind of protest activity. Then where would we be? There are no jobs for people like me."

No one said anything after that. Sunja called Noa in from the street. It was time for him to eat.

2

Each morning, Sunja walked to the police station and handed over three *onigin* made with barley and millet. If there was money in the budget for a chicken egg, she'd hard-boil it, soak the peeled egg in vinegary shoyu to supplement Isak's modest bento. No one could be sure if the food ever reached him, but she couldn't prove that it didn't. Everyone in the neighborhood knew someone who'd gone to jail, and the wildly varying reports were at best troubling and at worst terrifying. Yoseb wouldn't speak about Isak, but Isak's arrest had altered him considerably. Patches of gray smudged his once jet-black hair, and he suffered from intense stomach cramps. He stopped writing to his parents, who couldn't be told about Isak, so Kyunghee wrote to them instead, making excuses. At meals, Yoseb put aside much of his food for Noa, who sat beside him quietly. Yoseb and Noa shared a kind of unspeakable grief over Isak's absence.

Despite numerous personal appeals, no one had been allowed to see Isak, but the family believed he was alive, because the police had not told them otherwise. The elder minister and the sexton remained in jail as well, and the family hoped that the three of them sustained each other somehow, though no one knew how the prisoners were being housed. A day after the arrest, the police had come to the house to confiscate Isak's few books and papers. The family's comings and goings were monitored; a detective visited them every few weeks to ask questions. The police padlocked the church, yet the congregation continued to meet secretly in small groups led by the church elders. Kyunghee, Sunja, and Yoseb never met the parishioners for fear of putting them in danger. By now, most of the foreign missionaries back home and here had returned to their native countries. It was rare to see a white person in Osaka. Yoseb had written the Canadian missionaries about Isak but there'd been no reply.

Under considerable duress, the decision-making authority of the Presbyterian Church had deemed that the mandatory Shinto shrine ceremony was a civic duty rather than a religious one even though the Emperor, the head of the state religion, was viewed as a living deity. Pastor Yoo, a faithful and pragmatic minister, had believed that the shrine ceremony, where the townspeople were required to gather and perform rites, was in fact a pagan ritual drummed up to rouse national feeling. Bowing to idols was naturally offensive to the Lord. Nevertheless, Pastor Yoo had encouraged Isak, Hu, and his congregation to observe the Shinto bowing for the greater good. He didn't want his parishioners, many of them new to the faith, to be sacrificed to the government's predictable response to disobedience—prison and death. Pastor Yoo found support for such ideas in the letters of the apostle Paul. So whenever these gatherings at the nearest shrine took place, their frequency varying from town to town, the elder pastor, Isak, and Hu had attended when necessary along with whoever else was in the church building at the time. However, with his weakened vision, the elder pastor had not known that at every Shinto ceremony, the sexton Hu had been mouthing Our Father like an unbroken loop even as he bowed, sprinkled water, and clapped his hands like all the others. Isak had noticed Hu doing this, of course, but had said nothing. If anything, Isak had admired Hu's faith and gesture of resistance.

For Sunja, Isak's arrest had forced her to consider what would happen if the unthinkable occurred. Would Yoseb ask her and her children to leave? Where would she go, and how would she get there? How would she take care of her children? Kyunghee would not ask her to leave, but even so— she was only a wife. Sunja had to have a plan and money in case she had to return home to her mother with her sons.

So Sunja had to find work. She would become a peddler. It was one thing for a woman like her mother to take in boarders and to work alongside her husband to earn money, but something altogether different for a young woman to stand in an open market and sell food to strangers, shouting until she was hoarse. Yoseb tried to forbid her from getting a job, but she could not listen to him. With tears streaming down her face, she told her brother-in-law that Isak would want her to earn money for the boys' schooling. To this, Yoseb yielded. Nevertheless, he prohibited Kyunghee from working outdoors, and his wife obeyed. Kyunghee was allowed to put up the pickles with Sunja, but she couldn't sell them. Yoseb couldn't protest too much, because the household was desperate for cash. In a way, the two women tried to obey Yoseb in their disobedience—they did not want to hurt Yoseb by defying him, but the financial burdens had become impossible for one man to bear alone.

Her first day of selling took place one week after Isak was jailed. After Sunja dropped off Isak's food at the jail, she wheeled a wooden cart holding a large clay jar of kimchi to the market. The open-air market in Ikaino was a patchwork of modest retail shops selling housewares, cloth, tatami mats, and electric goods, and it hosted a collection of hawkers like her who peddled homemade scallion pancakes, rolled sushi, and soybean paste.

Kyunghee watched Mozasu at home. Nearby the peddlers selling *gochujang* and *doenjang*, Sunja noticed two young Korean women selling fried wheat crackers. Sunja pushed her cart toward them, hoping to wedge herself between the cracker stall and the soybean-paste lady.

"You can't stink up our area," the older of the two cracker sellers said. "Go to the other side." She pointed to the fish section.

When Sunja moved closer to the women selling dried anchovies and seaweed, the older Korean women there were even less welcoming.

"If you don't move your shitty-looking cart, I'll have my sons piss in your pot. Do you understand, country girl?" said a tall woman wearing a white kerchief on her head.

Sunja couldn't come up with a reply, because she was so surprised. None of them were even selling kimchi, and *doenjang* could smell just as pungently.

She kept walking until she couldn't see any more *ajumma*s and ended up near the train station entrance where the live chickens were sold. The intense funk of animal carcasses overwhelmed her. There was a space big enough for her cart between the pig butcher and the chickens.

Wielding an enormous knife, a Japanese butcher was cutting up a hog the size of a child. A large bucket filled with its blood rested by his feet. Two hogs' heads lay on the front table. The butcher was an older gentleman with ropy, muscular arms and thick veins. He was sweating profusely, and he smiled at her.

Sunja parked her cart in the empty lot by his stall. Whenever a train stopped, she could feel its deceleration beneath her sandals. Passengers would disembark, and many of them came into the market from the entrance nearby, but none stopped in front of her cart. Sunja tried not to cry. Her breasts were heavy with milk, and she missed being at home with Kyunghee and Mozasu. She wiped her face with her sleeves, trying to remember what the best market *ajumma*s would do back home.

"Kimchi! Delicious kimchi! Try this delicious kimchi, and never make it at home again!" she shouted. Passersby turned to look at her, and Sunja, mortified, looked away from them. No one bought anything. After the butcher finished with his hog, he washed his hands and gave her twenty-five sen, and Sunja filled a container for him. He didn't seem to mind that she didn't speak Japanese. He put down the kimchi container by the hogs' heads, then reached behind his stall to take out his bento. The butcher placed a piece of kimchi neatly on top of his white rice with his chopsticks and ate a bite of rice and kimchi in front of her.

"*Oishi! Oishi nee! Honto oishi,*" he said, smiling.

She bowed to him.

At lunchtime, Kyunghee brought Mozasu for her to nurse, and Sunja remembered that she had no choice but to recoup the cost of the cabbage, radish, and spices. At the end of the day, she had to show more money than they had spent.

Kyunghee watched the cart while Sunja nursed the baby with her body turned toward the wall.

"I'd be afraid," Kyunghee said. "You know how I'd said that I wanted to be a kimchi *ajumma*? I don't think I realized what it would feel like to stand here. You're so brave."

"What choice do we have?" Sunja said, looking down at her beautiful baby.

"Do you want me to stay here? And wait with you?"

"You'll get in trouble," Sunja said. "You should be home when Noa gets back from school, and you have to make dinner. I'm sorry I can't help you, Sister."

"What I have to do is easy," Kyunghee said.

It was almost two o'clock in the afternoon, and the air felt cooler as the sun turned away from them.

"I'm not going to come home until I sell the whole jar."

"Really?"

Sunja nodded. Her baby, Mozasu, resembled Isak. He looked nothing like Noa, who was olive-skinned with thick, glossy hair. Noa's bright eyes noticed everything. Except for his mouth, Noa looked almost identical to a young Hansu. At school, Noa sat still during lessons, waited for his turn, and he was praised as an excellent student. Noa had been an easy baby, and Mozasu was a happy baby, too, delighted to be put into a stranger's arms. When she thought about how much she loved her boys, she recalled her parents. Sunja felt so far away from her mother and father. Now she was standing outside a rumbling train station, trying to sell kimchi. There was no shame in her work, but it couldn't be what they'd wanted for her. Nevertheless, she felt her parents would have wanted her to make money, especially now.

When Sunja finished nursing, Kyunghee put down two sugared rolls and a bottle filled with reconstituted powdered milk on the cart.

"You have to eat, Sunja. You're nursing, and that's not easy, right? You have to drink lots of water and milk."

Kyunghee turned around so Sunja could tuck Mozasu into the sling on Kyunghee's back. Kyunghee secured the baby tightly around her torso.

"I'll go home and wait for Noa and make dinner. You come home soon, okay? We're a good team."

Mozasu's small head rested between Kyunghee's thin shoulder blades, and Sunja watched them walk away. When they were out of earshot, Sunja cried out, "Kimchi! Delicious Kimchi! Kimchi! Delicious kimchi! *Oishi desu! Oishi* kimchi!"

This sound, the sound of her own voice, felt familiar, not because it was her own voice but because it reminded her of all the times she'd gone to the market as a girl—first with her father, later by herself as a young woman, then as a lover yearning for the gaze of her beloved. The chorus of women hawking had always been with her, and now she'd joined them. "Kimchi! Kimchi! Homemade kimchi! The most delicious kimchi in Ikaino! More tasty than your grandmother's! *Oishi desu, oishi!*" She tried to sound cheerful, because back home, she had always frequented the nicest *ajummas*. When the passersby glanced in her direction, she bowed and smiled at them. "*Oishi! Oishi!*"

The pig butcher looked up from his counter and smiled at her proudly.

That evening, Sunja did not go home until she could see the bottom of the kimchi jar.

Sunja could sell whatever kimchi she and Kyunghee were able to make now, and this ability to sell had given her a kind of strength. If they could've made more kimchi, she felt sure that she could've sold that, too, but fermenting took time, and it wasn't always possible to find the right ingredients. Even when they made a decent profit, the price of cabbages could spike the following week, or worse, they might not be available at all. When there were no cabbages at the market, the women pickled radishes, cucumbers, garlic, or chives, and sometimes Kyunghee pickled carrots or eggplant without garlic or chili paste, because the Japanese preferred those kinds of pickles. Sunja thought about land all the time. The little kitchen garden her mother had kept behind the house had nourished them even when the boardinghouse guests ate double what they paid. The price of fresh food kept rising, and working people couldn't afford the most basic things. Recently, some customers would ask to buy a cup of kimchi because they couldn't afford a jar of it.

If Sunja had no kimchi or pickles to sell, she sold other things. Sunja roasted sweet potatoes and chestnuts; she boiled ears of corn. She had two carts now, and she hooked them together like the cars of a train—one cart with a makeshift coal stove and another just for pickles. The carts took up the better part of the kitchen because they had to keep them inside the house for fear of them getting stolen. She split the profits equally with Kyunghee, and Sunja put aside every sen she could for the boys' schooling and for their passage back home in case they had to leave.

When Mozasu turned five months old, Sunja also started selling candy at the market. Produce had been getting increasingly scarce, and by chance, Kyunghee had obtained two wholesale bags of black sugar from a Korean grocer whose Japanese brother-in-law worked in the military.

At her usual spot by the pork butcher's stall, Sunja stoked the fire beneath the metal bowl used to melt sugar. The steel box that functioned as a stove had been giving her trouble; as soon as she could afford it, Sunja planned on having a proper stove made up for her cart. She rolled up her sleeves and moved the live coals around to circulate the air and raise the heat.

"*Agasshi*, do you have kimchi today?"

It was a man's voice, and Sunja looked up. About Isak's age, he dressed like her brother-in-law—tidy without drawing much attention to himself. His face was cleanly shaven, and his fingernails were neat. The lenses of his eyeglasses were very thick and the heavy frames detracted from his good features.

"No, sir. No kimchi today. Just candy. It's not ready, though."

"Oh. When will you have kimchi again?"

"Hard to say. There isn't much cabbage to buy, and the last batch of kimchi we put up isn't ready yet," Sunja said, and returned to the coals.

"A day or two? A week?"

Sunja looked up again, surprised by his insistence.

"The kimchi might be ready in three days or so. If the weather continues to get warmer, then it might be two, sir. But I don't think that soon," Sunja said flatly, hoping he would let her start with the candy making. Sometimes, she sold a few bags to the young women getting off the train at about this time.

"How much kimchi will you have when it's ready?"

"I'll have plenty to sell you. Do you know how much you want? Most of my customers like to bring their own containers. How much do you think you need?" Her customers were Korean women who worked in factories and didn't have time to make their own *banchan*. When she sold sweets, her customers were children and young women. "Just stop by in three days, and if you bring your own container—"

The young man laughed.

"Well, I was thinking that maybe you can sell me everything you make." He adjusted his eyeglasses.

"You can't eat that much kimchi! And how would you keep the rest of it fresh?" Sunja replied, shaking her head at his foolishness. "It's going to be summer in a couple of months, and it's hot here already."

"I'm sorry. I should have explained. My name is Kim Changho, and I manage the *yakiniku* restaurant right by Tsuruhashi Station. News of your excellent kimchi has spread far."

Sunja wiped her hands on the apron that she wore over her padded cotton vest, keeping a close eye on the hot coals.

"It's my sister-in-law who knows what she's doing in the kitchen. I just sell it and help her make it."

"Yes, yes, I'd heard that, too. Well, I'm looking for some women to make all the kimchi and *banchan* for the restaurant. I can get you cabbage and—"

"Where, sir? Where do you get cabbage? We looked everywhere. My sister-in-law goes to the market early in the morning and still—"

"I can get it," he said, smiling.

Sunja didn't know what to say. The candy-making metal bowl was hot already, and it was time to put in the sugar and water, but she didn't want to start now. If this person was serious, then it was important to hear him out. She heard the train arrive. She had missed her first batch of customers already.

"Where's your restaurant again?"

"It's the big restaurant on the side street behind the train station. On the same street as the pharmacy—you know, the one owned by the skinny

Japanese pharmacist, Okada-san? He wears black glasses like mine?" He pushed his glasses up on his nose again and smiled like a boy.

"Oh, I know where the pharmacy is."

This was the shop where all the Koreans went when they were really sick and were willing to pay for good medicine. Okada was not a friendly man, but he was honest; he was reputed to be able to cure many ailments.

The young man didn't seem like anyone who was trying to take advantage of her, but she couldn't be sure. In the few short months working as a vendor, she'd given credit to a few customers and had not been repaid. People were willing to lie about small things and to disregard your interests.

Kim Changho gave her a business card. "Here's the address. Can you bring your kimchi when it's done? Bring all of it. I'll pay you in cash, and I'll get you more cabbage."

Sunja nodded, not saying anything. If she had only one customer for the kimchi, then she'd have more time to make other things to sell. The hardest part had been procuring the cabbage, so if this man could do that, then the work would be much easier. Kyunghee had been scouring the market with Mozasu on her back to track down these scarce ingredients and often returned home with a light market basket. Sunja promised to bring him what she had.

The restaurant was the largest storefront on the short side street parallel to the train station. Unlike the other businesses nearby, its sign was lettered handsomely by a professional sign maker. The two women admired the large black letters carved and painted into a vast wooden plaque. They wondered what the words meant. It was obviously a Korean *galbi* house— the scent of grilled meat could be detected from two blocks away—but the sign had difficult Japanese lettering that neither of them could read. Sunja grasped the handlebar of the carts loaded with all the kimchi they'd put up in the past few weeks and took a deep breath. If the kimchi sales to the restaurant were steady, they'd have a regular income. She could buy eggs more often for Isak's and Noa's meals and get heavy wool cloth for Kyunghee, who wanted to sew new coats for Yoseb and Noa.

Yoseb had been staying away from home, complaining of the sight and smell of all the kimchi ingredients spilling out from the kitchen. He didn't want to live in a kimchi factory. His dissatisfaction was the primary reason why the women preferred to sell candy, but sugar was far more difficult to find than cabbage or sweet potatoes. Although Noa didn't complain of it, the kimchi odor affected him the most. Like all the other Korean children at the local school, Noa was taunted and pushed around, but now that his clean-looking clothes smelled immutably of onions, chili, garlic, and shrimp paste, the teacher himself made Noa sit in the back of the classroom next to the group of Korean children whose mothers raised pigs in their homes. Everyone at school called the children who lived with pigs *buta*. Noa, whose *tsumei* was Nobuo, sat with the *buta* children and was called garlic turd.

At home, Noa asked his aunt for snacks and meals that didn't contain garlic, hoping this would keep the children from saying bad things to him. When she asked him why, Noa told his aunt the truth. Even though it cost more, Kyunghee bought Noa large milk rolls from the bakery for his breakfast and made him potato *korokke* or *yakisoba* for his school bento.

The children were merciless, but Noa didn't fight them; rather, he worked harder on his studies, and to the surprise of his teachers, he was the first or second in academic rank in his second grade class. At school, Noa didn't have any friends, and when the Korean children played in the streets, he didn't join them. The only person he looked forward to seeing was his uncle, but these days, when Yoseb was home, he was not himself.

In the street, Kyunghee and Sunja stood quietly in front of the restaurant, unable to enter. The door was ajar, but it was not open for business. Despite Kyunghee's initial excitement at the prospect of selling more kimchi, she'd been reasonably skeptical of the offer and had refused to let Sunja go to an unknown place by herself. She'd insisted on coming along, toting Mozasu on her back. They didn't tell Yoseb about coming here, but they planned on telling him everything after the first meeting.

"I'll stay out here with the cart and wait," Kyunghee said, patting Mozasu rhythmically with her right hand. The baby was resting calmly in the sling on Kyunghee's back.

"Shouldn't I bring the kimchi in?" Sunja said.

"Why don't you ask him to come outside?"

"We can both go in."

"I'll wait outside. But if you don't come outside soon, then I'll come in, all right?"

"But how will you push the cart and—"

"I can push the cart. Mozasu is fine." The baby was now laying his head drowsily on her back, and she kept up a reliable rocking motion.

"Go on inside, and I'll wait. Just ask Kim Changho to come out here. Don't keep talking to him inside, all right?"

"But I thought we'd talk to him together."

Sunja stared at her sister-in-law, not knowing what she should do, and then it occurred to her that her sister-in-law was afraid of going into the restaurant. If her husband asked her what had happened, she could say honestly that she was outside the whole time.

3

April 1940

It was the second restaurant she'd ever entered in her life. The main dining room was nearly five times the size of the udon shop in Busan that she'd gone to with Isak. The lingering smells of burnt meat and stale cigarettes from the previous night scraped against her throat. There were two rows of dining tables on a raised tatami-covered platform. Below the platform was a space for the guests' shoes. In the open kitchen, a teenage boy wearing a white undershirt washed beer glasses two at a time. With the water running and the clinking of the glasses, he didn't hear Sunja coming into the restaurant; she stared at his sharp profile as he concentrated on his work, hoping he'd notice her.

The man from the market had never specified the time of day for her to show up with the kimchi, and it had never occurred to her to ask whether to come by in the morning or afternoon. Kim Changho was nowhere to be seen. What if he was out today, or only came to work in the afternoons or evenings? If she went outside without speaking to anyone, Kyunghee wouldn't know what to do, either. Her sister-in-law was susceptible to endless worrying, and Sunja didn't want to trouble her.

The water in the sink stopped running, and the boy, exhausted from the night-to-morning shift, stretched his neck from side to side. The sight of the young woman surprised him. She wore Japanese trousers and a blue padded jacket that had faded from wear.

"*Agasshi*, we're not open right now," he said in Korean. She wasn't a customer, but she wasn't a beggar, either.

"Excuse me. I'm sorry to bother you, but do you know where Kim Changho is? He asked me to come by with the kimchi. I wasn't sure when I—"

"Oh! Is that you?" The boy grinned in relief. "He's just down the street. Boss told me to get him if you came by today. Why don't you sit down and wait. Did you bring the kimchi? The customers have been complaining about the side dishes for weeks. Are you going to work here, too? Hey, how old are you anyway?" The boy wiped his hands and opened the kitchen door in the back. The new girl was sweet looking, he thought. The last kimchi *ajumma* had been a toothless granny who'd yell at him for nothing. She'd been fired for drinking too much, but this one looked younger than he was.

Sunja was confused. "Wait, Kim Changho isn't here?"

"Have a seat. I'll be right back!"

The boy dashed out the door.

Sunja looked around, and, realizing that she was alone, she went outside.

Kyunghee whispered, "The baby's sleeping now."

She was sitting on the stubby market stool that normally hung on the side of the cart. In the bright sun, a slight breeze blew against the puffy tufts of Mozasu's hair and his smooth brow. It was early in the morning, and there were hardly any passersby on the street. The pharmacy hadn't even opened yet.

"Sister, the manager's on his way. Do you still want to wait outside?" Sunja asked.

"I'll be fine here. You go in and wait by the window so I can see you. But come out when he gets here, okay?"

Back inside the restaurant, Sunja was afraid to sit down, so she stood a foot away from the door. She knew they could have sold this kimchi today at the market. She was here because the man said he could get her cabbage—that alone was enough to make her stay and wait for him. Without the cabbage, they didn't have a business.

"How nice to see you!" Changho shouted, entering from the kitchen door. "Did you bring the kimchi?"

"My sister-in-law is watching the cart outside. We brought a lot."

"I hope you can make more."

"You haven't even tried it," she said quietly, confused by his enthusiasm.

"I'm not worried. I did my homework. I heard it's the most delicious kimchi in Osaka," he said, walking briskly toward her. "Let's go outside then."

Kyunghee bowed as soon as she saw him, but she didn't speak.

"Hello, my name is Kim Changho," he said to Kyunghee, a little startled by the woman's beauty. He couldn't tell how old she was, but the baby strapped to her back was not more than six months.

Kyunghee said nothing. She looked like a lovely, nervous mute.

"Is this your baby?" he asked.

Kyunghee shook her head, glancing at Sunja. This wasn't like talking to Japanese merchants—something she had to do to buy groceries or things needed for the house. Yoseb had told her on numerous occasions that money and business were men's issues, and suddenly she felt incapable of saying anything. Before getting here, it had been her plan to help Sunja with the negotiations, but now she felt like if she said anything at all, it would be unhelpful or wrong.

Sunja asked, "Do you know how much kimchi you'd like? On a regular basis, I mean. Do you want to wait to make an order after you try this batch?"

"I'll take all that you can make. I'd prefer it if you could make the kimchi here. We have refrigerators and a very cold basement that might be good for your purposes."

"In the kitchen? You want me to pickle the cabbages in there?" Sunja pointed to the restaurant door.

"Yes." He smiled. "In the mornings, you two can come here and make the kimchi and the side dishes. I have cooks who come in the afternoon to cut up the meat and fix the marinades, but they can't handle the kimchi and *banchan*. That sort of thing requires more skills. The customers want more home-style dishes for the pickles. Any fool can make a marinade and grill meat, but the customer needs a fine array of *banchan* to make him feel like he's dining like a king, wouldn't you say?"

He could see that they were still uncomfortable with the idea of working in a restaurant kitchen.

"Besides, you wouldn't want me to deliver boxes and boxes of cabbages and vegetables to your house, would you? That can't be very comfortable."

Kyunghee whispered to Sunja, "We can't work in a restaurant. We should make the kimchi at home, and we can bring it here. Or maybe they can send the boy to pick it up if we can't carry it all."

"You don't understand. I need you to make much, much more than whatever you were making before. I manage two more restaurants that require kimchi and *banchan*—this one is the central location and has the largest kitchen, though. I'd provide all your ingredients; you just tell me what you want. You'd be paid a good salary."

Kyunghee and Sunja looked at him, not understanding his meaning.

"Thirty-five yen a week. Each of you would get the same amount, so it's seventy yen in total."

Sunja opened her mouth in surprise. Yoseb earned forty yen per week.

"And every now and then, you could take some meat home," Kim said, smiling. "We'd have to see what we can do to make you enjoy working here. Maybe even some grains. If you need a lot of things for your personal use, I'd charge you what we pay for them. We can figure that out later."

After paying for the ingredients, Sunja and Kyunghee netted approximately ten to twelve yen a week from peddling. If they could earn seventy yen a week, they wouldn't worry about money. No one at home had eaten any chicken or fish in the past six months because of the cost; buying beef or pork had been impossible. Each week, they still bought soup bones and splurged on the occasional egg for the men, but Sunja wanted the boys, Isak, and Yoseb to eat other things besides potatoes and millet. With so much money, it would be possible to send more money to their parents, who were suffering far more than they let on.

"And I could be home when my older son, Noa, gets home?" Sunja blurted out without meaning to.

"Yes, of course," Kim said, as if he'd thought this through. "You could leave when you're done with your work. You could be finished before lunchtime even, I suppose."

"And my baby?" Sunja pointed to Mozasu, who slept on Kyunghee's back. "Can I bring him? He could stay in the kitchen with us," Sunja said, unable to imagine leaving him with one of the overwhelmed grannies in the neighborhood who watched the workingwomen's children. When there was no one to watch them at home, or if they couldn't afford to pay the grannies, a few women at the market tethered their very small children to their carts with ropes; the children with ropes crisscrossed around their torsos seemed happy to wander about or to sit by their mothers playing with cheap toys.

"The baby's not much trouble at all," Sunja said.

"Why not? As long as the work gets done, I don't care. There are no customers here at the time you're working, so they won't be in the way," he said. "If you need to stay late and your older son wants to come here from school, that's fine, too. There are no customers here until dinnertime."

Sunja nodded. She wouldn't have to spend another cold winter standing outside, waiting for customers, all the while worrying about Noa and Mozasu.

Seeing that Kyunghee looked more agitated than pleased at this job offer, which would change everything, Sunja said, "We have to ask. For permission—"

After the dinner table was cleared, Kyunghee brought her husband a cup of barley tea and his ashtray so he could have a smoke. Seated cross-legged near his uncle, Noa played with the brightly painted top that Yoseb had bought for him, and the child was mesmerized by how fast it could go. The wooden toy made a pleasant whirring sound against the floor. Sunja, who held Mozasu in her arms, watched Noa playing, wondering how Isak was. Ever since Isak's arrest, Sunja barely spoke at home for fear of upsetting her brother-in-law, whose temperament had altered greatly. When he got angry, he'd walk out of the house; sometimes, he wouldn't even bother coming home until very late. The women knew that Yoseb would be against their working at the restaurant.

After Yoseb lit his cigarette, Kyunghee told him about the jobs. They needed the work, she said, using the word "work" rather than "money."

"Have you lost your mind? First, you make food to sell under a bridge by a train station, and now both of you want to work in a restaurant where men drink and gamble? Do you know what kind of women go into such places? What, next you'll be pouring drinks for—?" Yoseb's unsmoked cigarette shook between his trembling fingers. He was not a violent man, but he'd had enough.

"Did you actually go into the restaurant?" he asked, not quite believing this conversation.

"No," Kyunghee replied. "I stayed outside with the baby, but it was a big, clean place. I saw it through the window. I went to the meeting with Sunja in case the place wasn't nice, because Sunja shouldn't go there by herself. The manager, Kim Changho, was a well-spoken young man, and you should meet him. We wouldn't go there if you didn't give us permission. *Yobo*—" Kyunghee could see how upset he was, and she felt terrible about it. She respected no one more than Yoseb. Women complained about their men, but there were no bad words to say about her husband; Yoseb was a truthful person who kept his word. He tried all he could; he was honorable. He did his best to care for them.

Yoseb put out his cigarette. Noa stopped spinning his top, and the boy looked frightened.

"Maybe if you met him..." Kyunghee knew they had to take this job, but she knew her husband would be humiliated by it. In their marriage, he had denied her nothing except for her ability to earn money. He believed that a hardworking man should be able to take care of his family by himself, and that a woman should remain at home.

"He could pay you instead of us; we'd just save the money for Isak's boys and send more to your parents. We could buy Isak better food and send him clothes. We don't know when he's—" Kyunghee stopped herself. Noa had sidled up closer to his uncle as if to protect him. He patted his uncle's leg the same way his uncle would pat his back when Noa fell down or got discouraged by something at school.

Although his head was full of arguments, Yoseb couldn't speak. He was working two full-time jobs—managing two factories for Shimamura-san, who paid him half the salary of one Japanese foreman. Lately, he repaired broken metal presses for a Korean factory owner after hours, but he couldn't count on that for a steady income. He hadn't mentioned this recent job to his wife, because he preferred for her to think of him working as a manager rather than as a mechanic. Before he got home, he'd scrub his hands ruthlessly with a bristle brush, using diluted lye to get out the machine oil stains from beneath his fingernails. No matter how hard he worked, there was never enough money—the yen notes and coins dropped out of his pockets as if they had gaping holes.

Japan was in trouble; the government knew it but would never admit defeat. The war in China pressed on without letting up. His boss's sons fought for Japan. The older one, who'd been sent to Manchuria, had lost a leg last year, then died of gangrene, and the younger one had been sent to Nanjing to take his place. In passing, Shimamura-san had mentioned that Japan was in China in order to stabilize the region and to spread peace, but the way he'd said all this hadn't given Yoseb the impression that Shimamura-san believed any of it. The Japanese were going deeper into the war in Asia, and there were rumors that Japan would soon be allied with Germany in the war in Europe.

Did any of this matter to Yoseb? He'd nodded at the right times and grunted affirmatively when his Japanese boss was talking about the war, because you were supposed to nod when the boss told you his stories. Nevertheless, to every Korean he knew, Japan's expanding war in Asia seemed senseless. China was not Korea; China was not Taiwan; China could lose a million people and still keep on. Pockets of it may fall, but it was an unfathomably vast nation; it would endure by sheer number and resolve. Did Koreans want Japan to win? Hell no, but what would happen to them if Japan's enemies won? Could the Koreans save themselves? Apparently not. So save your own ass—this was what Koreans believed privately. Save your family. Feed your belly. Pay attention, and be skeptical of the people in charge. If the Korean nationalists couldn't get their country back, then let your kids learn Japanese and try to get ahead. Adapt. Wasn't it as simple as that? For every patriot fighting for a free Korea, or for any unlucky Korean bastard fighting on behalf of Japan, there were ten thousand compatriots on the ground and elsewhere who were just trying to eat. In the end, your belly was your emperor.

Every minute of every day, Yoseb was worried about money. If he dropped dead, what would happen? What kind of man let his wife work in a restaurant? He knew this *galbi* place—who didn't? There were three of them, and the main one was by the train station. The gangsters ate there late at night. The owners set the prices high to keep out the regular people and the Japanese. When Yoseb had needed to borrow money for Isak and Sunja's passage to Japan, he'd gone there. Which was worse—his wife working for moneylenders or him owing money to them? For a Korean man, the choices were always shit.

4

May 1942

Noa Baek was not like the other eight-year-olds in the neighborhood. Each morning before he went to school, he'd scrub his face until his cheeks were pink, smooth three drops of oil on his black hair, then comb it away from his forehead as his mother had taught him to do. After a breakfast of barley porridge and miso soup, he'd rinse his mouth and check his white teeth in the small round hand mirror by the sink. No matter how tired his mother was, she made certain that Noa's shirts were ironed the night before. In his clean, pressed clothes, Noa looked like a middle-class Japanese child from a wealthier part of town, bearing no resemblance to the unwashed ghetto children outside his door.

At school, Noa was strong in both arithmetic and writing, and he surprised the gym teacher with his adept hand-eye coordination and running speed. After classes ended, he tidied the shelves and swept the classroom floors without being asked and walked home alone, trying not to draw any undue attention to himself. The boy managed to look unafraid of the tougher children while setting himself apart with a perimeter of quiet privacy that could not be disturbed. When he got home, Noa went directly into the house to do his schoolwork without lingering on the street with the neighborhood children who played until dinnertime.

When his mother and aunt moved the kimchi-making business to the restaurant, the house no longer smelled relentlessly of fermenting cabbage and pickles. Noa hoped he'd no longer be called garlic turd. If anything, lately, their house smelled less of cooking than the others in the neighborhood, because his mother and aunt brought home cooked food from the restaurant for their family meals. Once a week, Noa got to eat tidbits of grilled meat and white rice from the restaurant.

Like all children, Noa kept secrets, but his were not ordinary ones. At school, he went by his Japanese name, Nobuo Boku, rather than Noa Baek; and though everyone in his class knew he was Korean from his Japanized surname, if he met anyone who didn't know this fact, Noa wasn't forthcoming about this detail. He spoke and wrote better Japanese than most native children. In class, he dreaded the mention of the peninsula where his parents were born and would look down at his papers if the teacher mentioned anything about the colony of Korea. Noa's other secret: His father, a Protestant minister, was in jail and had not been home in over two years.

The boy tried to remember his father's face, but couldn't. When asked to tell family stories for class assignments, Noa would say that his father worked as a foreman at a biscuit factory, and if some children inferred that Uncle Yoseb was his father, Noa didn't correct them. The big secret that he kept from his mother, aunt, and even his beloved uncle was that Noa did not believe in God anymore. God had allowed his gentle, kindhearted father to go to jail even though he had done nothing wrong. For two years, God had not answered Noa's prayers, though his father had promised him that God listens very carefully to the prayers of children. Above all the other secrets that Noa could not speak of, the boy wanted to be Japanese; it was his dream to leave Ikaino and never to return.

It was a late spring afternoon; Noa returned home from school and found his snack, left out by his mother before she went to work, waiting for him on the low table where the family ate their meals and where Noa did his homework. Thirsty, he went to the kitchen to get some water, and when he returned to the front room, he screamed. Near the door, there was a gaunt and filthy man collapsed on the floor.

Unable to rise, the man leaned the weight of his torso on the crook of his left elbow and tried to push up to sitting, but couldn't manage it.

Should he scream again? Noa wondered. Who would help him? His mother, aunt, and uncle were at work, and no one had heard him the first time. The beggar didn't seem dangerous; he looked ill and dirty, but he could've been a thief, too. Uncle had warned Noa about burglars and thieves who could break into the house looking for food or valuables. He had fifty sen in his trouser pocket; he'd been saving it for an illustrated book on archery.

The man was sobbing now, and Noa felt bad for him. There were many poor people on his street, but no one looked as bad as this man. The beggar's face was covered with sores and black scabs. Noa reached into his pocket and pulled out the coin. Afraid that the man might grab his leg, Noa stepped just close enough to place the coin on the floor near the man's hand. Noa planned to walk backward to the kitchen and run out the back door to get help, but the man's crying made him pause.

The boy looked carefully at the man's gray-bearded face. His clothes were torn and grimy but the shape of them resembled the dark suits that his principal at school wore.

"It's *appa*," the man said.

Noa gasped and shook his head no.

"Where's your mother, child?"

It was his voice. Noa took a step forward.

"*Umma*'s at the restaurant," Noa replied.

"Where?"

Isak was confused.

"I'll go now. I'll get *umma*. Are you okay?" The boy didn't know what to do exactly. He was still a bit afraid, though it was certainly his father. The gentle eyes beneath the jutting cheekbones and scaly skin were the same. Perhaps his father was hungry. His shoulder bones and elbows looked like sharp tree branches beneath his clothing. "Do you want to eat something, *appa*?"

Noa pointed to the snack his mother had left for him: two rice balls made from barley and millet.

Isak shook his head, smiling at the boy's concern.

"*Aga*—can you get me some water?"

When Noa returned with the cup of cold water from the kitchen, he found his father slumped to the ground with his eyes closed.

"*Appa*! *Appa*! Wake up! I have your water! Drink your water, *appa*," Noa cried.

Isak's eyes fluttered open; he smiled at the sight of the boy.

"*Appa* is tired, Noa. *Appa* is going to sleep."

"*Appa*, drink your water." The boy held out the cup.

Isak raised his head and took a long drink, then closed his eyes again.

Noa bent over, close to his father's mouth, to check his breathing. He retrieved his own pillow and tucked it beneath Isak's bushy gray head. He covered him with the heavy quilt and closed the front door behind him quietly. Noa ran to the restaurant as fast as he could.

He burst into the dining room, but no one in the front area noticed him. None of the grown men working there minded the well-mannered boy who never said much beyond yes and no. The toddler, Mozasu, was sleeping in the storage room; when awake, the two-year-old tore through the dining room, but asleep, he looked like a statue of an angel. The manager, Kim, never complained about Sunja's children. He bought toys and comic books for the boys and occasionally watched Mozasu while he worked in the back office.

"*Uh-muh*." Kyunghee looked up from her work, alarmed at the sight of Noa, breathless and pale, in the kitchen. "You're sweating. Are you okay? We'll be done soon. Are you hungry?" She got up from her crouching position to fix him something to eat, thinking he'd come by because he was lonesome.

"*Appa* came home. He looks sick. He's sleeping on the floor at home."

Sunja, who'd been quiet, waiting for Noa to speak up, wiped her wet hands on her apron. "Can I go? Can we leave now?" She'd never left early before.

"I'll stay here and finish. You go. Hurry. I'll be right there after I'm done."

Sunja reached for Noa's hand.

*　　*　　*

Halfway down the street, Sunja shouted, "Mozasu!" and Noa looked up at her.

"*Umma*, Aunt will bring him home," he said calmly.

She clutched his hand tighter and walked briskly toward the house.

"You ease my mind, Noa. You ease my mind."

Without the others around, it was possible to be kind to her son. Parents weren't supposed to praise their children, she knew this—it would only invite disaster. But her father had always told her when she had done something well; out of habit, he would touch the crown of her head or pat her back, even when she did nothing at all. Any other parent might've been chided by the neighbors for spoiling a daughter, but no one said anything to her crippled father, who marveled at his child's symmetrical features and normal limbs. He took pleasure in just watching her walk, talk, and do simple sums in her head. Now that he was gone, Sunja held on to her father's warmth and kind words like polished gems. No one should expect praise, and certainly not a woman, but as a little girl, she'd been treasured, nothing less. She'd been her father's delight. She wanted Noa to know what that was like, and she thanked God with every bit of her being for her boys. On the days when it felt impossible to live another day in her husband's brother's house—to work through the whole day and night, then to wake up again before the sun to start again, to go to the jail and hand over a meal for her husband—Sunja thought of her father, who had never said a cross word to her. He had taught her that children were a delight, that her boys were her delight.

"Did *appa* look very ill?" Sunja asked.

"I didn't know it was him. *Appa* was usually so clean and nicely dressed, *nee*?"

Sunja nodded, having told herself long ago to expect the worst. The elders in her church had warned her that the Korean prisoners were usually sent home just as they were about to die, so that they would not die in jail. The prisoners were beaten, starved, and made to go without clothing to weaken them. Just that morning, Sunja had gone to the jail to drop off his meal and this week's clean set of undershirts. Brother had been right then; her husband must not have received any of these things. As she and

Noa walked down the busy street, oblivious to the crowds, it occurred to her that she'd never thought to prepare her son for Isak's return. If anything, she had been so busy preparing for his death by working and saving money that she had not thought about what the boy might think of his father's return, or worse, his death. She felt so sorry for not having told him what to expect. It must have been a terrible shock for Noa.

"Did you eat your snack today?" she asked him, not knowing what else to say.

"I left it for *appa*."

They passed a small throng of uniformed students streaming out of a confectionery, eating their treats happily. Noa looked down, but didn't let go of his mother's hand. He knew the children, but none were his friends.

"Do you have homework?"

"Yes, but I'll do it when I get home, *umma*."

"You never give me any trouble," she said, feeling his five perfect fingers in hers, and she felt grateful for his sturdiness.

Sunja opened the door slowly. Isak was on the floor, sleeping. She knelt by his head. Dark, mottled skin stretched across his eye sockets and high cheekbones. His hair and beard were nearly white; he looked years older than his brother, Yoseb. He was no longer the beautiful young man who had rescued her from disgrace. Sunja removed his shoes and peeled off his holey socks. Dried crusts of blood covered his cracked, raw soles. The last toe on his left foot had turned black.

"*Umma*," Noa said.

"Yes." She turned to him.

"Should I get Uncle?"

"Yes." She nodded, trying not to cry. "Shimamura-san may not let him leave early, Noa. If Uncle can't leave, tell him that I'm with him. We don't want Uncle to get in trouble at work. Okay?"

Noa ran out of the house, not bothering to slide the door fully shut, and the incoming breeze woke Isak; he opened his eyes to see his wife sitting next to him.

"*Yobo*," he said.

Sunja nodded. "You're home. We're so glad you're home."

He smiled. The once-straight white teeth were either black or missing—the lower set cracked off entirely.

"You've suffered so much."

"The sexton and the pastor died yesterday. I should've died a long time ago."

Sunja shook her head, unable to speak.

"I'm home. Every day, I imagined this. Every minute. Maybe that's why I am here. How hard it must have been for you," he said, looking at her kindly.

Sunja shook her head no, wiping her face with her sleeve.

The Korean and Chinese girls who worked at the factory smiled at the sight of Noa. The delicious scent of freshly baked wheat biscuits greeted him. A girl packing biscuit boxes near the door whispered in Korean how tall he was getting. She pointed to his uncle's back. He was crouched over the motor of the biscuit machine. The factory floor was long and narrow, designed like a wide tunnel for the easy inspection of workers; the owner had set up the imposing biscuit machine by his office with the conveyor belts moving toward the workers, who stood in parallel rows. Yoseb wore safety goggles and was poking about inside the service panel with a pair of pliers. He was the foreman and the factory mechanic.

The din of the heavy machine blocked out normal speaking voices. The girls weren't supposed to talk on the factory floor, but it was nearly impossible to catch them if they whispered and made minimal facial gestures. Forty unmarried girls, hired for their nimble fingers and general tidiness, packed twenty thin wheat biscuits into wooden boxes that would be shipped to army officers stationed in China. For every two broken biscuits, a girl was fined a sen from her wages, forcing her to work carefully as well as swiftly. If she ate even a broken corner of a biscuit, she'd be terminated immediately. At the end of the day, the youngest girl gathered the broken biscuits into a fabric-lined basket, packed them into small bags, and was sent out to the market to sell them at a discount. If they didn't sell, Shimamura sold the biscuits for a nominal amount to the girls who packed the most boxes without error. Yoseb never took broken biscuits home, because the girls made so little money, and even the biscuit crumbs meant so much to them.

Shimamura, the owner, was sitting in his glassed-in office, the size of a utility closet. The plate glass window allowed him to check the girls' work. If he found anything amiss, he'd call Yoseb in and tell him to give the girl a warning. On the second warning, the girl was sent home without pay even if she'd worked for six days. Shimamura kept a blue, cloth-bound ledger with warnings listed next to the names of the girls, written in his beautiful hand-lettering. His foreman, Yoseb, disliked punishing the girls, and Shimamura viewed this as yet another example of Korean weakness. The factory owner believed that if all Asian countries were run with a kind of Japanese efficiency, attention to detail, and high level of organization, Asia as a whole would prosper and rise—able to defeat the unscrupulous West. Shimamura believed he was a fair person with perhaps a too-soft heart, which explained why he hired foreigners when many of his friends wouldn't. When they pointed to the slovenly nature of foreigners, he argued how could the foreigners ever learn unless the Japanese taught them to loathe incompetence and sloth. Shimamura felt that standards must be maintained for posterity's sake.

Noa had been inside the factory only once, and Shimamura had not been pleased then. About a year ago, Kyunghee was sick with a high fever and had fainted in the market, and Noa was sent to fetch Yoseb. Shimamura had reluctantly allowed Yoseb to attend to his wife. The next morning, he explained to Yoseb that there would be no repeat of this incident. How could he, Shimamura asked, run two machine-based factories without the presence of a competent mechanic? If Yoseb's wife were to get sick again, she would have to rely on a neighbor or family member; Yoseb could not just leave the factory in the middle of the day. The biscuits were war orders, and they had to be met promptly. Men were risking their lives fighting for their country; each family must make sacrifices.

So when Shimamura spotted the boy again, only a year after that uncomfortable speech that he had not wanted to make, he was furious. He snapped open his newspaper, pretending not to see the boy tapping his uncle's lower back.

Yoseb, startled by Noa's light touch, turned around.

"*Uh-muh*, Noa, what are you doing here?"

"*Appa*'s home."

"Really?"

"Can you come home now?" Noa asked. His mouth made a small red O.

Yoseb removed his goggles and sighed.

Noa closed his mouth and looked down. His uncle would have to get permission, the way his mother had to ask Aunt Kyunghee or Mr. Kim— the same way he had to ask his teacher to go to the bathroom. Sometimes, when it was sunny outside, Noa dreamed of not telling anyone and going to Osaka Bay. He'd been there once with his father on a Saturday afternoon when he was very small, and he always thought it would be nice to go back.

"Is he all right?" Yoseb studied Noa's expression.

"*Appa*'s hair turned gray. He's very dirty. *Umma*'s with him. She said if you can't come, it's okay, but she wanted you to know. To know that *appa* is home now."

"Yes, that's right. I'm glad to know."

Yoseb glanced at Shimamura, who was holding up his newspaper, pretending to read, but was no doubt watching him very carefully. His boss would never allow him to go home now. Also, unlike when Kyunghee fainted, Shimamura knew Isak had gone to jail because the sexton had refused to observe the Shinto ceremony. Periodically, the police came by to question Yoseb as well as to speak with Shimamura, who defended Yoseb as a model Korean. If he left, Yoseb would lose his job, and if the police picked him up for questioning, he would lose his character reference.

"Listen, Noa, work will be done in less than three hours, and then afterwards, I'll hurry home. It's irresponsible for me to leave now without finishing my work. As soon as I'm done, I'll run home faster than you can run. Tell your *umma* that I'll come home right away. And if your *appa* asks, tell him that Brother will be there very soon."

Noa nodded, not understanding why Uncle was crying.

"I have to finish, Noa, so you run home. Okay?" Yoseb put on his safety goggles and turned around.

Noa moved quickly toward the entrance. The sweet scent of biscuits wafted out the door. The boy had never eaten one of those biscuits, never having asked for one.

5

Noa burst through the doors of the house, his head and heart pounding from the breathless run. Gulping in deep lungfuls of air, he told his mother, "Uncle can't leave work."

Sunja nodded, having expected this. She was bathing Isak with a wet towel.

Isak's eyes were closed but his chest rose and fell slightly, punctuated now and then by a series of painful coughs. A light blanket covered his long legs. Ridges of scar tissue furrowed diagonally across Isak's shoulders and discolored torso, making haphazard diamond-shaped intersections. Every time Isak coughed, his neck flushed red.

Noa approached his father quietly.

"No, no. Move back," Sunja said sternly. "*Appa* is very sick. He has a bad cold."

She pulled the blanket up to Isak's shoulders, though she wasn't nearly finished with cleaning him. In spite of the strong soap and several changes of basin water, his body emitted a sour stench; nits clung to his hair and beard.

Isak had been alert for a few moments, his violent coughs waking him, but now when he opened his eyes, he didn't say anything, and when he looked at her, he didn't seem to recognize her.

Sunja changed the compress on Isak's feverish head. The nearest hospital was a long trolley ride away, and even if she could move him by herself, an all-night wait wouldn't ensure that a doctor would see him. If she could tuck him into the kimchi cart and wheel him to the trolley stop, she could possibly get him into the car, but then what would she do with the cart itself? It wouldn't pass through the trolley door. Noa might be able to push it back home, but then how would she get Isak from the stop to the hospital without the cart? And what if the driver wouldn't let them board? More than once, she'd witnessed the trolley driver asking a sick woman or man to get off.

Noa sat by his father's legs to keep away from his coughing. He felt an urge to pat his father's sharp knee bone—to touch him, to make sure he was real. The boy pulled out his notebook from his satchel to do his homework, keeping close watch on Isak's breathing.

"Noa, you have to put your shoes back on. Go to the drugstore and ask Pharmacist Kong to come. Can you tell him that it's important—that *umma* will pay him double?" Sunja decided that if the Korean pharmacist wouldn't come, she'd ask Kyunghee to plead with the Japanese pharmacist to come by the house, though that was unlikely.

The boy got up and left without a murmur. She could hear him running down the street in his even, rapid steps.

Sunja wrung out the hand towel she was using to bathe Isak above the brass basin. Fresh welts from recent beatings and a number of older scars covered his wide, bony back. She felt sick as she washed his dark and bruised frame. There was no one as good as Isak. He'd tried to understand her, to respect her feelings; he'd never once brought up her shame. He'd comforted her patiently when she'd lost the pregnancies between Noa and Mozasu. Finally, when she gave birth to their son, he'd been overjoyed, but she'd been too worried about how they'd survive with so little money to feel his happiness. Now that he was back home to die, what did money matter, anyway? She should've done more for him; she should've tried to know him the way he had tried to know her; and now it was over. Even with his gashed and emaciated frame, his beauty was remarkable. He was the opposite of her, really; where she was thick and short, he was slender and long-limbed—even his torn-up feet were well shaped. If her eyes were small and anxious, his were large and full of acceptance. The basin water was now gray, and Sunja got up to change it again.

Isak woke up. He saw Sunja wearing farmer pants and walking away from him. He called out to her, "*Yobo*," but she didn't turn around. He felt like he didn't know how to raise his voice. It was as if his voice was dying while his mind was alive.

"*Yobo*," Isak mumbled, and he reached for her, but she was almost in the kitchen already. He was in Yoseb's house in Osaka. This had to be true because he was, in fact, waking from a dream where he was a boy. In the dream, Isak had been sitting on a low bough of the chestnut tree in his childhood garden; the scent of the chestnut blossoms still lingered in his nose. It was like many of the dreams he'd had in prison where, while he dreamed, he was aware that the dream itself wasn't real. In real life, he'd never been on a tree. When he was young, the family gardener would prop him below that very tree to get some fresh air, but he'd never been strong enough to climb it the way Yoseb could. The gardener used to call Yoseb "Monkey." In the dream, Isak was hugging the thick branches tightly, unable to break from the embrace of the dark green foliage, the clusters of white blossoms with their dark pink hearts. From the house, cheerful voices of the women called to him. He wanted to see his old nursemaid and his sister, though they had died years ago; in the dream, they were laughing like girls.

"*Yobo*—"

"*Uh-muh*." She put down the washbasin at the threshold of the kitchen and rushed back to him. "Are you all right? Can I get you something?"

"My wife," he said slowly. "How have you been?" Isak felt drowsy and uncertain, but relieved. Sunja's face was different than he remembered—a little older, more weary. "How you must've struggled here. I am so sorry."

"Shhh—you must rest," she said.

"Noa." He said the boy's name like he remembered something good. "Where is he? He was here before."

"He went to fetch the pharmacist."

"He looks so healthy. And bright." It was hard to get the words out, but his mind felt clear suddenly, and he wanted to tell her the things he'd been saving up for her.

"You're working at a restaurant now? Are you cooking there?" Isak began to cough and couldn't stop. Pindots of blood splattered on her blouse, and she wiped his mouth with a towel.

When he tried to sit up, she placed her left hand beneath his head and her right over his chest to calm him, fearful that he might hurt himself. The coughs wracked his body. His skin felt hot even through the blankets.

"Please rest. Later. We can talk later."

He shook his head.

"No, no. I—I want to tell you something."

Sunja rested her hands on her lap.

"My life wasn't important," he said, trying to read her eyes, so full of anguish and exhaustion. He needed her to understand that he was thankful to her—for waiting for him, for taking care of the family. It humbled him to think of her laboring and earning money for their family when he wasn't able to support them. Money must've been very hard with him gone and with inflation from the war. The prison guards had complained incessantly of the prices of things—no one had enough to eat, they said. *Quit complaining about the bugs in the gruel.* Isak had prayed constantly for his family's provision. "I brought you here and made your life more difficult."

She smiled at him, not knowing how to say—*you saved me*. Instead, she said, "You must get well." Sunja covered him with a thicker blanket; his body was burning hot, but he shivered. "For the boys, please get well." *How can I raise them without you?*

"Mozasu—where is he?"

"At the restaurant with Sister. Our boss lets him stay there while we work."

Isak looked alert and attentive, as if all his pain had vanished; he wanted to know more about his boys.

"Mozasu," Isak said, smiling. "Mozasu. He saved his people from slavery—" Isak's head throbbed so intensely that he had to close his eyes again. He wanted to see his two sons grow up, finish school, and get married. Isak had never wanted to live so much, and now, just when he wanted to live until he was very old, he'd been sent home to die. "I have two sons," he said. "I have two sons. Noa and Mozasu. May the Lord bless my sons."

Sunja watched him carefully. His face looked strange, yet peaceful. Not knowing what else to do, she kept talking.

"Mozasu is becoming a big boy—always happy and friendly. He has a wonderful laugh. He runs everywhere. So fast!" She pumped her arms to imitate the toddler's running, and she found herself laughing, and he laughed, too. It occurred to her then that there was only one other person in the world who'd want to hear about Mozasu growing up so well, and until now, she'd forgotten that she could express a prideful joy in her boys. Even when her brother- and sister-in-law were pleased with the children, she couldn't ignore their sadness at their lack; sometimes, she wanted to hide her delight from them for fear that it could be seen as a kind of boasting. Back home, having two healthy and good sons was tantamount to having vast riches. She had no home, no money, but she had Noa and Mozasu.

Isak's eyes opened, and he looked at the ceiling. "I can't go until I see them, Lord. Until I see my children to bless them. Lord, let me not go—"

Sunja bowed her head, and she prayed, too.

Isak closed his eyes again, his shoulders twitching in pain.

Sunja placed her right hand on his chest to check his faint breathing.

The door opened, and as expected, Noa had returned home alone. The pharmacist couldn't come now but promised to come later tonight. The boy returned to his spot by Isak's feet and did his sums while his father slept. Noa wanted to show Isak his schoolwork; even Hoshii-sensei, the hardest teacher in his grade, told Noa that he was good at writing his letters and that he should work hard to improve his illiterate race: "One industrious Korean can inspire ten thousand to reject their lazy nature!"

Isak continued to sleep, and Noa concentrated on his work.

Later, when Kyunghee arrived home with Mozasu, the house felt lively for the first time since Isak's arrest. Isak woke briefly to see Mozasu, who didn't cry at the sight of the skeletal man. Mozasu called him "Papa" and patted his face with both hands, the way he did when he liked someone. With his white, chubby hands, Mozasu made little pats on Isak's sunken cheeks. The toddler sat still in front of him briefly, but as soon as Isak closed his eyes, Kyunghee removed him, not wanting the baby to get sick.

When Yoseb returned home, the house grew somber again, because Yoseb wouldn't ignore the obvious.

"How could they?" Yoseb said, staring hard at Isak's body.

"My boy, couldn't you just tell them what they wanted to hear? Couldn't you just say you worshipped the Emperor even if it isn't true? Don't you know that the most important thing is to stay alive?"

Isak opened his eyes but said nothing and closed his eyes again. His eyelids felt so heavy that it was painful to keep them open. He wanted to speak with Yoseb, but the words would not come out.

Kyunghee brought her husband a pair of scissors, a long razor blade, a cup of oil, and a basin of vinegar.

"The nits and lice won't die. He should be shaved. It must be so itchy for him," she said, her eyes wet.

Grateful to his wife for giving him something to do, Yoseb rolled up his sleeves, then poured the cup of oil over Isak's head, massaging it into his scalp.

"Isak-ah, don't move," Yoseb said, trying to keep his voice normal. "I'm going to get rid of all these itchy bastards."

Yoseb made clean strokes across Isak's head and threw the cut hair into the metal basin.

"*Yah*—Isak-ah." Yoseb smiled at the memory. "You remember how the gardener used to cut our hair when we were kids? I used to holler like a crazy animal but you never did. You sat there like a baby monk, calm and peaceful, and you never once complained." Yoseb grew quiet, wanting what he saw in front of him not to be true. "Isak-ah, why did I bring you to this hell? I was so lonesome for you. I was wrong, you know, to bring you here, and now I'm punished for my selfishness." Yoseb rested his blade in the basin.

"I will not be all right if you die. Do you understand? You cannot die, my boy. Isak-ah, please don't die. How can I go on? What will I tell our parents?"

Isak continued to sleep, oblivious to his family encircling his pallet.

Yoseb wiped his eyes and shut his mouth, clamping down on his jaws. He picked up the blade again, working steadily to take off the bits of gray hair remaining on his head. When Isak's head was smooth, Yoseb poured oil over his brother's beard.

For the remainder of the evening, Yoseb, Kyunghee, and Sunja rid him of nits and lice, dropping the bugs into jars of kerosene, only stopping to put the boys to bed. Later, the pharmacist came to tell them what they already knew. There was nothing a hospital or a doctor could do for Isak now.

At dawn, Yoseb returned to work. Sunja remained with Isak, and Kyunghee went to the restaurant. Yoseb didn't bother complaining about Kyunghee going to work alone. He was too tired to argue, and the wages were badly needed. Outside the house, the street was filled with the morning bustling of men and women heading to work and children running to school. Isak slept in the front room, his breathing fast and shallow. He was clean and smooth like an infant—all the hair from his body shaved.

After Noa finished breakfast, he laid down his chopsticks neatly and looked up at his mother.

"*Umma*, may I stay home?" he asked, never having dared to ask for such a thing, even when things were awful at school.

Sunja looked up from her sewing, surprised.

"Are you feeling ill?"

He shook his head.

Isak, who was half-awake, had heard the boy's request.

"Noa—"

"Yes, *appa*."

"*Umma* told me that you're becoming a fine scholar."

The child beamed but, out of habit, looked down at his feet.

When Noa received high marks in school, he thought first of his father.

Yoseb had told the boy several times that his father had been a prodigy, having taught himself Korean, Classical Chinese, and Japanese from books with scant tutoring. By the time he went to seminary, Isak had already read the Bible several times.

When school felt difficult, knowing that his father was a learned man had strengthened the boy's resolve to learn.

"Noa."

"Yes, *appa*?"

"You must go to school today. When I was a boy, I wanted to go to school with the other children very much."

The boy nodded, having heard this detail about his father before.

"What else can we do but persevere, my child? We're meant to increase our talents. The thing that would make your *appa* happy is if you do as well as you've been doing. Wherever you go, you represent our family, and you must be an excellent person—at school, in town, and in the world. No matter what anyone says. Or does," Isak said, then paused to cough. He knew it must be taxing for the child to go to a Japanese school.

"You must be a diligent person with a humble heart. Have compassion for everyone. Even your enemies. Do you understand that, Noa? Men may be unfair, but the Lord is fair. You'll see. You will," Isak said, his exhausted voice tapering off.

"Yes, *appa*." Hoshii-sensei had told him that he had a duty to Koreans, too; one day, he would serve his community and make Koreans good children of the benevolent Emperor. The boy stared at his father's newly shaved head. His bald pate was so white in contrast to his dark, sunken cheeks. He looked both new and ancient.

Sunja felt bad for the child; he'd never had a day with both his parents and no one else. When she was growing up, even when there were others around, it had been just the three of them—her father, mother, and her—an invisible triangle. When she thought back to her life at home, this closeness was what she missed. Isak was right about school, but it wouldn't be much longer. Soon, Isak would be gone. She would have given anything to see her father again, but how could she go against Isak's wishes? Sunja picked up Noa's satchel and handed it to the boy, who was crestfallen.

"After school, come home straight away, Noa. We'll be here," Isak said.

Noa remained fixed to his spot on the floor, unable to take his eyes off his father for fear that he'd disappear. The child hadn't realized how much he'd missed his father until he returned. The ache of missing him had surfaced in his small, concave chest, and he felt anxious about the pain that was sure to return. If he remained home, Noa felt certain that his father would be okay. They wouldn't even have to talk. Why couldn't he study at home the way his father had? Noa wanted to ask this, but it was not in his nature to argue.

Isak, however, didn't want Noa to see him like this anymore. The boy was already afraid, and there was no need to make him suffer any more than he already had. There were many things he hadn't told the child yet about life, about learning, about how to talk to God.

"Is it very hard at school?" Isak asked.

Sunja turned to look at the boy's face; she'd never thought to ask him this.

Noa shrugged. The work was okay, not impossible. The good students, who were all Japanese, the ones he admired, wouldn't speak to him. They wouldn't even look at him. He believed that he could enjoy going to school if he were a regular person and not a Korean. He couldn't say this to his father or to anyone else, because it was certain he'd never be a regular Japanese. One day, Uncle Yoseb said, they would return to Korea; Noa imagined that life would be better there.

Carrying his book bag and bento, Noa lingered by the front door, memorizing his father's kindly face.

"Child, come here," Isak said.

Noa approached him and sat on bended knees. *Please God, please. Please make my father well. I'll ask this just once more. Please.* Noa shut his eyes tightly.

Isak took Noa's hand and held it.

"You are very brave, Noa. Much, much braver than me. Living every day in the presence of those who refuse to acknowledge your humanity takes great courage."

Noa chewed on his lower lip and didn't say anything. He wiped his nose with his hand.

"My child," he said, and Isak let go of his son's hand. "My dear boy. My blessing."

6

December 1944

Like most shops in Osaka with nothing to sell, the restaurant was shuttered frequently, but its three remaining workers showed up six days a week. Food had virtually disappeared from the markets, and even when the rations arrived and the shops opened for half a day to long lines, the offerings were unacceptably sparse and undesirable. You could wait six hours for fish and come home with a scant handful of dried anchovies, or worse, nothing at all. If you had high-level military connections, it was possible to obtain some of what you needed; of course, if you had a great deal of money, there was always the black market. City children were sent alone to the country by train to buy an egg or a potato in exchange for a grandmother's kimono. At the restaurant, Kim Changho, who was in charge of procuring food, kept two storage bins: one, which could be safely inspected by the neighborhood association leaders, who liked to make surprise visits to restaurant kitchens, and another, behind a false wall in the basement, for food bought from the black market. Sometimes, customers—usually wealthy businessmen from Osaka and travelers from abroad—brought their own meat and alcohol to the restaurant. The men who used to cook in the evening were gone now; Kim made up the whole of the evening staff; it was up to him to cook the meats and wash the dishes for the occasional customer.

It was the twelfth month of the year—a mild, wintry morning. When Sunja and Kyunghee arrived for work, Kim asked the women to have a seat at the square table pushed up against the wall outside the kitchen. This was where they usually took their meals and breaks. He'd already placed a pot of tea on the table. Once seated, Kyunghee poured each of them a cup.

"The restaurant will be closed tomorrow," Kim said.

"For how long?" Sunja asked.

"Till the war is over. This morning, I gave up the last of the metal things. The kitchen's almost empty now. All the steel rice bowls, basins, cooking pots, utensils, steel chopsticks were requisitioned. Even if I could find new ones and remain open, the police will know that we've kept things back and confiscate them. The government doesn't pay us for what they take. We can't keep replacing—" Kim took a sip of his tea. "Well, so it has to be."

Sunja nodded, feeling bad for Kim, who looked upset. He glanced briefly at Kyunghee.

"And what will you do?" Kyunghee asked him.

Kim, younger than Isak, addressed her as Sister. Lately, he depended on her to accompany him to the market to support his civilian status when stopped. Suspicious of military service dodgers, the police and neighborhood association leaders routinely questioned any male not in uniform. To put them off, he'd taken to wearing the dark glasses of a blind man on the streets.

"Can you find another job?" Kyunghee asked.

"Don't worry about me. At least I don't have to fight"—he laughed, touching his eyeglasses; his poor vision had kept him from fighting and from working in the mines when other Koreans had been conscripted—"which is good, since I'm a coward."

Kyunghee shook her head.

Kim stood up.

"We have some customers coming this evening from Hokkaido. I kept back two cooking pans and a few bowls for the meal; we can use those. Sister, I wonder if you can come with me to the market," he said, then he turned to Sunja. "Will you stay here and wait for the liquor man to come? He's supposed to bring a package by. Oh, the customer has asked for your bellflower *muchim* for tonight. I left a packet of dried bellflowers in the downstairs cupboard. You'll find the other ingredients there."

Sunja nodded, wondering how he'd found dried bellflowers and sesame oil.

Kyunghee got up and put on her old blue coat over her sweater and worker pants. She was still a lovely woman, clear skinned and slender, but now, fine crinkles around her eyes and marionette lines by her mouth appeared when she smiled. Heavy kitchen work had ruined her once-supple white hands, but she did not mind. Yoseb, who held her small right hand when they slept, didn't seem to notice the red scaly patches on her palms resulting from day after day of pickling. After Isak died, Yoseb had become a different man—sullen, brooding, and uninterested in anything but work. His change had transformed their household and their marriage. Kyunghee tried to cheer up her husband, but she could do little to dispel his gloom and silence. At home, no one seemed to talk except for the boys. Yoseb was almost unrecognizable from the boy she had loved from girlhood. He had become this cynical, broken man—something she could never have predicted. So it was only at the restaurant that Kyunghee behaved like herself. Here, she teased Kim like a younger brother and giggled with Sunja while they cooked. Now, even this place would be gone.

After Kim and her sister-in-law left for the market, Sunja shut the door behind them. As she turned toward the kitchen, she heard the knock.

"Did you forget something?" Sunja asked, opening the door.

Hansu stood before her, wearing a black coat over a gray wool suit. His hair was still dark and his face more or less the same, with a slight thickening along his jawline. Reflexively, Sunja checked to see if he was wearing the white leather shoes he used to wear long ago. He wore black leather lace-up shoes.

"It's been a long time," Hansu said calmly, entering the restaurant. Sunja stepped several paces away from him.

"What are you doing here?"

"This is my restaurant. Kim Changho works for me."

Her head felt foggy, and Sunja slumped down on the nearest seat cushion.

*   *   *

Hansu had located her eleven years ago when she'd pawned the silver pocket watch he'd given her. The pawnbroker had tried to sell him that watch, and the rest had been simple detective work. Since then, Hansu had been tracking her daily. After Isak went to prison, he knew she needed money and created this job for her. Sunja learned that the moneylender who'd loaned Yoseb the money worked for him as well. In fact, Hansu's wife was the eldest daughter of a powerful Japanese moneylender in Kansai, and Hansu had been legally adopted by his father-in-law, Morimoto, because the man did not have a son. Koh Hansu, whose legal name was Haru Morimoto, lived in an enormous house outside of Osaka with his wife and three daughters.

Hansu led her back to the table where she'd sat only a few moments ago with Kim and Kyunghee.

"Let's have some tea. You stay here, and I'll get a cup. You seem troubled by my appearance."

Familiar with where everything was, Hansu returned from the kitchen right away with a teacup.

Sunja stared at him, still unable to speak.

"Noa is a very smart boy," he said proudly. "He's a handsome child and an excellent runner."

She tried not to look afraid. How did he know these things? She now recalled every conversation she'd ever had with Kim about her sons. There had been numerous occasions when Noa and Mozasu had been with her at the restaurant when there'd been no school for Noa.

"What do you want?" she asked finally, trying to appear calmer than she felt.

"You have to leave Osaka immediately. Convince your sister and your brother-in-law to go. For the safety of the children. However, if they don't want to go, there's little you can do. I have a place for you and the boys."

"Why?"

"Because the real bombing will start soon here."

"What are you talking about?"

"The Americans are going to bomb Osaka in a matter of days. The

B-29s have been in China. Now they found more bases on the islands. The Japanese are losing the war. The government knows it can never win but won't admit it. The Americans know that the Japanese military has to be stopped. The Japanese military would kill every Japanese boy rather than admit its error. Fortunately, the war will end before Noa is recruited."

"But everyone says Japan is doing better."

"You mustn't believe what you hear from the neighbors or what the newspapers say. They don't know."

"Shhh—" Sunja looked around instinctively at the plate glass window and the front door. If anyone was caught saying such treacherous things, he could be sent to jail. She had repeatedly told her boys to never, ever say anything negative about Japan or the war. "You shouldn't talk like this. You could get in trouble—"

"No one can hear us."

She bit her lower lip and stared, still unable to believe the sight of him. It had been twelve years. Yet here was the same face—the one she had loved so much. She had loved his face the way she had loved the brightness of the moon and the cold blue water of the sea. Hansu was sitting across from her, and he returned her gaze, looking kindly at her. However, he remained composed, certain of every measured word he uttered. There had never been any hesitation in him. He was unlike her father, Isak, her brother-in-law, or Kim. He was unlike any other man she had ever known.

"Sunja-ya, you have to leave Osaka. There's no time to think about it. I came here to tell you this, because the bombs will destroy this city."

Why had he not come sooner? Why had he kept back like a watchful shadow over her life? How many times had he seen her when she had not seen him?

The anger she felt toward him surprised her. "They won't leave, and I can't just—"

"You mean your brother-in-law. He might be a fool, but that's not your problem. The sister-in-law will go if you tell her. This city is made of wood and paper. It'll take no more than a match for it to incinerate. Imagine what will happen with an American bomb." He paused. "Your sons will be killed. Is that what you want? I've already sent my daughters away a long time ago. A parent must be decisive; a child cannot protect himself."

She understood then. Hansu was worried about Noa. He had a Japanese wife and three daughters. He had no son.

"How do you know? How do you know what will happen?"

"How did I know that you needed work? How did I know where Noa goes to school, that his math teacher is a Korean who pretends to be Japanese, that your husband died because he didn't get out of prison in time, and that you're alone in this world. How did I know how to keep my family safe? It's my job to know what others don't. How did you know to make kimchi and sell it on a street corner to earn money? You knew because you wanted to live. I want to live, too, and if I want to live, I have to know things others don't. Now, I'm telling you something valuable. I'm telling you something so you can save your sons' lives. Don't waste this information. The world can go to hell, but you need to protect your sons."

"My brother-in-law will not abandon his house."

He laughed. "The house will be a pile of ashes. The Japanese will not give him a sen for his pain when it's gone."

"The neighbors said that the war will end soon."

"The war will end soon, but not the way they think. The wealthy Japanese have already sent their families to the country. They've already converted their cash into gold. The rich do not care about politics; they will say anything to save their skin. You're not rich, but you're smart, and I'm telling you that you have to leave today."

"How?"

"Kim will take you, your brother-in-law and sister-in-law, and the boys to a farm outside Osaka prefecture. A sweet-potato farmer owes me a favor. He has a big place, and there'll be plenty of food there. All of you will have to work for him until the war's over, but you'll have a place to sleep and more than enough to eat. Tamaguchi-san has no children; he won't harm you."

"Why did you come?" Sunja began to cry.

"It's not the time to discuss this. Please don't be a foolish woman. You're smarter than that. It's time to take action. The restaurant will be destroyed no different than your house will be," he said, speaking quickly. "This building is made of wood and a few bricks. Your brother-in-law should sell his house immediately to the next idiot and get out. Or at the very least, he should take his ownership papers with him. Soon, people will be fleeing here like rats, so you have to leave now before it's too late. The Americans will finish this stupid war. Maybe tonight, maybe in a few weeks, but they're not going to put up with this nonsense war for very long. The Germans are losing, too."

Sunja folded her hands together. The war had been going on for so long. Everyone was sick of it. Without the restaurant, the family would have starved even though everyone was working and earning money. Their clothes were threadbare and holey. Cloth, thread, and needles were unavailable. How were Hansu's shoes so shiny when no one had any shoe polish? She and Kyunghee loathed the neighborhood association's endless meetings, yet if they didn't go, the leaders would take it out on their rations. The latest military drills had become ludicrous—on Sunday mornings, grandmothers and little children were required to practice spearing the enemy with sharpened bamboo spears. They said American soldiers raped women and girls and that it would be better to kill yourself than to surrender to such barbarians. Back in the restaurant office, there was a cache of bamboo spears for the workers and the customers in case the Americans landed. Kim kept two hunting knives in his desk drawer.

"Can I go back home? To Busan?"

"There's nothing to eat there, and it isn't safe for you. Women are being taken away from smaller villages in greater numbers."

Sunja looked puzzled.

"I've told you this before: Never listen to anyone who tells you there's good factory work in China or any of the other colonies. Those jobs don't exist. Do you understand me?" His expression grew severe.

"Is my mother all right?"

"She's not young so they won't take her. I'll try to find out."

"Thank you," she said quietly.

Worried about her boys, Sunja hadn't paid enough attention to her mother's welfare. In Yangjin's sparse letters, written for her by a harried schoolteacher, she'd say that she was fine, expressing more concern for Sunja and the boys than for herself. Sunja hadn't seen her mother in as many years as she had not seen Hansu.

"Can you be ready to go tonight?"

"Why would my brother-in-law listen to me? How can I possibly explain—"

"Tell him that Kim told you that you must leave today. He's talking to your sister-in-law now. Tell him that he learned this privileged information from his boss. I can send Kim to speak to him at your house."

Sunja said nothing. She didn't believe that anyone could convince Yoseb to leave.

"There should be no hesitation. The boys have to be protected."

"But Sister will—"

"So what about her? Listen to me. Choose your sons over everyone else. Don't you know this by now?"

She nodded.

"Bring everyone here at dusk. Kim will keep the restaurant open. No one should know where you're going. You want to get out of here before everyone else tries to as well." Hansu got up and looked at her soberly. "Leave the others if you have to."

7

1945

On the day that Hansu told her to take the boys to the country, Yoseb got a job offer. Earlier that afternoon, a friend of a friend had stopped by Yoseb's biscuit factory and told him of the position: A steel factory in Nagasaki needed a foreman to manage its Korean workers. There would be a housing camp for men, including room and board, but Yoseb couldn't bring his family. The pay was almost triple his current salary. The family would be separated for a while. When Yoseb came home, excited about the offer, Kyunghee and Sunja had news of their own. Hansu's hand was in everything, but what could Sunja say?

At dusk, Kim moved the women and boys to Tamaguchi's farm. The next morning, Yoseb quit his job at the factory, packed one bag, and locked up the house. That afternoon, Yoseb headed to Nagasaki, recalling the time he left Pyongyang for Osaka—the last time he'd left on a journey by himself.

Short months passed before the bombings started, but once they began, the bombing continued through the summer. Hansu was wrong about the timing, but he was right that the neighborhood would turn to ashes.

Tamaguchi, a fifty-eight-year-old sweet-potato farmer, did not mind having the extra pairs of hands. His regular workers and seasonal ones had been conscripted years ago, and there were no able-bodied men to replace them. Several of his former workers had already died in Manchuria, with two badly disabled in battle, and there had been scant news of the others sent to Singapore and the Philippines. Each morning, as Tamaguchi rose from his futon, he suffered from the routine aches that accompanied aging; however, he was relieved to be old, since he would not have to fight the stupid war. The shortage of men impaired his ambitions for his farm, especially at a time when there was a growing demand for potatoes. Tamaguchi could command any illegal price he wanted, it seemed, and now that he had tasted wealth, so much so that he'd been forced to hide troves of treasure in various parts of the farm, he was willing to do whatever it took to squeeze every golden drop from this national calamity.

Night and day, Tamaguchi cultivated potato slips, turned the earth, and planted. Without men, it was nearly impossible to complete the endless chores of the farm, and without men, there was no one to marry his wife's two sisters, whom he'd been forced to take in—worthless city girls not built for any kind of work. With their chatter and made-up ailments, the sisters distracted his wife from her labors, and he hoped he wouldn't be saddled with them for much longer. Thankfully, his wife's parents were dead. For seasonal work, Tamaguchi had been hiring the elderly men and women in the village, but they were given to endless whining about the difficult nature of planting in the warm weather and harvesting in the cold.

It would never have occurred to Tamaguchi to hire city Koreans or to board them on his farm when he'd turned away many city Japanese who'd sought refuge, but Koh Hansu he could not refuse.

Upon the receipt of Hansu's telegram, the farmer and his overworked wife, Kyoko, configured the barn to make it habitable for the Korean family from Osaka. Only days after their arrival, however, Tamaguchi learned that it was he who'd gotten the better end of the bargain. Hansu had furnished him with two strong women who could cook, clean, and plow; a young man who couldn't see well but could dig and lift; and two clever boys who took instruction perfectly. The Koreans ate plenty, but they earned their keep and bothered no one. They didn't ever complain.

From the first day, Tamaguchi put Noa and Mozasu in charge of feeding the three cows, eight pigs, and thirty chickens; milking the cows;

collecting the eggs; and cleaning the henhouse. The boys spoke Japanese like natives, so he was able to take them to the market to help sell; the older one was excellent with calculations, and his letters were neat enough for the ledger. The two Korean women, sisters-in-law, were fine housekeepers and hardy outdoor workers. The skinny married one was not young but very pretty, and her Japanese was good enough that Kyoko tasked her with the cooking, washing, and mending. The shorter one, the quiet widow, tended the kitchen garden ably and worked in the fields alongside the young man. The two labored like a pair of oxen. For the first time in years, Tamaguchi felt relaxed; even his wife was less irritable, scolding him and her sisters less than usual.

Four months after their arrival, Hansu's truck drove up to the farm at dusk. Hansu stepped out of the truck, and he had with him an older Korean woman. Tamaguchi rushed to meet him. Normally, Hansu's men came by in the evenings to pick up the produce for sale in the city, but it was rarely the boss himself.

"Tamaguchi-san." Hansu bowed. The old woman bowed to Tamaguchi from the waist. She wore a traditional dress and in each hand she clutched fabric parcels.

"Koh-san." Tamaguchi bowed, smiling at the older woman. As he drew closer, Tamaguchi could see that the woman was not very old; in fact, she might have been younger than he was. Her brown face was drawn and malnourished.

"This is Sunja's mother. Kim Yangjin *desu*," Hansu said. "She arrived from Busan earlier today."

"Kim-u Yangjin-san." The farmer said each syllable slowly, realizing that he had a new guest. He scanned her face, searching for any resemblance to the young widow, mother to the two boys. There was some similarity around the mouth and jaw. The woman's brown hands were strong like a man's, with large knobbed fingers. She would make a good worker, he thought. "Sunja's mother? Is that so? Welcome, welcome," he said, smiling.

Yangjin, her eyes downcast, appeared afraid. She was also exhausted. Hansu cleared his throat.

"And how are the boys? I hope they're not giving you any trouble."

"No, no. Not at all. They're excellent workers! Wonderful boys." Tamaguchi meant this. He had not expected the boys to be so capable. With no children of his own, he had expected city children to be spoiled and lazy like his sisters-in-law. In his village, prosperous farmers complained about their foolish sons, so the childless Tamaguchi and his wife had not envied parents very much. Also, Tamaguchi hadn't had any idea of what Koreans would be like. He was not a bigoted man, but the only Korean he knew personally was Koh Hansu, and their relationship had begun with the war and was not an ordinary one. An open secret, several of the larger farms sold their produce on the city's black markets through Koh Hansu and his distribution network, but no one discussed this. Foreigners and yakuza controlled the black market, and there were serious repercussions for selling produce to them. It was an honor to help Koh Hansu; favors created obligations, and the farmer was determined to do anything he could for him.

"Koh-san, please come inside the house for tea. You must be thirsty. It is very hot today." Tamaguchi walked into the house, and even before taking off his own shoes, the farmer offered house slippers to his guests.

Shaded by ancient, sturdy poplars, the interior of the large farmhouse was pleasantly cool. The fresh grass smell of new tatami mats greeted the guests. In the main room, paneled in cedar, Tamaguchi's wife, Kyoko, sat on a blue silk floor cushion, sewing her husband's shirt; her two sisters, lying on their stomachs with their ankles crossed, flipped through an old movie magazine they'd read so many times before that they'd memorized its text. The three women, exceptionally well dressed for no one in particular, looked out of place in the farmhouse. Despite the rationing of cloth, the farmer's wife and her sisters had not suffered any privation. Kyoko wore an elegant cotton kimono, more suited for a Tokyo merchant's wife, and the sisters wore smart navy skirts and cotton blouses, looking like college co-eds from American films.

When the sisters lifted their chins to see who'd walked into the house, their pale, pretty faces emerged from the long bangs of their stylishly bobbed haircuts. The war had brought priceless treasures to the

Tamaguchi home—valuable calligraphy scrolls, bolts of fabric, more ki-monos than the women could ever wear, lacquered cupboards, jewels, and dishes—possessions of city dwellers who'd been willing to trade heir-looms for a sack of potatoes and a chicken. However, the sisters yearned for the city itself—new films, Kansai shops, the unblinking electric lights. They were sick of the war, the endless green fields, and farm life in gen-eral. Bellies full and well housed, they had only contempt for the smell of lamp oil, loud animals, and their hick brother-in-law, who was always talking about the prices of things. The American bombs had burned down the cinemas, department stores, and their beloved confectioneries, but glittering images of such urban pleasures called to them still, feeding their growing discontent. They complained daily to their elder sister—the plain and sacrificial one—whom they had once mocked for marrying their distant country cousin, who now prepared gold and kimonos for their dowries.

When Tamaguchi cleared his throat, the girls sat up and tried to look busy. They nodded at Hansu and stared at the filthy hem of the Korean woman's long skirt, unable to keep from making a face.

Yangjin bowed deeply to the three women and remained by the door, not expecting to be invited in, and she was not. From where she stood, Yangjin could see a portion of the bent back of a woman working in the kitchen, but it didn't look like Sunja.

Hansu spotted the woman in the kitchen as well and asked Tamaguchi's wife, "Is that Sunja-san in the kitchen?"

Kyoko bowed to him again. The Korean seemed too confident for her taste, but she recognized that her husband needed the fellow more than ever.

"Koh-san, welcome. It's so nice to see you," Kyoko said, rising from her seat; she gave her sisters a reproving look, which stirred them suffi-ciently to stand up and bow to the guest. "The woman in the kitchen is Kyunghee-san. Sunja-san is planting in the fields. Please, sit down. We shall get you something cool to drink." She turned to Ume-chan, the younger of the two sisters, and Ume trudged to the kitchen to fetch cold oolong-*cha*.

Hansu nodded, trying not to show his irritation. He'd expected Sunja to work, but it hadn't occurred to him that she'd be doing outdoor labor.

Kyoko sensed the man's displeasure. "Surely, you must want to see your daughter, ma'am. Tako-chan, please accompany our guest to her daughter."

Tako, the middle of the three sisters, complied because she had no choice; it was pointless to defy Kyoko, who could hold a grudge for days in punitive silence. Hansu told Yangjin in Korean to follow the girl who'd take her to Sunja. As Tako put on her shoes in the stone-paved foyer, she caught a whiff of the old woman's sour, peculiar odor, only aggravated by two days of travel. Filthy, she thought. Tako walked briskly ahead of her, keeping as many paces between them as she could.

After Kyoko poured the tea that Ume had brought from the kitchen, the women disappeared, leaving the men to speak alone in the living room.

The farmer asked Hansu for news of the war.

"It can't last much longer. The Germans are being crushed, and the Americans are just getting started. Japan will lose this war. It's a matter of when." Hansu said this without a trace of regret or joy. "It's better to stop this madness sooner than later than to have more nice boys get killed, is it not?"

"Yes, yes. That is so, isn't it?" Tamaguchi replied in a whisper, dispirited. Of course, he wanted Japan to win, and no doubt Hansu knew the realities, but even if Japan would not win, the farmer had no wish for the war to end just yet. There had been talk of fermenting sweet potatoes into airplane fuel; if that happened, and even if the government paid only a little—if anything at all—the farmer expected prices to rise even higher on the black market, because the cities were desperate for food and alcohol. With just one or two more harvests, Tamaguchi would have enough gold to buy the two vast tracts of land beside his. The owner of the plots was only getting older and less interested in working. To own the entire south side of the region in one unbroken lot had been his grandfather's dearest wish.

Hansu interrupted the farmer's reverie.

"So, how is it? Having them here?"

Tamaguchi nodded favorably. "They help a great deal. I wish they didn't have to work so much, but, as you know, I'm short on men—"

"They'd expected to work." Hansu nodded reassuringly, fully cognizant that the farmer was getting back his room and board and making a large profit, but this was okay with him as long as Sunja and her family weren't being mistreated.

"Will you stay with us tonight?" Tamaguchi asked. "It's too late to travel, and you must have dinner with us. Kyunghee-san is an exceptional cook."

Tako didn't have to walk the old woman far. When Yangjin spotted her daughter bent over in the vast, dark field, she grabbed the tail end of her long skirt and wound it around her body to free her legs. She ran as fast as she could in the direction of her daughter.

Sunja, who heard the rushed footfalls, looked up from her planting. A tiny woman in an off-white-colored *hanbok* was running toward her, and Sunja dropped her hoe. The small shoulders, the gray bun gathered at the base of the neck, the bow of the short blouse knotted neatly in a soft rectangle: *Umma*. How was that possible? Sunja trampled the potato slips in her path to get to her.

"Oh, my child. My child. Oh, my child."

Sunja held her mother close, able to feel the sharpness of Yangjin's collarbone beneath the blouse fabric. Her mother had shrunk.

Hansu ate his dinner quickly, then went to the barn to speak with the others. He wanted merely to sit with them, not to have them fuss over him. He would have preferred to eat with Sunja and her family, but he didn't want to offend Tamaguchi. During the meal, he had thought only of her and the boy. They had never shared a meal. It was hard to explain, even to himself, his yearning to be with them. In the barn, he realized that Kyunghee had made two dinners in the Tamaguchi kitchen—a Japanese one for the Tamaguchi family and a Korean for the others. In the barn, the Koreans ate their meals on a low, oilcloth-covered table that Kim had built for them with leftover beams. Sunja had just cleared the dinner dishes. Everyone looked up when he walked in.

The animals were quieter in the evening, but they were not silent. The smells were stronger than Hansu remembered, but he knew the odor would be less noticeable soon enough. The Koreans were housed in the back part of the barn, and the animals were nearer the front, with haystacks between them. Kim had built a wooden partition, and he and the boys slept on one side with the women on the other.

Yangjin, who'd been sitting on the ground between her grandsons, got up and bowed to him. On the way to the farm, she'd thanked him numerous times, and now, reunited with her family, she kept repeating thank you, thank you, clutching on to her grandsons, who looked embarrassed. She bawled like an old Korean woman.

Kyunghee was still in the farmhouse kitchen, washing the dinner dishes. When she finished with that, she would prepare the guest room for Hansu. Kim was in the shed behind the barn that was used for bathing, busy heating water for everyone's bath. Kyunghee and Kim had taken over Sunja's evening chores to allow her to remain with her mother. None of them suspected the reasons why Hansu had gone through the trouble of getting Yangjin from Korea. As Yangjin sobbed, Sunja observed Hansu, unable to make sense of this man who had never left her life.

Hansu sat down on the thick pile of hay, opposite the boys.

"Did you eat enough dinner?" Hansu asked them in plain Korean.

The boys looked up, surprised that Hansu spoke Korean so well. They'd thought that the man who'd brought their grandmother might be Japanese, because he was so well dressed and since Tamaguchi-san had treated him with such deference.

"You are Noa," Hansu said, considering the boy's face carefully. "You are twelve years old."

"Yes, sir," Noa replied. The man wore very fine clothes and beautiful leather shoes. He looked like a judge or an important person in a movie poster.

"How do you like being on the farm?"

"It is good, sir."

"I'm almost six years old," Mozasu interrupted, something he did out of habit whenever his older brother spoke. "We eat a lot of rice here. I can eat bowls and bowls of rice. Tamaguchi-san said that I need to eat well to grow. He told me not to eat potatoes but to eat rice! Do you like rice, sir?" the boy asked Hansu. "Noa and I will have baths tonight. In Osaka, we couldn't take baths often because there was no fuel for hot water. I like the baths on the farm better because the tub is smaller than the one at the *sento*. Do you like baths? The water is so hot, but you get used it, *nee*, and the tips of my fingers get wrinkled like an old man when I don't come out of the water." Mozasu opened his eyes wide. "My face doesn't wrinkle, though, because I am young."

Hansu laughed. The younger child had none of Noa's formality. He seemed so free.

"I'm glad you're eating well here. That's good to know. Tamaguchi-san said that you boys are excellent workers."

"Thank you, sir," Mozasu said, wanting to ask the man more questions but stopping himself when the man addressed his brother.

"What are your chores, Noa?"

"We clean the stalls here, feed the animals, and take care of the chickens. I also keep records for Tamaguchi-san when we go to the market."

"Do you miss school?"

Noa did not reply. He missed doing math problems and writing Japanese. He missed the quiet of doing his work—how no one bothered him when he was doing his homework. There was never any time to read at the farm, and he had no books of his own.

"I was told that you're a very good student."

"Last year, there wasn't much school."

Back home, school had been canceled often. Unlike the other boys, Noa had disliked the bayonet practices and pointless air raid drills. Although he had not wanted to be separated from Uncle Yoseb, the farm was better than being in the city, because he felt safe here. At the farm, he never heard any planes, and there were far fewer bomb shelter drills. Meals were abundant and delicious. They ate eggs every day and drank fresh milk. He slept deeply and woke up feeling well.

"When the war ends, you will return to school, I suppose. Would you like that?" Hansu asked.

Noa nodded.

Sunja wondered how they would manage then. After the war, she had planned on going back to Yeongdo, but her mother said there was nothing left. The government had assessed taxes on the boardinghouse owner, and the owner had sold the building to a Japanese family. The servant girls had taken factory jobs in Manchuria, and there had been no news of them. When Hansu had located Yangjin, she had been working as a housekeeper for a Japanese merchant in Busan, sleeping in the storeroom.

Hansu pulled out two comic books from his jacket pocket.

"Here."

Noa accepted them with both hands, the way his mother had taught him. The writing was in Korean.

"Thank you, sir."

"Do you read Korean?"

"No, sir."

"You can learn," Hansu said.

"Aunt Kyunghee can help us read this," Mozasu said. "Uncle Yoseb isn't here, but when we see him next time, we can surprise him."

"You boys should know how to read Korean. One day, you may return," Hansu said.

"Yes, sir," Noa said. He imagined that Korea would be a peaceful place where he would be normal. His father had told him that Pyongyang, where he'd grown up, was a beautiful city, and Yeongdo, his mother's hometown, was a serene island with abundant fish in blue-green waters.

"Where are you from, sir?" Noa asked.

"Jeju. It isn't far from Busan, where your mother is from. It's a volcanic island. They have oranges there. The people from Jeju are descendants of gods." He winked. "I will take you there one day."

"I don't want to live in Korea," Mozasu cried. "I want to stay here at the farm."

Sunja patted Mozasu's back.

"*Umma*, we should live on the farm forever. Uncle Yoseb will come here soon, right?" Mozasu asked.

Kyunghee walked in then, having finished her work. Mozasu ran to her with the comic books.

"Can you read this for me?"

Mozasu led her to the pile of folded futons, which they used as chairs. Kyunghee nodded.

"Noa, come. I'll read these to you boys."

Noa bowed quickly to Hansu and joined Kyunghee and Mozasu. Yangjin followed Noa, leaving Sunja at the table. When Sunja started to get up, Hansu gestured for her to sit down.

"Stay." Hansu looked serious. "Stay for a little while. I want to know how you are."

"I'm well. Thank you." Her voice was shaky. "Thank you for bringing my mother here," Sunja said. There was more she needed to say, but it was hard.

"You asked for news of her, and I thought it would be better for her to come here. It's very bad in Japan, but it's worse in Korea right now. When the war ends, it may get better, but it'll be worse before it stabilizes."

"What do you mean?"

"When the Americans win, we don't know what the Japanese will do. They'll pull out of Korea, but who'll be in charge of Korea? What will happen to all those Koreans who supported the Japanese? There will be confusion. There will be more bloodshed. You don't want to be around it. You don't want your sons around it."

"What will you do?" she asked.

He looked directly at her.

"I'll take care of myself and my people. You think I'd trust my life to a bunch of politicians? The people in charge don't know anything. And the ones who do don't care."

Sunja thought about this. Perhaps that was right, but why should she trust him? She pushed herself off the ground with her hands, but Hansu shook his head.

"Is it so difficult to talk with me? Please sit."

Sunja sat down.

"I have to take care of my sons. You should understand that."

The boys were staring intently at the comic book pages. Kyunghee was reading the lines with feeling, and even Yangjin, who was unable to read, found herself laughing with the children at the silly things the characters were saying. They were absorbed in the comic book, and their faces seemed softer somehow, like they were calm.

"I'll help you," Hansu said. "You don't have to worry about money or—"

"You're helping us now because I have no choice. When the war ends, I'll work to take care of them. I'm working now to earn our keep—"

"When the war ends, I can find you a home and give you money to take care of the boys. The boys should be going to school, not pushing cow dung around. Your mother and sister-in-law can stay, too. I can get your brother-in-law a good job."

"I can't explain you to my family," Sunja said. She felt like she was lying all the time. What was he thinking? she wondered. Surely, he could not desire her anymore. She was a twenty-nine-year-old widow with two young children to feed and educate. Sunja was not old, but she could not imagine that any man would want her now. If she had never been beautiful before, she was not even appealing now. She was a plain woman with a country face, her skin spotted and wrinkled by the sun. Her body was strong and stout, larger than when she had been a girl. In her life, she'd been desired by two men; it was difficult to imagine having that again. Sometimes, she felt like a serviceable farm animal who'd one day be useless. Before that day arrived, it was important to make sure her boys would be okay when she was gone.

"You have children, don't you?"

"Three daughters."

"And what would your daughters say about me? About us?" she whispered.

"My family has nothing to do with you."

"I understand." Sunja swallowed, her mouth dry. "I'm grateful for this opportunity—to work and to be safe. But when the war ends, I'll get another job and support the boys and my mother. I'll work until I cannot work anymore."

Sunja got up from the floor and brushed the hay off her work pants.

Unable to breathe normally, she turned from him and stared at the oxen—their enormous dark eyes, full of eternal suffering. Had the others noticed them talking? They seemed to be focused on the comic book. Sunja covered her left hand with her right; despite her washing, her cuticles were still brown from the dirt.

8

Again, Hansu was not wrong. The war did end, faster than he had predicted, but even he could not have imagined the final bombs. A bunker had shielded Yoseb from the worst, but when he finally climbed out to the street, a burning wall from a nearby wooden shed struck his right side, engulfing him in orange-and-blue flames. Someone he knew from the factory floor put out the fire, and Hansu's men found him at a pathetic hospital in Nagasaki at last.

It was a starry evening, breathlessly quiet after an extended season of cicadas, when Hansu brought Yoseb to Tamaguchi's farm on an American military truck. Mozasu was the first to spot the truck, and the small and quick boy darted to the pig stalls to retrieve the bamboo spears. The family stood by the half-open barn door, observing the truck as it came closer.

"Here," Mozasu said, handing out the rattling, hollow spears to his mother, grandmother, brother, and aunt, keeping back two. Kim Changho was having his bath. He whispered to his brother, "You have to get *ajeossi* from the bath. Give him his weapon." The child gave Noa a spear for Kim and kept one for himself. Mozasu clutched his spear tightly, preparing for attack. Noa's holey hand-me-down sweater hung loosely over Mozasu's flour-sack work pants. He was tall for a six-year-old.

"The war's over," Noa reminded Mozasu firmly. "It's probably Hansu *ajeossi*'s men. Put that thing down before you hurt yourself."

The truck stopped, and two Koreans working for Hansu brought out a stretcher carrying Yoseb, who was bandaged and deeply sedated.

Kyunghee let go of the spear, letting it fall on the soft earth, and she put her hand on Mozasu's shoulder to steady herself.

Hansu stepped out of the cab of the truck while the driver, a ginger-haired American GI, stayed behind. Mozasu snuck glances at the soldier. The driver had light, freckled skin and pale, yellow-reddish hair like fire; he didn't look mean, and Hansu *ajeossi* didn't look afraid. Back in Osaka, Haru-san, the leader of the neighborhood association, who was most often in charge of rations, had warned the neighborhood children that Americans kill indiscriminately so everyone must flee at the sight of any American soldiers. Death at your own hands was preferable to capture. When the driver noticed Mozasu looking at him, he waved, showing his straight, white teeth.

Kyunghee approached the stretcher slowly. At the sight of his burns, she clasped her mouth with both her hands. Despite the terrifying news reports about the bombings, she had believed that Yoseb was alive, that he would not die without letting her know. She had prayed for him continually, and now he was home. She dropped to her knees and bowed her head. Everyone was silent until she rose. Even Kim was crying.

Hansu nodded at the slight, pretty woman who was weeping and gave her a large parcel wrapped in paper and a military-sized tub of burn liniment from America.

"You'll find some medicine in there. Mix a very small spoon of the powder with water or milk and give it to him at night so he can sleep. When it runs out, there's no more, so you have to wean him off it little by little. He'll beg you for more, but you have to tell him that you're trying to make it last."

"What is it?" she asked. Sunja stood by her sister-in-law and said nothing.

"He needs it. For the pain, but it's not good to keep taking it, because it's addictive. Anyway, keep changing the bandages. They must be sterile. Boil the fabric before you use it. There's more in there. He'll need the liniment because his skin is getting tighter. Can you do this?"

Kyunghee nodded, still staring at Yoseb. His mouth and cheek were half gone, as if he had been consumed by an animal. He was a man who had done everything he could for his family—this had happened to him because he had gone to work.

"Thank you, sir. Thank you for all that you've done for us," Kyunghee said to Hansu, who shook his head and said nothing. He left them to speak to the farmer. Kim, who had returned by then, having finished his bath, followed Hansu as he walked to the farmer's house.

The women and the boys led the men carrying the stretcher inside the barn and made a place for him in an empty horse stall. Kyunghee moved her pallet there.

A short while later, Hansu and the men drove off without saying good-bye.

The farmer didn't complain about having one more Korean on his property, because the other Koreans did Yoseb's share of the work as well as their own; harvest season was approaching, and he would need them. Though none of them had mentioned it, Tamaguchi sensed that soon enough, they'd ask him for money to leave, and the farmer was determined to get as much work as he could out of them before they left for home. He had told them they were welcome to stay for as long as they liked, and the farmer meant this. Tamaguchi had been hiring returning veterans for small jobs, but they grumbled about the dirtier tasks and openly refused to work alongside foreigners. Even if he could replace all the Koreans with Japanese veterans, Tamaguchi needed Hansu to transport his sweet potatoes to the markets. All the Koreans could stay.

The transport truck returned regularly, but Hansu didn't come back for weeks. Yoseb suffered. He had lost the hearing in his right ear. He was either shouting in anger or crying in agony. The medicine powder was now gone, and Yoseb wasn't much better. In the evenings, he cried like a child, and there was little anyone could do. During the day, he tried to help out on the farm, repairing tools or attempting to sort the potatoes, but the pain was too great for him to work. Now and then, Tamaguchi, who abhorred alcohol, gave him some holiday sake out of pity. However, when Kyunghee started to beg him each day for more, he told her that he couldn't spare any, not because he was a stingy man, because Tamaguchi wasn't, but because he had no intention of having a drunk on his property.

A month later, Hansu returned. The afternoon sun had dimmed only a little, and the workers had just returned to the fields after their midday meal to begin their second shift. In the cold barn, Yoseb was alone, lying down on his straw-filled pallet.

Hearing the footfalls, Yoseb lifted his head, then laid it back down again on the straw pillow.

Hansu placed two enormous crates in front of him, then sat down on the thick slab of wood by the pallet, which was being used as a bench. Despite his well-tailored suit and highly polished leather brogues, Hansu appeared at ease in the barn, indifferent to the harsh smells of the animals and the cold drafts.

Yoseb said, "You're the father of the boy, aren't you?"

Hansu studied the man's scarred face, the ragged edges of a once-sloping jawline. Yoseb's right ear was now a tight bud of a flower, folding into itself.

"That's why you do all this," Yoseb said.

"Noa is my son," Hansu said.

"We owe you a debt—something we may never be able to repay."

Hansu raised his eyebrows but said nothing. It was always better to say less.

"But you have no business being around him. My brother gave the child a name. He should never know anything else."

"I can give him a name, too."

"He has a name. It's wrong to do this to the boy."

Yoseb frowned; the smallest movement hurt. Noa had his younger brother's mannerisms—from the way he spoke in Isak's measured cadences to the way he ate his meals in modest bites, chewing neatly. He behaved exactly like Isak. Whenever Noa had any time to spare, he would take his old exercise books from school and practice writing, though no one told him to do so. Yoseb would never have believed that this yakuza was Noa's biological father except that the upper half of Noa's face was

virtually a mirror image of Hansu's. In time, Noa would see this. He had
not mentioned it to Kyunghee, but even if she had guessed at the truth
herself, she would have kept her suspicions from Yoseb to protect Sunja,
who was closer to her than a sister.

"You don't have a son," Yoseb said, taking another guess.

"Your brother was kind to help Sunja, but I would've taken care of her
and my son."

"She must not have wanted that."

"I'd offered to take care of her, but she didn't want to be my wife in
Korea. Because I have a Japanese wife in Osaka."

Lying on his back, Yoseb stared at the barn roof. Jagged slats of light
broke through the beams. Column slivers of dust floated upward in diag-
onal lines. Before the fire, he had never noticed such small things; also, he
had never hated anyone. Though he shouldn't, Yoseb hated this man—
his expensive clothes, flashy shoes, his unchecked confidence, reeking of
a devilish invulnerability. He hated him for not being in pain. He had no
right to claim his brother's child.

Hansu could see Yoseb's anger.

"She wanted me to go, so I left at first, planning to come back. When I
returned, she was gone. Already married. To your brother."

Yoseb didn't know what to believe. He had learned almost nothing
about Sunja from Isak, who had seemed to believe that Noa's origins were
best forgotten.

"You should leave Noa alone. He has a family. After the war, we'll do
everything possible to repay you."

Hansu folded his arms close to his chest and smiled before speaking.

"You son of a bitch, I paid. I paid for your life. I paid for everyone's
life. Everyone would be dead without me."

Yoseb shifted to his side a little and winced from the pain. Sometimes
he felt like he was still on fire.

"Did Sunja tell you?" Hansu asked.

"Just look at the child's face. It doesn't make sense for anyone to go
through all this trouble, and I know you're not some sort of saint. I know
what you are—"

Hansu laughed out loud. It was almost out of respect for Yoseb's directness.

"We're going back home," Yoseb said, and closed his eyes.

"Pyongyang's controlled by the Russians, and the Americans are in charge of Busan. You want to go back to that?"

"It's not going to be like that forever," Yoseb said.

"You'll starve there."

"I'm done with Japan."

"And how will you go back to Pyongyang or Busan? You can't even walk down the length of this farm."

"The company owes me my wages. When I'm well enough, I'll go back to Nagasaki to collect my pay."

"When's the last time you read a newspaper?" Hansu pulled out a sheaf of Korean and Japanese newspapers he'd brought for Kim from the crates. He put the stack beside Yoseb's pallet.

Yoseb glanced at the papers but refused to pick them up.

"There's no money for you." Hansu spoke to him slowly as if Yoseb were a child. "The company will never pay you. Never. There are no records for your work, and you can't prove it. The government wants nothing more than for every poor Korean to go back, but it won't give you the fare or a sen for your troubles. Ha."

"What do you mean? How do you know?" Yoseb asked.

"I know. I know Japan," Hansu said, looking privately disappointed. He had lived among the Japanese for all of his adult life. His father-in-law was unquestionably the most powerful Japanese moneylender in Kansai. Hansu could say with confidence that the Japanese were pathologically intractable when they wanted to be. In this, they were exactly like the Koreans except their stubbornness was quieter, harder to detect.

"Do you know how hard it is to get money out of the Japanese? If they don't want to pay you, they will never ever pay you. You're wasting your time."

Yoseb's body felt itchy and warm.

"Every day, for every one boat that heads out to Korea filled with idiots wanting to go home, two boats filled with refugees come back because there's nothing to eat there. The guys who come straight from Korea are even more desperate than you. They'll work for week-old bread. Women will whore after two days of hunger, or one if they have children to feed. You're living for a dream of a home that no longer exists."

"My parents are there."

"No. No, they're not."

Yoseb turned to look at Hansu's eyes.

"Why do you think I brought back only Sunja's mother. Do you really think I couldn't find your parents and your in-laws?"

"You don't know what happened to them," Yoseb said. Neither he nor Kyunghee had heard from them in over a year.

"They were shot. All landowners who were foolish enough to stick around were shot. Communists see people only in simple categories."

Yoseb wept and covered his eyes.

The lie had to be told, and Hansu did not mind telling it. If the parents weren't dead already, Yoseb's and Kyunghee's parents would starve to death or die of old age inevitably. They could have very well been shot. The conditions in the communist-occupied North were awful. There were numerous landowners who'd been rounded up, killed, and shoved into mass graves. No, he didn't know for certain if Yoseb's parents were alive or not, and yes, he could have learned the truth if he didn't mind risking some of his men to find them, but he didn't see the point of it. He didn't see how their lives could be useful for his purposes. It had been easy to find Sunja's mother—barely two days of his man's time. In the scheme of things, it was preferable for Yoseb and Kyunghee to lose their parents, because Sunja would have followed them blindly out of some preposterous sense of duty. Yoseb and Kyunghee would be better off in Japan for now, anyway. Hansu would never allow his son to go to Pyongyang.

Hansu opened one of the parcels and withdrew a large bottle of soju. He opened it and passed it to Yoseb, then left the barn to see Tamaguchi about a payment.

After finishing her work, Sunja finally returned to the barn, and she found Hansu waiting for her. He was sitting by himself by the feed bins at the far end of the barn, a good distance away from the boys, who were read-ing. Yoseb was sleeping soundly. Kyunghee and Yangjin were in the house cooking dinner while Kim loaded the sacks of potatoes in the cold shed. Hansu said hello to her first and waved her toward him openly, no longer feeling the need to be discreet.

Sunja stood by the bench opposite Hansu.

"Sit, sit," he insisted, but she refused.

"Tamaguchi tells me that he wants to adopt your sons," Hansu said quietly, smiling.

"What?"

"I told him you'd never let them go. He offered to take just one of them even. The poor man. Don't worry. He can't take them."

"Soon, we'll go to Pyongyang," she said.

"No. That's not going to happen."

"What do you mean?"

"Everyone there is dead. Kyunghee's parents. Your in-laws. All shot for owning property. These things happen when governments change. You have to get rid of your enemies. Landlords are enemies of the workers," Hansu said.

"*Uh-muh.*" Sunja sat down at last.

"Yes, it's sad, but nothing can be done."

Sunja was a pragmatic woman, but even she thought Hansu was un-usually cruel. The more she got to know this man, the more she realized that the man she'd loved as a girl was an idea she'd had of him—feelings without any verification.

"You should be thinking about Noa's education. I brought him some books to study for his college entrance examinations."

"But—"

"You cannot return home. You're going to have to wait until things are more stable."

"It's not your decision to make. My boys have no future here. If we can't go back home now, we'll go back when it's safer."

Her voice had trembled, but she'd said what she'd needed to say.

Hansu remained silent for a moment.

"Whatever you decide to do later is one thing, but in the meantime, Noa should be studying for university. He's twelve."

Sunja had been thinking of Noa's schooling but hadn't known how to help him. Also, how would she pay for school? They didn't even have enough money for the passage home. Out of Yoseb's hearing, the three women talked about this all the time. They had to get back to Osaka to figure out a way to make money again.

"Noa should study while he's in this country. Korea will be in chaos for a long time. Besides, he's already a good Japanese student. When he goes back, he'll have a degree from a good Japanese university. That's what all the rich Koreans are doing, anyway—sending their kids abroad. If Noa gets into a university, I'll pay for it. I'll pay for Mozasu as well. I could get them some tutors when they return—"

"No," she said loudly. "No."

He decided not to fight her, because she was stubborn. He had learned this. Hansu pointed to the crates by Yoseb's pallet.

"I brought meat and dried fish. There's also canned fruit and chocolate bars from America. I brought the same things for Tamaguchi's family, too, so you don't have to give them any of yours. There's fabric in the bottom crate; all of you need clothing, I think. There's scissors, thread, and needles," he added, proud of himself for having brought these things. "I'll bring wool next time."

Sunja didn't know what she was supposed to do anymore. It wasn't that she was ungrateful. Mostly, she felt ashamed of her life, her powerlessness. With her sun-browned hands and dirty fingernails, she touched her uncombed hair. She didn't want him to see her this way. It occurred to her that she would never be lovely again.

"I brought some newspapers. Have someone read them to you. The stories are the same—you can't go back now. It would be terrible for the boys."

Sunja faced him.

"That's how you got me to come here, and now that's how you're trying to get me to stay in Japan. You'd said it would be better for the boys so I brought them to the farm."

"I wasn't wrong."

"I don't trust you."

"You are trying to hurt me, Sunja. That makes no sense." He shook his head. "Remember, your husband would have wanted the boys to go to school. I also want what's best for the boys and for you, Sunja. You and I—we're good friends," he said calmly. "We will always be good friends. We will always have Noa."

He waited to see if she would say anything, but it was as if her face had closed like a door. "And your brother-in-law knows. About Noa. I didn't tell him. He figured it out."

Sunja covered her mouth with her hand.

"You needn't worry. Everything will be fine. If you want to move back to Osaka, Kim will make the arrangements. Refusing my help would be selfish. You should give your sons every advantage. I can give both your sons many advantages."

Before she could speak, Kim had returned to the barn. He walked past the boys, who were still absorbed in their books.

"Boss," Kim said. "It's good to see you. Can I get you something to drink?"

Hansu said no.

Sunja realized she'd failed to offer him anything.

"So, are you ready to return to Osaka?" Hansu asked Kim.

"Yes, sir," Kim said, smiling. Sunja appeared distressed, but he said nothing to her for now.

"Boys," Hansu shouted across the length of the barn, "how are the books?"

Kim waved at them to come closer, and the boys ran to him.

"Noa, do you want to go back to school?" Hansu asked.

"Yes, sir. But—"

"If you want to go back to school, you need to go back to Osaka right away."

"How about the farm? And Korea?" Noa asked, straightening his back.

"You can't go back to Korea for a while, but in the meantime, you can't let your head become empty," Hansu said, smiling. "What do you think of those exam books I brought you? Are they difficult?"

"Yes, sir, but I want to learn them. I need a dictionary, I think."

"We'll get you one," Hansu said proudly. "You study, and I will send you to school. A boy shouldn't have to worry about school fees. It's important that older Koreans support young Koreans in their studies. How else will we have a great nation unless we support our children?"

Noa beamed, and Sunja could not say anything.

"But I want to stay at the farm," Mozasu interrupted. "That's not fair. I don't want to go back to school. I hate school."

Hansu and Kim laughed.

Noa pulled Mozasu toward him and bowed. They headed to the other side of the barn.

When they were far enough away from the grown-ups, Mozasu said to Noa, "Tamaguchi-san said we could live here forever. He said we were like his sons."

"Mozasu, we can't keep living in this barn."

"I like the chickens. I didn't get pecked even once this morning when I got the eggs. The barn is nice to sleep in, especially since Aunt Kyunghee made us those hay blankets."

"Well, you'll feel differently when you get older," Noa said, cradling the thick volumes of the examination books in his arms. "*Appa* would've wanted us to go to university and become educated people."

"I hate books," Mozasu said, scowling.

"I love them. I could read books all day and do nothing else. *Appa* loved to read, too."

Mozasu plowed into Noa in an attempt to wrestle him, and Noa laughed.

"Brother, what was *appa* like?" Mozasu sat up and looked at his brother soberly.

"He was tall. And he had light-colored skin like you. He wore glasses like me. He was very good at school and good at teaching himself things from books. He loved learning. He was happy when he was reading; he told me so."

Noa smiled.

"Like you," Mozasu said. "Not like me. Well, I like manga."

"That's not real reading."

Mozasu shrugged.

"He was always nice to *umma* and me. He used to tease Uncle Yoseb and make him laugh. *Appa* taught me how to write my letters and remember the multiplication tables. I was the first one in school to know them by heart."

"Was he rich?"

"No. Ministers can't be rich."

"I want to be rich," Mozasu said. "I want to have a big truck and a driver."

"I thought you wanted to live in a barn," Noa said, smiling, "and collect chicken eggs every morning."

"I'd rather have a truck like Hansu *ajeossi*."

"I'd rather be an educated man like *appa*."

"Not me," Mozasu said. "I want to make a lot of money, then *umma* and Aunt Kyunghee wouldn't have to work anymore."

9

Osaka, 1949

After the family returned to Osaka, Hansu gave Kim the job of collecting fees from the store owners at Tsuruhashi market. In exchange for these fees, Hansu's company gave the owners protection and support. Naturally, no one wanted to pay these not-insignificant sums, but there was little choice in the matter. On the rare instances when someone cried poor or foolishly refused to pay, Hansu sent his other men, not Kim, to address the situation. For a store owner, such fee payments were a long-established practice—just one more cost of doing business.

Any agent who worked for Hansu had to look the part of the larger organization, and the men who worked for Hansu, both Japanese and Korean, took special pains to keep a low profile, avoiding any unnecessary negative attention. Except for his nearsightedness, corrected with his thick eyeglasses, Kim was a pleasant-looking man—humble, diligent, and well-spoken. Hansu preferred Kim to do the collection because Kim was effective and unfailingly polite; he was the clean wrapper for a filthy deed.

It was Saturday evening, and Kim had just collected the week's payments—over sixty packets of cash, each covered in fresh paper and labeled with the name of the business. No one had missed a payment. When he reached Hansu's parked sedan, Kim bowed to his boss, who was just stepping out of the car. His driver would pick them up later.

"Let's have a drink," Hansu said, patting Kim on the back. They walked in the direction of the market. Along the road, men continuously bowed to Hansu, and he acknowledged them with nods. He stopped for no one, however.

"I'm going to take you to a new place. Pretty girls there. You must want one after living in a barn for so long."

Kim laughed out of surprise. His boss didn't normally discuss such things.

"You like the married one," Hansu said. "I know."

Kim kept walking, unable to reply.

"Sunja's sister-in-law," Hansu said, looking straight ahead as they walked down the narrow market street. "She's still good-looking. Her husband can't do it anymore. He's drinking more, *nee*?"

Kim removed his glasses and cleaned the lenses with his handkerchief. He liked Yoseb and felt bad for not saying something. Yoseb drank a lot, but he was not a bad man. It was clear that the men in the neighborhood still admired him. At home, when Yoseb felt well enough, he helped the boys with schoolwork and taught them Korean. On occasion, he fixed machines for some factory owners he knew, but in his condition, he couldn't work regularly.

"How's the house?" Hansu asked.

"I've never lived so well."

Kim was telling the truth. "The meals are delicious. The house is very clean."

"The women need a workingman to watch over them. But I worry that you're too attached to the married one."

"Boss, I've been thinking more about going back home. Not to Daegu, but to the North."

"This again? No. End of discussion. I don't care if you go to those socialist meetings, but don't start believing that horseshit about returning to the motherland. The heads of *Mindan* are no better. Besides, they'll kill you in the North, and they'll starve you in the South. They all hate Koreans who've been living in Japan. I know. If you go, I will never support it. Never."

"The leader Kim Il Sung fought against Japanese imperialism—"

"I know his guys. Some of them might actually believe the message, but most of them are just trying to collect a pay envelope each week. The ones in charge who live here are never going back. You watch."

"But don't you think we must do something for our country? These foreigners are cutting up the nation into—"

Hansu put both his hands on Kim's shoulders and faced him squarely.

"You haven't had a girl in such a long time that you can't think straight." Hansu smiled, then looked serious again. "Listen, I know the heads of both the Association and *Mindan*"—he snorted—"I know them very, very well—"

"But *Mindan*'s a mere puppet of the American—"

Hansu smiled at Kim, amused by the young man's sincerity.

"How long have you worked for me?"

"I must've been twelve or thirteen when you gave me a job."

"How many times have I really talked politics with you?"

Kim tried to remember.

"Never. Not really. I'm a businessman. And I want you to be a businessman. And whenever you go to these meetings, I want you to think for yourself, and I want you to think about promoting your own interests no matter what. All these people—both the Japanese and the Koreans— are fucked because they keep thinking about the group. But here's the truth: There's no such thing as a benevolent leader. I protect you because you work for me. If you act like a fool and go against my interests, then I can't protect you. As for these Korean groups, you have to remember that no matter what, the men who are in charge are just men—so they're not much smarter than pigs. And we eat pigs. You lived with that farmer Tamaguchi who sold sweet potatoes for obscene prices to starving Japanese during a time of war. He violated wartime regulations, and I helped him, because he wanted money and I do, too. He probably thinks he's a decent, respectable Japanese, or some kind of proud nationalist—don't they all? He's a terrible Japanese, but a smart businessman. I'm not a good Korean, and I'm not a Japanese. I'm very good at making money. This country would fall apart if everyone believed in some samurai crap. The Emperor does not give a fuck about anyone, either. So I'm not going to tell you not to go to any meetings or not to join any group. But know this:

Those communists don't care about you. They don't care about anybody. You're crazy if you think they care about Korea."

"Sometimes, I'd like to see my home again," Kim said quietly.

"For people like us, home doesn't exist." Hansu took out a cigarette, and Kim rushed to light it.

Kim had not been back home in over twenty years. His mother had died when he was a toddler, and his tenant farmer father died not much later; his older sister did what she could for him but eventually married, then disappeared, leaving him to beg. Kim wanted to go to the North to help with the reunification efforts, but he also wanted to go to Daegu to clean his parents' graves and do a proper *jesa* now that he could afford it.

Hansu took a long drag of his cigarette.

"You think I like it here? No, I don't like it here. But here, I know what to expect. You don't want to be poor. Changho-ya, you've worked for me, you've had enough food and money, so you've started to think about ideas—that's normal. Patriotism is just an idea, so is capitalism or communism. But ideas can make men forget their own interests. And the guys in charge will exploit men who believe in ideas too much. You can't fix Korea. Not even a hundred of you or a hundred of me can fix Korea. The Japs are out and now Russia, China, and America are fighting over our shitty little country. You think you can fight them? Forget Korea. Focus on something you can have. You want that married one? Fine. Then either get rid of the husband or wait until he's dead. This is something you can fix."

"She's not going to leave him."

"He's a loser."

"No, no, he's not," Kim said gravely. "And she's not the kind of woman who'd just—" He couldn't talk about this anymore. He could wait until Yoseb died, but it was wrong to want a man to die. He believed in many ideas, including the idea that a wife must be loyal to her husband. If Kyunghee left a broken man, she would be less worthy of his devotion.

At the end of the street, Hansu stopped walking and tilted his head toward a plain-looking bar.

"You want a girl now, or do you want to go back to the house and want someone else's wife?"

Kim stared at the handle of the door, then pulled it open, letting his boss enter first before following him inside.

The new house in Osaka was two tatami mats larger than the old one and sturdier—built out of tile, solid wood, and brick. As Hansu had predicted, the bombings had razed the original house. Kyunghee had sewn their legal documents in the lining of her good coat, and when it came time, Hansu's lawyer made the municipal government recognize Yoseb's property rights. With the gift money Tamaguchi had given them when they left the farm, Yoseb and Kyunghee bought the vacant lot adjacent to their original house. They rebuilt their home with the help of Hansu's construction company. Again, Yoseb told none of their neighbors that he was the owner of the house—it always being wiser to appear poorer than you are. The exterior of the house was nearly identical to the other dwellings on their street in Ikaino. The family had agreed that Kim should live with them, and when Yoseb asked him, he did not refuse. The women papered the walls with good-quality paper and bought strong, thick glass for their little windows. They spent a little extra for better fabric to make warm quilts and floor cushions and bought a low Korean dining table for meals and for the boys to do their homework.

Though from the facade the house didn't look like much more than a roomy shack, inside was an exceptionally clean and well-organized house with a proper kitchen that had enough space to store their food carts overnight. It had an attached outhouse, which could be entered from the kitchen door. Yangjin, Sunja, and the boys slept in the middle room, which during the day served as the main room; Yoseb and Kyunghee slept in the large storage room by the kitchen, and Kim slept in the tiny front room, its two walls made up of paper screen doors. All seven of them—three generations and one family friend—lived in the house in Ikaino. Considering the neighborhood, their accommodations were almost luxurious.

Late in the evening, when Kim finally returned home from the bar, everyone was asleep. Hansu had paid for a Korean girl, an exceptionally attractive one, and Kim went to the back room with her. Afterward, he'd wanted to go to a bathhouse, but the ones near the house were closed for the night. He washed up as well as he could in the sink by the outhouse, but he still had the waxy flavor of the girl's frosty pink lipstick in his mouth.

The girl had been young, twenty if that, and when she wasn't in the back rooms, she worked as a waitress. The war and the American occupation had toughened her, like the other girls who worked at the bar, and because she was so pretty, she had been with many men. She went by the name Jinah.

In one of the back rooms reserved for paying customers, Jinah shut the door and took off her floral-print dress right away. She wore no underwear. Her body was long and thin, with the round, high breasts of a young girl who didn't need a brassiere and the skinny legs of a hungry peasant. She sat on his lap, making a soft grinding gesture, and made him hard, then gingerly led him to an oxblood-colored pallet on the floor. She undressed him, wiped him expertly with a warm, wet towel, then put a prophylactic on him with her painted mouth. It had been a long time since he had been with a girl. He'd only been with whores, but this one had the loveliest face and figure, and he could understand why she cost so much even though he wasn't paying this time. Jinah called him *Oppa*, and asked if he wanted to enter her now, and he had nodded, astonished by her skillfulness—at once charming and professional. She pushed him down gently and clambered on his hips and pulled him inside her in a single thrust. She kissed his forehead and hair, letting him bury his head between her breasts as they fucked. He didn't know if she was pretending, but she seemed to like what she was doing, unlike the other whores, who'd pretended to be virginal. There was no false protest, and Kim found himself deeply excited by her and came almost right away. She lay in his arms for a little while, then got up to get a towel for him. As she cleaned him, she called him her handsome brother and asked him to return to see her soon, because Jinah would be thinking about his eel. Kim almost wanted to stay the night to try to have her again, but Hansu was waiting for him at the bar, so Kim promised to return.

In his room, someone had already unfolded his pallet to make his bed. Kim lay down on his clean, starched cotton pallet, imagining Kyunghee's slender fingers smoothing down the blankets on which he rested, and as usual, he imagined making love to her. A married woman could not be surprised by sex, he thought, but he wondered if she could enjoy it the way Jinah seemed to. What would he think of her if she did? In the barn, he'd always fallen asleep before the women, and he was grateful for this schedule, because he could not bear the idea of Yoseb being on top of her. Fortunately, he never heard any noises, and in this house, he did not hear them, either. He felt sure that Yoseb no longer slept with his wife, and this knowledge gave him permission to love her and to not hate him. This way, she was his, too. Hansu had detected his feelings, because he was obvious about them; he could not resist watching her soft face, her graceful quiet movements. He thought if he could be with her, he would die. What would it be like to be with her each night? When they'd worked beside each other at the restaurant, and when he was alone with her at the farm, it had been almost maddening to keep from clasping her body to his. What kept him from doing so was the knowledge that she would never respond to him; she loved her husband, and she loved *Yesu Kuristo*, her god, whom Kim could not believe in and who did not allow his followers to have sex outside of marriage.

Kim closed his eyes, wanting her to open the thin paper door to his room. She could slip off her dress the way the whore had done and put her mouth over him. He would pull her up to him and tuck her into his body. He would make love to her and wish for his death, because his life would have been perfect at that moment. Kim could envision her small breasts, pale stomach and legs, the shadow of her pubis. He grew hard again and laughed quietly, thinking that he was like a boy tonight, because he felt he could do it again and again and never have enough. Hansu was wrong to think that a pretty whore would take his mind off Kyunghee; in fact, he wanted her more now, far more than he ever had. He had tasted something sweet and cool tonight, and now he wanted an immense tubful of it—enough to bathe deeply in its refreshment.

Kim rubbed himself and fell asleep with his glasses on.

In the morning, Kim rose before the others and went to work without having breakfast. That evening, as he walked home, he noticed a pair of slight shoulders pushing a confection cart down the street. He ran to catch up with her.

"Let me."

"Oh, hello." Kyunghee smiled in relief. "We were worried about you this morning when you were gone. We didn't see you last night. Did you eat today?"

"I'm all right. You don't need to worry about me."

He noticed that the stack of bags used to pack up the candies were all gone. "You're out of bags. You did well today?"

She nodded, smiling again. "I sold everything, but the price of black sugar has gone up again. Maybe I can make jellies. They require less sugar. I need to find some new recipes." Kyunghee stopped walking to wipe her brow with the back of her hand.

Kim took the cart from her to push it.

"Is Sunja at home already?" he asked.

Kyunghee nodded, looking worried.

"What's the matter, Sister?"

"I'm hoping there won't be a fight tonight. My husband's being too hard on everyone lately. Also, he's—" She didn't want to say any more. Yoseb's health was declining precipitously, but he was unfortunately well enough to feel the horrible discomfort of his burns and injuries. Every little thing upset him, and when he was angry, he never held back anymore. His poor hearing made him shout, a thing he had never done before the war.

"It's about the boys' school. You know."

Kim nodded. Yoseb had been telling Sunja that the boys had to go to a Korean school in the neighborhood because the family had to be ready to go back. The boys had to learn Korean. Hansu was telling Sunja the opposite. Sunja couldn't say anything, but everyone knew it was a terrible time to return.

The road to their house was empty. As the sun set, the dusk gave off a muted gray-and-pink light.

"It's nice when it's quiet," she said.

"Yes." Kim grasped the cart handle a little tighter.

Strands of her bun had come loose, and Kyunghee smoothed her hair behind her ears. Even at the end of a long workday, there was still something so clean and bright in her expression; it could not be defiled.

"Last night, he yelled at her again about the schools. My husband means well. He's also in a lot of pain. Noa wants to go to Japanese school. He wants to go to Waseda University. Can you imagine? Such a big school like that!" She smiled, feeling proud of his grand dream. "And, well, Mozasu never wants to go to school at all." She laughed. "Of course, it isn't clear when we can return now, but the boys need to learn how to read and write. Don't you think?" Kyunghee found herself crying, but couldn't explain why.

From his coat pocket, Kim dug out a handkerchief that he used to clean his glasses and gave it to her.

"There are so many things we can't control," he said.

She nodded.

"Do you want to go home?"

Without looking at his face, she said, "I can't believe my parents are dead. In my dreams, they seem alive. I'd like to see them again."

"But you can't go back now. It's dangerous. When things get better—"

"Do you think that will be soon?"

"Well, you know how we are."

"What do you mean?" she asked.

"Koreans. We argue. Every man thinks he's smarter than the next. I suppose whoever is in charge will fight very hard to keep his power." He repeated only what Hansu had told him, because Hansu was right, especially when it came to seeing the worst in people—in this, he was always right.

"So you're not a communist, then?" she asked.

"What?"

"You go to those political meetings. I thought if you went to them, then perhaps they're not so bad. And they're against the Japanese government, and they want to reunify the country, right? I mean, aren't the Americans trying to break up the country? I hear things at the market from the others, but it's hard to know what to believe. My husband said that the communists are a bad lot; they're the ones who shot our parents. You know, my father smiled at everyone. He always did good things."

Kyunghee could not understand why her parents were killed. Her father had been the third son, so his plot had been very small. Had the communists killed all the landowners? Even the insignificant ones? She was curious as to what Kim thought, too, because he was a good man and knew a lot about the world.

Kim leaned in to the cart, and he looked at her carefully, wanting to comfort her. He knew she was looking to him for advice, and it made him feel important. With a woman like this by him, he wondered if he would even care about politics anymore.

"Are there different kinds of communists?" she asked.

"I think so. I don't know if I'm a communist. I am against the Japanese taking over Korea again, and I don't want the Russians and the Chinese to control Korea, either. Or the Americans. I wonder why Korea can't be left alone."

"But you just said, we quarrel. I suppose it's like when two grannies have a dispute, and the villagers constantly whisper in their ears about the wickedness of the other one. If the grannies want to have any peace, they have to forget everyone else and remember that they used to be friends."

"I think we should put you in charge," he said, pushing the cart toward the house. Even if it was just this brief walk, he felt happy to be with her, but of course, it made him want more. He'd gone to those meetings to get out of the house, because sometimes being near her was too much. He lived in that house because he needed to see her every day. He loved her. This would never change, he thought. His situation was impossible.

Only a few paces from home, the two walked slowly, murmuring this and that about their day, content and only a little less shy. He would continue to suffer with love.

IO

Osaka, January 1953

Worried about money, Sunja had woken up in the middle of the night to make candies to sell. When Yangjin noticed that her daughter wasn't in bed, she went to the kitchen.

"You don't sleep anymore," Yangjin said. "You'll get sick if you don't sleep."

"*Umma*, I'm fine. You should go back to bed."

"I'm old. I don't need to sleep so much," Yangjin said, putting on her apron.

Sunja was trying to make extra money for Noa's tutoring fees. He had failed his first attempt at the Waseda exams by a few points, and he felt certain that he'd be able to pass on his next try if he could be tutored in mathematics. The fees for the tutors were exorbitant. The women had been trying to earn more so Noa could leave his job as a bookkeeper to study full time, but it was difficult enough to manage their household costs and Yoseb's medical bills on his salary and their earnings from selling food. Each week, Kim gave them money for his room and board. He had tried to add to Noa's tutoring fund, but Yoseb forbade the women from taking any more than what was a reasonable sum. Yoseb would not allow Sunja to accept any money from Hansu for Noa's schooling.

"Did you sleep at all last night?" Yangjin asked.

Sunja nodded, laying a clean cloth over the large chunks of black sugar to muffle the sound of the mortar and pestle.

Yangjin was exhausted herself. In three years, she'd turn sixty. When she was a girl, she'd believed that she could work harder than anyone under any circumstances, but she no longer felt that way. Lately, Yangjin felt tired and impatient; small things bothered her. Aging was supposed to make you more patient, but in her case, she felt angrier. Sometimes, when a customer complained about the small size of the portions, she wanted to tell him off. Lately, what upset her most was her daughter's impossible silence. Yangjin wanted to shake her.

The kitchen was the warmest room in the house, and the electric lights emitted a steady light. Against the papered walls, the two bare lightbulbs attached to the ceiling by their electric cords made stark shadows, resembling two lonely gourds hanging from leafless vines.

"I still think about our girls," Yangjin said.

"Dokhee and Bokhee? Didn't they find work in China?"

"I shouldn't have let them go with that smooth-talking woman from Seoul. But the girls were so excited about traveling to Manchuria and earning money. They promised to return when they made enough to buy the boardinghouse. They were good girls."

Sunja nodded, recalling their sweetness. She didn't know people like that anymore. It seemed as if the occupation and the war had changed everyone, and now the war in Korea was making things worse. Once-tenderhearted people seemed wary and tough. There was innocence left only in the smallest children.

"At the market, I hear that the girls who went to work in factories were taken somewhere else, and they had to do terrible, terrible things with Japanese soldiers." Yangjin paused, still confounded. "Do you think this can be true?"

Sunja had heard the same stories, and Hansu had warned her on more than one occasion of the Korean recruiters, working for the Japanese army, falsely promising good jobs, but she didn't want her mother to worry any more. Sunja ground the sugar as finely as she could.

"What if the girls were taken? For that?" Yangjin asked.

"*Umma*, we don't know," Sunja whispered. She lit the fire in the stove and poured sugar and water into the pan.

"That's what happened. I just feel it." Yangjin nodded to herself. "Your *appa*—it would make him so sad that we lost our boardinghouse—*aigoo*. And now this fighting in Korea. We can't go back yet because the army would take Noa and Mozasu. Isn't that right?"

Sunja nodded. She could not let her sons become soldiers.

Yangjin shivered. The draft seeping through the kitchen window stung her dry, brown skin, and she tucked a towel around the sill. Yangjin pulled her shabby cotton vest tightly over her nightclothes. She started to crush sugar for the next batch while Sunja watched the bubbling pot on the low flame.

Sunja stirred the pot as the sugar caramelized. Busan seemed like another life compared to Osaka; Yeongdo, their little rocky island, stayed impossibly fresh and sunny in her memory, though she hadn't been back in twenty years. When Isak had tried to explain heaven, she had imagined her hometown as paradise—a clear, shimmering beauty. Even the memory of the moon and stars in Korea seemed different than the cold moon here; no matter how much people complained about how bad things were back home, it was difficult for Sunja to imagine anything but the bright, sturdy house that her father had taken care of so well by the green, glassy sea, the bountiful garden that had given them watermelons, lettuces, and squash, and the open-air market that never ran out of anything delicious. When she was there, she had not loved it enough.

The news reports from back home were so horrific—cholera, starvation, and soldiers who kidnapped your sons, even little boys—that their meager life in Osaka and their pathetic attempts to scrounge up enough money to send Noa to college seemed luxurious in contrast. At least they were together. At least they could work toward something better. The war in Korea roused commerce in Japan, and there were more jobs to be had by all. At least here, the Americans were still in charge, so the women were able to find sugar and wheat. Although Yoseb prohibited Sunja from taking money from Hansu, when Kim found any of the scarce ingredients the women needed through his connections, the women knew enough not to ask too many questions or to talk about it with Yoseb.

As soon as the taffy cooled on the metal pan, the women worked quickly to cut the candy into neat squares.

"Dokhee used to tease me about the sloppy way I cut onions," Sunja said, smiling. "And she couldn't bear how slowly I washed the rice pots. And every morning when I would clean the floors, she would say without fail, 'Always use two rags to clean the floors. First, sweep, then wipe with a clean rag, and then wipe it again with a fresh one!' Dokhee was the cleanest person I have ever met." As she spoke the words, Sunja could recall Dokhee's round and simple face growing somber while giving instructions. Her expressions, mannerisms, and voice were equally vivid, and Sunja, who did not pray often, prayed to God in her heart for the girls. She prayed that they were not taken for the soldiers. Isak used to say that we could not know why some suffered more than others; he said we should never hasten to judgment when others endured agony. Why was she spared and not them? she wondered. Why was she in this kitchen with her mother when so many were starving back home? Isak used to say that God had a plan, and Sunja believed this could be so, but it gave her little consolation now, thinking of the girls. Those girls had been more innocent than her sons when they were very little.

When Sunja looked up from her task, her mother was weeping.

"Those girls lost their mother, then their father. I should've done more for them. Tried to help them get married, but we had no money. A woman's lot is to suffer. We must suffer."

Sunja sensed that her mother was right that the girls had been tricked. They were likely dead now. She put her hand on her mother's shoulder. Her mother's hair was nearly all gray, and during the day, she wore the old-fashioned bun at the base of her neck. It was night, and her mother's gray, scant braid hung down her back. The years of outdoor work had creased her brown oval face with deep grooves on her forehead and around her mouth. For as long as she could remember, her mother had been the first to rise and the last to go to bed; even when the girls had worked with them, her mother had worked as hard as the younger one. Never one to talk much, as she'd gotten older her mother had a lot more to say, but Sunja never seemed to know what to say to her.

"*Umma*, remember digging up the potatoes with *appa*? *Appa*'s beautiful potatoes. They were fat and white and so good when you baked them in the ashes. I haven't had a good potato like that since—"

Yangjin smiled. There had been happier times. Her daughter had not forgotten Hoonie, who had been a wonderful father to her. So many of their babies had died, but they'd had Sunja. She had her still.

"At least the boys are safe. Maybe that's why we're here. Yes." Yangjin paused. "Maybe that's why we're here." Her face brightened. "You know, your Mozasu is such a funny one. Yesterday, he said he wants to live in America and wear a suit and hat like in the movies. He said he wants to have five sons!"

Sunja laughed, because that sounded like Mozasu.

"America? What did you say?"

"I told him it's okay as long as he visited me with his five sons!"

The kitchen smelled of caramel, and the women worked nimbly until sunlight filled the house.

School was a misery. Mozasu was thirteen and tall for his age. With broad shoulders and well-muscled arms, he appeared more manly than some of his teachers. Because he could not read or write at grade level—despite Noa's prodigious efforts to teach him kanji—Mozasu had been placed in a class full of ten-year-olds. Mozasu spoke Japanese just as well as his peers; if anything, he had tremendous verbal facility, which served him well in his regular battles with the older children. In arithmetic, he could keep up with the class, but writing and reading Japanese lamed him brutally. His teachers called him a Korean fool, and Mozasu was biding his time so he could be done with this hell. In spite of the war and all their academic privations, Noa had finished high school, and whenever he wasn't working, he was studying for his college entrance examinations. He never left the house without an exam study book and one of his old English-language novels, which he bought from the bookseller.

Six days a week, Noa worked for Hoji-san, the cheerful Japanese who owned most of the houses in their neighborhood. It was rumored that Hoji-san was in fact part *burakumin* or Korean, but no one said too much about his shameful blood, since he was everyone's landlord. It was possible that the vicious rumor that he was not pure Japanese could have been started by an unhappy tenant, but Hoji-san did not seem to care. As his bookkeeper and secretary, Noa kept Hoji-san's ledgers in excellent order and wrote letters to the municipal offices in beautiful Japanese on his behalf. Despite his smiles and jokes, Hoji-san was ruthless when it came to getting his rent money. He paid Noa very little, but Noa did not complain. He could've made more money working for Koreans in the pachinko business or in *yakiniku* restaurants, but Noa didn't want that. He wanted to work in a Japanese office and have a desk job. Like nearly all Japanese business owners, Hoji-san would not normally hire Koreans, but Hoji-san's nephew was Noa's high school teacher, and Hoji-san, a man who knew how to find bargains, hired his nephew's most brilliant pupil.

In the evening, Noa helped Mozasu with his schoolwork, but they both knew it was pointless, since Mozasu had no interest in memorizing kanji. As his long-suffering tutor, Noa focused on teaching his brother sums and basic writing. With remarkable patience, Noa never got upset when Mozasu did poorly on his examinations. He knew how it was for most Koreans at school; most of them dropped out, and he didn't want this to happen to Mozasu, so he did not focus on exam grades. He even asked Uncle Yoseb and his mother to refrain from getting upset with Mozasu's report cards. He told them that the goal was to make sure that Mozasu had better-than-average skills as a worker. If Noa hadn't tried so hard and taught him with such care, Mozasu would've done what nearly all the other Korean boys in the neighborhood did rather than go to school— collect scrap metal for money, search for rotting food for the pigs their mothers bred and raised in their homes, or worse, get in trouble with the police for petty crimes.

Ever the student, after Noa helped Mozasu, he studied English with a dictionary and a grammar book. In the only academic reversal, Mozasu, who was more interested in English than Japanese or Korean, would help his older brother learn new vocabulary words by drilling Noa on English words and phrases.

At the dreadful local school, Mozasu hung back and kept to himself during lunch and recess. There were four other Koreans in the class, but they all went by their Japanese pass names and refused to discuss their background, especially in the presence of other Koreans. Mozasu knew with certainty who they were, because they lived on his street and he knew their families. All of them were only ten years old, so the Koreans in his grade were smaller than he was, and Mozasu stayed away from them, feeling both contempt and pity.

Most Koreans in Japan had at least three names. Mozasu went by Mozasu Boku, the Japanization of Moses Baek, and rarely used his Japanese surname, Bando, the *tsumei* listed on his school documents and residency papers. With a first name from a Western religion, an obvious Korean surname, and his ghetto address, everyone knew what he was— there was no point in denying it. The Japanese kids would have nothing to do with him, but Mozasu no longer gave a shit. When he was younger, getting picked on used to bother him, though far less than it had bothered Noa, who had compensated by outperforming his classmates academically and athletically. Every day, before school began and after school ended, the bigger boys told Mozasu, "Go back to Korea, you smelly bastard." If there was a crowd of them, Mozasu would keep walking; however, if there were only one or two assholes, he would hit them as hard as he could until he saw blood.

Mozasu knew he was becoming one of the bad Koreans. Police officers often arrested Koreans for stealing or home brewing. Every week, someone on his street got in trouble with the police. Noa would say that because some Koreans broke the law, everyone got blamed. On every block in Ikaino, there was a man who beat his wife, and there were girls who worked in bars who were said to take money for favors. Noa said that Koreans had to raise themselves up by working harder and being better. Mozasu just wanted to hit everyone who said mean things. In Ikaino, there were homely old women who cussed and men who were so drunk that they slept outside their houses. The Japanese didn't want Koreans to live near them, because they weren't clean, they lived with pigs, and the children had lice. Also, Koreans were said to be even lower than *burakumin* because at least *burakumin* had Japanese blood. Noa told Mozasu that his former teachers had told him he was a good Korean, and Mozasu understood that with his own poor grades and bad manners, those same teachers would think Mozasu was a bad one.

So the fuck what? If the other ten-year-olds thought he was stupid, that was okay. If they thought he was violent, that was okay. If necessary, Mozasu was not afraid to clean out all the teeth right from their mouths. You think I'm an animal, Mozasu thought, then I can be an animal and hurt you. Mozasu did not intend to be a good Korean. What was the point in that?

Before spring, a few months before the war in Korea ended, a new boy from Kyoto joined his class. He was eleven, going on twelve. Haruki Totoyama was obviously a poor kid, evident from his shabby uniform and pathetic shoes. He was also wiry and nearsighted. The boy had a small, triangular face, and he might have been acceptable to the others, but unfortunately, someone let it out that he lived on the border street between the Korean ghetto and the Japanese poor. Quickly, rumors spread that Haruki was a *burakumin*, though he wasn't. Then it was discovered that Haruki had a younger brother with a head shaped like a dented summer melon. Even as a Japanese, it had been difficult for Haruki's mother to find a better place for them to live, because many of the Japanese landlords thought the family was cursed. Haruki did not have a father; this would have been understandable if his father had died in the war as a soldier, but the truth was that at Haruki's brother's birth, the father had taken one look at the child and left.

Unlike Mozasu, Haruki cared deeply about fitting in and tried very hard, but even the kids with the lowest social status wouldn't give him a chance. He was treated like a diseased animal. The teachers, who followed the cues of the student leaders, kept their distance from Haruki. The new boy had been hoping that this school might be different from his old one in Kyoto, but he saw that he didn't have a chance here, either.

At lunchtime, Haruki sat at the end of the long table with two seat gaps around him like an invisible parenthesis while the other boys in their dark woolen uniforms stuck together like a tight row of black corn kernels. Not far from this table, Mozasu, who always sat alone, watched the new boy trying to say something now and then to the group of boys, though, of course, Haruki never got a reply.

After a month of this, Mozasu finally said something to him in the boys' washroom.

"Why do you try to make those kids like you?" Mozasu asked.

"What choice do I have?" Haruki replied.

"You can tell them to fuck off and get a life of your own."

"And what kind of life do you have?" Haruki asked. He didn't mean to be rude; he just wanted to know if there was an alternative.

"Listen, if people don't like you, it's not always your fault. My brother told me that."

"You have a brother?"

"Yeah. He works for Hoji-san, you know, the landlord."

"Is your brother the young guy in the glasses?" Haruki asked. Hoji-san was their landlord, too.

Mozasu nodded, smiling. He was proud of Noa, who cut an impressive figure in the neighborhood. Everyone respected him.

"I better go back to class," Haruki said. "I'll get in trouble if I'm late."

"You're a pussy," Mozasu said. "Do you really give two shits if the teacher yells at you? Kara-sensei is an even bigger pussy than you are."

Haruki gulped.

"If you want, I'll let you sit with me during recess," Mozasu said. He had never made such an offer before, but he didn't think he could bear it if Haruki tried to talk to those assholes one more time and was rejected. In a strange way, just watching his efforts was painful and embarrassing.

"Truly?" Haruki said, smiling.

Mozasu nodded, and even when they were men, neither one ever forgot how they became friends.

II

October 1955

Mozasu kept a photograph of the wrestler Rikidozan taped to the inside lid of his trunk, where he kept his special things like his favorite comics, old coins, and his father's eyeglasses. Unlike the Korean wrestler, Mozasu did not like to get too close to his opponent and tussle for too long. Rikidozan was known for his famous karate chop, and similarly, Mozasu had deadly aim with his strikes.

Over the years, he had hit many different kinds of boys: He had hit them when they called him names; when they picked on his friend Haruki; and when they hassled his mother or grandmother at their confectionery stall at Tsuruhashi Station. By this time, Sunja had gotten used to the notes and visits from teachers, counselors, and angry parents. There was little she could do to stop her son from fighting, and she was terrified that he would get into serious trouble or argue with the wrong boy. After each incident, Yoseb and Noa would speak to him, and the fighting would stop for a while. Nevertheless, once incited, Mozasu would pound anyone who deserved it.

When Sunja asked him what happened, she could always expect two things from him: a sincere apology to her and his family for bringing them shame, and the defense that he didn't start it. Sunja believed him. By nature, her boy, who was sixteen, was not violent. He avoided fights when he could and for as long as he could, but when things got bad, he would put a stop to the harassment with a quick, effective punch to the instigator's face. Mozasu had broken the noses of several boys and blackened as many eyes. By now, only a stubborn fool or a new bully at school would bother Mozasu. Even the teachers respected the boy's physical authority, and everyone knew that he did not abuse his power and preferred to be left alone.

To keep him out of trouble, Mozasu was required to go to the confectionery stand after school. Kyunghee stayed at home with Yoseb, and Noa wanted Mozasu to help their mother and grandmother. When the family had enough money to buy a store, it was hoped that Mozasu would help his mother and grandmother run it. Mozasu did not want to do this. Working in the market was women's work, and though the boy respected the women, he did not want to make candy or sell *taiyaki* for the rest of his life.

For now, he did not mind helping his mother and grandmother by fetching more coal for the box stove beneath the *taiyaki* griddle and candy burner. At the end of the day, Sunja and Yangjin were relieved to have a strong boy to push the carts home, since they had been working since dawn. However, between the hours of four and seven, there wasn't enough for Mozasu to do, because Sunja and Yangjin were able to cook the sweets and handle the customers without him. It was never that busy then.

It was a late fall afternoon, when business was exceedingly slow and the market women were busy talking with each other since there were so few customers; Mozasu made excuses about getting some *gimbap* on the other side of the market, and no one seemed to mind. Mozasu went to see Chiyaki, the girl who sold socks.

She was an eighteen-year-old Japanese orphan whose parents had died in the war. She lived and worked with her elderly grandparents, who owned the large sock store. Petite and curvy, Chiyaki was a flirt. She didn't like other girls very much and preferred the company of the boys who worked in the market. Chiyaki teased Mozasu because she was two years older than he was, but of all the boys she liked, she thought he was the most handsome. It was a pity, she thought, that he was Korean, because her grandparents would disown her if she dated him. They both knew this, but there was no harm in talking.

When Chiyaki's grandparents went home in the afternoon and left her alone to manage and close the shop, Mozasu or other boys came by to keep her company. Chiyaki had quit school years before because she hated all the stuck-up girls who ruled the school. Besides, her grandparents couldn't see the point in her finishing. They were arranging her marriage to the tatami maker's second son, who Chiyaki thought was boring. Chiyaki liked sharp dressers who talked a good game. Despite her interest in boys, she was very innocent and had never done anything with a boy. She would inherit her grandparents' store, and she was pretty enough to get a guy to take her to a café if she wanted. Her value was obvious, and what she liked best was to make a man give her his devotion.

When Mozasu knocked on the doorframe of the stall and handed her his grandmother's famous *taiyaki*, still warm from the griddle, Chiyaki smiled and licked her lips. She smelled it appreciatively at first, then took a little bite.

"*Oishi*! *Oishi*! Mo-san, thank you so much," she said. "A handsome young man who can make sweets. You are perfect, *nee*?"

Mozasu smiled. She was adorable; there was no one like her. She had a reputation for talking to a lot of guys, but he still enjoyed being in her company. Also, he'd never seen her with another guy, so he didn't know if the rumors were true. She had a cute figure and wore a berry-colored lipstick, which made her small mouth look delicious.

"How's business?" he asked.

"Not bad. I don't care. I know we made enough for the week, because Grandfather said so."

"The sandal lady is looking at us," Mozasu said. Watanabe-san owned the store opposite Chiyaki's, and she was best friends with Chiyaki's grandmother.

"That old bat. I hate her. She's going to tell Grandmother about me again, but I don't care."

"Are you going to get in trouble for talking to me?"

"No. I'll only get in trouble if I keep letting you give me sweets," she said.

"Well, I'll stop then."

"*Iyada!*" Chiyaki took another bite of her cake and shook her head like a willful little girl.

They both looked up when a young man dressed like an office worker stopped in front of the shop. Chiyaki gestured to the empty stool in the corner of the shop, and Mozasu sat down and busied himself with the newspaper.

"May I help you, sir?" Chiyaki asked the man. He had been by earlier when her grandparents were there, but had returned. "Did you want to see those black socks again?"

"You remember me?" the man said excitedly.

"Sure. You were here this morning."

"A pretty girl like you remembered me. I like that. I'm glad I came back for you."

Mozasu looked up from the paper, then looked down again.

"How many would you like?"

"How many do you have?"

"At least twenty pairs your size," she said. Sometimes a person would buy ten pairs. Once, a mother bought two boxes for her son who was at university.

"I'll take two, but I'll take more if you put them on me."

Mozasu folded the paper and glanced at the man, who didn't seem to notice his irritation.

"I'll wrap up these two, then," Chiyaki said.

"What's your name?" he asked.

"Chiyaki."

"I have a cousin with that name. Gosh, you are very beautiful. You got a boyfriend?"

Chiyaki got quiet.

"No? I think you should be my girlfriend then." The man put money in her hand and held it.

Chiyaki smiled at him. She had dealt with this sort of fellow before, and she knew what he was implying. She pretended not to understand. Mozasu was jealous, but she didn't mind. She stuck out her chest a little.

In the bathhouse, the older women always stared at her high, round breasts and told her she was lucky.

The man stared exactly where Chiyaki wanted him to and said, "Nice. When can I pick you up tonight? I'll buy you some yakitori."

"You can't," she said, putting the money away in the cashbox. "You're too old for me."

"You little tease."

"You're not my type," Chiyaki said, unafraid.

"You're too young to have a type. I make good money, and I know how to fuck." The man pulled her to him and put his hands on her behind and squeezed her. "Nice and full back there. Good tits, too. Close the shop. Let's go."

Mozasu got up from his chair quietly and walked over to the man. He hit him square in the mouth as hard as he could. The man fell over and blood poured down his lip. From the pain in his knuckles, Mozasu knew that he had loosened some of the man's teeth.

"You should take the socks and go home now," he said.

The man stared at the blood on his blue shirt and trousers as if the blood belonged to someone else.

"I'm calling the police," he said.

"Go ahead, call the police," Chiyaki said to the man. She waved frantically to the sandal lady, who was now rushing over.

"Mo-san, go now," she said. "Hurry, get out. Go. I'll deal with this."

Mozasu walked briskly toward the confection stand.

The police found him in no time. Only a few minutes before, Mozasu had come back to the stall with blood on his hand and told his mother and grandmother what had happened with Chiyaki.

The police officer confirmed the story.

"Your son hit a gentleman who was buying some socks. This sort of behavior warrants an explanation. The young lady said that that man was trying to molest her and your son was protecting her, but the customer denies it," the officer said.

Goro-san, the pachinko parlor owner, who was heading to the stand for his afternoon snack, rushed toward them when he saw the police-man.

"Hello, officer." He winked at Sunja. "Is everything okay?" Goro asked.

Mozasu sat on the old wooden stool by the cart, looking guilty for troubling his mother and grandmother.

"Mozasu was defending a young lady who works at the sock store from a man who grabbed her. Mozasu hit him in the face," Sunja said calmly. She kept her head high and refused to apologize for fear of admitting guilt on his behalf. Her heart was pounding so hard that she thought they could hear it. "He was only trying to help."

Yangjin nodded firmly and patted Mozasu's back.

"*Maji?*" Goro said, laughing. "Is that right, officer?"

"Well, that's what the young lady said in the shop, and Watanabe-san agreed with her version of the events. The man who was hit denies it, but I've heard from some other store owners that he is a creep who often bothers the younger girls who work here." The police officer shrugged. "Nevertheless, the man thinks his jaw is broken. His two lower teeth are loose. I wanted to warn the young man that he can't just hit people even if they're wrong. He should have called the police."

At this, Mozasu nodded. He had been in trouble before, but no one had ever called the police. All his life, he had known about his father, who had been wrongfully imprisoned. Lately, Noa was warning him that since the Koreans in Japan were no longer citizens, if you got in trouble, you could be deported. Noa had told him that no matter what, Mozasu had to respect the police and be very deferential even if they were rude or wrong. Only a month ago, Noa had said a Korean had to be extra good. Once again, Mozasu felt bad for messing up and dreaded the look of disappointment that would surely appear on Noa's face.

Goro considered the boy and Sunja, one of his favorite *ajummas* in the market.

"Officer, I know this family. They're very hardworking, and Mozasu is a good kid. He won't get in trouble again. Right, Mozasu?" Goro stared directly at Mozasu.

"*Hai*," Mozasu replied.

The officer repeated his speech about how citizens should never take the law into their own hands, and Mozasu, Sunja, and Goro nodded as if the officer were the Emperor himself. After he left, Goro lightly smacked Mozasu in the back of head with his felt hat. Mozasu winced, but of course it hadn't hurt.

"What are you going to do with this boy?" Goro asked the women, both exasperated and amused.

Sunja looked at her hands. She had tried everything she could, and now she had to ask a stranger. Yoseb and Noa would be angry with her, but she had to try something else besides what they were doing now.

"Could you help him?" Sunja asked. "Could he work for you? You wouldn't have to pay him very much—"

Goro waved her away and shook his head and turned his attention to Mozasu. That was all he needed to hear.

"Listen, you're going to quit school tomorrow morning and start working for me. Your mother doesn't need this shit. After you tell the school that you're done, you're going to head to my shop, and you're going to work very hard. I'm going to pay you what you deserve. I don't steal from my employees. You work, you get paid. You got it? And stay away from the sock girl. She's trouble."

"Does your parlor need a boy?" Sunja asked.

"Sure, but no fighting. That's not the only way to be a man," he said, feeling sorry for the kid who didn't have a father. "Being a man means you know how to control your temper. You have to take care of your family. A good man does that. Okay?"

"Sir, you are gracious to give him a chance. I know he'll work—"

"I can see that," Goro said to Sunja, smiling. "We'll make him a pachinko boy and keep him off the streets."

Mozasu got up from his stool and bowed to his new boss.

12

March 1956

Goro was a fat and glamorous Korean, notably popular with beautiful women. His mother had been an abalone diver in Jeju Island, and in the neighborhood of Ikaino where Goro lived in a modest stand-alone house by himself, there was talk of Goro having once been an agile and powerful swimmer. That said, it was rather difficult to imagine him doing much beyond telling funny stories and eating the tasty snacks he liked to fix for himself in his kitchen. There was something plush and sensual about his thickly rounded arms and swollen belly; it might have been the smoothness of his clear, tawny skin, or the way he fit into a well-made suit, resembling a self-satisfied seal gliding across a city street. He was a good talker—the sort of man who could sell lumber to a woodcutter. Though he made plenty of money from his three pachinko parlors, he lived simply and preferred to avoid expensive habits. He was known for being generous with women.

For six months, Mozasu had been working for Goro in his main pachinko parlor, doing whatever was needed. In that time, the sixteen-year-old had learned more about the world than in all his years of school. Making money was ten times easier and more pleasant than trying to stuff the kanji he had no use for into his head. It was a tremendous relief to forget the dry books and exams. At work, nearly everyone was Korean, so nothing stupid was said about his background. At school, Mozasu hadn't thought that the taunts had bothered him much, but when the mean remarks had utterly disappeared from his daily life, he realized how peaceful he could feel. He hadn't had a single fight since he'd started working for Goro.

Each Saturday evening, Mozasu handed his pay envelope to his mother who, in turn, gave him an allowance. She used what she needed for the household expenses, but she was saving as much as she could, because Mozasu wanted to be his own boss one day. Each morning, Mozasu rushed to work and stayed as late as he could keep his eyes open; he was happy just to sweep up the cigarette butts or to wash the dirty teacups when Kayoko, the kitchen girl, was busy.

It was a mild morning in March, only a couple of hours after dawn. Mozasu ducked into the back door of the shop and found Goro setting up the pins on his chosen machine. Each day, before the store opened, Goro would gently tap a few straight pins on the vertical pachinko machines with his tiny rubber-coated hammer. He was tapping the pins very, very slightly to alter the course of the metal balls to affect the machine's payout. You never knew which machine Goro would choose, or which direction Goro would direct the pins. There were other pachinko parlors in the area that had decent businesses, but Goro was the most successful, because he had a kind of touch—a true feel for the pins. The minuscule adjustments he made were sufficiently frustrating to the regular customers who'd studied the machines before closing hours for better payouts in the morning, yet there was just enough predictability to produce attractive windfalls, drawing the customers back to try their luck again and again. Goro was teaching Mozasu how to tap the pins, and for the first time in his life, Mozasu had been told that he was a good student.

"Good morning, Goro-san," Mozasu said, running into the shop.

"Early again, Mozasu. Good for you. Kayoko has made some chicken rice; you should eat some breakfast. You're a big kid, but you need to fill out some more. Women like to have something to grab on to!" Goro laughed heartily, raising his eyebrows. "Isn't that so?"

Mozasu smiled, not minding the teasing. Goro-san talked to him as if Mozasu, too, had many women when in fact, he'd never once been with a girl.

"My mother made soup this morning, so I already ate. Thank you." Mozasu sat down beside his boss.

"How is your mother?"

"Good, good."

Despite Noa's strict disapproval of Mozasu working in a pachinko parlor, Sunja had relented in the end. She had allowed him to work with Goro, a widely respected man in Ikaino. Mozasu had fought against the other schoolboys so often that she'd feared for his safety and let him leave school for good. Mozasu would never finish school, but Noa was still trying to get into Waseda, and this was the family consolation—at least one of the boys would be educated like their father.

"How's her business? Sugar is an addictive substance. Good for making money, *nee*?" He laughed while tapping gently at one pin then another.

Mozasu nodded. He was proud of the confectionery stall his mother, aunt, and grandmother ran in the open market by the train station. They wanted to have a proper shop of their own, but they'd have to wait until they had the money to buy the building, because no one would rent good locations to Koreans. Mozasu wanted to make enough money to pay for Noa's tutoring and to buy his mother a beautiful shop.

Goro handed Mozasu the hammer.

"Try it."

Mozasu tapped the pins while Goro watched him.

"So, last night, I met my lady friend Miyuki, and we drank too much. Mozasu, don't be like me and spend all your free time with fast girls," Goro said, smiling. "Well, unless they are very pretty. Ha."

"Miyuki-san is pretty," Mozasu said.

"*Soo nee*. Beautiful tits and a stomach like a mermaid. Women are so tasty. Like candy! I don't know how I'll ever settle down," Goro said. "Then again, I don't see why I should. You see, Mozasu, I don't have a mother or a father anymore, and though this makes me sad, no one cares enough for me to get married and is willing to arrange it." He nodded, not looking at all troubled by this.

"And who were you out with last night?" Goro asked.

Mozasu smiled.

"You know I was here until the closing. Then I went home."

"So you didn't even chase Kayoko around the kitchen?"

"No." Mozasu laughed.

"Ah, yes, I suppose that was me. Poor girl. She is so very ticklish. Not bad looking and will one day have a fine figure, but for now, she is too young. One day, someone will buy her some rouge and powder, and she will leave us. And so this is the way of women."

Mozasu couldn't understand why his boss would be interested in the kitchen girl when he regularly escorted actresses and dancers.

"Kayoko is perfectly suitable for tickling, however. She has a cute laugh." Goro knocked against Mozasu's knee with his own. "You know, Mozasu, I like having you kids here. It makes this place feel more jolly." Goro kept Mozasu at the main shop because he had a wonderful energy about him. Goro could now afford to hire enough employees in all his shops. It wasn't that long ago that, as a new owner, he did the same work Mozasu did. Goro looked up and down at the boy and frowned.

Mozasu looked at his boss, puzzled.

"You wear the same white shirt and black trousers each day. You look clean, but you look like a janitor. You have two shirts and two pairs of trousers. Isn't that so?" Goro said this kindly.

"Yes, sir." Mozasu glanced down. His mother had ironed his shirt the night before. He didn't look bad, but Goro-san was right—he didn't look important. There was no extra money for clothing. After food, tutoring, and transportation, Uncle Yoseb's doctor's bills ate up all their spare cash. He'd been getting worse and remained in bed most of the day.

"You need some more clothes. Let's go." Goro shouted, "Kayo-chan, I'm going to go out with Mozasu for a few minutes. Don't let anyone in. Okay?"

"Yes, sir," Kayoko shouted from the kitchen.

"But I need to put the trays of balls out and sweep the front. The machines need to be cleaned, and I wanted to help Kayoko with the hand towels—" Mozasu listed his morning duties, but his boss was already at the door.

"Mozasu, come on! I don't have all day. You can't look like that anymore!" he shouted, while smiling, not the least bit ruffled by the boy's confusion.

The woman who answered the small wooden door was surprised to see the tall boy standing by her customer, Goro-san.

Mozasu recognized Haruki's mother immediately. He'd never been to his friend's house before but had met her on the street several times, and Haruki had introduced her to him.

"Totoyama-san! Hello." Mozasu bowed deep from the waist.

"Mozasu-san, hello. Welcome. I'd heard that you were working for Goro-san."

Goro smiled. "He is a good boy. I'm sorry to come so early, Totoyama-san, but Mozasu needs a few things."

As Mozasu entered, he was surprised by the smallness of the living quarters. The space was a third the size of his house. It was basically one small room divided by a wall-to-wall screen—the front part held the sewing machine, dressmakers' dummies, work table, and fabrics. Some sort of sandalwood incense covered the shoyu and mirin smells from cooking. The room was meticulously clean. It was hard to believe that Haruki lived somewhere so cramped with his mother and brother. Seeing this made him miss his friend more. Mozasu had not seen Haruki since he left school and started work.

"Mozasu is going to be my new morning foreman. My youngest one yet."

"*Ehh?*" Mozasu said out loud.

"But a foreman cannot look like the boy who cleans the machines and passes out hand towels and cups of tea," Goro said. "Totoyama-san, please make him two proper jackets and matching trousers."

Totoyama nodded gravely, unspooling her measuring tape to gauge the size of his shoulders and arms. With a stubby pencil, she took notes on a pad made out of used wrapping paper.

"Mama! Mama! Can I come out now?"

It was the voice of a larger male but with the pleading tone of a small boy.

"Excuse me. My son is curious. We don't usually have customers so early in the morning."

Goro-san waved her away, letting her check on her son.

When she left the room, Goro made a sad face. "The boy is—"

Mozasu nodded, because he knew about Haruki's younger brother. It had been almost six months since he had last seen Haruki, who was still in school. Haruki wanted to become a police officer. Neither had realized that school had made their relationship possible until one of them left; there'd been no chance to see him since Mozasu worked all the time.

The sliding walls between the rooms were made of paper and thin slats of wood, and Goro and Mozasu could hear everything.

"Daisuke-chan, Mama will be right back, *nee*? I'm in the next room. You can hear me, *nee*?"

"Mama, is brother back home from school?"

"No, no, Daisuke-chan. Haruki left only an hour ago. We must wait for him patiently. He will not be home until much later. Mama has to make some jackets for Haruki's good friend. Can you stay here and do your puzzle?"

"Is this Mozasu-san?"

Startled at hearing his name, Mozasu glanced at the closed screen door.

"I want to meet him, Mama. This is the Korean boy. Can I meet him, please? Brother said Mozasu curses. I want to hear that!" Daisuke burst out laughing.

Goro patted Mozasu's back as if he was trying to assure him somehow. Mozasu could feel Goro's sympathy and kindness.

"Oh, Mama! Mama! I want to meet the Korean friend. Oh, Mama, please?"

Suddenly, it got quiet, and Totoyama's voice lowered to a low murmur like a bird cooing. "Daisuke-chan, Daisuke-chan, Daisuke-chan," she chanted. Haruki's mother repeated his name until the boy quieted.

"You should stay here and do your puzzle and help Mama. Okay? You are my good child. Haruki will be home in a few hours. He will want to see your progress on your puzzles."

"Yes, Mama, yes. I will play with my top first. Then I will do my puzzles. Can we have rice today, do you think? If we have customers, can we have rice? Sometimes you buy rice when we have customers. I want a big rice ball, Mama."

"Later, Daisuke-chan. We will talk later. Daisuke-chan, Daisuke-chan, Daisuke-chan," she murmured.

Totoyama returned to the room and apologized. Goro said it was nothing. For the first time, Mozasu saw that Goro could look troubled. He smiled a lot at Totoyama, but his downward-sloping eyes showed his anguish at the sight of her stoic yet gentle face.

"Maybe you should make the boy two jackets, two sets of trousers, and a proper winter coat. He is always wearing some shabby thing. I want my customers to see that the employees of my shops are neat and well dressed."

Goro-san handed her some bills, and Mozasu turned away. He looked for signs of his friend in the tiny room, but there were no photographs, books, or images. There was a portrait-sized mirror on the wall beside the curtained dressing area.

"I will send Kayoko later today so you can make her something that matches Mozasu's uniform. I think they should wear a striped tie or some striped thing that matches each other. I saw that in a Tokyo parlor last month. She should wear a neat dress with an apron. Maybe the apron could be striped. What do you think? Well, I leave that to you. She should have two or three uniforms made. They should be sturdy." Goro peeled off some more bills and put them in her hands.

Totoyama bowed and bowed again. "It is too much," she said, looking at the money.

Goro gestured to Mozasu. "We should go back now. The customers will be itchy to touch their machines!"

"Goro-san, I shall have the jackets and trousers ready by the end of the week. I will work on the coat last. Mozasu-san will come again to try on the jacket, please. Can you come by in three days?"

Mozasu glanced at Goro-san, who nodded firmly.

"Come along, Mozasu. We mustn't keep the customers waiting."

Mozasu followed his boss out the door, unable to find out anything about his friend, who would be suffering through morning classes about now.

Totoyama bowed when they left and remained at the threshold until they turned the corner and could no longer see her. She shut the door tight and locked the door behind her. There would be money for rent and food that month. Totoyama sat down in front of her door and cried from relief.

13

1957

There has to be a way to raise that money," Kyunghee said.

"We have whatever's left from the savings for the shop," Yangjin said.

"It's mostly gone," Sunja whispered. Trying to save money while paying medical bills was like pouring oil into a broken jar.

The women were speaking in low voices in the kitchen for fear of waking Yoseb. His latest skin infection made him itch terribly and kept him from resting. He had only just gone to bed after taking a large draft of Chinese medicine. The herbalist had given him a very strong dose this time, and it had worked. After all these years, the women were used to paying a lot for the medications, but this concoction had been shockingly expensive. Regular medicines no longer worked for his ailments, and he continued to suffer a great deal. Mozasu, who gave his full pay envelope each week to his mother, said that whatever they had left after living expenses should go toward the best possible care for Uncle Yoseb. Noa felt the same way. Despite the family's thrift and diligence, the savings seemed to vanish with each visit to the pharmacy. How would they pay for Waseda?

At last, Noa had passed the entrance exam. This should have been a good day, perhaps the greatest day in the family's life, but they didn't know how to pay even a portion of his first tuition bill. Also, the school was in Tokyo, and he would need room and board in the most expensive city in the country.

Noa intended to continue working for Hoji-san up until almost the first day of school, then get a job in Tokyo while going to university. Sunja didn't know how that could be possible. Koreans didn't get jobs so easily, and they knew no one in Tokyo. Noa's boss, Hoji-san, was furious that his best bookkeeper was going to quit working to study something as useless as English literature. Hoji-san would never help Noa get a job in Tokyo.

Kyunghee thought they should buy another cart and set up in another part of town to try to double their earnings, but Yoseb could not be left alone. He could no longer walk, and the muscles in his legs had atrophied so much that what had once been thick, powerful calves were now bony stalks sheathed with scabs.

He was not asleep, and he could hear them. The women were in the kitchen worrying about Noa's tuition. They were worried when he was studying for his exams, and now that he had finally passed, they were worried about how they would pay. Somehow, they had to live without Noa's salary, come up with the cost of the boy's education, and pay for his medicines. It would have been better if he were dead. Everyone knew it. As a young man, the only thing Yoseb had wanted to do was to take care of his family, and now that he was helpless to do so, he could not even die to help them. The worst thing had happened: He was eating up his family's future. Back home, in the olden days, he could have asked someone to carry him off to the mountains to die, perhaps to be eaten by tigers. He lived in Osaka, and there were no wild animals here—only expensive herbalists and doctors who could not help him get well, but rather keep him from just enough agony to fear death more while hating himself.

What surprised him was that as he felt closer to death, he felt the terror of death, its very finality. There were so many things he had failed to do. There were even more things he should never have done. He thought of his parents, whom he should never have left; his brother, whom he should never have brought to Osaka; and he thought of the job in Nagasaki he should never have taken. He had no children of his own. Why did God bring him this far? He was suffering, and in a way, he could manage that;

but he had caused others to suffer, and he did not know why he had to live now and recall the series of terrible choices that had not looked so terrible at the time. Was that how it was for most people? Since the fire, in the few moments when he felt clear and grateful to breathe without pain, Yoseb wanted to see the good in his life, but he couldn't. He lay on his well-laundered pallet, dwelling on the mistakes that seemed so obvious in hindsight. He was no longer angry at Korea or Japan; most of all, he was angry about his own foolishness. He prayed that God would forgive him for being an ungrateful old man.

Softly, he called out "*Yobo*." He didn't want to wake the boys, who were sleeping in the back room, and Changho, who slept in the room by the front door. Yoseb tapped the floor gently in case Kyunghee could not hear him.

When he saw her at the threshold, he asked her to bring Sunja and Yangjin.

The three women sat on the floor by his pallet.

"You can sell my tools first," he said. "They're worth something. Maybe they'll pay for his books and his moving fees. You should sell all the jewelry you have. That will help, too."

The women nodded. Among the three of them, they had two gold rings left.

"Mozasu should ask his boss, Goro-san, for an advance against his salary equal to Noa's tuition, room, and board. And the three of you and he can work down the debt. During the school breaks, Noa can find whatever temporary jobs he can get and save. The boy has to go to Waseda. He deserves to go. Even if no one hires Koreans here, with his degree he can go back to Korea and work for a better salary. Or move to the United States. He'll know how to speak English. We have to think of his education as an investment."

He wanted to say more. He wanted to apologize for not providing for them and for the expense he caused them, but he couldn't say these things now.

"The Lord will provide," Kyunghee said. "He's always taken care of our every need. When the Lord saved your life, he saved our lives."

"Send Mozasu to me when he comes home. I'll tell him that he must ask for an advance from Goro-san so he can pay for the tuition."

Sunja shook her head slightly.

"Noa won't allow his younger brother to pay for his tuition," she said. "He's already told me so." She didn't look at him while speaking. "Koh Hansu has said that he would pay for the tuition and board. Even if Mozasu got an advance—"

"No. That's the foolish talk of an unthinking woman! You can't take that bastard's money! It's filthy."

"Shhh," Kyunghee said gently. "Please don't get upset." She didn't want Kim Changho to hear them talking about his boss. "Noa said that he'll get a job in Tokyo, and it's true, he did say that Mozasu cannot pay for the tuition. That he'll manage. You know Noa won't go if Mozasu pays."

"I should be dead," Yoseb said. "I'd rather be dead than listen to this. How can that boy work and go to a school like Waseda? Impossible. A boy who studied hard like this must go. I'll ask Goro-san myself if Noa can borrow the money. I'll tell Noa that he has to take it from him."

"But we don't know if Goro-san will lend it. And asking him could hurt Mozasu's job. I don't want to let Koh Hansu pay for the fees, either, but how else? We can make it a loan, and we can pay it back in increments so that Noa doesn't owe him anything," Sunja said.

"Borrowing from Goro-san and hurting Mozasu's future in pachinko is far better than taking money from Koh Hansu," Yoseb said firmly. "That Koh Hansu is bad. Take money from him for Noa, and there will be no end to him. He wants to control the boy. You know that. For Goro-san, it's just money."

"But why is Goro's pachinko money cleaner than Koh Hansu's money? Koh Hansu owns construction companies and restaurants. There's nothing wrong with those things," Kyunghee said.

"Shut up."

Kyunghee pursed her lips. The Bible said that a wise person must rein in his tongue. Not everything you wanted to say should be said.

Sunja said nothing as well. She had never wanted anything from Hansu before, but she reasoned that it would be preferable to ask a man who had already offered the money than bother a total stranger. Goro had already been so gracious to Mozasu, and Mozasu was very happy in his job. She didn't want to bring shame to Mozasu, who had only just started out. The boy had been talking of opening his own parlor one day. Besides, she knew Noa wouldn't allow Mozasu to borrow that money. Yoseb could insist all he wanted, but Noa would not listen to this.

"How about Kim Changho? Can he help?" Yangjin asked.

"That man works for Koh Hansu. Changho doesn't have that kind of money, and if he got it, he would have gotten it from his boss. These debts are not easy, but Goro-san is the best option. He won't charge some exorbitant rate, or hurt Noa. Mozasu will be fine," Yoseb replied. "I'm going to rest now."

The women left the room and closed the door.

The next day, Hansu asked Noa to come by his office in Osaka with his mother. That same evening, without telling the family, the mother and son went to see Hansu. The office had two receptionists, dressed in matching black suits and crisp white shirts, and one of them brought them tea in thin blue porcelain cups on a lacquer tray lined in white gold foil. The waiting area was filled with beautiful floral arrangements. As soon as Hansu's call ended, the older one ushered them into Hansu's immense, wood-paneled office. Hansu sat on a tufted black-leather chair behind a mahogany partners desk from England.

"Congratulations!" Hansu said, getting up from his big chair. "I'm so glad you could come. We should go have sushi! Can you go now?"

"No, no, thank you. We have to get home," Sunja replied.

Noa glanced at his mother, wondering why she wouldn't go to dinner. They didn't have any plans. After the meeting, they would likely just go back home and eat something simple that Aunt Kyunghee made.

"I asked you to come today because I want Noa to know that he has achieved something great. Not just for himself or his family but for all Koreans. You are going to university! And to Waseda, an excellent Japanese university! You are doing everything a great man can do in his time—you are pursuing your education. So many Koreans could not go to school, but you kept studying and studying. And even when the exams were not good, you persevered. You deserve a great reward! How wonderful! I'm so proud. So proud." Hansu beamed.

Noa smiled shyly. No one had fussed nearly this much. Everyone at home had been happy, but mostly they had been anxious about the cost. Noa had been concerned, too, about the money, but he felt that somehow, everything would be okay. He had worked since high school, and he would keep working even at Waseda. After getting into Waseda, he felt like he could do anything. He didn't mind working in any kind of job as long as he could go to classes and study.

"I am sorry to ask this, but a while ago, you had said that you may be able to help Noa with the fees," Sunja said. "Do you think you could help us?"

"*Umma*, no." Noa flushed. "I can get a job. That's not why we're here. Kim-san said that Koh-san wanted us to come by to congratulate me. *Nee*?" Noa was surprised by his mother's request. She didn't like to ask for anything. She didn't even like taking free samples at the bakery.

"Noa, I'm asking for a loan. We would pay everything back. With interest," Sunja said. She hadn't wanted to ask now, but it was better this way, she thought. Now he would know the terms from the beginning. There was no way to do this perfectly, so she had to just say it. "The tuition is due now, and if you could help us, then we can write up a loan paper, and I will stamp it with my *hanko*. I brought it." Sunja nodded for emphasis. For a second, she wondered: What would she do if he said no?

Hansu laughed and shook his head dismissively.

"That's not necessary, and Noa need never worry about tuition, board, and fees. I've already taken care of it. As soon as I heard the great news from Kim Changho, I sent the money to the school. I called my friend in Tokyo and found a good room near the school, which I will take you to see next week. Then I asked Kim Changho to ask you and Noa to come by so I could invite you to dinner. So, now, let's go eat sushi. The boy deserves a magnificent meal!"

Hansu looked at Sunja's face with pleading in his eyes. He wanted so much to celebrate his son's great accomplishment.

"You sent the money? And found a room in Tokyo? Without my permission? It's supposed to be a loan," she said, feeling more anxious.

"Sir, it's far too generous. My mother is right. We should return the money to you. I will get a job in Tokyo. Perhaps you can help me with that rather than pay the fees. I'd like to earn it myself. I feel like I can do that."

"No. You have to study. You had to take that exam again and again, not because you are not smart. You are very smart. You didn't have the time to study like a normal student. You took much longer than you needed because you didn't have schooling and you had to work full time to support your family. You didn't have all the proper tutoring that the average Japanese middle-class child would have had. And during the war, you were in that farm without any lessons. No. I will no longer watch idly while you and your mother pretend that the rules of human performance do not apply to you. A hardworking scholar should not have to worry about money. I should have forced my way earlier. Why should it take many more years for you to graduate from school? Do you want to be an old man by the time you finish Waseda? You study and learn as much as you can. I will pay," Hansu said, laughing. "Do it my way. Be smart, Noa. This is what I can do for the next generation as a responsible Korean elder."

Noa bowed.

"Sir, you have been very kind to our family. I am very grateful."

Noa looked at his mother, who remained seated quietly by his side. Her hands twisted the handle of her homemade canvas bag, stitched from Mozasu's leftover coat material. He felt sorry for her, because she was a proud woman, and this was humiliating for her. He knew she wanted to pay for his tuition.

"Noa, can you go outside and ask Mieko-san to call the restaurant for us?" Hansu asked.

Noa looked again at his mother, who seemed lost in her heavily upholstered chair.

"*Umma?*"

Sunja glanced up at her son, who was already standing by the door. She could see that he wanted to go to dinner with Hansu. The boy looked so handsome and pleased. She couldn't imagine what this must have meant to him. Noa had not refused Hansu. He had already accepted the money, because the boy wanted so much to go to this university. In her mind, she could hear Yoseb yelling at her—to stop this now, that she was a foolish woman who had not thought this through. But the boy, her first child, was happy. He had done this tremendous, near impossible thing, and she could not imagine unmaking it to the thing it was yesterday, before he had passed—this glittering, brilliant object that could be taken away at a moment's notice through lack of money. She nodded, and her son understood that they would dine with Hansu.

When the door closed, and Hansu and Sunja were alone in his office, she tried again:

"I want this to be a loan. And I want papers so I can show Noa that I paid for his school."

"No, Sunja. This, this I get to do. He's my son. If you don't let me do this, I will tell him."

"Are you crazy?"

"No. Paying for his school is nothing to me financially, but it is everything to me as his father."

"You're not his father."

"You don't know what you're saying," Hansu said. "He is my child. He has my ambition. He has my abilities. I will not let my own blood rot in the gutters of Ikaino."

Sunja gathered her bag and got up. Yoseb was not wrong, and she could not take this back.

"Let us go then. The boy is waiting outside. He must be hungry," he said.

Hansu opened the door and let her out first.

14

December 1959

On a Saturday morning when the others would be at work, Kyunghee wanted to go to church. Missionaries from America who spoke Japanese but not Korean were visiting their church, and the minister had asked her to help him greet them since her Japanese was so good. Normally, she couldn't get out of the house because she wouldn't leave Yoseb by himself, but Changho offered to watch Yoseb. It wouldn't be for very long, and Changho wanted to do one last thing for her.

Changho sat cross-legged on the warm floor near Yoseb's bedding to help him do some of the stretches the doctor had recommended.

"You've made up your mind, then?" Yoseb asked.

"Brother, I should go. It's time I went home."

"Really, tomorrow?"

"In the morning, I'll take the train to Tokyo, then head to Niigata from there. The ship leaves next week."

Yoseb said nothing. His face contorted a little in pain as he lifted his right leg toward the ceiling. Changho kept his right hand beneath Yoseb's thigh to steady him down slowly. They switched to the left leg.

Yoseb exhaled audibly after doing two more sets.

"If you wait until I die, then you can take my ashes and bury me there. That would be a good thing, I suppose. Though I think it doesn't much matter in the end. You know, I still believe in heaven. I believe in Jesus, even after all this. I suppose being married to Kyunghee will do that. Her faith brought me closer to the Lord. I am not a good man, but I believe that I am saved. My father once said that when you die and go to heaven, you get your body back. I can finally get rid of this one. That will be good. And I feel ready to go home, too."

Changho put his right arm beneath Yoseb's head, and Yoseb raised his arms above his head slowly, then lowered them. His arms were much stronger than his legs.

"Brother, you can't talk that way. It's not time. You're still here, and I can still feel the power in your body."

Changho grasped Yoseb's good hand, which was unmarred by burns. He could feel the man's delicate bones. How had he survived for so long?

"And...if you wait...if you wait until I die, then you can marry her," Yoseb said. "But you can't take her there. I ask that. I ask that of you."

"What?" Changho shook his head.

"I don't trust the communists. I wouldn't want her to go back home when they're in charge. And this can't last forever. Japan will be a rich country again soon, and Korea won't always be divided. You still have your health. You can make money here and take care of my..." Yoseb couldn't say her name then.

"I've made her suffer so much. She loved me when I was just a boy. I always knew that we'd be together, even when we were kids. She was the most beautiful girl I had ever seen. You know, I've never wanted to be with another woman. Ever. Not just because she's so lovely, but because she's so good. Never, not once, did she complain about me. And I have not been a husband to her for such a long time." He sighed. His mouth felt dry. "I know you care for her. I trust you. I wish you didn't work for that thug, but there aren't that many jobs here. I understand. Why don't you just wait until I die?" The more he said these things, the more Yoseb felt that it was right. "Stay here. I'll die soon. I feel it. You're needed here, too. You can't fix that country. No one can."

"Brother, you're not going to die."

"No, I must. We must try to build a nation again. We can't only think of our own comfort." Even as Yoseb said this, Changho felt the possibility of being with her again, something he had given up.

*　　*　　*

As Kyunghee walked home from church, she saw Changho sitting on the bench in front of the convenience store, a block from the house. He was reading a newspaper and drinking juice from a glass bottle. Changho was friendly with the owner, and he liked this quiet spot beneath the tarpaulin awning on the busy intersection.

"Hello," she said. Kyunghee was happy to see him. "Is he okay? It's not easy being cooped up, is it? Thank you so much for watching him. I better go back. You stay."

"He's fine. I just stepped out. Before he went to sleep, he asked me to get him some papers for when he wakes up. He wanted me to get some air."

Kyunghee nodded and turned from him to rush home.

"Sister, I was hoping I'd get a chance to speak with you."

"Oh? Let's go back home. I better start dinner. He'll be hungry."

"Wait. Can you sit with me? Can I get you a juice from the store?"

"No, no. I'm all right." She smiled at him and sat down, her hands folded over her lap. She was wearing her winter Sunday coat over her navy wool dress with her nice leather shoes.

Without delay, Changho told her what her husband said, almost word for word. He was nervous, but he knew he had to do it now.

"You could come with me. The first ship leaves next week, but we can go later. Korea needs more people who have the energy to rebuild a nation. We're supposed to get our own apartment with all the latest appliances, and we'll be in our own country. White rice three times a day. We can take his ashes there, and we can visit your parents' graves. Do a proper *jesa*. We can go home. You can be my wife."

Stunned, Kyunghee said nothing. She could not imagine that Yoseb would have offered her to him, but she could not imagine that Changho would lie to her. The only thing that made sense was that Yoseb was worried enough about her to suggest such a plan. After the meeting at the church broke up, she had asked the minister to pray for Changho's journey and well-being in Pyongyang. Changho didn't believe in God or Christianity, but Kyunghee had wanted to pray for him, because she didn't know what else she could do for him. If the Lord watched over him, then she would not worry.

He had told her that he was leaving only a week ago, and it was difficult to think of him being gone, but it was the right thing. He was a young man who believed in building a great country for others. She admired him, because he didn't even have to go there. He had a good job and friends. Pyongyang wasn't even his home—Changho was from Kyungsangdo. It was she who was from the North.

"Is it possible?" he asked.

"But you said—that you wanted to go. I thought you'd marry someone back home."

"But you know that—that I've cared. That I do—"

Kyunghee looked around. The shopkeeper of the convenience store was seated in the back and couldn't hear them over the noise of his radio program. On the road, a few cars and bicycles passed by, but not many, because it was Saturday morning. The red-and-white pinwheels attached to the store awning spun slowly in the light winter breeze.

"If you said it is possible—"

"You can't talk that way," she said softly. She didn't want to hurt him. All these years, his adoration and kindness had nourished her but had also caused her anguish, because she could not care for him in that way. It was wrong to do so. "Changho, you have a future. You must find a young woman and have children. There isn't a day when I don't feel heartbroken that my husband and I couldn't have them. I know it was the Lord's plan for me, but I think you might have some. You'd make a wonderful husband and father. I couldn't ask you to wait. It would be sinful."

"It's because you don't want me to wait. Because I would if you told me to."

Kyunghee bit her lip. She felt cold suddenly and put on her blue wool mittens.

"I have to make dinner."

"I leave tomorrow. Your husband said I should wait. Isn't that what you wanted? For him to give you permission? Wouldn't that make it okay in the eyes of your god?"

"It isn't up to Yoseb to change God's laws. My husband is alive, and I wouldn't want to hasten his death. I care for you very much, Changho. You have been the dearest friend to me. I'm not sure if I can bear it when you go, but I know we're not supposed to be man and wife. To even talk about it while he is alive cannot be right. I pray that you'll understand."

"No. I don't understand. I will never understand. How could your faith allow such suffering?"

"It isn't just suffering. It isn't. I pray that you will forgive me. That you will—"

Changho laid down the juice bottle carefully on the bench and got up.

"I'm not like you," he said. "I'm just a man. I don't want to be holy. I'm a minor patriot." He left, walking away from the direction of the house and didn't return until late in the evening when everyone was asleep.

Early in the morning, when Kyunghee went to the kitchen to get water for Yoseb, she saw that Changho's room door was open. She looked in, and he was gone. The bedding had been folded neatly. Changho had never had many possessions, but the room looked even more empty without his pile of books, his extra pair of glasses resting on top of them. The family was supposed to have accompanied him to Osaka Station to see him off, but he had taken an earlier train.

Kyunghee stood by his door crying, when Sunja touched her arm. She was wearing her work apron over her nightclothes.

"He left in the middle of the night. He told me to tell everyone goodbye. I only saw him because I got up to make candy."

"Why didn't he wait? Until we could go with him to the train station?"

"He said he didn't want to make a fuss. He said he had to go. I tried to make him breakfast, but he said he'd buy something later. That he couldn't eat."

"He wanted to marry me. After Yoseb died. Yoseb had told him that it was okay."

"*Uh-muh*," Sunja gasped.

"But that's not right, is it? He should be with someone young. He has a right to have children. I couldn't give him any. I don't even have blood anymore."

"Maybe you're more important than children."

"No. I could not disappoint two men," she said. "He is a good man."

Sunja held her sister-in-law's hand.

"You told him no?" Her sister-in-law's face was wet with tears, and Sunja wiped it with a corner of her apron.

"I have to get water for Yoseb," Kyunghee said, remembering suddenly why she'd gotten out of bed.

"Sister, he would not have cared about children. He would have been happy to have just been with you. You are like an angel in this world."

"No. I'm selfish. Yoseb isn't."

Sunja didn't understand.

"It was selfish to keep him here, but I did because he meant so much to me. I prayed every day for the courage to let him go, and I know the Lord wanted me to let him go. It cannot be right to have two men care for you that way and to allow it."

Sunja nodded, but it didn't make sense. Were you supposed to have only one person in your life? Her mother had her father and no one else. Was her person Hansu or Isak? Did Hansu love her or had he just wanted to use her? If love required sacrifice, then Isak had really loved her. Kyunghee had served her husband faithfully without complaint. There was no one as kindhearted and lovely as her sister-in-law—why couldn't she have more than one man love her? Why did men get to leave when they didn't get what they wanted? Or had Changho suffered enough waiting? Sunja wanted her sister-in-law to make Changho wait, but it wouldn't have been Kyunghee if she had made him do so. Changho had loved someone who would not betray her husband, and perhaps that was why he had loved her. She could not violate who she was.

Kyunghee moved toward the kitchen, and Sunja followed, a few steps behind. Morning sunlight broke through the kitchen window, and it was hard to see straight ahead, but the light cast a glowing outline around her sister-in-law's slight frame.

15

Tokyo, 1960

It took some time, but after two years at Waseda, Noa finally felt comfortable about his place there. Always an excellent student with good habits, after a few hiccups and several thoughtful attempts, Noa learned how to write English literature papers and take university-level exams. University life was glorious in contrast to secondary school, where he had learned and memorized many things he no longer valued. None of his requirements even seemed like work; Waseda was pure joy to him. He read as much as he could without straining his eyes, and there was time to read and write and think. His professors at Waseda cared deeply about the subjects they taught, and Noa could not understand how anyone could ever complain.

Hansu had procured for him a well-appointed apartment and gave him a generous allowance, so Noa did not have to worry about housing, money, or food. He lived simply and managed to send some money home each month. "Just study," Hansu had said. "Learn everything. Fill your mind with knowledge—it's the only kind of power no one can take away from you." Hansu never told him to study, but rather to learn, and it occurred to Noa that there was a marked difference. Learning was like playing, not labor.

Noa was able to buy every book he needed for his classes, and when he couldn't find one at the bookstore, all he had to do was go to the immense university library, which was deeply underutilized by his peers. He didn't understand the Japanese students around him, because they seemed so much more interested in things outside of school rather than learning. He knew well enough from schools past that the Japanese didn't want much to do with Koreans, so Noa kept to himself, no different than when he was a boy. There were some Koreans at Waseda, but he avoided them, too, because they seemed too political. During one of their monthly lunches, Hansu had said that the leftists were "a bunch of whiners" and the rightists were "plain stupid." Noa was alone mostly, but he didn't feel lonely. Even after two years, he was still in thrall with just being at Waseda, with just having a quiet room to read in. Like a man starved, Noa filled his mind, ravenous for good books. He read through Dickens, Thackeray, Hardy, Austen, and Trollope, then moved on to the Continent to read through much of Balzac, Zola, and Flaubert, then fell in love with Tolstoy. His favorite was Goethe; he must have read *The Sorrows of Young Werther* at least half a dozen times.

If he had an embarrassing wish, it was this: He would be a European from a long time ago. He didn't want to be a king or a general—he was too old for such simple wishes. If anything, he wanted a very simple life filled with nature, books, and perhaps a few children. He knew that later in life, he also wanted to be let alone to read and to be quiet. In his new life in Tokyo, he had discovered jazz music, and he liked going to bars by himself and listening to records that the owners would select from bins. Listening to live music was too expensive, but he hoped that one day, when he had a job again, he would be able to go to a jazz club. At the bar, he would have one drink that he'd barely touch to pay for his seat, then he'd go back to his room, read some more, write letters to his family, then go to sleep.

Every few weeks, he saved some of his allowance and took an inexpensive train ride home and visited his family. At the beginning of each month, Hansu took him for a sushi lunch to remind Noa of his mission in the world for some higher purpose that neither could articulate fully. His life felt ideal, and Noa was grateful.

That morning, as he walked across campus to his George Eliot seminar, he heard someone calling his name.

"Bando-san, Bando-san," a woman shouted. It was the radical beauty on campus, Akiko Fumeki.

Noa stopped and waited. She had never spoken to him before. He was, in fact, a little afraid of her. She was always saying contrary things to Professor Kuroda, a soft-spoken woman who had grown up and studied in England. Though the professor was polite, Noa could tell that she didn't like Akiko much; the other students, especially the females, could barely tolerate her. Noa knew it was safer to keep his distance from the students that the professors disliked. In the seminar room, Noa sat one seat away from the professor, while Akiko sat in the very back of the room below the high windows.

"Ah, Bando-san, how are you?" Akiko asked, flushed and out of breath. She spoke to him casually, as if they had talked many times before.

"Well, thank you. How are you?"

"So what do you think of Eliot's final masterpiece?" she asked.

"It's excellent. Everything by George Eliot is perfect."

"Nonsense. *Adam Bede* is a bore. I almost died reading that thing. *Silas Marner* is barely tolerable."

"Well, *Adam Bede* was not as exciting or developed as *Middlemarch*, but it remains a wonderful depiction of a brave woman and an honest man—"

"Oh, please." Akiko rolled her eyes, and she laughed at him.

Noa laughed, too. He knew she was a Sociology major, because everyone had had to introduce himself or herself on the first day of class.

"You have read everything by George Eliot? That's impressive," he said, never having met anyone else who had done so.

"You're the one who's read absolutely everything. It's sickening, and I'm almost irritated at you for doing so. But I admire it, too. Although, if you like everything you read, I can't take you that seriously. Perhaps you didn't think about these books long enough." She said this with a serious face, not in the least bit concerned about offending him.

"*Soo nee.*" Noa smiled. It had not occurred to him that any book that a professor would choose and admire could be inferior even in relation to that author's own works. Their professor had loved *Adam Bede* and *Silas Marner*.

"You sit so close to the professor. I think she's in love with you."

In shock, Noa halted.

"Kuroda-san is sixty years old. Maybe seventy." Noa moved toward the building door and opened it for her.

"You think women want to stop having sex just because they're sixty? You're absurd. She's probably the most romantic woman in Waseda. She's read far too many novels. You're perfect for her. She'd marry you tomorrow. Oh, the scandal! Your George Eliot married a young man, too, you know. Although her groom did try to kill himself on their honeymoon!" Akiko laughed out loud, and the students who were walking up the staircase to their classroom stared at her. Everyone seemed puzzled by their interaction, since Noa was almost as famous as the campus beauty, but for being aloof.

Once in their classroom, she sat at her old seat in the back, and Noa returned to his seat by the professor. He opened his notebook and retrieved his fountain pen, then looked down at the sheet of white paper lined in pale blue ink. He was thinking about Akiko; she was even prettier up close.

Kuroda-san sat down to give her lecture. She wore a pea-green sweater over her Peter Pan–collar white blouse and a brown tweed skirt. Her tiny feet were shod with a childish pair of Mary Janes. She was so small and thin that she gave the impression that she could almost fly away like a sheet of paper or a dry leaf.

Kuroda-san's lecture was primarily an extensive psychological portrait of the heroine in *Daniel Deronda*, the self-centered Gwendolen Harleth, who changes as a result of her suffering and the goodness of Daniel. The professor put great emphasis on a woman's lot being determined by her economic position and marriage prospects. Unsurprisingly, the professor compared Gwendolen to the vain and greedy Rosamond Vincy of *Middlemarch*, but argued that in contrast, Gwendolen achieves the Aristotelian anagnorisis and peripeteia. Kuroda-san spent most of the lecture on Gwendolen, then right before the period ended, she spoke a little about Mirah and Daniel, the Jews of the book. Kuroda-san gave some background on Zionism and the role of Jews in Victorian novels.

"Jewish men are often seen as exceptionally brilliant, and the women are often beautiful and tragic. Here we have a situation where a man does not know his own identity as an outsider. He is like Moses, the infant in Genesis who learns that he is Jewish and not Egyptian—" As Kuroda-san was saying this, she glanced at Noa, but he was not aware of it, because he was taking notes.

"However, when Daniel learns that he is indeed a Jew, Daniel is free to love the virtuous Mirah, another talented singer like his Jewish mother, and they will go east to Israel." Kuroda-san sighed quietly, as if she was pleased by Eliot's ending.

"So are you saying that it is better for people to only love within their race, that people like the Jews need to live apart in their own country?" Akiko asked, without raising her hand. She did not seem to believe in that formality.

"Well, I think George Eliot is arguing that there is great nobility in being Jewish and wanting to be part of a Jewish state. Eliot recognizes that these people were often persecuted unfairly. They have every right to a Jewish state. The war has taught us that bad things happened to them, and that can't happen again. The Jews have done no wrong, but the Europeans—" Kuroda-san spoke more quietly than usual, as if she was afraid that someone might overhear her and she would get in trouble. "It's complicated, but Eliot was far ahead of her contemporaries to think about the issue of discrimination based on religion. *Nee?*"

There were nine students in the class, and everyone nodded, including Noa, but Akiko looked irritated nonetheless.

"Japan was an ally of Germany," Akiko said.

"That is not part of this discussion, Akiko-san."

The professor opened her book nervously, wanting to change the subject.

"Eliot is wrong," Akiko said, undeterred. "Maybe the Jews have a right to have their own state, but I see no need for Mirah and Daniel to have to leave England. I think this nobility argument or a greater nation for a persecuted people is a pretext to eject all the unwanted foreigners."

Noa did not look up. He found himself writing down everything Akiko said, because it upset him to think that this could be true. He had admired Daniel's courage and goodness throughout the book, and he had not thought much about Eliot's political design. Was it possible that Eliot was suggesting that foreigners, no matter how much she admired them, should leave England? At this point in the course, everyone in the room despised Akiko, but suddenly he admired her courage to think so differently and to suggest such a difficult truth. He felt lucky to be at a university and not in most other settings, where the person in charge was always right. Nevertheless, until he really listened to Akiko disagree with the professor, he had not thought for himself fully, and it had never occurred to him to disagree in public.

After class, he walked home alone, deep in thoughts of her, and he knew that he wanted to be with her, even if it would not be easy. The following Tuesday, before the seminar began, Noa went early to class to claim the chair next to hers. The professor tried not to show that she was hurt by this defection, but of course, she was.

16

Osaka, April 1960

At some point in the past four years, Mozasu had worked as a foreman at all six of Goro's pachinko parlors. Goro had opened new parlors in rapid succession, and Mozasu had helped him to start each new one. Mozasu was twenty years old, and he did little else but mind the shops and fix whatever needed fixing while Goro scouted for new locations and came up with inspired ideas for his growing empire, which oddly seemed to work out. In business, Goro could not miss, it seemed, and he credited some of his good fortune to Mozasu's willingness to labor without ceasing.

It was April and early in the morning when Mozasu arrived at the manager's office at Paradaisu Six—the newest pachinko parlor.

"*Ohayo*. The car is waiting. I'm taking you to Totoyama-san's for new clothes. Let's go," Goro said.

"*Maji?* Why? I have enough suits for this year and next. I'm the best-dressed foreman in Osaka," Mozasu said, laughing. Unlike his brother, Noa, Mozasu had never cared for nice clothing. He wore the well-tailored clothes Goro wanted him to wear only because his boss was fastidious about how his staff should look. Goro's employees were an extension of himself, he believed, and Goro was strict about their personal hygiene as well.

Mozasu had too much to do, and he didn't feel like going down to Totoyama-san's place. He was eager to phone the newspapers to put out ads for more workers. Paradaisu Six needed men to work the floor on the late shift, and since the interiors of Paradaisu Seven would be finished in a month, he had to start thinking about hiring for Seven as well.

"You have the right clothes for a foreman, but you'll need new suits to be the manager of Seven."

"*Ehh?* I can't be manager of Seven!" Mozasu replied, startled. "That's Okada-san's job."

"He's gone."

"What? Why? He was looking forward to being manager."

"Stealing."

"What? I don't believe it."

"*Honto desu,*" Goro said, nodding. "I caught him. I had suspected it, and it was confirmed."

"That's terrible." Mozasu couldn't fathom anyone stealing from Goro. It would be like stealing from your father. "Why did he do that?"

"Gambling. He owed some goons money. He said he was going to pay me back, but the losses got bigger. You know. Anyway, his mistress came by this morning to apologize for him. She's pregnant. He finally gets her pregnant and then he loses his job. Moron."

"Oh, shit." Mozasu recalled all the times Okada had spoken of wanting a son. Even a daughter would do, he'd said. Okada was crazy about kids and pachinko. Even with all his experience, no pachinko parlor in Osaka would hire him if Goro had gotten rid of him for stealing. No one stole from Goro. "Did he say he was sorry?"

"Of course. Cried like a child. I told him to get out of Osaka. I don't want to see his face anymore."

"*Soo nee,*" Mozasu said, feeling bad for Okada, who had always been nice to him. He had a Korean mother and a Japanese father, but he always said he felt like a full Korean because he was such a passionate man. "Is his wife okay?" Mozasu knew Goro got along with both women.

"Yeah. His wife and mistress are fine," Goro replied. "But I told the mistress that he shouldn't show up around here. I wouldn't be so nice next time."

Mozasu nodded.

"Let's go to Totoyama-san's. I'm tired of feeling sad. Seeing To-toyama's girls will cheer me up," Goro said.

Mozasu followed his boss to the car. He knew enough not to ask about his new salary; Goro didn't like to talk about money, strangely enough. The manager's salary would be better than that of a foreman. Mozasu had been saving carefully for his mother's confection shop, and they were pretty close to having enough to buy a small store near the train station. With Uncle Yoseb's health worsening, Aunt Kyunghee couldn't make candy to sell when she was home. With only his mother and grandmother working in the stall and with Noa in his third year at Waseda in Tokyo, any extra money would be good for the family, he figured. Each Saturday evening, Mozasu felt proud handing his mother his fat pay envelope; she'd tried to increase his allowance, but he had refused except for his bus fare. He didn't need much, since he ate his meals at the employee cafeteria and Goro bought him his work clothes. Mozasu worked seven days a week and slept at home; if it was very late, he slept in one of the spare employee dorm rooms at the parlors.

The shop door shut behind them after they exited.

"Boss, I don't know. Do you think the guys will listen to me? Like the way they do Okada?" Mozasu asked. It wasn't that Mozasu wasn't ambitious; it was that he enjoyed being the morning or evening foreman at the shops; he was very good at it. Being a manager was more serious; everyone looked up to the manager. He would be in charge whenever Goro wasn't there. Okada was almost thirty-five and tall like a baseball player.

"I'm flattered and grateful, but you know, I think some of the other managers might—"

"Shut up, kid. I know what I'm doing. You're smarter than the other managers, and you know how to solve problems by yourself. This is the most important shop. If I'm running around checking the others, I need you to be sharp."

"But Seven is going to need almost fifty employees. How am I supposed to find fifty men?"

"Actually, you're going to need at least sixty men and twenty pretty girls for the prize counters."

"Really?" Mozasu was always game for Goro's outlandish plans, but this seemed a bit much, even for him. "How will I find—"

"You will. You always do. And you can hire any kind of girl you want for the prize counters—Okinawans, *burakumin*, Koreans, Japanese, I don't care. They just have to be cute and pretty, but not so slutty they'll scare the men. The girls are always important. Ha."

"I didn't realize that the dorm could accommodate so many—"

"You worry a lot. That's why you'll be perfect." Goro smiled widely.

Mozasu thought about that and had to agree. No one worried about the shops nearly as much as he did.

In the car ride to Totoyama's workshop, the driver and Goro talked about wrestling, while Mozasu sat quietly. In his mind, he was making lists of all the things that had to be done for Seven. As he pondered over which of the men he would shuffle around from the other shops, he realized that maybe he was ready after all to become a manager of a shop, and it made him smile a little. Goro was never wrong; maybe he wasn't wrong about him, either. Mozasu wasn't smart like his brother, who was now studying English literature at Waseda in Tokyo and who could read thick novels in English without a dictionary. Noa wanted to work for a real Japanese company; he wouldn't have wanted to work in a pachinko parlor. Noa thought that after the family bought the confectionery, Mozasu should work with the family. Like most Japanese, Noa thought pachinko parlors were not respectable.

The car stopped in front of a squat redbrick building that had been used as a textile factory before the war. A large persimmon tree shaded the gray metal door. As Goro's exclusive uniform maker, Totoyama had earned and saved enough to move her shop here from her home-cum-workshop near Ikaino. She and her sons, Haruki and Daisuke, now lived in three of the back rooms, and she used the rest of the building as the workroom. She employed half a dozen assistants who worked six days a week filling orders for uniforms. By word of mouth, she had picked up work from other Korean business owners in Osaka and now made uniforms for *yakiniku* restaurants and other pachinko parlors in the Kansai region, but Goro's work always came first, because it was he who had told the others to hire her.

When Goro rang the bell, Totoyama answered the door herself. A hired girl, another apprentice, brought them hot fragrant tea and imported wheat biscuits on a lacquered tray. Totoyama led Mozasu to the mirror so she could take his measurements. With pins in her mouth, she measured the width of his long arms.

"You are getting thinner, Mozasu-san," Totoyama said.

"*Soo nee*," he answered. "Goro-san tells me I need to eat more."

Goro nodded as he munched on the biscuits and drank a second cup of *genmaicha*. He was seated on a cedar bench covered with indigo fabric–covered cushions. He felt peaceful, watching Totoyama work. He always felt better when he solved problems. Okada had turned out to be a crook, so he got rid of him. Now he was going to promote Mozasu.

The large and airy workroom had been whitewashed recently, but the wood floors were shabby and old. The floors were cleaned each day, but the morning's bits of fabric and thread littered the areas around the worktables. In the slant of light from the skylight, a pale column of dust motes pierced the room. The long workroom was lined with six sewing machines, and a girl sat behind each one. They tried not to look at the men, but couldn't help being drawn to the young one who came by the shop at least once a year. Mozasu had grown noticeably more attractive. He had his father's purposeful gaze and welcoming smile. He liked to laugh, and this was one of the reasons why Goro liked the boy so much. Mozasu was enthusiastic, not prone to moodiness. He was wearing a foreman's uniform that had been made in this workshop, and the girls who had worked on his clothing felt connected to him in this way but could hardly admit this. They knew he didn't have a girlfriend.

"There's a new face here," Goro said, folding his arms over his chest. He scanned the girls carefully and smiled. He got up from his seat and walked toward them. He bowed deeply, and this was funny because he was such an important person. The girls rose up simultaneously and bowed. Goro shook his head and made a silly face, scrunching up his nose to make them laugh.

"Sit, sit," he said.

He had a kind of comic facility combined with a physical smoothness. To make women laugh, he could walk while wiggling his shoulders. He was a stout little man with funny movements who liked flirting with all kinds of women. You remembered him. You wanted him to like you. Because he could be silly, it was possible to forget that he was a powerful businessman and wealthy enough to own seven pachinko parlors. With a word, he could make grown men leave Osaka for good.

"Eriko-san, Reiko-san, Midori-san, Hanako-san, and Motoko-san, *nee*?" Goro recited their names perfectly, then stopped in front of the new girl.

"Goro *desu*," he said, presenting himself to the new girl. "You have lovely hands."

"Yumi *desu*," the young woman replied, slightly annoyed at him for distracting her from her sewing.

Totoyama looked up from her measurements and frowned at the new girl. Yumi's sewing was neater than the others', but she was often too purposely aloof, taking lunch alone or reading during her breaks rather than talking. Her skills and personal nature were secondary to the fact that she had to respect Goro-san, to humor him even. To Totoyama, Goro-san was a great man who was truly good. Though he joked with girls, he was never inappropriate. Goro had never asked any of the girls out or done any of the bad things her other male customers had tried to do. Yumi had been working for her for two months. From her papers, Totoyama knew she was Korean, but Yumi went by her pass name and never brought up her background. Totoyama didn't care about a person's background as long as the employee did her job. Yumi was an elegant girl with good skin and a high bosom. She did not have a good figure for a kimono but had the sort of curves that men liked. It was natural that Goro-san would have noticed her.

"Goro-san, so Mozasu-san is the new manager of Seven?" Totoyama asked. "How wonderful for such a young man."

Mozasu looked down, avoiding the looks of curiosity and wonder in the eyes of the seamstresses, except for Yumi, who continued her sewing.

"Yes. Mozasu-san will need three dark suits. Use a good fabric, please. He will need some nice neckties. Something different from the others. Something elegant, older looking."

Mozasu stood in front of the three-way mirror and noticed Yumi, who was working diligently. She was lovely. Her shoulders were thin and wide and her neck long, reminding him of an illustration of a swan on a box of detergent.

When Totoyama finished taking Mozasu's measurements, the men returned to the car.

"Yumi-san, the new girl, is very pretty. A terrific ass," Goro said.

Mozasu nodded.

Goro laughed. "Finally, some interest from the hardworking boy! She'd be a good one for you."

The following week, when he returned alone for another fitting, Totoyama was finishing up with a customer and asked Yumi to get him his suit.

Yumi handed him the partially finished suit and pointed to the dressing room behind the indigo fabric curtain.

"Thank you," he said in Japanese.

She said nothing at all, but stood there coolly, waiting to be discharged from her duties by Totoyama.

When Mozasu came out, Yumi was standing in front of the mirror holding a scarlet wool pincushion. Totoyama was still occupied with another customer on the other side of the room.

Yumi looked at his neckline and cocked her head. The lapel needed some work, she noticed.

"I'm Mozasu Boku. It's a pleasure to meet you."

Yumi frowned at the lapel and pulled out a pin from the cushion to mark the place.

"You're not going to poke me, are you?" he said, laughing.

Yumi walked behind him to check the yoke.

"You're not going to speak to me? Really?"

"I'm not here to speak with you. I'm here to check your fit."

"If I buy you dinner, maybe you can find a few words for me," Mozasu said, repeating a line he'd heard Goro use on women. Mozasu had never asked a girl out. He was a manager now at Paradaisu Seven. A girl might find that impressive, he thought.

"No dinner. No thank you."

"You have to eat." This was another one of Goro's stock phrases. "You finish work around seven thirty. I know because I've been here before to pick up uniforms."

"I go to school after work. I don't have time for nonsense."

"I'm nonsense?"

"Yes."

Mozasu smiled at her. She didn't talk like anyone he knew.

"What are you studying anyway?"

"English."

"I know English. I can help you."

"You don't know English."

"Hello, Miss Yumi. My name is Moses Park. How are you?" He repeated the lines he'd practiced with Noa from his English books. "What kind of weather are you having in Tulsa, Oklahoma?" he asked. "Is it rainy or dry? I like hamburgers. Do you like hamburgers? I work at a place called Paradise."

"Where did you learn that? You didn't even finish high school," Yumi said.

"How do you know that?" He smiled.

"Never mind," she said, seeing Totoyama approaching them.

"Miss Yumi, do you like the fascinating novels of Mr. Charles Dickens? He is my brother's favorite author. I think his books are very long. There are no pictures in his books."

Yumi smiled a little, then bowed to her boss before pointing out the areas that needed work. She bowed again before leaving them to return to her sewing machine.

"I'm so sorry to keep you waiting, Mozasu-san. How are you? How is Goro-san?"

Mozasu answered her politely, and when she was nearly done with the pins, he turned and sneezed dramatically, curving his back as if to bend forward and ripping the carefully basted seams.

"Oh, I'm a fool. I'm so sorry," he said, glancing at Yumi, who was trying not to laugh. "Should I come back tomorrow or the next day? I may be able to come by before you close."

"Oh, yes, please," Totoyama said, assessing the torn seams, oblivious to the two young people studying each other. "We'll have it ready for you by tomorrow night."

17

October 1961

Mozasu leaned against the maple tree opposite Totoyama-san's work-shop, his profile only slightly obscured by its trunk. This was their ar-ranged meeting place. Three nights a week, Mozasu met Yumi after work. For over a year, he'd been accompanying her to the English class at the church, then heading back to her rented room where she'd fix them a simple dinner. Often, they would make love before Mozasu returned to Paradaisu Seven, where he worked until closing before falling asleep in his quarters at the employee dormitory.

It was already October, and though the early evening breezes had yet to lose the supple warmth of summer, the leaves on the trees were begin-ning to turn gold and shiny. The tall tree above him formed a burnished metallic lace against the blurry evening sky. Laborers and other men in uniform were returning home from work, and small children popped out of their homes to greet their fathers. In the past year, the road where To-toyama had her new workshop had improved, with families moving into the abandoned houses near the river. A local vegetable seller had done so well in his once-desolate spot that he was now able to rent the adja-cent lot for his brother-in-law to sell dry goods. The new bakery selling Portuguese-style sponge cakes, which perfumed the street invitingly, had achieved sufficient fame in Osaka to command long lines each morning.

The seamstresses at Totoyama-san's were working later than usual, so Mozasu studied his crumpled list of homework words. He'd never thought much of his memory when he was at school, but he found that he was able to remember English words and phrases very well. His recall was useful for impressing Yumi. Unlike most girls, who cared about gifts of cash, dresses, or trinkets, Mozasu's girlfriend cared only about learning. Yumi seemed happiest with him when he gave the right answers when their teacher, the Reverend John Maryman, called on him. Yumi, who wanted to live in America, believed that she had to learn English well if she was to live there one day.

There was only a little natural light left to read by, but when a man's shadow passed over him, he couldn't make out the words on the page. Noticing the solemn pair of men's work shoes a few paces from him, Mozasu glanced up.

"Is it possible that you are studying, Mo-san? *Honto?*"

"Hey, Haruki!" Mozasu shouted. "Is that you? I haven't seen you since I don't know when!" He clasped his friend's hand heartily and shook it. "I'm always asking your mother about you. She's real proud of you. Not like she's bragging, but you know, in her quiet, polite Totoyama-san way. And look at you! Haruki, the—police officer!" Mozasu whistled at Haruki's academy uniform. "You look really serious. Makes me want to commit a crime. You're not going to tell on me, right?"

Haruki smiled and hit Mozasu on the shoulder lightly with his fist, feeling shy around his old school friend. It had been difficult to keep away from Mozasu, but Haruki had done so because his feelings for him had been too strong. There had been other infatuations over the years and encounters with strangers. Recently, there was a fellow at the academy, Koji, another tough and funny guy. As he had done with Mozasu, Haruki did his best to keep away from Koji, because he knew well enough to draw a thick line between what was public and what was private.

"What the hell are you doing around here? Don't you live near the academy?"

Haruki nodded. "I have the week off."

"So? When do you become a cop? I mean detective." Mozasu chuckled, pretending to bow formally.

"Two years."

Upon seeing Mozasu by the maple tree, Haruki had been afraid to cross the street. The mere image of him had been overwhelming. As a boy, Haruki had worshipped Mozasu, who had saved him from the anguish of school. When Mozasu had dropped out to work for Goro-san and then disappeared into his job, Haruki had felt the loss like a deadly punch to the chest. After Mozasu left to work at the pachinko parlors, the sheep, witches, and ghouls of their high school emerged to the fore, forcing Haruki to retreat to any available sanctuary. During his free periods, he had filled his burgeoning sketchbooks with pencil drawings in the safety of a kindhearted art teacher's classroom. Home was always the same: His younger brother would never grow up, and his mother could never quit working until her eyes failed. His art teacher, whose husband and brothers were police detectives, had given Haruki the suggestion to go to the police academy. Interestingly, the teacher had not been wrong. Haruki loved the academy with its rules and hierarchy. He did what he was told to do, and he did it very well. Also, it was easier just to start again in a new place where no one knew you.

"Why are you standing out here?" Haruki asked. The sun was very low, and its orange-red color moved him.

"I'm waiting for Yumi. She works for your mother. No one's supposed to know about us, though. Of course, I don't think your mother would care. I'm not such a terrible guy."

"I won't say anything," Haruki said, thinking that Mozasu had become more appealing. He had always admired Mozasu's smooth brow, the strong nose, and neat white teeth, but in his manager suit he looked like a grown man in charge of his life. Haruki wanted to follow him.

The workshop windows were still brightly lit, and the girls labored with their dark heads bowed at their worktables. Mozasu could imagine Yumi's thin fingers flying across the fabric. When she focused on her work, Yumi could not be distracted. She was like that about everything and could be left alone working for hours. Mozasu couldn't imagine being so quiet all the time; he would miss the bustle of the pachinko parlor. He loved all the moving pieces of his large, noisy business. His Presbyterian minister father had believed in a divine design, and Mozasu believed that life was like this game where the player could adjust the dials yet also expect the uncertainty of factors he couldn't control. He understood why his customers wanted to play something that looked fixed but which also left room for randomness and hope.

"Do you see her?" Mozasu pointed with pride. "There! She's the fourth desk from the—"

"Yumi-san. Yes, I've met her. She's a good seamstress. A very elegant person. You're lucky," Haruki said. "And how's your work? Have you made your fortune?"

"You should come by. I'm at the Paradaisu Seven now. Come tomorrow. I'm there all day and night nearly, except for when I meet Yumi and take her to the English class."

"I don't know. I have to see my brother while I'm home."

"I hear he's been a little down."

"That's why I came home. Mother said he's getting a little strange. Not giving her trouble or anything, but she says that he talks less and less. The doctors don't know what to do. They want him to go live in an institution. They say he might be happier living with other people like himself, but I doubt that. Those places can be—" Haruki sucked wind between his clenched teeth. "Of course, Mother would never allow it. Daisuke is a very good child." Haruki said this quietly, having known for as long as he could remember that Daisuke would be his responsibility after his mother could no longer care for him. Who Haruki married would be determined by her willingness to be good to Daisuke and his aging mother.

"Yumi says that it might be good for him in America. Then again, she thinks everyone is better off in America. She said it's not like it is here in Japan, where a person can't be different."

Mozasu thought his girlfriend was irrationally biased in favor of America and anything from America. Like his brother, Noa, Yumi thought English was the most important language and America was the best country.

"Yumi said there are better doctors in America." Mozasu shrugged.

"That's probably true."

Haruki smiled, having often wished that he could live somewhere else, where he didn't know anyone.

As Yumi walked toward the meeting spot, she recognized her employer's older son. It would have been awkward to turn around so she stayed her course.

"You know Haruki-san," Mozasu said to Yumi, smiling. "He was my only friend in high school. And now he will be fighting crime!"

Yumi nodded, smiling uncomfortably.

"Yumi-san. It's good to see you again. I'm grateful to you that I got to see my friend again after so many, many years."

"You are home from the academy, Haruki-san?" Yumi kept her posture both formal and demure.

Haruki nodded, then made excuses about Daisuke waiting for him at home. Before leaving them, however, Haruki promised to visit Mozasu at the pachinko parlor the following morning.

Their English class met in the large conference room in the offices of the new Korean church, built recently with large donations from some wealthy *yakiniku* families. Despite his European name, the teacher, John Maryman, was a Korean who had been adopted as an infant by American missionaries. English was his first language. As a result of his superior diet, rich in both protein and calcium, John was significantly taller than the Koreans and Japanese. At nearly six feet, he caused a commotion wherever he went, as if a giant had descended from heaven. Though he spoke Japanese and Korean proficiently, he spoke both languages with an American accent. In addition to his size, his mannerisms were distinctly foreign. John liked to tease people he didn't know well, and if something was funny, he laughed louder than most. If it hadn't been for his patient Korean wife, who possessed masterful *noonchi* and was able to explain to others tactfully that John just didn't know any better, he would have gotten into trouble far more often for his many cultural missteps. For a Presbyterian pastor, John seemed far too jovial. He was a good man whose faith and intelligence were irreproachable. His mother, Cynthia Maryman, an automobile tire heiress, had sent him to Princeton and Yale

Divinity School, and to his parents' delight, he had returned to Asia to spread the gospel. His lovely coloring was more olive than golden and his fringed, ink-black eyes, constantly bemused, invited women to linger in his presence.

A girl normally hard to win over, Yumi admired her teacher, whom all the students called Pastor John. To her, John represented a Korean being from a better world where Koreans weren't whores, drunks, or thieves. Yumi's mother, a prostitute and alcoholic, had slept with men for money or drinks, and her father, a pimp and a violent drunk, had been imprisoned often for his criminality. Yumi felt that her three elder half sisters were as sexually indiscriminate and common as barn animals. Her younger brother had died as a child, and soon after, at fourteen years old, Yumi ran away from home with her younger sister and somehow supported them with small jobs in textile factories until the younger sister died. Over the years, Yumi had become an excellent seamstress. She refused to acknowledge her family, who lived in the worst sections of Osaka. If she spotted a woman who had even a passing resemblance to her mother on any street, Yumi would cross to the other side or turn around to walk away. From watching American movies, she had decided that one day she would live in California and planned on becoming a seamstress in Hollywood. She knew Koreans who had returned to North Korea and many more who had gone back to the South, yet she could not muster any affection for either nation. To her, being Korean was just another horrible encumbrance, much like being poor or having a shameful family you could not cast off. Why would she ever live there? But she could not imagine clinging to Japan, which was like a beloved stepmother who refused to love you, so Yumi dreamed of Los Angeles. Until Mozasu, with his swagger and enormous dreams, Yumi had never let a man into her bed, and now that she had attached herself to him, she wanted both of them to go to America to make another life where they wouldn't be despised or ignored. She could not imagine raising a child here.

The English class had fifteen pupils who attended three nights a week. Until Mozasu showed up, Yumi had been Pastor John's best student. Mozasu had an enormous advantage over her since he had been uninten-

tionally studying with his brother, Noa, for years by being his at-home
English quiz partner, but Yumi did not mind. She was relieved that he was
better than she was at this, that he made more money than she did, and
that he was relentlessly kind to her.

Each class began with Pastor John going around the room asking each
person a series of questions.

"Moses," Pastor John said in his teaching voice, "how is the pachinko
parlor? Did you make a lot of money today?"

Mozasu laughed. "Yes, Pastor John. Today, I earned lot money. Tomorrow, I make more! Do you need money?"

"No, thank you, Moses. But please remember to help the poor, Moses.
There are many among us."

"The pachinko money isn't mine, Pastor John. My boss is rich, but I
am not a rich man yet. One day, I will rich."

"You will *be* rich."

"Yes, I will *be* rich man, Pastor John. A man must have money."

John smiled at Moses kindly, wanting to disabuse him of such idola-
trous notions, but he turned to Yumi.

"Yumi, how many uniforms did you make today?"

Yumi smiled and color rushed to her face.

"Today, I made two vests, Pastor John."

John moved on to the others, encouraging the reserved students to talk
to each other as well as to the class. He wanted the Koreans to speak well;
he wanted no one ever to look down on them. He had left his beautifully
comfortable life in Princeton, New Jersey, because he felt sorry for the
impoverished Koreans in Japan. In his wonderful childhood, filled with
the warmth of his loving parents, he had always felt bad for the Koreans
who had lost their nation for good. People like Moses and Yumi had never
been to Korea. There was always talk of Koreans going back home, but
in a way, all of them had lost the home in their minds for good. His parents had adopted him alone, and he had no known siblings. Because John
had always felt so happy with his parents, he'd felt guilty that many others
hadn't been chosen the way he was. Why was that? He wanted to know.
There were unhappy adoptions, to be sure, but John knew his lot was bet-

ter than almost anyone's. "Chosen" was always the word his mother had used with him.

"We chose you, our darling John. You had the loveliest smile, even as a small baby. The ladies at the orphanage loved holding you, because you were such an affectionate child."

Teaching English class wasn't part of his job as a pastor. He didn't proselytize his students, most of whom were not parishioners. John loved the sound of English words, the sounds of Americans talking. He wanted to give this to the poor Koreans in Osaka. He wanted them to have another language that wasn't Japanese.

Like his students, John was born in Japan to Korean parents. His biological parents had left him with their landlord. John didn't know how old he was exactly. His parents had given him the birthday of Martin Luther, November 10. The only fact he knew about his birth parents was that they had left their rented room in the early hours of the morning without paying the rent and had left him behind. His adoptive mother said this must have been because the landlord had money and shelter, and wherever his biological parents were going, they may not have been able to give these things to him. Their sacrifice of leaving him was an act of love, his mother had said every time John had asked about them. Nevertheless, whenever John saw an older Korean woman or man who could be the age of his parents, he wondered. He could not help it. He wished he could give them money now, for John was a very wealthy man, and he wished he could meet his biological parents and give them a house to keep them warm and food to eat when they were hungry.

As Pastor John teased the two sisters in the back about their fondness for sweets, Mozasu knocked his knee gently against Yumi's. Mozasu had long thighs, and he had to move his thigh only a little to graze the skirt fabric covering Yumi's pretty legs. She tapped him back in slight annoyance, though she did not mind.

Pastor John had asked the younger sister about what she did when it rained, and instead of listening to the girl stumble in English, casting about for the word "umbrella," Mozasu found himself staring at Yumi. He loved to look at her soft profile, the way her dark, sad eyes met her high cheekbones.

"Moses, how can you learn English if you are just staring at Yumi?" John asked, laughing.

Yumi blushed again. "Behave," she whispered to Mozasu in Japanese.

"I cannot stop, Pastor John. I love her," Mozasu declared, and John clapped in delight.

Yumi looked down at her notes.

"Will you two marry?" Pastor John asked.

Yumi appeared stunned at this question, though she shouldn't have been. Pastor John was liable to say anything.

"She will marry me," Mozasu said. "I am confident."

"What?" Yumi cried.

The women in the back were near tears laughing. Two men in the middle of the class pounded on their desks, cheering loudly.

"This is fun," John said. "I think we are witnessing a proposal. 'Pro-po-sal' means an invitation to marry."

"Of course, you will marry me, Yumi-chan. You love me, and I love you very much. We will marry. You see," Mozasu said calmly in English, "I have plan."

Yumi rolled her eyes. He knew she wanted to go to America, but he wanted to stay in Osaka and open his own pachinko parlor in a few years. He intended to buy his mother, aunt, uncle, and grandmother a huge house when he was rich. He said that if they wanted to move back to Korea, he would make so much money that he would build them castles. He couldn't make this kind of money in Los Angeles, he'd explained. He couldn't leave his family, and Yumi knew this.

"You and I love each other. *Soo nee*, Yumi-chan?" Mozasu smiled at her and took her hand.

The pupils clapped loudly and stamped their feet as if watching a baseball game.

Yumi bent her head down, mortified by his behavior, but she couldn't be angry at him. She could never be angry with him. He was the only friend she'd ever had.

"We'll have to plan a wedding then," John said.

18

Tokyo, March 1962

Is he married?" Akiko asked. Her eyes brightened with anticipation.

"Yes. He's married, and his wife is expecting in a few months," Noa answered, almost flattening his voice.

"I want to know more about your family. C'mon," she pleaded.

Noa got up to get dressed.

She couldn't help it. Akiko was training to be a sociologist. She collected pieces of data, and her lover was her favorite puzzle. Yet the more she inquired, the more reticent he grew. When he answered her in his pithy manner, she had a habit of saying, "*Sooo?*" as if the facts of his life were something marvelous to behold. Everything about him was fascinating to her, but Noa didn't want to be fascinating. He wanted just to be with her. He didn't mind when she turned her headlights on strangers; it was far more interesting to hear her attempts at demystifying others.

He was Akiko's first Korean lover. In bed, she wanted him to speak Korean.

"How do you say 'pretty'?" she'd asked just a few hours before.

"*Yeh-puh-dah.*" Such a simple word felt strange in his mouth when he'd said it to her. Akiko was stunning; "pretty" wouldn't suffice in describing her beauty. "*Ah-reum-dop-da,*" he should have said, but Noa didn't. She was an excellent social scientist not to have asked for the Korean word for love, because he would have no doubt revealed his hesitation in the translation.

Not wishing to be a specimen under her glass, Noa didn't talk about his mother, who had peddled kimchi and, later, confections so he could go to school, or his father, who'd died from harsh imprisonment during the colonial era. These aspects of his biography had happened a long time ago as far as he was concerned. He wasn't ashamed of his past; it wasn't that. He resented her curiosity. Akiko was a Japanese girl from an upper-class family who had grown up in Minami-Azabu; her father owned a trading company and her mother played tennis with expatriates in a private club. Akiko adored rough sex, foreign books, and talking. She had pursued him, and Noa, who had never had a serious girlfriend before, did not know what to make of her.

"Come back to me," she said flirtatiously, fingering her white cotton top.

Noa retreated to the futon.

After making love between classes, they had been lolling in Noa's rented room—an exceptionally large living space for a university student, with two square windows that let in the morning light and immense floor space for a double futon and a furry beige rug. Thick piles of novels covered his large pine desk—Dickens, Tolstoy, Balzac, and Hugo. The fancy electric lamp with a green glass shade was off. Noa couldn't have conceived of anything as nice as this room and could not believe his luck at the incredibly low rent. Hansu's friend was the landlord, and it had come furnished with new, elegant things—ideal for a student studying literature and English. Noa had had to bring only his clothes packed in his father's old suitcase.

Akiko claimed that none of the other students lived in a place as nice, even if they lived at home in Tokyo. She lived in a beautiful apartment with her family in Minami-Azabu, but in a room half the size of his; she spent all her free time between classes at his place. Her things were on his desk, in his bathroom, and in his closet. The commonplace idea that girls were neater than boys was not true in her case.

Despite Akiko's best efforts, Noa couldn't do it again so soon. Embarrassed, he finished dressing. She, too, rose to fix herself a cup of tea.

There was no kitchen here, but Noa had an electric kettle that Hansu had bought for him. All Noa had to do was study, Hansu had said. "Learn everything you can. Learn for all the Koreans, for every Korean who couldn't go to a school like Waseda." Hansu paid the tuition in full before the start of each term. Freed from worrying about money, Noa studied more fervently than he ever had. He reread books and studied as many critical essays as he could find. His only relief from work was this lovely girl whom he had fallen for. She was brilliant, sensual, and creative.

"What is he like?" Akiko asked, sprinkling tea leaves into the iron teapot.

"Who?"

"Koh Hansu, your benefactor. You're leaving me in ten minutes to meet him. You do this on the first of the month."

Noa hadn't told her, but of course, she had guessed. Akiko wanted to meet Hansu. She had asked numerous times if she could tag along, but Noa did not think it was appropriate.

"He's a good friend of the family. I told you. My mother and grand-mother knew him before they came to Japan. He's from Jeju, which is not very far from Busan. He owns a construction company."

"Is he good-looking?"

"What?"

"Like you. Korean men are really good-looking."

Noa smiled. What could he say to this? Of course, not all Korean men were good-looking, and not all Korean men were bad-looking, either. They were just men. Akiko liked to make positive generalizations about Koreans and other foreigners. She reserved her harshest words for well-off Japanese.

Akiko put down her teacup and pushed him down on the futon play-fully, and Noa fell on his back. She straddled him and removed her shirt. She wore a white cotton bra and panties. She looked so beautiful, he thought. Her black hair fell like glossy, iridescent feathers around her face.

"Is he like you?" She rubbed against him.

"No, no. We're very different." Noa exhaled and removed her gently from his hips, puzzled himself by his answer. "I mean, I don't know. He's a generous man. I told you before: He doesn't have a son, and his daughters don't want to go to university, so he has been supporting me. I intend to pay him back. He's helped my family in difficult times. He's my benefactor; that's all."

"Why do you have to pay him back? Isn't he loaded?"

"I don't know." Noa went to get his socks from the dresser. "It doesn't matter. It's a debt. I will pay him back."

"Don't you want to stay with me?" Akiko removed her brassiere to reveal her champagne glass–sized tits.

"You are tempting me, my beauty," he said. "But I must get going. I will see you tomorrow, *nee*?"

There was absolutely no time to have sex again, he told himself, even if he could get another erection, which he doubted.

"Can't I come and meet him, Noa-chan? When will I meet your family?"

"He's not my family, and I don't know. I haven't met yours, either."

"You don't want to meet Mother and Father. They are racists," she said. "*Honto desu.*"

"Oh," Noa said. "I will see you tomorrow. Lock up, please."

The *sushi-ya* was less than a mile away from his place. The interior was recently repaneled in fresh cedar, and the walls gave off the faint scent of clean, new wood. Hansu preferred to meet Noa here each month in the private room in the back. No one ever disturbed them except to bring them course after course of exceptional delicacies, brought in from various remote fishing villages in Japan.

Normally, the two men talked about his classes, because Hansu was curious about what it was like to attend such a wondrous and fabled university. He had never attended secondary school or university. Hansu had taught himself both how to read and write Korean and Japanese from books, and as soon as he could afford it, Hansu had hired tutors to learn the kanji and *hanja* necessary to read difficult Japanese and Korean newspapers. He knew many rich men, strong men, and brave men, yet he was most impressed with educated men who could write well. He sought friendships with great journalists, because he admired their well-composed thoughts and points of view on the issues of the day. Hansu did not believe in nationalism, religion, or even love, but he trusted in education. Above all, he believed that a man must learn constantly. He loathed waste of any kind, and when all three of his daughters forsook school for baubles and gossip, he grew to despise his wife, who had allowed this to happen. The girls had good minds and unlimited resources, and she had let them throw these things away like garbage. The girls were lost to him, but he now had Noa. It thrilled him that Noa could read and write English so beautifully—a language he knew was essential in the world. Noa had recommended books to him, and Hansu had read them, because he wanted to know the things his son knew.

The young man's extraordinary scholarship was something Hansu knew he had to nurture. Hansu was not sure what he wanted Noa to do when he graduated; he was careful not to say too much, because it was clear that Noa had some of his own ideas. Hansu wanted to back him, the way he wanted to back good business plans.

The two sat cross-legged on the pristine tatami floor with a low acacia wood table between them.

"You should have more of the sea urchin. The chef had it brought for us from Hokkaido last night," Hansu said. He enjoyed watching Noa, a poor student, eat these rare things that he himself consumed regularly.

Noa nodded in appreciation and finished his portion. He didn't enjoy eating this way or even this kind of food. Noa knew how proper Japanese people behaved and could imitate their mannerisms faultlessly, so he ate whatever was put in front of him and was grateful. However, he preferred to eat a nourishing bowl of simple food quickly and be done with it. He ate the way most working Koreans did: Tasty food was merely necessary fuel, something to be eaten in a rush so you could return to your work. Well-off Japanese considered this sort of eating— high volume, strong flavors, and deliberate speed—nothing short of vulgar. In his benefactor's presence, Noa aped the ruling-class Japanese, not wishing to disappoint Hansu, yet Noa was simply not interested in food or sitting still very long for a meal. Akiko teased him about this as well, but they did not go to luxurious restaurants, so it was of little consequence in their relationship.

Noa liked being with Hansu, but it was tedious watching another person drink while eating so little. Obviously, Hansu could drink a great deal and somehow manage a successful construction company, but Noa was suspicious of any form of drinking. As a little boy on his way to school, he used to have to step over grown men who were sleeping off their drunken binges from the night before. When he worked as a bookkeeper for the real estate company in Ikaino, he had seen many fathers unable to pay the rent, resulting in their families being thrown out of their homes—the trouble having started with a few harmless drinks on payday. And every winter, homeless alcoholic Koreans froze to death near the Sumida River, their bodies unaware of the deadly frost. Noa didn't drink. Hansu could drink bottles of sake or soju without any visible effect, so in accordance with Korean tradition, Noa poured his elder's drink, cup after cup, dragging the precious meal out even further.

As Noa was pouring the sake into the Oribe sake cup, the gentle knock on the paper screen door startled him.

"Enter," Hansu said.

"Excuse me, Koh-san," said the young waitress, who had no makeup on. She wore a simple indigo day kimono with a mushroom-colored obi.

"Yes?" Hansu said.

Noa smiled at the waitress, who looked and behaved like a well-mannered girl child.

"There is a lady who says she would like to say hello to you."

"Really?" Hansu said. "To me?"

"Yes." The waitress nodded.

"Very well," Hansu said. Few people knew that he ate at this restaurant. It was possible that one of his boss's secretaries was bringing a private message for him, but that was odd, because more commonly, young men from the company were sent on such errands. Hansu's driver and bodyguard were outside the restaurant standing guard; they would have prevented anyone dangerous from reaching him. They would have examined her for certain.

The waitress closed the door, and in a few moments knocked again.

This time, Noa rose to his feet and opened the door himself. It felt good to stretch his legs.

"Akiko," Noa said, his mouth momentarily agape.

"Hello," she said, standing by the waitress, waiting to be invited in.

"Is this your friend, Noa?" Hansu asked, smiling at this gorgeous thing who looked Japanese.

"Yes."

"Welcome. Please have a seat. You wanted to see me?"

"Noa thought I should stop by and say hello to his benefactor, so I came by at his insistence," Akiko said, smiling.

"Yes," Noa said, not sure why he was agreeing to this story but lacking an alternative narrative. "I should have mentioned that Akiko might be stopping by. I'm sorry if I took you by surprise."

"Not at all. I'm very happy to meet a friend of Noa. You must join us for lunch."

Hansu looked up at the waitress, who was still standing by the door.

"Please bring another setting and a sake cup for Noa's friend," Hansu said, feeling both curious and pleased that the boy would want him to meet his girlfriend. He wanted to welcome her.

Immediately, a place setting and a wine cup appeared before her. The chef himself brought them a dish of fried oysters sprinkled with transparent flakes of English salt. Noa poured Hansu a cup of wine, then Hansu poured a cup for Akiko.

"To new friends," Hansu said, raising his cup.

19

The young couple remained standing by the restaurant door as Hansu got into his car. Akiko and Noa bowed deep from the waist in the direction of the rear passenger seat, where Hansu was seated. The chauffeur closed the passenger door, bowed to the couple, then got behind the wheel to take Hansu to his next meeting.

"I don't see why you're so upset," Akiko said, still smiling like a proper Japanese schoolgirl, though Hansu was already gone. "Koh-san is wonderful. I'm glad I met him."

"You lied," Noa said, his voice trembling. He didn't want to speak for fear of saying something awful, but he couldn't help himself. "I . . . I didn't invite you to the lunch. Why did you say that to Koh-san? The lunch could have turned out badly. This man is important to our family. He's supporting my education. I owe him a great deal."

"Nothing happened. It was an ordinary lunch with relatives at a fancy *sushi-ya*. Big deal. I've been to dozens of them. I behaved perfectly. He liked me," Akiko said, puzzled by his irritation. She had always been confident of her ability to win grown-ups over.

"Are you ashamed of me?" Akiko asked, laughing, strangely delighted to be having a fight with Noa, who was normally so calm and silent that she didn't know what went through his mind. Besides, it was his fault: He was so difficult to understand, she'd felt compelled to go to this lunch without an invitation. She hadn't done it to upset him. He should have been pleased that she cared enough about him to get to know his friends.

"You would never have let me. I was right to go." She touched his arm, and he moved away.

"Akiko, why, why do you always have to be right? Why do you always have to have the upper hand? Why can't I decide when and where you can meet someone personal to me? I would never do this to you. I would respect your privacy," Noa sputtered, and he put his hand over his mouth.

Akiko stared at him, not understanding. She was not used to a man saying no to her. His cheeks were flushed; he was having trouble getting the words out. This wasn't the same man who would explain difficult passages of her sociology texts to her or help her with her statistics homework. Her gentle and wise Noa was furious.

"What is it? Is it that you are embarrassed that you are Korean?"

"What?" Noa took a step back. He looked around to see if anyone could hear their argument. "What are you saying?" He looked at her as if she was deranged.

Akiko grew calm and she spoke slowly.

"I'm not embarrassed that you are Korean. I think it's great that you are Korean. It doesn't bother me at all. It might bother any ignorant person or even my racist parents, but I love that you are Korean. Koreans are smart and hardworking, and the men are so handsome," she said, smiling at him like she was flirting. "You are upset. Listen, if you want, I can arrange for you to meet my whole family. They'd be lucky to meet such an excellent Korean. It would change the way they—"

"No," he said, shaking his head. "No. No more of this."

Akiko moved closer to him. An older woman passed by and glanced at them, but Akiko didn't pay her any attention.

"Noa-chan, why are you so angry with me? You know that I think you're the best. Let's go home, and you can fuck me."

Noa stared at her. She would always believe that he was someone else, that he wasn't himself but some fanciful idea of a foreign person; she would always feel like she was someone special because she had condescended to be with someone everyone else hated. His presence would prove to the world that she was a good person, an educated person, a liberal person. Noa didn't care about being Korean when he was with her; in fact, he didn't care about being Korean or Japanese with anyone. He wanted to be, to be just himself, whatever that meant; he wanted to forget himself sometimes. But that wasn't possible. It would never be possible with her.

"I will pack up your things and have them sent to your house by messenger. I don't want to see you anymore. Please never come see me again."

"Noa, what are you saying?" Akiko said, astonished. "Is this the Korean temper that I've never seen before?" She laughed.

"You and I. It cannot be."

"Why?"

"Because it cannot." There was nothing else he could think of, and he wanted to spare her the cruelty of what he had learned, because she would not believe that she was no different than her parents, that seeing him as only Korean—good or bad—was the same as seeing him only as a bad Korean. She could not see his humanity, and Noa realized that this was what he wanted most of all: to be seen as human.

"He's your father, isn't he?" Akiko said. "He looks exactly like you. You told me your father died, but he's not dead. You just didn't want him to meet me, because you didn't want me to meet your yakuza papa. And you didn't want me to know that he's a gangster. How else do you explain that ridiculous car and uniformed chauffeur? How else can he put you up in that enormous apartment? Even my father can't afford that apartment, and he owns a trading company! Come on, Noa, how can you get mad at me when all I wanted was to learn more about you? I don't care about what he does. It doesn't matter—I don't mind that you're Korean. Don't you see?"

Noa turned around and walked away. He walked until he couldn't hear her scream his name anymore. He walked rigidly and calmly, not believing that a person you loved—yes, he had loved her—could end up being someone you never knew. Perhaps he had known all along about her, but he couldn't see it. He just couldn't. When Noa reached the train station, he went down the stairs to the platform slowly. He felt like he might fall down. He would take the first train to Osaka.

*   *   *

It was early evening when he reached the house. His Aunt Kyunghee started when she answered the door. He was distraught and wanted to speak to his mother. Uncle Yoseb was sleeping in the back room, and his mother was in the front room sewing. He wouldn't take off his coat. When Sunja came to the door, Noa asked if they could go outside to talk.

"What? What's the matter?" Sunja asked, putting on her shoes.

Noa wouldn't answer. He went outside to wait for her.

Noa led her away from the shopping street to a spot where there were very few people.

"Is it true?" Noa asked his mother. "About Koh Hansu."

He couldn't say the words out loud exactly, but he had to know.

"Why he pays for my school, and why he's always been around. You were together—" he said. It was easier to say this than the other thing.

Sunja had been buttoning her faded woolen coat, and she stopped walking and stared at her son's face. She understood. Yoseb had been right all along. She shouldn't have allowed Hansu to pay for his education. But she hadn't been able to find another way. Noa had gone to work each day and saved every bit of his earnings and studied every night until his eyes were red-rimmed in the morning, and he had finally passed the entrance examination for Waseda.

How could she have said no? There were no loans for this. There was no one else who could help. She had always been afraid of Hansu's presence in Noa's life. Would that money keep Noa tied to Hansu? she had wondered. But not to take the money. Was that possible?

A child like Noa, a child who worked so hard, deserved to fulfill his wish to study and to become someone. Throughout his life, Noa's teachers had said that he was an ideal student, far smarter than anyone else; "A credit to your country," they'd said, and this had pleased her husband, Isak, so much, because he knew the Japanese thought Koreans were worth so little, fit only for the dirty, dangerous, and demeaning tasks. Isak had said that Noa would help the Korean people by his excellence of character and workmanship, and that no one would be able to look down on him. Isak had encouraged the boy to know everything as well as he could, and

Noa, a good son, had tried his best to be the very best. Isak had loved the boy so much. Sunja could not say anything, and her mouth was dry. All she could think of was how good Isak had been to give Noa a name and to give them his protection.

"How could this be?" Noa shook his head. "How could you betray him?"

Sunja knew he meant Isak, and she tried to explain.

"I met him before I met your father. I didn't know Koh Hansu was married. I was a girl, and I believed that he would marry me. But he couldn't, because he was already married. When I was pregnant with you, your father, Isak, stayed at our inn; he married me even when he knew. Baek Isak wanted you as his son. Blood doesn't matter. Can you understand that? When you are young, you can make serious mistakes. You can trust the wrong people, but I am so grateful to have you as my son and so grateful to your father for marrying me—"

"No." He looked at her with disdain. "This kind of mistake I cannot understand. Why didn't you tell me sooner? Who else knows?" His voice grew colder.

"I didn't think it was necessary to tell anyone. Listen to me, Noa, the man who chose to be your father is Baek—"

Noa acted like he didn't even hear her.

"Then Uncle Yoseb and Aunt Kyunghee—do they know?" His mind couldn't accept that no one had told him this.

"We've never discussed it."

"And Mozasu? He is Baek Isak's son? He doesn't look like me."

Sunja nodded. Noa called his father Baek Isak; he'd never done that before.

"My half brother then—"

"I met Koh Hansu before your father. I've always been faithful to Baek Isak—my only husband. Koh Hansu found us when your father was in prison. He was worried that we didn't have money."

A part of her had always feared Noa finding out, but even against such a possibility, she had trusted that Noa would understand, because he was so smart and had always been such an easy child—the one who never made her worry. But the young man who stood in front of her was like cold metal, and he looked at her as if he could not remember who she was to him.

Noa stopped moving and took a deep breath, then exhaled, because he felt so dizzy.

"That's why he's always helping us—why he found that farm for us during the war. Why he brought us things."

"He was trying to make sure that you were okay. He wanted to help you. It had nothing to do with me. I was someone he knew a long time ago."

"You know that he's a yakuza? Is that right?"

"No. No, I do not know that. I do not know what he does. He used to be a wholesale fish broker who lived in Osaka when I knew him. He bought fish in Korea for Japanese companies. He was a businessman. He owns a construction company and restaurants, I think. I don't know what else he does. I hardly ever speak to him. You know that—"

"Yakuza are the filthiest people in Japan. They are thugs; they are common criminals. They frighten shopkeepers; they sell drugs; they control prostitution; and they hurt innocent people. All the worst Koreans are members of these gangs. I took money for my education from a yakuza, and you thought this was acceptable? I will never be able to wash this dirt from my name. You can't be very bright," he said. "How can you make something clean from something dirty? And now, you have made me dirty," Noa said quietly, as if he was learning this as he was saying it to her. "All my life, I have had Japanese telling me that my blood is Korean— that Koreans are angry, violent, cunning, and deceitful criminals. All my life, I had to endure this. I tried to be as honest and humble as Baek Isak was; I never raised my voice. But this blood, my blood is Korean, and now I learn that my blood is yakuza blood. I can never change this, no matter what I do. It would have been better if I were never born. How could you have ruined my life? How could you be so imprudent? A foolish mother and a criminal father. I am cursed."

Sunja looked at him with shock. If he had been a little boy, she might have told him to hush, to mind his manners, never to dishonor your parents, but she couldn't say that now. How could she defend gangsters? There were organized criminals everywhere, she supposed, and she knew that they did bad things, but she knew that many of the Koreans had to work for the gangs because there were no other jobs for them. The government and good companies wouldn't hire Koreans, even educated ones. All these men had to work, and there were many of them who lived in their neighborhood who were far kinder and more respectful than the men who didn't work at all. She couldn't say this to her son, however, because Noa was someone who had studied, labored, and tried to lift himself out of their street, and he thought all the men who hadn't done so weren't very bright, either. He would not understand. Her son could not feel compassion for those who did not try.

"Noa," Sunja said, "forgive me. *Umma* is sorry. I just wanted you to go to school. I know how much you wanted that. I know how hard you—"

"You. You took my life away. I am no longer myself," he said, pointing his finger at her. He turned around and walked back to the train.

20

Osaka, April 1962

They didn't receive letters often, and when one arrived, the family gathered around Yoseb's bedside to hear it read. He was lying on his back, his head propped up by a buckwheat-filled pillow. Of course, Sunja recognized her son's handwriting on the envelope. Though illiterate, she was able to make out her name and signs in both Japanese and Korean. Normally, Kyunghee read the letters out loud, asking Yoseb for help when there were difficult characters she could not recognize. Yoseb's vision had worsened; he was unable to read his beloved newspapers, so Kyunghee read them to him. If Kyunghee described the image of the character, Yoseb could sometimes guess it from the context. Kyunghee read in her clear, mild-toned voice. Sunja's face was white with fear, and Yangjin stared at the thin sheet of paper, wondering what her grandson had to say. Yoseb's eyes were closed, but he was awake.

Umma,

I have withdrawn from Waseda. I have moved out of the apartment. I am in a new city and have found a job.

This may be very difficult for you to understand, but I ask that you not look for me. I have thought about this very deeply. This is the best way for me to live with myself and to maintain my integrity. I want to start a new life, and to do that there is no other way.

I have had to pay some bills in starting out, and as soon as I earn some more money, I will send you something as often as I can. I will not neglect my duties. Also, I will earn enough money to repay Koh Hansu. Please make sure that he never reaches me. I do not wish to know him.

I send regards to you, Uncle Yoseb, Aunt Kyunghee, Grandmother, and Mozasu. I am sorry I did not get a chance to say good-bye properly, but I will not be returning. Please do not worry about me. This cannot be helped.

Your son,
Noa

Noa had written his brief message in simple Japanese rather than Korean, a language he had never written well. When Kyunghee finished reading, no one said anything. Yangjin patted her daughter's knee, then got up to go to the kitchen to fix dinner, leaving Kyunghee to put her arm around her sister-in-law, who now sat wordless and pale.

Yoseb exhaled. Would anything bring the boy back? he wondered. He did not think so. This life had too much loss. When Isak died, Yoseb had thought of his brother's little boys and vowed to watch over them. Noa and Mozasu were not his own, but what did that matter? He had wanted to be a good man for them. Then after the war, after his accident, he had resigned himself to death and looked forward only to the boys' future. The stupid heart could not help but hope. Life had seemed almost bearable; though Yoseb was nearly cut off from the living, confined to his pallet, his family had persisted. Life continued. To Yoseb, Noa had seemed so much like Isak that it had been possible to forget that the boy's blood father was someone else—someone wholly different from his gentle Isak. But now, the poor boy had learned somehow that he had descended from another line. The boy had decided to leave them, and his departure was punishment. Yoseb could understand the boy's anger, but he wanted another chance to talk to him, to tell Noa that a man must learn to forgive—to know what is important, that to live without forgiveness was a kind of death with breathing and movement. However, Yoseb did not have enough energy to rise from his pallet, let alone search for his dear nephew, a boy who was like his own flesh.

"Could he have gone to the North?" Kyunghee asked her husband. "He wouldn't do something like that, isn't that so?"

Sunja glanced at her brother-in-law.

"No, no." Yoseb's pillow made a gravelly noise as he moved his head from side to side.

Sunja covered her eyes with her hands. No one who went to the North came back. There was still hope as long as he had not gone there. Kim Changho had left in the last month of 1959, and in more than two years, they'd heard from him only twice. Kyunghee rarely spoke of him, but it made sense that her first thought was Pyongyang.

"And Mozasu? What do we tell him?" Kyunghee asked. Still holding Noa's letter, she patted Sunja's back with her free hand.

"Wait until he asks about him. The boy is so busy as it is. If he asks, just say you don't know. Then later, if you have to, tell him that his brother ran away," Yoseb said, his eyes still shut. "Tell him that school was too hard for Noa, so he left Tokyo and he was too ashamed to return home after all those attempts to get into school. For all we know, that could be the reason." It sickened Yoseb to say these words, so he said nothing else.

Sunja couldn't speak. Mozasu would never believe that, yet she couldn't tell him the truth, either, because he would go look for his brother. And she could not tell Mozasu about Hansu. Mozasu was hardly sleeping lately, because he had so many responsibilities at work, and Yumi had miscarried only a few weeks before. The boy did not need any more worries.

Since that evening when Noa had come home from school to speak to her, Sunja had thought daily of going to Tokyo to talk to him, but she could not do so. A month had passed and now this. What did he say to her? *You took my life away.* He had withdrawn from Waseda. Sunja felt unable to think, to breathe even. All she wanted was to see her son again. If that wasn't possible, it would be better to die.

Wiping her wet hands on her apron, Yangjin came out of the kitchen and told them that dinner was ready. Yangjin and Kyunghee stared at Sunja.

"You should eat something," Kyunghee said.

Sunja shook her head. "I have to go. I have to find him."

Kyunghee clutched her arm, but Sunja broke free and got up.

"Let her go to him," Yangjin said.

It turned out that Hansu lived only thirty minutes away by train. His preposterously immense house stood out prominently on the quiet street. A pair of tall, carved mahogany doors, flanked by grand picture windows, centered the two-story limestone structure like a giant maw. The house had been the residence of an American diplomat after the war. Heavy drapery shaded the interiors, making it impossible to look inside. As a young girl, Sunja had imagined where he might live, but she could never have conceived of anything like this. He lived in a castle, it seemed to her. The taxi driver assured her that this was the address.

A young, short-haired servant girl wearing a shimmering white apron answered the door, opening it only halfway. The master of the house was not in, she said in Japanese.

"Who's that?" an older woman asked, emerging from the front parlor. She tapped the servant girl lightly, and she moved aside. The door opened fully to expose the grand entryway.

Sunja realized who this must be.

"Koh Hansu, please," she said in her best Japanese. "Please."

"Who are you?"

"My name is Boku Sunja."

Hansu's wife, Mieko, nodded. The beggar was no doubt a Korean who wanted money. The postwar Koreans were numerous and shameless, and they took advantage of her husband's soft nature toward his countrymen. She did not begrudge his generosity, but she disapproved of the beggars' boldness. It was evening, and this was no time for a woman of any age to beg.

Mieko turned to the servant girl, "Give her what she wants and send her away. There's food in the kitchen if she is hungry." This was what her husband would do. Her father had also believed in hospitality toward the poor.

The servant bowed as the mistress walked away.

"No, no," Sunja said in Japanese. "No money, no food. Speak Koh Hansu, please. Please." She clasped her hands together as if in prayer.

Mieko returned, taking deliberate steps. Koreans could be insistent like unruly children. They could be loud and desperate, with none of the coolness and placidity of the Japanese. Her children were half of this blood, but fortunately, they did not raise their voices or have slovenly habits. Her father had loved Hansu, claiming that he was not like the others and that it would be good for her to marry him, because he was a real man and he would take care of her. Her father was not wrong; under her husband's direction, the organization had only grown stronger and wealthier. She and her daughters had enormous wealth in Switzerland as well as innumerable fat packets of yen hidden in the stone walls of this house. She lacked for nothing.

"How did you learn that he lives here? How do you know my husband?" Mieko asked Sunja.

Sunja shook her head, because she didn't understand exactly what the woman was asking. She understood the word "husband." His wife was clearly Japanese—early sixties with gray hair, cut short. She was very beautiful, with large dark eyes fringed with unusually long lashes. She wore a light green kimono over her elegant frame. The rouge on her lips was the color of *umeboshi*. She looked like a kimono model.

"Fetch the garden boy. He speaks Korean." Hansu's wife extended her left hand and gestured to Sunja to remain by the door. She noted the rough and worn cotton clothing and the tired hands, spotted from outdoor work. The Korean could not be very old; there was some prettiness in her eyes, but her youth was spent. Her waist was thick from childbearing. She was not attractive enough to be one of Hansu's whores. To her knowledge, all of Hansu's whores were Japanese hostesses, some younger than their daughters. They knew better than to grace her doorstep.

The garden boy came running to the front of the house from the backyard, where he'd been weeding.

"Yes, ma'am," he said, bowing to the mistress of the house.

"She's a Korean," Mieko said. "Ask her how she learned where the master lives."

The boy glanced at Sunja, who looked terrified. She wore a light gray coat over her cotton work clothes. She was younger than his mother.

"*Ajumoni*," he said to Sunja, trying not to alarm her. "How can I help you?"

Sunja smiled at the boy, then, seeing the concern in his eyes, she burst into tears. He had none of the hardness of the house servant and the wife. "I'm looking for my son, you see, and I think your master knows where he is. I need to speak"—she had to stop speaking to breathe through her tearful gulps—"to your master. Do you know where he is?"

"How does she know my husband lives here?" Hansu's wife asked again calmly.

In his wish to help the desperate woman, the boy had forgotten his mistress's request.

"The mistress wants to know how you know that the master lives here. *Ajumoni*, I have to give her an answer; do you understand?" The boy peered into Sunja's face.

"I worked for Kim Changho at a restaurant your master owned. Kim Changho gave me your master's address to me before he left for the North. Did you know Mr. Kim? He went to Pyongyang."

The boy nodded, recalling the tall man with the thick eyeglasses who always gave him pocket money for candy and played soccer with him in the backyard. Mr. Kim had offered to take the boy with him to the North on the Red Cross ship, but his master had forbidden it. The master never spoke about Mr. Kim and would get angry if anyone brought him up.

Sunja stared hard at the boy as if he could find Noa himself.

"You see, your master might know where my son is. I have to go find him. Do you think you can tell me where your master is? Is he here now? I know he would see me."

The boy looked down and shook his head, and at that moment, Sunja looked up and started to take in the interior of Hansu's house.

The magnificent, cavernous foyer behind the boy resembled the interior of an old train station with its high ceilings and pale white walls. She imagined Hansu descending the carved cherrywood staircase to ask what was the matter. This time, she would beg for his help in a way she had never done before. She would plead for his mercy, for all of his resources, and she would not leave his side until her son was found.

The boy turned to the mistress and translated everything Sunja had said.

Hansu's wife studied the weeping woman.

"Tell her that he is away. That he will be gone for a long time." Mieko turned around and while walking away said, "If she needs any train fare or food, send her to the back and give her what she needs; otherwise, send her away."

"*Ajumoni*, do you need any money or food?" he asked.

"No, no. I just need to speak to your master. Please, child. Please help me," Sunja said.

The boy shrugged, because he didn't know where Hansu was. The servant, her white apron glinting in the brilliant electric lights of the foyer, stood by the door like a maiden sentry and looked off into the distance as if to give these poor, messy people some privacy.

"*Ajumoni*, I'm sorry, but my mistress wants you to leave. Would you like to go to the kitchen? In the back of the house? I can get you something to eat. The mistress said—"

"No. No."

The maid closed the front door quietly, while the boy remained outside. He had never walked through the front door and never expected to do so.

Sunja turned to the darkened street. A half-moon was visible in the navy-colored sky. The mistress had returned to the parlor to study her flower magazines, and the servant resumed her work in the pantry. From the house, the boy watched Sunja walking toward the main road. He wanted to tell her that the master came home every now and then, but rarely slept at home when he returned. He traveled all over the country for his work. The master and the mistress were very polite to one another, but they did not seem like an ordinary husband and wife. Perhaps this was the way of rich people, the boy thought. They were nothing like his own parents. His father had been a carpenter before he died from a bad liver. His mother, who never stopped working, had doted on him, though he'd never made any money. The gardener boy knew that the master stayed in a hotel in Osaka sometimes; the head servants and the cook talked about his mansion apartment in Tokyo, but none of them had been there except for the driver, Yasuda. The boy had never given it much thought. He had never been to Tokyo or anywhere else besides Osaka, where he was born, and Nagoya, where his family now lived. The only people who would ever know for certain where the master would be were Yasuda and his brawny guard Chiko, but it had never occurred to the boy to ask them the master's whereabouts. Sometimes, the master went to Korea or Hong Kong, they said.

The streets were empty except for the Korean woman's small figure walking slowly toward the train station, and the gardener boy ran quickly to catch up with her.

"*Ajumoni, ajumoni*, where, where do you live?"

Sunja stopped and turned to the boy, wondering if he might know something.

"In Ikaino. Do you know the shopping street?"

The boy nodded, hunched over and holding his knees to catch his breath. He stared at her round face.

"I live three blocks from the shopping street by the large bathhouse. My name is Baek Sunja or Sunja Boku. I live in the house with my mother, brother-in-law, and sister-in-law, Baek Yoseb and Choi Kyunghee. Just ask anyone where the lady who sells sweets lives. I also sell confections in the train station market with my mother. I'm always at the market. Will you come find me if you know where Koh Hansu is? And when you see him, will you tell him that I need to see him?" Sunja asked.

"Yes, I will try. We don't see him often." The boy stopped there, because it didn't seem right to tell her that Hansu was never home. He had not seen him in many months, maybe even a year. "But if I see my master, I'll tell him that you came by. I'm sure the mistress will tell him, too."

"Here." Sunja fished in her purse to find some money for the boy.

"No, no, thank you. I have everything I need. I'm all right." The boy looked at the worn rubber soles of her shoes; they looked identical to the ones his mother wore to the market.

"You're a good boy," she said, and Sunja started to cry again, because all her life, Noa had been her joy. He had been a steady source of strength for her when she had expected so little from this life.

"My *umma* works in a market in Nagoya; she helps another lady who sells vegetables," he found himself telling her. He had not seen his mother and sisters since New Year's. The only person he spoke to in Korean here was with the master himself.

"She must wish to see you, too."

Sunja smiled weakly at the boy, feeling sorry for him. She touched his shoulder, then walked to the train station.

BOOK III

Pachinko

1962–1989

I propose the following definition of the nation: it is an imagined political community—and imagined as both inherently limited and sovereign.

It is *imagined* because the members of even the smallest nation will never know most of their fellow-members, meet them, or even hear of them, yet in the minds of each lives the image of their communion...

The nation is imagined as *limited* because even the largest of them, encompassing perhaps a billion living human beings, has finite, if elastic, boundaries, beyond which lie other nations...

It is imagined as *sovereign* because the concept was born in an age in which Enlightenment and Revolution were destroying the legitimacy of the divinely-ordained, hierarchical dynastic realm...

Finally, it is imagined as a *community*, because, regardless of the actual inequality and exploitation that may prevail in each, the nation is always conceived as a deep, horizontal comradeship. Ultimately it is this fraternity that makes it possible, over the past two centuries, for so many millions of people, not so much to kill, as willingly die for such limited imaginings.

—Benedict Anderson

I

Nagano, April 1962

Noa hadn't meant to linger at the café by the Nagano train station, but it wasn't as if he knew where to go exactly. He hadn't made a plan, which was unlike him, but after he'd left Waseda, his days had made little sense to him. Reiko Tamura, a cheerful middle school teacher who had been kind to him, was from Nagano, and for some reason, he'd always considered her hometown as a place populated with gentle, benevolent Japanese. He recalled his teacher's childhood stories of the snowstorms that were so severe that when she walked outside her little house to go to school, she could hardly see the streetlights. Osaka had snow occasionally, but nothing resembling Tamura-san's storms. He had always wanted to visit his teacher's hometown—in his mind, it was always blanketed with fresh snow. This morning, when the man at the ticket counter had asked him where to, he'd replied, "Nagano, please." Finally, he was here. He felt safe. Tamura-san had also spoken of school trips to the famed Zenkoji temple, where she'd eat her modest bento outdoors with her classmates.

Seated alone at a small table not far from the counter, Noa drank his brown tea and took only a few bites of his omelet rice while considering a visit to the temple. He was raised as a Christian, but he felt respectful of Buddhists, especially those who had renounced the spoils of the world. The Lord was supposed to be everywhere, which was what Noa had learned at church, but would God keep away from temples or shrines?

Did such places offend God, or did He understand those who may wish to worship something, anything? As always, Noa wished he'd had more time with Isak. The thought of him saddened Noa, and the thought of Hansu, his biological father, shamed him. Koh Hansu didn't believe in anything but his own efforts—not God, not Jesus, not Buddha, and not the Emperor.

The heavyset waiter came by with a teapot.

"Is everything to your satisfaction, sir?" the waiter asked him while re-filling Noa's cup. "Is the meal not to your liking? Too much scallion? I always tell the cook that he is too heavy with the—"

"The rice is very good, thank you," Noa replied, realizing that it had been some time since he had spoken to anyone at all. The waiter had a broad smile, thin, tadpole eyes, and uneven teeth. His ears were large and his lobes thick—physical features Buddhists admired. The waiter stared at Noa, though most Japanese would have looked away out of politeness.

"Are you visiting for a while?" The waiter glanced at Noa's suitcase, which was set by the empty chair.

"Hmm?" Noa was surprised by the waiter's personal question.

"I apologize for being so nosy. My mother always said I would get in trouble because I am far too curious. Forgive me, sir, I am just a chatty country boy," the waiter said, laughing. "I haven't seen you here before. Please forgive the café for being so quiet. Normally we have many more customers. Very interesting and respectable ones. I cannot help but have questions when I meet someone new, but I know I should not ask them."

"No, no. It's natural to want to know things. I understand. I am here to visit, and I heard such nice things about Nagano that I thought I would like to live here." Noa was surprised to hear himself say this. It felt easy to talk to this stranger. It had not occurred to him before to live in Nagano, but why not? Why not for a year at least? He would not return to Tokyo or Osaka—this much he had resolved.

"Move here? To live? *Honto*? How wonderful. Nagano is a very special place," the waiter said with pride. "My entire family is from here. We have always been from here. Eighteen generations, and I am the dumbest one in my family. This is my little café, which my mother bought for me to keep me out of trouble!" The waiter laughed. "Everyone calls me Bingo. It is a game from America. I have played it once."

"Nobuo *desu*," Noa said, smiling. "Nobuo Ban *desu*."

"Ban-san, Ban-san," Bingo chirped happily. "I once loved a short girl from Tokyo named Chie Ban, but she did not love me. Of course! Lovely girls do not love me. My tall wife is not lovely, but she loves me nonetheless!" Again, he laughed. "You know, you are smart to wish to settle in Nagano. I have been to Tokyo only once, and that was enough for me. It's dirty, expensive, and full of fast—" The waiter stopped himself. "Wait, you're not from Tokyo, are you?"

"No. I'm from Kansai."

"Ah, I love Kansai. I have been to Kyoto twice, and though it is too expensive for a simple man like myself, I am fond of truly delicious udon, and I believe one can eat delicious udon there for a reasonable sum. I prefer the chewy kind of udon."

Noa smiled. It was pleasant to listen to him talk.

"So what will you do for work?" the waiter asked. "A man must have work. My mother always says this, too." Bingo clasped his right hand over his mouth, embarrassed at being so forward, but he was unable to keep from talking so much. The stranger seemed so attractive and humble, and Bingo admired quiet people. "Did you have a job you liked in Kansai?" he asked, his sparse eyebrows raised.

Noa looked down at his barely eaten meal.

"Well, I have worked as a bookkeeper. I can also read and write in English. Perhaps a small business may need a bookkeeper. Or maybe a trading company may wish to have documents translated—"

"A young man like you could work in lots of places. Let me think." Bingo's round face grew serious. He tapped his small chin with his index finger. "You seem very smart."

"I don't know about that, but that's kind of you to say." Noa smiled.

"Hmm." The waiter made a face. "Sir, I don't know if you're picky, but if you need work right away, the pachinko parlor hires people from out of town. Office jobs are not so common lately."

"Pachinko?" Noa tried not to look offended. Did the waiter think he was Korean? Most Japanese never assumed he was Korean until he told them his Korean surname, Boku. His identification card from Waseda stated his *tsumei* name, Nobuo Bando. Noa wasn't sure why he had dropped the "-do" from his surname when he'd introduced himself to Bingo, but now it was too late to change it back. "I don't know much about pachinko. I have never—"

"Oh, I didn't mean to offend you. They pay very well, I hear. Takano-san, the manager of the best parlor in Nagano, is a great gentleman. Maybe you wouldn't work in any ordinary pachinko parlor, but Cosmos Pachinko is a grand establishment run by an old family from the area. They change their machines very often! However, they do not hire foreigners."

"Eh?"

"They do not hire Koreans or Chinese, but that will not matter to you since you are Japanese." Bingo nodded several times.

"*Soo desu*," Noa agreed.

"Takano-san is always looking for office workers who are smart. He pays handsomely. But he cannot hire foreigners." Bingo nodded again.

"Yes, yes," Noa said sympathetically, sounding as if he understood. Long ago, he had learned how to keep nodding even when he didn't agree, because he noticed that the motion alone kept people talking.

"Takano-san is a regular customer. He was here just this morning. Every day, he takes his coffee at the window table." Bingo pointed. "Black coffee and two sugar cubes. Never any milk. This morning, he tells me, 'Bingo-san, I have a headache that will not go away, because it is so hard to find good workers. The fools here have pumpkins for heads, and seeds are not brains.'" The waiter clasped his thick meaty fingers over his head in a comic imitation of the anguished Takano-san.

"Hey, why don't you go over there and tell Takano-san that I sent you," Bingo said, smiling. This was the sort of thing he loved to do best—help people and make introductions. He had already arranged three marriages for his high school friends.

Noa nodded and thanked him. Years later, Bingo would tell anyone that he was Ban-san's first friend in Nagano.

Takano-san's business office was located in another building, separate from the immense pachinko parlor, almost two city blocks away. From the conservative appearance of the brick building, it would have been impossible to know the purpose of this office. Noa might have missed it altogether if Bingo hadn't drawn a map for him on a sheet of notepaper. Except for its number, the building had no sign.

Hideo Takano, the parlor manager, was a sharp-looking Japanese in his late thirties. He wore a beautiful dark woolen suit with a striped purple necktie and a matching pocket handkerchief; each week, he paid a neighborhood boy to shine all his leather shoes to a mirror sheen. He dressed so well that he looked more like a clothing salesman than a man who worked in an office. Behind his desk were two black safes, the size of doors. His large office was adjacent to half a dozen modest-sized rooms, each filled with office workers wearing white shirts—mostly young men and plain-faced office ladies. Takano had a small bump on the bridge of his handsome nose and round black eyes that sloped downward, and when he spoke, his velvety eyes were expressive and direct.

"Sit down," Takano said. "My secretary said you are looking for a clerk position."

"My name is Nobuo Ban *desu*. Bingo-san from the café said that you were looking for workers. I recently arrived from Tokyo, sir."

"Ha! Bingo sent you? But I don't need anyone to pour my coffee here." From behind his large metal desk, Takano leaned forward in his chair. "So, Bingo is listening to my sad troubles after all. I thought I was mostly listening to his."

Noa smiled. The man seemed genial enough; he didn't seem like someone who hated Koreans. He was glad to have worn a clean shirt and a tie today; Koh Hansu had mentioned often that a man should look his best each day. For Koreans, this was especially important: Look clean and be well groomed. In every situation, even in ones when you have a right to be angry, a Korean must speak soberly and calmly, he'd said.

"So, friend of Bingo-san, what can you do?" Takano asked.

Noa sat up straighter. "I'm trained as a bookkeeper and have worked for a landlord in Kansai. I've collected rents and kept books for several years before I went to university—"

"Yeah? University? Really? Which one?"

"Waseda," Noa answered, "but I haven't finished my degree in literature. I was there for three years."

"Literature?" Takano shook his head. "I don't need an employee who will be reading books when he should be working. I need a bookkeeper who's smart, neat, and honest. He needs to show up to work each morning when he's supposed to, not hungover and not dealing with girl problems. I don't want any losers. I fire losers." Takano tilted his head after saying all this. Noa looked very respectable; he could see why Bingo would send him over.

"Yes, sir. Of course. I am a very precise bookkeeper, and I am very good at writing letters, sir."

"Modest."

Noa did not apologize. "I will do my best if you hire me, sir."

"What's your name again?"

"Nobuo Ban *desu*."

"You're not from here."

"No, sir. I'm from Kansai."

"Why did you leave school?"

"My mother died, and I didn't have enough money to finish my degree. I was hoping to earn money to return to school one day."

"And your father?"

"He is dead."

Takano never believed it when out-of-towners said their parents were dead, but he didn't care either way.

"So why should I train you so you can leave to continue your study of literature? I'm not interested in helping you finish your university education. I need a bookkeeper who will stick around. Can you do that? I won't pay you very well when you start, but you'll be able to get by. What the hell are you going to do with literature, anyway? There's no money in that. I never finished high school, and I can hire you or fire you a hundred times. Your generation is foolish."

Noa didn't reply. His family thought he wanted to work in a company, but that wasn't entirely true. It had been a private dream of his to be a high school English teacher. He'd thought that if he graduated from Waseda then it might be possible to get a good job at a private school. Public schools didn't hire Koreans, but he thought the law may be changed one day. He had even considered becoming a Japanese citizen. He knew he could at least work as some sort of private tutor.

"Well, you don't have the money for university now, and you need a job, or else you wouldn't be here. So where are you living?"

"I arrived in Nagano today. I was going to find a boardinghouse."

"You can sleep in the dormitory behind the shop. You'll have to share a room at first. No smoking in the rooms, and you cannot bring girls. You are allowed three meals in the cafeteria. As much rice as you want. There's meat twice a week. As for girls, there are hotels for that sort of thing. I don't care what you do on your time off, but your first duty is to the company. I am a very generous manager, but if you mess up, you will be terminated instantly without any back pay."

Noa wondered if his younger brother spoke this way to employees. The fact that he was going to work for a pachinko business, no different than Mozasu, a kid who had flunked out of school essentially, was stunning to Noa.

"You can start today. Find Ikeda-san in the office next to mine. He has gray hair. Do whatever he tells you. He's my head accountant. I'll try you out for a month. If you do okay, I'll pay you a good enough salary. You have no overhead. You can save quite a bit."

"Thank you, sir."

"Where are your people from?"

"Kansai," Noa replied.

"Yeah, you said. Where in Kansai?"

"Kyoto," Noa replied.

"What do your parents do?"

"They're dead," Noa replied, hoping to end the questions.

"Yeah, you said. So what did they do?"

"My father worked in a udon shop."

"Yeah?" Takano looked puzzled. "So a noodle man sends his son to Waseda? Really?"

Noa said nothing, wishing he was a better liar.

"You're not a foreigner, right? You swear."

Noa tried to look surprised by such a question. "No, sir. I am Japanese."

"Good, good," Takano replied. "Get out of my office and see Ikeda-san."

The dormitory of the pachinko parlor slept sixty employees. On his first night, Noa slept in one of the smallest rooms, sharing it with an older worker who snored like a broken motor. Within a week, he established a routine. When he woke up, Noa washed his face quickly, having bathed the night before in the public bath, and he went down to the cafeteria where the cook served rice, mackerel, and tea. He worked methodically and won over Ikeda-san, who had never met such a smart bookkeeper. When the trial month passed, Noa was kept on. Years later, Noa learned that the Japanese owner had liked Noa from the start. After the first month, the owner told Takano to give Noa a raise and a better room at the year's end, but not before, because the others might fuss over any favoritism. The owner suspected that Nobuo Ban was a Korean, but he said nothing, because as long as no one else knew, it didn't matter.

2

Osaka, April 1965

In three years, Yumi had lost two pregnancies, and she found herself pregnant again. Against the advice of her husband, Mozasu, she'd worked through the previous pregnancies. In her quiet and deliberate way, Yumi's boss, Totoyama-san, insisted that she work from home for this pregnancy. Yumi refused.

"Yumi-chan, there isn't much work this season, and you need to rest," Totoyama-san would say, and only occasionally, Yumi went home before it got too dark.

It was a late spring afternoon. Yumi had just completed an order of bow ties for hotel uniforms when she felt sharp pains along her lower abdomen. This time, Totoyama-san refused to hear a word of protest from Yumi. She sent for Mozasu, who picked up his wife, and he took her to a famous Japanese baby doctor in downtown Osaka, whom Totoyama-san had learned of, rather than to Yumi's regular doctor in Ikaino.

"It's elementary, Boku-san. You have very high blood pressure. Women like you often fight pregnancy," the doctor said calmly.

He walked away from the examination table and returned to his desk. His office had been painted recently, and the faint smell of paint lingered. Except for a medical chart of a woman's reproductive organs, everything in the office was white or stainless steel.

Yumi said nothing and thought about what he said. Could it be true?

she wondered. Could she have somehow aborted her prior pregnancies by fighting them?

"I am less worried about the previous miscarriages. It is a sad thing, of course, but miscarriages reveal the wisdom of nature. It's for the best that you don't give birth when it isn't good for your health. A miscarriage indicates that the woman can conceive, so it is not necessarily a fertility matter. But, as for this pregnancy, I do not see much danger to the child; there is danger only to the mother; so for the remainder of the pregnancy, you must remain in bed."

"But I have to work," Yumi said, looking terrified.

The doctor shook his head.

"Yumi-chan," Mozasu said, "you have to listen to the doctor."

"I can work less. Go home early, the way Totoyama-san wants me to."

"Boku-san, it's possible for the mother to die of preeclampsia. As your physician, I cannot allow you to work. My patients must listen to me, or else we cannot work together."

The famous doctor looked away from her, pretending to glance at the few papers on his desk, confident that Yumi would remain his patient. She'd be a fool to choose otherwise. He jotted down some notes about her diet, advising her to avoid sweets or too much rice. She must not gain much weight, since she'd be retaining an enormous amount of water, and the baby would be too big to deliver vaginally.

"Please call me any time you do not feel comfortable. This is critical. If we have to deliver early, then we need to take precautions. Boku-san, there is no need to be stoic. That can come after you have the child. A woman has a right to be a little difficult before she has her first child." The doctor smiled at both of them. "Make a fuss about your food cravings, or if you want extra pillows at night."

Mozasu nodded, grateful for the doctor's humor and inflexible tone. Any good doctor would need to match his wife's stubbornness. Mozasu had never had reason to disagree with Yumi on anything important, but he wondered if he had not done so because he'd sensed that she would not have listened to him anyway.

When the couple returned home, Yumi lay down on the futon, her dark hair mussed and spread out across the narrow pillow. Mozasu was seated on the bed, cross-legged by her side, not knowing what else to say to his wife, who did not want a glass of water or anything to eat. With her, he felt a little dumb, because she was so stalwart and clever. Her goals had always seemed absurdly fantastic. Sometimes, he wondered how she allowed herself to dream for so much. He had never seen her cry or complain about anything difficult. He knew Yumi did not want to be at home by herself, unable to work or go to her English classes.

"Would you like your English books?" he asked.

"No," she said, not looking at him. "You have to go back to work, *nee*? I'll be fine. You can go."

"Can't I get you something? Anything?"

"Why can't we go to America? We could have a good life there."

"You remember what the immigration lawyer said. It would be impossible almost."

"The minister Maryman-san may be able to sponsor us."

"Why would he do that? I'm not going to become a missionary and neither are you. You don't even believe in God. Besides, what could I do in America that would make as much money as I do here? I'm not going back to school. I'm not a college boy; I'm your oaf. I count on you to think for the two of us, and soon, for the three of us." He laughed, hoping she would smile.

"Yumi-chan, very soon I will open my own parlor in Yokohama, and if it is successful, I'll make more money than twenty college graduates. Can you imagine? Then I can buy you anything you want. If it's not successful, I can still work for Goro-san and make us a nice life."

"I know how to make money."

"Yes, I know. I know you are independent. But it would give me pleasure to buy something for you that you cannot get for yourself. And I promise you will like Yokohama; it's an international city. There are lots of Americans there. As soon as you have the baby, and the doctor says it is okay, I will take you to visit. We can stay in a beautiful hotel, and you can see what it's like. And it will be easier for you to study English there. We can find you a tutor, and you can go to school if you like," Mozasu said. Although he tried not to think of Noa because it made him too sad, Mozasu could not help but think of his brother, who had quit Waseda and run away without explanation.

"The Japanese do not like us. How will our baby live here?" Yumi asked.

"Some Japanese like us very much. The baby will live here with us. She will live like us." From the very first pregnancy, Mozasu had determined that the baby was a girl—a child just like Yumi.

Mozasu stroked her forehead. His dark hand looked enormous on her small, pale brow. For a very young woman, his wife could appear ancient in her sternness, able to push herself through the most difficult tasks, but when sad, she had the face of a disappointed child, lost and bereft. He loved her face, how it showed every trace of feeling; she could be silent, but she was incapable of hiding herself from others.

"What else can we do?" Mozasu asked, looking to her for the answer. "Besides go to America?" He had never understood what she thought she'd find there. Sometimes, he wondered if Noa had gone to the States— this magical place so many Koreans in Japan idealized. "What else, Yumi-chan, what else would you like to do?"

She shrugged. "I don't want to stay in the house until the baby comes. I don't like to be lazy."

"You will never be lazy. It's impossible." He laughed. "When the baby comes, and it will be soon," he said, "you will be chasing after her. You and she will be the fastest moving females in Osaka—never ever bound by the house."

"Mozasu, I can feel her moving. I didn't lose the baby."

"Of course not. The doctor said the baby is fine. Baby-chan will look just like you. We'll give her a wonderful home. You're going to be a wonderful mother."

She smiled, not believing him but wanting him to be right.

"I called my mother. She'll come here tonight."

Yumi crinkled her eyes, worried.

"You like her, *nee*?"

"Yes," Yumi said. It was true; Yumi admired her mother-in-law, yet they were strangers to one another. Sunja was not like most mothers of sons; she never said anything intrusive, and her reluctance to speak her mind had only increased after Noa disappeared. When Mozasu and Yumi had asked her and Mozasu's grandmother to move into their house, Sunja had declined, saying that it would be better for the young couple to live without old women bothering them.

"I thought she wanted to stay with her mother and Aunt Kyunghee."

"Yes, but she wants to help us. She will come by herself. It will not be permanent. Grandmother will stay with Aunt Kyunghee to help with the store. I'll hire some girls for them to replace my mother while she's here."

After two weeks of bed rest, Yumi felt like she was going out of her mind. Mozasu had bought her a television, but she had no interest in watching it, and heartburn kept her from reading. Her wrists and ankles were so swollen that if she pushed her thumb lightly onto her wrist, she could make a deep impression in her flesh. Only the baby's movements and occasional hiccups kept Yumi glued to her futon and from fleeing out of doors. Since her arrival, her mother-in-law remained by herself in the small room beside the kitchen—no matter how many times Mozasu insisted that she stay in the larger, unused room by the master bedroom. Sunja did all the cooking and cleaning. At whatever hour of the night Mozasu came home, she had his dinner ready.

It was morning when Sunja knocked on Yumi's door to bring her breakfast.

"Come in, *omoni*," Yumi said. Her own mother could not make a pot of rice or a cup of tea, in contrast to Mozasu's mother, who had supported her family on her cooking.

As usual, Sunja carried in a tray with an assortment of tempting dishes, all covered with a clean white cloth. She smiled at her daughter-in-law.

Yumi, who would normally have relished such good meals, felt bad, because all she could manage to keep down lately was rice porridge.

"I feel terrible that I'm lying in bed all day while you work so much,"

Yumi said, hoping that Sunja would stay and talk with her. "Have you eaten breakfast?"

"Yes, I ate. You work hard all the time. But now, you're supposed to be resting. A pregnancy is not an easy thing. My mother had six miscarriages before having me," she said. "She wanted to come and take care of you, but I told her to stay at home."

"Six miscarriages. I've only had two."

"Two is not easy, either," Sunja said. "You should have your breakfast. You and the baby need nourishment."

Yumi sat up a bit. "Mozasu left early today for Yokohama."

Sunja nodded. She'd fixed his breakfast before he got on the morning train.

"You saw him then." Yumi admired the tray. "This looks delicious."

Sunja hoped her daughter-in-law would eat. She was terrified that she would miscarry again, but didn't want to appear worried. She regretted having mentioned the number of her mother's miscarriages. The minister at the church had warned against the sins of the careless tongue; it was always better to speak less, Sunja thought.

"Thank you for taking such good care of us."

Sunja shook her head.

"This is nothing. You'll do this for your children," Sunja said.

Unlike the *ajumma*s in the open market with their tight, black, permanent-wave curls, Sunja hadn't colored her graying hair and wore it cut short like a man's. Her mature figure was solid, neither small nor large. She had worked out of doors for so many years that the sun had carved thin grooves into her round, dark face. Like a Buddhist nun, Sunja wore no makeup, not even moisturizer. It was as if she had decided some time ago that she would not care what she looked like beyond being clean, as if to pay penance for having once cared about such things, when in fact she had not.

"Did Mozasu tell you about my mother?" Yumi picked up the spoon.

"That she worked in a bar," Sunja said.

"She was a prostitute. My father was her pimp. They weren't married."

Sunja nodded and stared at the tray of uneaten food. When Mozasu had told her about Yumi's family, Sunja had imagined as much. The occupation and the war had been difficult for everyone.

"I'm sure she was a good person. I'm sure she cared for you very much."

Sunja believed this. She had loved Hansu, and then she had loved Isak. However, what she felt for her boys, Noa and Mozasu, was more than the love she'd felt for the men; this love for her children felt like life and death. After Noa had gone, she felt half-dead. She could not imagine any mother feeling differently.

"My mother isn't a good person. She beat us. She cared more about drinking and getting money than anything else. After my brother died, if my sister and I hadn't run away, she would have put us to work. Doing what she did. Not once did she ever say a kind thing to me," Yumi said. She'd never told anyone this.

"Mozasu told me your sister passed away."

Yumi nodded. After she and her sister had left home, they'd found shelter in an abandoned clothing factory. In the winter, they both got sick with a high fever, but her sister had died in her sleep. Yumi had slept beside her sister's dead body for nearly a day, waiting to die herself.

Sunja shifted her seat and moved toward her.

"My child, you have suffered too much."

Yumi did not deliver a girl. Her baby Solomon was an enormous boy, over nine pounds, even larger than the famous doctor had expected. The birth took over thirty hours, and the doctor had to call in a colleague to help him through the night. The baby was strong and well. In a month's time, Yumi recovered fully and returned to work, bringing Solomon with her to the workshop. On his first birthday ceremony, Solomon clutched the crisp yen note over the ink brush, string, or cakes—signifying that he would have a rich life.

3

Yokohama, November 1968

When the floor manager came by to tell Mozasu that the police were waiting in his office to see him, he assumed that it was about the pachinko machine permits. It was that time of the year. Once he reached his office, he recognized the young men from the precinct and invited them to sit down, but they remained standing and bowed, not saying a word at first. The floor manager, who remained by the door, was unable to meet his glance; preoccupied earlier, Mozasu hadn't noticed that the floor manager's face was so solemn.

"Sir," the shorter of the two officers said, "your family is in the hospital at the moment, and we've come to take you there. The captain would have come himself, but—"

"What?" Mozasu left his side of the desk and went to the door.

"Your wife and son were hit by a taxi this morning. A block from your son's school. The driver was inebriated from the night before and had fallen asleep while driving."

"Are they all right?"

"Your son broke his ankle. Otherwise, he is well."

"And my wife?"

"She died in the ambulance before reaching the hospital."

Mozasu ran out of the office without his coat.

*   *   *

The funeral was held in Osaka, and Mozasu would always be able to recall some parts of it vividly and some not at all. During the service, he had held on to Solomon's small hand, fearing that if he let go, the boy might disappear. The three-and-a-half-year-old boy stood, leaning on his crutches, insisting on greeting each person who'd come to pay his respects to his mama. After an hour, he agreed to sit down but did not leave his father's side. Several witnesses had recounted that Yumi had pushed her son onto the sidewalk when the taxi lost control. At the funeral, Mozasu's childhood friend Haruki Totoyama had observed that Yumi must have had incredible hand-eye control in a moment of such intense pressure.

Several hundred guests came. They were people Mozasu knew from his business and many more from his father's church, where his grandmother and Aunt Kyunghee still worshipped. Mozasu did his best to greet them, but he could hardly speak; it was as if he had forgotten both Korean and Japanese. He didn't want to go on anymore without Yumi, but this was something he could not say. She was his lover, but more than anything, she was his wise friend. He could never replace her. And he felt he had done her a great injustice by not having told her this. He had expected to have a long life with her, not a few years. Who would he tell when a customer did something funny? Who would he tell that their son had made him so proud, standing on crutches and shaking the hands of grown-ups and being braver than any other person in the room? When the mourners wept at the sight of the little boy in the black suit, Solomon would say, "Don't cry." He calmed one hysterical woman by telling her, "Mama is in California." When the mourner looked puzzled, neither Solomon nor Mozasu explained what this meant.

He had never taken her there. They'd meant to go. With some difficulty, it was possible now for them to get the passports, but he hadn't bothered. Most Koreans in Japan couldn't travel. If you wanted a Japanese passport, which would allow you to reenter without hassles, you had to become a Japanese citizen—which was almost impossible, and no one he knew would do that anyway. Otherwise, if you wanted to travel, you could get a South Korean passport through *Mindan*, but few wanted to be affiliated with the Republic of Korea, either, since the impoverished country was run by a dictator. The Koreans who were affiliated with North Korea couldn't go anywhere, though some were allowed to travel to North Korea. Although nearly everyone who had returned to the North was suffering, there were still far more Koreans in Japan whose citizenship was affiliated with the North than the South. At least the North Korean government still sent money for schools for them, everyone said. Nevertheless, Mozasu wouldn't leave the country where he was born. Where would he go, anyway? So Japan didn't want them, so fucking what?

Images of her filled his mind, and even as the mourners spoke to him, all he could hear was her practicing English phrases from her language books. No matter how many times Mozasu had said he would not emigrate to the United States, Yumi had not given up hope that one day they would live in California. Lately, she had been suggesting New York.

"Mozasu, don't you think it would be wonderful to live in New York City or San Francisco?" she'd ask him occasionally, and it was his job to say that he couldn't decide between the two coasts.

"There, no one would care that we are not Japanese," she'd say. *Hello, my name is Yumi Baek. This is my son, Solomon. He is three years old. How are you?* Once, when Solomon asked her what California was, she had replied, "Heaven."

After most of the funeral guests left, Mozasu and Solomon sat down at the back of the funeral hall. Mozasu patted the boy's back, and his son leaned into him, fitting into the crook of his father's right arm.

"You're a good son," Mozasu said to him in Japanese.

"You are a good papa."

"Do you want to get something to eat?"

Solomon shook his head and looked up when an older man approached them.

"Mozasu, are you okay?" the man asked him in Korean. He was a virile-looking gentleman in his late sixties or early seventies, wearing an expensive black suit with narrow lapels and a dark necktie.

The face was familiar, but Mozasu couldn't place it. He felt unable to answer him. Not wanting to be rude, Mozasu smiled, but he wanted to be left alone. Perhaps it was a customer or a bank officer; Mozasu couldn't think right now.

"It's me. Koh Hansu. Have I aged that much?" Hansu smiled. "Your face is the same, of course, but you've become a man. And this is your boy?" Hansu touched Solomon's head. Throughout the day, nearly everyone had patted the boy's glossy chestnut-colored hair.

Mozasu shot up from his seat.

"*Uh-muh.* Of course, I know who you are. It's been so long. Mother had been looking for you for a while but couldn't get ahold of you. To see if you might know where Noa is. He's disappeared."

"It's been too long." Hansu shook his hand. "Have you heard from Noa?"

"Well, yes and no. He sends Mother money each month, but he won't give his whereabouts. He sends a lot of money actually, so he can't be too badly off. I just wish we knew where he—"

Hansu nodded. "He sent me money, too. To pay me back, he said. I wanted to return it, but there's no way. I thought I'd give it to your mother for her to keep for him."

"Are you still in Osaka?" Mozasu asked.

"No, no. I live in Tokyo now. I live near my daughters."

Mozasu nodded. He felt weak suddenly and wanted to sit again. When Hansu's driver appeared, Hansu promised to call on Mozasu another day.

"Sir, I am very sorry to bother you, but there is a small matter outside. The young woman said it was an emergency."

Hansu nodded and walked out of the building with his driver.

As he approached the car, Hansu's new girl, Noriko, beckoned him from within.

The long-haired beauty clapped when she saw him open the door. Her pink pearl nail polish glinted from her fingertips.

"Uncle is here!" she cried happily.

"What's the matter?" Hansu asked. "I was busy."

"Nothing. I was bored, and I missed my uncle," she replied. "Take me shopping, please. I have waited for so long and so patiently for you to come back in this car. And the driver is no fun! My friends in Ginza told me cute bags from France came in this week!"

Hansu closed the car door. The bulletproof windows shut out all daylight. The interior lamps of the Mercedes sedan lit up Noriko's oval-shaped face.

"You called me in here because you wanted to go shopping, *nee*?"

"Yes, Uncle," she said sweetly, and extended her pretty small hand on his lap like a kitten's paw. Her rich clients loved her petulant-niece routine. Men wanted to buy girls nice things. If Uncle wanted to remove her white cotton panties, he'd have to buy her as many luxury items from France as she wanted for months and months. Koh Hansu was the most important patron of the hostess bar where Noriko worked; Noriko's mama-san had promised her that Koh Hansu liked spoiling his new girls. This was their second lunch date, and on their first, he had bought her a Christian Dior purse before lunch. Noriko, an eighteen-year-old former beauty contestant, was not used to being kept waiting in a car. She had worn her most expensive peach-colored georgette silk dress with matching heels and a real pearl necklace, borrowed from mama-san.

"Did you ever go to high school?" he asked.

"No, Uncle. I'm not a good schoolgirl," she said, smiling.

"No, of course not. You are stupid. I can't stand stupid."

Hansu hit the girl's face so hard that blood gushed from her pink mouth.

"Uncle, Uncle!" she cried. She swatted at his thick, clenched fist.

He hit her again and again, banging her head against the side lamp of the car until she stopped making any noise. Blood covered her face and the front of her peach-colored dress. The necklace was splattered with red spots. The driver sat motionless in the front until Hansu was finished.

"Take me to the office, then take her back to her mama-san. Tell the mama-san that I don't care how pretty a girl is, I cannot bear a girl who does not have any sense. I was at a funeral. I will not return to the bar until this ignorant thing is removed from my sight."

"I'm sorry, sir. She said it was an emergency. That she had to speak to you or else she would start to scream. I didn't know what to do."

"No hooker is ever to be given precedence over a funeral. If she was sick, then you should have taken her to hospital. Otherwise, she could have screamed her head off. What does it matter, you oaf?"

The girl was still alive. She sat crumpled and half-awake in the corner of the expansive backseat like a crushed butterfly.

The driver was terrified, because he could still be punished. He should never have listened to some bar girl and her stories. A lieutenant he knew in the organization had lost part of his ring finger for failing to line up the guests' shoes properly outside Koh Hansu's apartment when he was much younger and training through the ranks.

"I am sorry, sir. I am very sorry. Please forgive me, sir."

"Shut up. Go to the office." Hansu closed his eyes and leaned his head against the leather-covered rest.

After the driver dropped Hansu off, he took Noriko to the bar where she worked. The horrified mama-san took her to the hospital, and even after the surgeons did their work, the girl's nose would never look the same again. Noriko was ruined. The mama-san couldn't recover her expenses so she sent Noriko off to a *toruko* where she would have to bathe and serve men in the nude until she was too old to work that job. Her tits and ass would last half a dozen years at most in the hot water. Then she would have to find something else to do.

Six days a week, Sunja took her grandson to school and picked him up. Solomon attended an international preschool where only English was spoken. At school, he spoke English and at home, Japanese. Sunja spoke to him in Korean, and he answered in Japanese sprinkled with a few words in Korean. Solomon loved going to school, and Mozasu thought it was good to keep him occupied. He was a cheerful child who wanted to please his teachers and elders. Wherever he went, the news of his mother's death preceded him, wrapping the child in a kind of protective cloud; teachers and mothers of his friends were watchful on his behalf. Solomon was certain that he would see his mama in heaven; he believed that she could see him. She visited him in his dreams, he said, and told him that she missed holding him.

In the evenings, grandmother, father, and son ate dinner together even if Mozasu had to return to work immediately after his meal. Twice, Mozasu's friend Haruki Totoyama had come from Osaka to visit, and once, they'd gone to Osaka to see the family, since Uncle Yoseb was too frail to travel.

Another school day almost over, Sunja waited patiently outside the preschool alongside the sweet-natured Filipina nannies and the friendly Western mothers who were also waiting to collect their children. Sunja couldn't speak to them, but she smiled and nodded in their presence. As usual, Solomon was one of the first to run out. He shouted good-bye to his teachers, then bolted outside to hug his grandmother's torso before joining the other boys to race to the corner candy store. Sunja tried to keep up with his pace. She was oblivious to Hansu, who'd been watching her from his car.

Sunja was wearing a black wool coat, nothing expensive but not shabby, either. It looked store-bought. She had aged considerably, and Hansu felt sorry for her. Only a little over fifty, she looked much older than that. As a girl, she had been bright and taut, so very appealing. The memory of her fullness and vitality aroused him. The years in the sun had darkened her face and covered her hands lightly with pale brown spots. Shallow crags had settled in her once-smooth brow. In place of the maiden's dark, glossy braids, she now kept her hair short, and it was gray mostly. Her middle had thickened. Hansu remembered her large breasts and lovely pink nipples. They had never spent more than a few hours together, and it had always been a wish of his to make love to her more than once in the course of a day. He'd had many women and girls, yet her innocence and trust had excited him more than even the sexiest of whores who were willing to do anything.

Her pretty eyes were still the same—bright and hard like river stones—the light shimmered in them. He had loved her passionately, the way an older man could love a young girl who could restore his youth and vigor; he had loved her with a kind of gratitude. He knew that he'd loved her more than any other girl. She was not beautiful anymore, but he desired her still. The recollection of taking her in the forest often made him hard, and if he had been alone in the car, he would have jerked off, happy for the rare erection.

Several times each day, Hansu thought of her. What was she doing at the moment? Was she all right? Did she think of him? His mind turned to her as often as it did toward his dead father. When Hansu learned that she was looking for him to find out where Noa was, he did not contact her, because he had no news. He could not imagine disappointing Sunja. He had used every resource to locate the boy but to no avail. Noa had disappeared so perfectly that if Hansu hadn't had the mortuary logs inspected regularly throughout Japan, he might have thought that the boy was dead. At the funeral, he learned that Noa still sent his mother money. That was a relief. The boy was alive, then, and living somewhere in Japan. It had been Hansu's plan to find Noa first, then to contact Sunja, but Yumi's funeral had reminded him that time was not always in his favor. Then last month, his doctor had diagnosed him with prostate cancer.

As Sunja walked past his car, Hansu rolled down the car window.

"Sunja, Sunja."

She gasped.

Hansu told his driver to stay and opened the car door himself to get out.

"Listen, I got to Yumi's funeral late. Mozasu said you'd left. You live with him now, right?"

Sunja stood on the pavement and stared at him. He didn't seem to age. Had it really been eleven years since she last saw him? It had been at his office with Noa, then that expensive dinner to celebrate Noa's admission to Waseda. Noa had been gone six years now. Sunja glanced in the direction of her grandson, who'd run into the store with the other boys to look over comics and debate over which candies to purchase. Without replying, Sunja walked in Solomon's direction. Mozasu had mentioned that Hansu had come to the funeral, that when asked about Noa, Hansu had said nothing.

"Can't you stop for a moment to speak with me? The little boy's fine. He's in the shop. You can see him through the glass." Solomon was in the cluster of boys standing by the rotating comic-book kiosk.

"I begged your wife to tell you that I was looking for you. The gardening boy. I'm sure he gave you my message even if she didn't. Since I've known you, I've done everything I could to never be a burden to you; I have asked you for nothing. Six years have passed since I went to your house. Six."

Hansu opened his mouth, but Sunja spoke again.

"Do you know where he is?"

"No."

Sunja walked toward the candy store.

Hansu touched her arm, and Sunja pushed him back hard with the palm of her hand, knocking him back a step. The chauffeur and body-guard, who'd been standing near the car, ran toward him, but he waved them away.

"I'm fine," he mouthed to them.

"Go back to your car," she said. "Go back to your crooked life."

"Sunja—"

"Why do you bother me now? How can you not see that you've de-stroyed me? Why can't you let me alone? Noa is gone from me. There is nothing between us."

Her wet, shining eyes blinked, lit up like lanterns. Her young face shone through the old one.

"Can I drive you and Solomon home? Maybe we can go to a café? I need to speak to you."

Sunja looked down at the large squares of concrete below her feet, un-able to stop the flow of tears.

"I want my son. What did you do to him?"

"How can you blame me for that? I just wanted to send him to school."

Sunja sobbed. "It's my fault that I let you know him. You're a selfish person who'd take whatever you want, no matter the consequences. I wish I'd never met you."

Passersby gaped until Hansu stared back at them, forcing them to look away. The boy was still in the shop.

"You're the worst kind of man, because you won't let go until you get your way."

"Sunja, I'm dying."

4

Cradling his copies of *Tetsuwan Atomu* and *Ultraman*, Solomon sat quietly between Sunja and Hansu in the backseat of the large sedan.

"How old are you?" Hansu asked.

Solomon held up three fingers.

"*Soo nee*. Are you going to read those now?" Hansu asked, pointing to the boy's new comics. "Can you read already?"

Solomon shook his head. "I'm going to wait until Toto comes tonight so he can read them to me." He opened up his red satchel and put the comics inside.

"Who is Toto?" Hansu asked.

"He's my papa's friend from when they were boys. He's a real Japanese policeman. He's caught murderers and robbers. I've known him since I was born."

"Is that so? All that time?" Hansu smiled.

The small boy nodded gravely.

"Grandma, what will you make Toto for dinner?" Solomon asked.

"Fish *jeon* and chicken *jorim*," Sunja replied. Mozasu's friend Haruki Totoyama would arrive this evening and stay for the weekend, and she'd already planned all the meals.

"But Toto likes *bulgogi*. It's his favorite meal."

"I can make that tomorrow night. He won't leave until Sunday afternoon."

Solomon looked worried.

Hansu, who'd been observing Solomon carefully, said, "I love chicken *jorim*. That's the kind of dish you can only get at a nice home. Anyone can have *bulgogi* at a restaurant, but only your grandmother can make—"

"Do you want to meet Toto? He's my best grown-up friend."

Sunja shook her head, but Hansu ignored her.

"I've known your father since he was a boy your age. I'd love to have dinner at your house. Thank you, Solomon."

In the front hall, Sunja removed her coat and helped Solomon with his. With his right forearm raised and his left tucked close to his body, the boy ran to the den to watch *Tetsuwan Atomu*. Hansu followed Sunja to the kitchen.

She poured shrimp chips into a small basket and retrieved a yogurt drink from the refrigerator and arranged them on the round Ultraman tray.

"Solomon," she called out.

The boy came to the kitchen to take the tray, and he carried it carefully back to the den to watch his programs.

Hansu sat down by the Western-style breakfast table.

"This is a good house."

Sunja didn't reply.

It was a brand-new three-bedroom in the Westerners' section of Yokohama. Of course, Hansu had driven past it before; he'd seen the exterior of every place she'd ever lived. With the exception of the farmhouse during the war, this was the first one he'd been inside. The furnishings resembled sets from American films—upholstered sofas, high wooden dining tables, crystal chandeliers, and leather armchairs. Hansu guessed that the family slept on beds rather than on the floor or on futons. There were no old things in the house—no traces of anything from Korea or Japan. The spacious, windowed kitchen looked out onto the neighbors' rock garden.

Sunja wasn't speaking to him, but she didn't seem angry, either. She was facing the stove with her back turned to him. Hansu could make out the outline of her body in her camel-colored sweater and brown woolen

trousers. The first time he'd spotted her, he'd noticed her large, full bosom beneath the traditional Korean blouse. He'd always preferred a girl
with big breasts and a pillowy bottom. He had never seen her completely naked; they'd only made love outside, where she had always worn
a *chima*. His famously beautiful wife had no chest, hips, or ass, and he had
dreaded fucking her because she'd loathed being touched. Before bed, he
had to bathe, and after lovemaking she had to have a long bath at no matter
what hour. After she gave birth to three girls, he quit trying for a son; even
his father-in-law, whom Hansu loved, had said nothing about the other
women.

He believed that she'd been foolish for refusing to be his wife in
Korea. What did it matter that he had a marriage in Japan? He would
have taken excellent care of her and Noa. They would have had other
children. She would never have had to work in an open market or in a
restaurant kitchen. Nevertheless, he had to admire her for not taking his
money the way any young girl did these days. In Tokyo, it was possible
for a man to buy a girl for a bottle of French perfume or a pair of shoes
from Italy.

If Hansu was comfortable reminiscing in her kitchen, Sunja was more
than a little unsettled at the sight of him sitting at the breakfast table. From
the moment she'd met him, she'd felt his presence all around her. He was
an unwanted constant in her imagination. And after Noa vanished, it was
as if she were continually haunted by both father and son. Hansu was now
in her kitchen waiting patiently for her attention. He was staying for dinner. In all these years, they had never eaten a meal together. Why had he
come? When would he go? It was his way to appear then disappear, and
as she boiled water for their tea, she thought, I could turn around and he
could be gone. Then what?

Sunja opened a blue tin of imported butter cookies and put some on a
plate. She filled the teapot with hot water and floated a generous pinch of
tea leaves. It was easy to recall a time when there was no money for tea and
a time when there was none to buy.

"On the first of each month, Noa sends me cash with a brief note saying
that he's well. The postmarks are always different," she said.

"I've looked for Noa. He doesn't want to be found. I'm looking for him still. Sunja, he's my son, too."

How can you blame me for that? Hansu had once said to her. She poured him a cup of tea and excused herself.

The reflection in the bathroom mirror disappointed her. She was fifty-two years old. Her sister-in-law, Kyunghee, who'd been diligent about wearing her hat and gloves to protect her from spots and lines, looked much younger than she did, though Kyunghee was fourteen years older. Sunja touched her short, graying hair. She had never been lovely, and certainly now, she didn't believe that any man would ever want her. That part of her life had ended with Mozasu's father. She was plain and wrinkled; her waist and thighs were thick. Her face and hands belonged to a poor, hardworking woman, and no matter how much money she had in her purse now, nothing would make her appealing. A long time ago, she had wanted Hansu more than her own life. Even when she broke with him, she had wanted him to return, to find her, to keep her.

Hansu was seventy, yet he had changed very little; if anything, his features had improved. He still trimmed his thick white hair carefully and tamed it with scented oil; in his fine wool suit and handmade shoes, Hansu looked like an elegant statesman—a handsome grandfather. No one would have pegged him for a yakuza boss. Sunja didn't want to leave the bathroom. Before she'd left the house, she hadn't even bothered to look in the mirror. She wasn't hideous or shameful to look at, but she had prematurely reached the stage in a woman's life when no one noticed her entering or leaving a room.

Sunja opened the cold-water spigot and washed her face. Despite everything, she wanted him to desire her a little—this knowledge was embarrassing. In her life, there had been two men; that was better than none, she supposed; so that had to be enough. Sunja dried her face on a hand towel and turned off the light.

In the kitchen, Hansu was eating a biscuit.

"Are you okay living here?"

She nodded.

"And the little boy. He's well behaved."

"Mozasu checks in on him all the time."

"When will he be home?"

"Soon. I better make dinner."

"Can I help you cook?" Hansu pretended to take off his suit jacket. Sunja laughed.

"At last. I thought you'd forgotten how to smile."

They both looked away.

"Are you dying?" she asked.

"It's prostate cancer. I have very good doctors. I don't think I'll die of this. Not very soon, anyway."

"You lied then."

"No, Sunja. We're all dying."

She felt angry with him for lying, but she felt grateful, too. She had loved him, and she could not bear the thought of him being gone from this life.

Solomon shrieked with happiness when the door opened. Rolling up his red sweater sleeves hastily, Solomon raised his left arm, bent into a sharp L, and his right hand bisected his left forearm to make an off-centered cross. The child made static sounds to announce the laser beams emitting from his left hand and held his fierce pose.

Haruki fell down onto the floor. He moaned, then made the sound of an explosion.

"Ah, the *kaiju* has been defeated!" Solomon shouted, and jumped on top of Haruki.

"It's very good to see you again," Mozasu said to Hansu. "This is my friend Haruki Totoyama."

"*Hajimemashite*. Totoyama *desu*."

Solomon resumed his pose.

"Have mercy, Ultraman. *Kaiju* Toto must say hello to your grandmother."

"It's good to see you," Sunja said.

"Thank you for having me."

Solomon moved in between Sunja and Haruki.

"*Kaiju* Toto!"

"*Hai!*" Haruki bellowed.

"Papa bought me a new *Ultraman* yesterday."

"Lucky, lucky," Haruki said, sounding envious.

"I'll show you. C'mon!" Solomon pulled on Haruki, and the grown man hurtled dramatically toward Solomon's room.

Hansu kept a file on every person in Sunja's life. He knew all about Detective Haruki Totoyama, the elder son of a seamstress who owned a uniform manufacturer in Osaka. He had no father and a younger brother who was mentally disabled. Haruki was a homosexual who was engaged to an older woman who worked for his mother. In spite of his relative youth, Haruki was highly regarded in his precinct.

The dinner table talk was happy and relaxed.

"Why can't you move to Yokohama and live with us?" Solomon asked Haruki.

"Hmm. Tempting, *nee*? Then I can play Ultraman every day. *Soooo*. But, Soro-chan, my mother and brother live in Osaka. I think I'm supposed to live there, too."

"Oh," Solomon sighed. "I didn't know you had a brother. Is he older or younger?"

"Younger."

"I'd like to meet him," Solomon said. "We could be friends."

"*Soo nee*, but he's very shy."

Solomon nodded.

"Grandma is shy, too."

Sunja shook her head, and Mozasu smiled.

"I wish you could move here with your brother," Solomon said quietly.

Haruki nodded. Before Solomon was born, he had not been very interested in children. From a young age, having a handicapped brother had made him wary of the responsibilities of caring for another person.

"My girlfriend Ayame prefers Tokyo over Osaka. Perhaps she would be happier here, too," Haruki said.

"Maybe you can move here when you get married," Solomon said.

Mozasu laughed. "*Soo nee.*"

Hansu sat up straighter.

"The Yokohama chief of police is a friend. Please let me know if I can be of service if you'd like to transfer," Hansu said, making an offer he could realize. He took out his business card and handed it to the young officer, and Haruki received it with two hands and a small bow of the head.

Mozasu raised his eyebrows.

Sunja, who had been quiet, continued to observe Hansu. Naturally, she was suspicious of his help. Hansu was not an ordinary person, and he was capable of actions she could neither see nor understand.

5

Nagano, January 1969

A maze of filing cabinets and metal desks created a warren of office workers in the business offices of Cosmos Pachinko. In the thicket of furniture, Risa Iwamura, the head filing clerk, was not very noticeable. By any conventional measure, Risa was, in fact, appealing in her face and form. However, she possessed a distant manner, preventing ease or intimacy with those around her. It was as if the young woman were turning down her lights to minimize any possibility of attraction or notice. She dressed soberly in white blouses and inexpensive black poly skirts requiring little maintenance; she wore the black leather shoes of an old woman. In the winter, one of her two gray wool cardigans graced her thin shoulders like a cape—her only ornament, an inexpensive silvertone wristwatch, which she consulted often, though she never seemed to have anywhere to go. When she performed her tasks, Risa needed little guidance; she anticipated the needs of her employers faultlessly and executed the tasks without any reminders.

For nearly seven years, Noa had been living in Nagano, passing as a Japanese called Nobuo Ban. He had worked assiduously for the owner of Cosmos Pachinko and had settled into a small, invisible life. He was a valued employee, and the owner left him alone. The only thing that the owner brought up every January when he gave Noa his bonus and New Year's lecture was marriage: A man of his age and position should have his own home and children. Noa had been the head of the business offices ever since

Takano, the man who had hired him, had moved to Nagoya to run the multiple Cosmos businesses there. Nevertheless, Noa continued to live in the pachinko parlor dorms and took his meals regularly in the pachinko staff cafeteria. Although he had already paid Hansu back for the Waseda tuition and board, Noa still sent money to his mother each month. He spent almost nothing on himself beyond what was absolutely necessary.

After this year's New Year's lecture, Noa thought deeply about his boss's advice. He had been aware of Risa. Although she never spoke of it, everyone knew that she came from a middle-class family with a sad scandal.

When Risa was fourteen or so, her father, a beloved doctor at the local clinic, had dispensed improper medication to two patients during the flu season, resulting in their deaths. Shortly thereafter, the doctor took his own life, rendering his family both destitute and tainted. Risa was effectively unmarriageable, since a suicide in a family could indicate mental illness in her blood; even worse, her father was perceived to have done something so shameful that he felt that he needed to die. The relatives did not come to the funeral, and they no longer called on Risa and her mother. Risa's mother never recovered from the shock and no longer left the house even to run errands. After Risa completed secondary school, Takano, a former patient of Risa's father, hired her to do clerical work.

Noa had noticed her beautiful handwriting on the files even before he noticed her. It was possible that he was in love with the way she wrote the number two—her parallel lines expressing a kind of free movement inside the invisible box that contained the ideograph's strokes. If Risa wrote even an ordinary description on an invoice, Noa would pause to read it again, not because of what it said, but because he could detect that there was a kind of dancing spirit in the hand that wrote such elegant letters.

When Noa asked her to dinner one winter evening, she replied, in shock, "*Maji?*" Among the file clerks, Nobuo Ban was a fascinating topic of discussion, but after so many years, with so little change in his behavior, the interested girls had long since given up. It took two dinners, perhaps even less time than that, for Risa to fall in love with Noa, and the two intensely private young people married that winter.

On their wedding night, Risa was frightened.

"Will it hurt?"

"You can tell me to stop. I'd rather hurt myself than hurt you, my wife."

Neither had realized the loneliness each had lived with for such a long time until the loneliness was interrupted by genuine affection.

When Risa got pregnant, she quit her job and stayed home and raised her family with as much competence as she had run the file rooms of a successful pachinko business. First, she had twin girls; then a year later, Risa gave birth to a boy; then a year after that, another girl.

Every month, Noa traveled for work for two days, but otherwise he kept to a kind of reliable schedule that made it possible to work six days a week for Cosmos and raise his family attentively. Curiously, he did not drink or go out to clubs, even to entertain the police or to be entertained by pachinko machine salesmen. Noa was honest, precise, and could handle any level of business complication from taxes to machine licenses. Moreover, he was not greedy. The owner of Cosmos respected that Noa avoided *mizu shobai*. Naturally, Risa was grateful; it was easy to lose the affections of a husband to an ambitious bar hostess.

Like all Japanese mothers, Risa volunteered at the children's schools and did everything else she could to make sure that her four children were well and safe. Having so many little constituents kept her from having to involve herself with those outside her family. If her father's death had expelled her from the tribe of ordinary middle-class people, she had effectively reproduced her own tribe.

The marriage was a stable one, and eight years passed quickly. The couple did not quarrel. Noa did not love Risa in the way he had his college girlfriend, but that was a good thing, he thought. Never again, he swore, would he be that vulnerable to another person. Noa remained careful around his new family. Though he valued his wife and children as a kind of second chance, in no way did he see his current life as a rebirth. Noa carried the story of his life as a Korean like a dark, heavy rock within him. Not a day passed when he didn't fear being discovered. The only thing he continued to do from before was to read his English-language novels.

After marrying, he no longer ate at the employees' cafeteria. Now he allowed himself lunch at an inexpensive restaurant where he ate alone. Over lunch, for thirty minutes a day, he reread Dickens, Trollope, or Goethe, and he remembered who he was inside.

It was spring when the twin girls turned seven, and the family went to Matsumoto Castle for a Sunday picnic. Risa had planned the outing to cheer up her mother, who seemed to be retreating further into herself. The children were overjoyed, since they would get ice cream on the way home.

The doctor's widow, Iwamura-san, had never been a competent woman; in fact, she was often helpless. She had remained childishly pretty—soft, pale cheeks, naturally red lips, and dyed black hair. She wore simple beige smocks and cardigans, closed only on the top button. Her expression was perpetually one of a small child who had been disappointed by her birthday present. That said, she was hardly ignorant. She had been a doctor's wife, and though his death had destroyed her cherished social ambitions, she had not relinquished her wishes for her only child. It was bad enough that her daughter worked in pachinko, but now she had married a man who worked in the sordid business, cementing her caste in life. On her initial meeting with Nobuo Ban, she had guessed that there was something unusual about his past, since he had no family. No doubt, he was foreign. She felt suspicious of his character; however, there was also something so sad beneath his fine manners that reminded her of her dear husband, that the widow felt compelled to overlook his background as long as no one ever found out.

A sparse crowd was forming in front of Matsumoto-jo. A famous docent, popular with the locals, was about to lecture about Japan's oldest existing castle. The old man with wispy white eyebrows and a slight hunch had brought an easel with him and was setting up his poster-sized photographs and visual aids. Noa's third child, who had barely eaten anything except for half a rice ball, bolted from his seat and darted toward the guide. Risa was packing up the empty bento boxes and asked Noa to stand near Koichi, a tiny six-year-old boy with a remarkably well-shaped face and head. He had no fear of strangers and would talk to anyone. Once, at the market, he told the greengrocer that his mother had burned the eggplant the week before. Adults enjoyed talking with Koichi.

"*Sumimasen, sumimasen!*" the boy shouted, pushing his little body through the group listening carefully to the guide's introduction to the castle's history.

The crowd parted to let the boy stand in the front. The guide smiled at Koichi and continued.

The boy's mouth was open a little, and he listened intently while his father stood in the back.

The guide turned to the next image on the easel. In the old black-and-white photograph, the castle leaned dramatically as if the edifice might collapse. The crowd gasped politely at the famous image. Tourists and children who had never seen it before looked at the image closely.

"When this magnificent castle started to list this much, everyone remembered Tada Kasuke's curse!" The guide widened his heavy-lidded eyes for emphasis.

The adults from the region nodded in recognition. There wasn't a soul in Nagano who didn't know about the seventeenth-century Matsumoto headman who'd led the Jokyo Uprising against unfair taxes and was executed with twenty-seven others, including his two young sons.

"What is a curse?" Koichi asked.

Noa frowned, because the child had been reminded repeatedly that he must not blurt out questions whenever he wished.

"A curse?" the guide said, then paused silently for dramatic effect.

"A curse is a terrible, terrible thing. And a curse with moral power is the worst! Tada Kasuke was unfairly persecuted when he was just trying to save all the good people of Nagano from the exploitation of those who lived in this castle! At his death, Tada Kasuke uttered a curse against the greedy Mizuno clan!" The guide grew visibly impassioned by his own speech.

Koichi wanted to ask another question, but his twin sisters, who were now standing by him, pinched the little bit of flesh around his right elbow. Koichi had to learn not to talk so much, they thought; policing him was a family effort.

"Almost two hundred years after Tada Kasuke's death, the ruling clan tried everything in their power to appease the spirit of the martyr to lift the curse. It must have worked, because the castle structure is straight again!" The guide raised both arms dramatically and gestured toward the building behind him. The crowd laughed.

Koichi stared at the poster-sized image of the listing castle. "How? How do you reverse a curse?" Koichi asked, unable to control himself.

His sister Ume stepped on his foot, but Koichi did not care.

"To appease the spirits, the ruling clan proclaimed that Tada Kasuke was a martyr and gave him an afterlife name. They had a statue built. Ultimately, the truth must be acknowledged!"

Koichi opened his mouth again, but this time Noa walked over and picked up his son gently and carried him back to his mother, who was seated with her mother on a bench. Even though he was in kindergarten, Koichi still loved to be picked up. The crowd smiled.

"Papa, that was so interesting, *nee?*"

"*Hai,*" Noa replied. When he held the boy, he always recalled Mozasu, who would fall asleep easily in his arms, his round head resting on Noa's shoulder.

"Can I put a curse on someone?" Koichi asked.

"What? Who do you want to put a curse on?"

"Umeko. She stepped on my foot on purpose."

"That's not very nice, but it doesn't warrant a curse, *nee?*"

"But I can reverse a curse if I want."

"Oh, it isn't so easy to do so, Koichi-chan. And what would you do if someone put a curse on you?"

"*Soo nee.*" Koichi sobered at the thought of this, then broke into a smile when he saw his mother, whom he loved more than anyone. Risa was knitting a sweater as she chatted with her mother. The picnic bags rested at her feet.

The Ban family walked around the castle grounds, and when the children grew bored, Noa took them to eat ice cream, as he had promised.

6

Yokohama, July 1974

Haruki Totoyama married Ayame, the foreman of his mother's uniform shop, because his mother had wanted him to do so. It turned out to be a wise decision. When his mother was diagnosed with stomach cancer and could no longer manage the shop or take care of Haruki's brother, Daisuke, Ayame knew exactly what to do. For two years, Ayame managed the business ably, nursed her ailing mother-in-law, and took good care of Daisuke. When Totoyama-san finally died after a great deal of suffering, Haruki asked his exhausted wife what he should do with his mother's shop, and Ayame's answer surprised him.

"We should sell it and move to Yokohama. I don't want to live in Osaka anymore. I never liked working at the shop. I did it because I could never disappoint your mother. We don't have to worry about money anymore. If there's any free time, I want to learn how to bake cakes. Daisuke likes cakes. I will stay home and take care of him."

Haruki didn't know what to make of this, but he couldn't refuse her.

With the money from the sale of the business and his inheritance, Haruki bought a three-bedroom mansion-style apartment near the old cemetery in Yokohama. The apartment had a double wall oven for Ayame. One phone call to Mozasu led to a call from the Yokohama police chief, who offered Haruki the same job he had in Osaka. Naturally, Mozasu and Solomon were happy that Haruki was finally moving to Yokohama. Nevertheless, upon Haruki's family's arrival, Solomon was not allowed to visit

Haruki's house or to meet Haruki's younger brother, who was terrified of children.

Daisuke was almost thirty years old, but he was not much older than five or six mentally. He could not go outside often, because noise, crowds, and bright lights upset him. His mother's illness and death had been catastrophic for him, but Ayame, a longtime employee of his mother, was able to keep Daisuke calm. She created a predictable routine for him at their new home, and because there were so many foreigners in Yokohama, Ayame was able to find an American special education teacher who was willing to come to the house and work with him five days a week. Daisuke would never be able to go to a normal school, get a job, or live alone, but Ayame believed that he could do more and that he should know more than what was expected of him, which was very little. Haruki was grateful for her thoughtfulness. He could not help but admire his wife's ability to solve problems and manage so many new things without ever complaining. She was five years older than he was, the eldest daughter raised in a deeply conservative Buddhist family, and he assumed that her strict upbringing had much to do with her ability to forbear and endure. His mother told him on more than one occasion that Ayame loved him, though he didn't deserve it.

Daisuke took a nap in the early afternoon, ate a late lunch, then had three hours of at-home school with lessons, games, and story time with his teacher, Miss Edith. During his lessons, Ayame went to the public bath, then did her food shopping. The July heat in Yokohama was milder than back home, and Ayame didn't mind walking around after her bath. Invariably, street dust and humidity would spoil that pure feeling that came from a bath, but Ayame felt happy to be alone. She had well over an hour before Miss Edith would leave, so she took the greener path cutting through the wooded park by the cemetery. It was not yet dusk, and there was still a bluish light left over from the day. Beneath the canopy of bright green leaves, Ayame felt clean and joyful. For dinner, she planned on picking up a few sticks of the yakitori that Daisuke was so fond of, which an elderly couple sold a few blocks from their apartment.

As she walked past a thicket of evergreens, she heard the light rustle of branches. From childhood, Ayame had loved birds, even the enormous black crows that most children feared, and she gingerly approached the dense cluster of trees. As she moved closer to the sounds, she could see a nice-looking man leaning against a wide tree trunk with his eyes closed. His trousers were pulled down to his knees and another man knelt in front of him, his head hovering over the standing man's pale hips. Ayame held her breath and retreated quietly to the main path. The men had not seen her. She was not in danger, but she walked faster, her heart beating as if it would pound itself out of her body. The dry grass poked her sandaled feet. Ayame ran until she reached the pavement border, where she could see pedestrians.

On the crowded street opposite the cemetery, no one noticed her. Ayame wiped the perspiration from her brow. When was the last time her husband had wanted her? It had been his mother's suggestion that they marry, and in their brief courtship, Haruki had been thoughtful and kind. She was not a virgin when she married, having had sex with two men who had refused to marry her. There had been one other man, a fabric distributor who pursued her for months, but when Ayame learned that he was married, she refused to go to the love motel with him, because she had only slept with the others as a way to get married, and with this one there was really no point. Unlike the other men, Haruki had never asked her to go with him to a motel. She reasoned that it may have been awkward for him since she worked with his mother. She could not help admiring his high-mindedness and good manners.

Their marriage was consummated. In the beginning, when she and Haruki were trying to have a baby, he made love to her regularly—quickly and cleanly, respecting her wishes when it was not the right time of the month. After they had been attempting to have a child for two years, the doctors determined that she was infertile, and it seemed that Daisuke would effectively become her son. They did not make love again. She had never been interested in being the sexy lady, and he did not approach her for such transactions.

Ayame kept to Daisuke's schedule and went to bed early, while Haruki woke up late and went to bed late. Their varying sleep times prevented regular encounters in bed. She may not have been interested in sex, but she was not unaware that in general, men needed sex, and that it was a preferable situation to have a husband who had sex periodically with his own wife. If Haruki and she no longer made love, Ayame blamed herself. She was older. Her yellowing face was ordinary and round, and she was far too thin, with spindly legs and arms. Wanting to fill out, she ate as much as she could, especially sweetmeats, but it was impossible for her to gain weight. When she was growing up, her brothers had teased her that her chest was more even than the floor. If she'd wanted, she could have worn clothing for middle school girls. Out of practicality and habit, each day, Ayame wore one of the many dark-colored jumpers that she'd sewed for herself. She had midi-length jumpers in every fabric and color. In the summer, her jumpers were made of linen or seersucker.

When Ayame reached Daisuke's favorite yakitori stand, she fished out her purse from the string bag holding her bath things and asked the old woman for grilled chicken wings, gizzards, and pieces of white meat with scallion. As the woman behind the smoky stand filled the order, Ayame recalled the man leaning against the tree—his rapturous face. Did Haruki want her to kneel before him? Of course, she knew of many things that men and women did, but she had never seen anyone else make love. She'd read two D. H. Lawrence novels. At thirty-seven years old, Ayame wanted to know even more about the things she had never done. Would Haruki be embarrassed for her?

Ayame checked her slender wristwatch with its tiny face, a birthday present from Haruki's mother. There were still forty minutes left until she had to head home. Ayame turned around.

When she returned to the thicket of evergreens, the two men were gone, but now there were at least five other couples; women and men were lying together in the more secluded areas, and two men who were not wearing pants stroked each other while whispering. One couple was lying on thick sheets of brown butcher paper that made noise with their movements. When a tall woman spotted her looking, she didn't flinch; rather, she closed her eyes and made noises of pleasure as the man beside her continued to massage her small breasts. It felt as if the tall woman wanted Ayame to study them, and Ayame felt emboldened to move closer. The sounds of quiet moaning from the lovers were like evening bird calls. She remembered Daisuke, who would want his dinner.

Three days later, after another long bath, Ayame went directly to the park behind the cemetery. She recognized a woman and man from before, and there were others who did not seem to mind her solitary presence. Everyone here belonged to each other's secret, and Ayame felt safe among them. As she was leaving, a lovely girl approached her.

"Why do you come so early? It's more wonderful in the evening."

Ayame didn't know what to say, but she felt it would be impolite not to reply.

"What do you mean?"

"There are more people later if you want to do things." The girl laughed. "Don't you like to do things?"

Ayame shook her head.

"I, I...No."

"If you have money, I can do things for you. I prefer to be do things with girls."

Ayame held her breath. The girl was plump in a very pretty way, with vivid color in her cheeks. She had beautiful white arms, full and smooth like those of a woman in an Italian painting. In her sheer georgette blouse in a *cha* color and navy print skirt, she looked like an attractive office lady. The girl took Ayame's left hand and slipped it in her blouse; Ayame could feel the smooth rise of the girl's large nipple.

"I like this bone between your neck and shoulders. You're very cute. Come see me. I'm here in the evenings. Today, I started early, because I have a meeting, but he's a little late. I'm usually near the shrubs over there." She giggled. "I love to put things in my mouth. *Nee?*" She wet her lips with her strawberry-colored tongue. "And I can bring you toys," she said, before returning to her spot.

Stunned, Ayame nodded and walked home. Her left hand felt like it was burning, and with it, she stroked her collarbone, never having given it any thought.

For three months after, Ayame stuck to her old route to the *sento* and went straight from there to the market streets to do her shopping. She returned faithfully to her routines with Daisuke, and when she took her baths at the *sento*, she tried not to think of that girl. Ayame was not ignorant; even as a girl, she knew that others did many curious things. What puzzled her was that so late in her life, she wanted to know more but had no one to ask. Her husband never seemed to change: He was hardworking, polite, and rarely home. He was affectionate with Daisuke. When he had time off, he went to see his Korean friend Mozasu and his son, Solomon, or took his brother for walks in the park or to the *sento* to give her some time alone. Occasionally, the three of them went to the same *yakiniku* restaurant, where the owner gave them a private room in the back. Daisuke liked cooking his meals on the grill. After Daisuke fell asleep for the night, her evenings were quiet. She read recipe books and sewing magazines and crocheted lace.

Despite her strong efforts, it was no longer just at the *sento*. Ayame wondered about the girl all day—when she was baking a golden sponge cake or merely dusting the furniture. What confused her was that the girl in the green blouse had looked so wholesome and amused, nothing at all like what she'd seen in maudlin films about a fallen woman from a bad family. The girl was luscious like a costly melon sold in a department store.

It was a Saturday evening at the end of November, and Daisuke had fallen asleep earlier than usual. Haruki was at the office catching up on writing reports where it was quiet enough for him to work undisturbed. In the living room, Ayame was trying to read a book about English baking techniques, but she found her mind drifting. Closing the book, she decided to have another bath, though she'd had one earlier that day. Daisuke was snoring quietly when she left the house.

At the *sento*, she soaked in the hot bathwater, fearing that someone could see the desire in her face. She wondered if she could find the nerve to ask her husband to make love to her. When the tips of her fingers were horribly wrinkled, she dressed and combed her hair. Outside, the streetlamps shone brightly, and the black pavement glistened in the night. Ayame walked toward the cemetery.

Even in the cold, there were too many lovers to count. Couples watched others make love and masturbate each other. Naked bodies humped beneath large trees. Men lined up in a row while others on their knees bobbed their heads against them. Watching the men's faces thrilled her. She wanted Haruki to take her into his arms and make violent love to her there. There was only a little light in the evening sky, only a small misshapen moon and the faintest spray of winter stars. Ayame walked through the arrangements of men and women. By an impressive oak, two men embraced in lovemaking, and the taller man, whose arms clasped the younger one, wore a gray suit much like the one she had made for her husband. Ayame looked closer and saw him, his eyes shut tightly as he held on to the young man in the white cotton undershirt who was gasping with excitement. She retreated to the other side of the foliage to hide herself. Ayame held her breath, and she watched her husband making love. It was. It was him.

When Haruki and the young man in the white shirt were done, they put on their clothes without talking and walked away from one another without a bow or a good-bye. She didn't see Haruki giving the young man any money, but that could have happened earlier; she couldn't be sure of how these things worked. Would it matter if the man had been paid? she wondered.

Ayame sat down on the roots of an old tree not far from a couple having breathless intercourse, and she stared at the pads of her fingers, which were smooth again. There was no choice but to wait until he was long gone, but if he reached the house before she did, she'd have to tell him that she was at the *sento*, which wasn't true.

"Hi."

The girl wore a white blouse this time, and it shimmered in the dark, making her look like an angel.

"Did you bring money?"

The girl crouched down to Ayame's level and heaved her bosom toward her face as if readying to nurse her. She opened her blouse and pulled out her breasts, propping them over the fabric cups of her underwire brassiere.

The girl was beautiful. Ayame wondered why she could not possess features as lovely and alluring on her withered body that could neither conceive nor be loved.

"You can pay me after if you want." The girl glanced at Ayame's string bag. "You've had your bath like a good baby, and you're clean. Come to Mama. Here, you can put your mouth on them. I like that. Then I can do it to you. *Aka-chan*, you look afraid, but why? This will feel so nice and sweet." The girl took Ayame's right hand and pushed it up her skirt, and Ayame felt another woman for the first time. It was soft and plush.

"*Daijoubu?*" On her knees, the girl moved closer and took Ayame's left hand and put her ring finger into her mouth as she climbed onto Ayame's lap. She sniffed Ayame's wet hair. "I can almost drink your shampoo. You smell so pretty. *Aka, aka*, you'll feel better as we make love. You'll be in paradise."

Ayame folded herself into the warmth of the girl's body.

As she opened her mouth, the girl pulled the string bag to her.

"Do you have money here? I need a lot. Mama has to buy many things to look pretty for her baby."

Ayame recoiled and heaved the girl off her body, making her fall on her back.

"You're disgusting. Disgusting." She got up.

"You skinny old cunt!" the girl shouted, and Ayame could hear her throaty laugh from a distance. "You have to pay for love, you bitch!"

Ayame ran back to the *sento*.

When she finally returned home, Haruki was fixing his brother a snack.

"*Tadaima*," she said quietly.

"Where were you, A-chan?" Daisuke asked, his face folded with worry. He had the lopsided face of a pale, gaunt man with the extraordinary eyes of a very young child—unguarded and capable of expressing joy. He wore the yellow pajamas that she had ironed for him that morning.

Haruki nodded and smiled at her. He had never before found his brother alone. Daisuke had been crying on his bed mat, asking for his mother. He didn't want to tell Ayame this for fear of making her feel bad about being late.

"I was at the bath, Dai-chan. I'm very sorry I'm late. I thought you were sleeping, and it was cold so I went to have another bath."

"I was afraid. I was afraid," Daisuke said, his eyes beginning to well up again. "I want Mama."

She felt unable to look at Haruki's face. He had not yet removed his suit jacket.

Daisuke went to her, leaving Haruki by the kitchen counter to put away the box of *senbei*.

"A-chan is clean. She had a bath. A-chan is clean. She had a bath." He sang the line that he liked to repeat after she came home from the *sento*.

"Are you tired now?" she asked him.

"No."

"Would you like me to read to you?"

"*Hai*."

Haruki left them in the living room with her reading a picture book about old trains, and she nodded to him when he said good night before going to bed.

7

Yokohama, March 1976

A retiring detective had failed to complete a report of a suicide, and eventually it landed on Haruki's desk. A twelve-year-old Korean boy had jumped off the roof of his apartment building. The mother was too hysterical to finish the interview at the time, but the parents were willing to meet Haruki tonight after they finished work.

The boy's parents lived not far from Chinatown. The father was a plumber's assistant, and the mother worked in a glove factory. Tetsuo Kimura, the jumper, was the oldest of three and had two sisters.

Even before the apartment door opened, the familiar smells of garlic, shoyu, and the stronger miso that Koreans favored greeted him in the damp hallway. All the tenants of the six-story building owned by a Korean were also Koreans. The boy's mother, her face downcast and meek, let him into the three-room apartment. Haruki slipped off his street shoes to put on the slippers she gave him. In the main room, the father, wearing a workman's clean overalls, was already seated cross-legged on a blue floor cushion. The mother set out a discount-store tray brimming with teacups and wrapped biscuits from the *conbini*. The father held a bound book in his lap.

After handing the father his business card with two hands, Haruki sat down on a floor cushion. The mother poured him a cup of tea and sat with her knees folded.

"You didn't get a chance to see this." The father handed the book to

Haruki. "You should know what happened. Those children should be punished."

The father, a long-waisted man with an olive complexion and a square jaw, didn't make eye contact when speaking.

The book was a middle school graduation album. Haruki opened the thick volume to the page marked with a slip of blank notepaper. There were rows and columns of black-and-white photographs of students, all of them wearing uniforms—a few smiling, some showing teeth, with little variation overall. Right away he spotted Tetsuo, who had his mother's long face and his father's small mouth—a mild-looking boy with thin shoulders. There were a few handwritten messages over the faces of the photographs.

"Tetsuo—good luck in high school. Hiroshi Noda."

"You draw well. Kayako Mitsuya."

Haruki must have looked confused, because he didn't notice anything unusual. Then the father prompted him to check the flyleaf.

"Die, you ugly Korean."

"Stop collecting welfare. Koreans are ruining this country."

"Poor people smell like farts."

"If you kill yourself, our high school next year will have one less filthy Korean."

"Nobody likes you."

"Koreans are troublemakers and pigs. Get the hell out. Why are you here anyway?"

"You smell like garlic and garbage!!!"

"If I could, I'd cut your head off myself, but I don't want to get my knife dirty!"

The handwriting was varied and inauthentic. Some letters slanted right or left; multiple authors had tried purposefully to shield their identities.

Haruki closed the book and laid it beside him on the clean floor. He took a sip of tea.

"Your son, he never mentioned that others were bothering him?"

"No," the mother answered quickly. "He never complained. Never. He said he was never discriminated against."

Haruki nodded.

"It was not because he was Korean. That sort of thing was from long ago. Things are better now. We know many kindhearted Japanese," the mother said.

Even with the cover closed, Haruki could see the words in his mind. The electric fan on the floor circulated a constant flow of warm air.

"Did you speak with his teachers?" the mother asked.

The retired detective had. The teachers had said that the boy was a strong student but too quiet.

"He had top marks. The children were jealous of him because he was smarter than they were. My son learned to read when he was three," the mother said.

The father sighed and laid his hand gently on his wife's forearm, and she said no more.

The boy's father said, "Last winter, Tetsuo asked if he could stop going to school and instead work in the vegetable store that his uncle owns. It's a small shop near the little park down the street. My brother-in-law was looking for a boy to break down boxes and work as a cashier. Tetsuo said he wanted to work for him, but we said no. Neither of us finished high school, and we didn't want him to quit. It didn't make any sense for him to work in a job like that and to give up school when he's such a good student. My brother-in-law is barely getting by himself, so my son would not have made much of a salary. My wife wanted him to get a good job in an electronics factory. If he had finished high school, then—"

The father covered his head with his large, rough hands, pressing down on his coarse hair. "Working in the basement of a grocery store. Counting inventory. That's not an easy life for anyone, you know," he said. "He was talented. He could remember any face and draw it perfectly. He could do many things we didn't know how to do."

The mother said calmly, "My son was hardworking and honest. He never hurt anyone. He helped his sisters do their homework—"

Her voice broke off.

Suddenly, the father turned to face Haruki.

"The boys who wrote that should be punished. I don't mean go to jail, but they shouldn't be allowed to write such things." He shook his head.

"He should've quit school. It would've been better if he'd worked in a basement of a grocery store or peeling bags of onions in a *yakiniku* restaurant. I'd rather have my son than no son. My wife and I are treated badly here, but it's because we're poor. There are rich Koreans who are better off. We thought it could be different for our children."

"You were born here?" Haruki asked. Their accent was no different than that of native Japanese speakers from Yokohama.

"Yes, of course. Our parents came from Ulsan."

Ulsan was in what was now South Korea, but Haruki guessed that the family was affiliated with the North Korean government, as were many of the ethnic Koreans. *Mindan* was much less popular. The Kimuras probably lacked the tuition for the North Korean schools and sent them to the local Japanese school.

"You're *Chosenjin*?"

"Yes, but what does that matter?" the father said.

"It doesn't. It shouldn't. Excuse me." Haruki glanced at the album. "Does the school know? About this? There was nothing in the report about any other kids."

"I took the afternoon off to show it to the principal. He said it was impossible to know who wrote those things," the father said.

"*Soo, soo,*" Haruki said.

"Why can't the children who wrote this be punished? Why?" the mother asked.

"There were several people who witnessed him jump with no one else on the roof. Your son was not pushed. We cannot arrest everyone who says or writes something mean-spirited—"

"Why can't the police make the principal—" The father looked directly at him, then, seeing Haruki's defeated expression, the father stared at the door instead. "You people work together to make sure nothing ever changes. *Sho ga nai. Sho ga nai.* That's all I ever hear."

"I'm sorry. I am sorry," he said before leaving.

*   *   *

Paradaisu Yokohama was crowded at eight o'clock in the evening. The volcanic rush of tinny bells, the clanging of tiny hammers across miniature metal bowls, the beeping and flashing of colorful lights, and the throaty shouts of welcome from the obsequious staff felt like a reprieve from the painful silence in his head. Haruki didn't even mind the thick swirls of tobacco smoke that hung like a layer of gray mist above the heads of the players seated opposite the rows upon rows of vertical, animated machines. As soon as Haruki stepped into the parlor, the Japanese floor manager rushed to him and asked if he would like tea. Boku-san was in the office in a meeting with a machine salesman and promised to be down shortly. Haruki and Mozasu had a standing dinner arrangement every Thursday, and Haruki was here to pick him up.

It was fair to say that almost everyone at the parlor wanted to make some extra money by gambling. However, the players also came to escape the eerily quiet streets where few said hello, to keep away from the loveless homes where wives slept with children instead of husbands, and to avoid the overheated rush-hour train cars where it was okay to push but not okay to talk to strangers. When Haruki was a younger man, he had not been much of a pachinko player, but since moving to Yokohama, Haruki allowed himself to find some comfort here.

It took no time for him to lose several thousand yen, so he bought another tray of balls. Haruki wasn't reckless about his inheritance, but his mother had saved so much that he'd have enough even if he was fired, and even if he lost a fortune. When Haruki paid young men to sleep with him, he could afford to be generous. Of all the vices, pachinko seemed like a petty one.

The small metal balls zigzagged rhythmically across the rectangular face of the machine, and Haruki moved the dial steadily to keep the action going. *No*, he had wanted to tell Tetsuo's father, *how can I prove guilt for a crime that doesn't exist? I cannot punish and I cannot prevent.* No, he could not say such things. Not to anyone. So much he could never say. Since he was a child, Haruki had wanted to hang himself, and he thought of it still. Of all the crimes, Haruki understood murder-suicides the best;

if he could have, he would've killed Daisuke, then himself. But he could never kill Daisuke. And now he could not do such an unspeakable thing to Ayame. They were innocent.

The machine died suddenly. He looked up and saw Mozasu holding the plug to the extension cord. He wore a black suit with a red Paradaisu Yokohama pin on his jacket lapel.

"How much did you lose, dummy?"

"A lot. Half my pay?"

Mozasu pulled out his wallet and handed Haruki a sheaf of yen notes, but Haruki wouldn't take it.

"It's my own fault. Sometimes I win, right?"

"Not that often." Mozasu tucked the money into Haruki's coat pocket.

At the *izakaya*, Mozasu ordered beer and poured Haruki his first drink from the large bottle. They sat at the long counter on carved wooden stools. The owner laid out the dish of warm, salted soybeans, because they always started with those.

"What's the matter with you?" Mozasu asked. "You look like shit."

"A kid jumped off a building. Had to talk with his parents today."

"Ugh. How old?"

"Middle school. Korean."

"*Ehh?*"

"You should have seen what the rotten kids wrote on his yearbook."

"Probably the same shit kids wrote in mine."

"*Maji?*"

"Yeah, every year, a bunch of knuckleheads would tell me to go back to Korea or to die a slow death. Just mean kid stuff."

"Who? Anyone I know?"

"It was a long time ago. Besides, what are you going to do? Arrest them?" Mozasu laughed. "So, you're sad about that? About the kid?"

Haruki nodded.

"You have a weakness for Koreans," Mozasu said, smiling. "You idiot."

Haruki started to cry.

"What the hell? Hey, hey." Mozasu patted his back.

The owner behind the counter looked away and wiped down the counter space of a customer who'd just left.

Haruki clasped his head with his right hand and closed his wet eyes.

"The poor kid couldn't take any more."

"Listen, man, there's nothing you can do. This country isn't going to change. Koreans like me can't leave. Where we gonna go? But the Koreans back home aren't changing, either. In Seoul, people like me get called Japanese bastards, and in Japan, I'm just another dirty Korean no matter how much money I make or how nice I am. So what the fuck? All those people who went back to the North are starving to death or scared shitless."

Mozasu patted down his pockets for cigarettes.

"People are awful. Drink some beer."

Haruki took a sip and coughed, having swallowed wrong.

"When I was a boy, I wanted to die," Haruki said.

"Me too. Every fucking day, I thought it would be better if I died, but I couldn't do it to my mother. Then after I left school, I didn't feel that way anymore. But after Yumi died, I didn't know if I was going to make it. You know? But then I couldn't do it to Solomon. And my mother, well, you know, she changed after Noa disappeared. I can never let her down like that. My mother said that my brother left because he couldn't handle Waseda and was ashamed. I don't think that's true. Nothing in school was ever hard for him. He's living somewhere else, and he doesn't want us to find him. I think he just got tired of trying to be a good Korean and quit. I was never a good Korean."

Mozasu lit his cigarette.

"But things get better. Life is shitty, but not all the time. Etsuko's great. I didn't expect her to come along. You know, I'm going to help her open a restaurant."

"She's a nice lady. Maybe you'll get married again." Haruki liked Mozasu's new Japanese girlfriend.

"Etsuko doesn't want to get married again. Her kids hate her enough already. It'd be hell for her if she married a Korean pachinko guy." Mozasu snorted.

Haruki's sad expression remained.

"Man, life's going to keep pushing you around, but you have to keep playing."

Haruki nodded.

"I used to think if my father hadn't left, then I'd be okay," Haruki said.

"Forget him. Your mother was a great lady; my wife thought she was the best of the best. Tough and smart and always fair to everyone. She was better than having five fathers. Yumi said she was the only Japanese she'd ever work for."

"Yeah. Mama was a great lady."

The owner brought out the fried oysters and *shishito* peppers.

Haruki wiped his eyes with a cocktail napkin, and Mozasu poured him another glass of beer.

"I didn't know kids wrote that stuff on your yearbooks. You were always watching out for me. I didn't know."

"Forget it. I'm okay. I'm okay now."

8

Nagano, August 1978

Hansu's driver found her waiting at the north gate of Yokohama Station as instructed, and he led Sunja to the black sedan, where Hansu was sitting in the back.

Sunja arranged herself in the plush velvet backseat, pulling down her suit jacket to cover the swell of her *ajumma* abdomen. She wore an imported French designer dress and Italian leather shoes that Mozasu's girlfriend, Etsuko, had selected for her. At sixty-two years, Sunja looked like what she was—a mother of two grown men, a grandmother, and a woman who had spent most of her life working outdoors. Despite the clothes of a wealthy Tokyo matron, her wrinkled and spotted skin and short white hair couldn't help but make her look rumpled and ordinary.

"Where are we going?"

"Nagano," Hansu replied.

"Is that where he is?"

"Yes. He goes by Nobuo Ban. He's been there continuously for sixteen years. He's married to a Japanese woman and has four children."

"Solomon has four cousins! Why couldn't he tell us?"

"He is now Japanese. No one in Nagano knows he's Korean. His wife and children don't know. Everyone in his world thinks he is pure Japanese."

"Why?"

"Because he does not want anyone to know about his past."

"Is it so easy to do this?"

"It's easy enough, and in his world, no one cares enough to dig around."

"What do you mean?"

"He runs a pachinko parlor."

"Like Mozasu?" There were Koreans in every aspect of the pachinko business, from the parlors and the *keihin* to the machine manufacturers, but she would have never expected Noa to do the same thing as Mozasu.

"*Soo nee.* How is Mozasu?" Hansu asked.

"Good." She nodded, having a hard time concentrating.

"His business okay?"

"He bought another parlor in Yokohama."

"And Solomon? He must be very big now."

"He's doing well at school. Studying hard. I want to know more about Noa."

"He is well off." Hansu smiled.

"Does he know we're coming to see him?"

"No."

"But—"

"He doesn't want to see us. Well, he doesn't want to see me. He may want to see you, but if he had, surely he would've let you know sooner."

"Then—"

"We should not speak to him today, but I thought if you wanted to see him with your own eyes, you could. He is going to be at his main office."

"How do you know this?"

"I just do," Hansu said, closing his eyes and leaning against the white lace-covered headrest. He was taking several medications, and they made him feel foggy.

It was his plan to wait until Noa came out of his office as he usually did to have lunch at the *soba-ya* across the street. Each weekday, he ate a simple lunch at a different restaurant, and on Wednesdays he ate soba. Hansu's private investigators had detailed Noa's life in Nagano in a twenty-six-page report, and what was most notable was his unwavering need for routine. Noa did not drink alcohol, gamble, or fool around with women. He had no apparent religion, and his wife and four children lived like a middle-class Japanese family in a modest house.

"Will he eat lunch by himself, do you think?"

"He always eats lunch by himself. Today is Wednesday so he will eat *zaru soba*, taking less than fifteen minutes. He will read a little of his English novel, then return to his office. This is why he is so successful, I think. He does not make mistakes. Noa has a plan." There was a kind of territorial pride in Hansu's voice.

"Do you think he'll see me?"

"It's hard to tell," he said. "You should wait in the car and get a glimpse of him, then the driver will take us back to Yokohama. We can return next week if you like. Maybe you can write to him first."

"What's the difference between today and next week?"

"Maybe if you see him and know that he is well, then you will not need to see him so much. He has chosen this life, Sunja, and maybe he wants us to respect that."

"He's my son."

"And mine."

"Noa and Mozasu. They're my life."

Hansu nodded. He had never felt this way about his children. Not really.

"I've lived only for them."

This was wrong to say. At church, the minister preached about how mothers cared too much about their children and that worshipping the family was a kind of idolatry. One must not love one's family over God, he'd said. The minister said that families could never give you what only God could give. But being a mother who loved her children too much had helped her to understand a little of what God went through. Noa had children of his own now; perhaps he could understand how much she'd lived for him.

"Look. He's coming out," Hansu said.

Her son's face had changed only a little. The graying hair along the temples surprised her, but Noa was forty-five years old and no longer the university student. He wore round, golden spectacles much like those

Isak used to wear, and his black suit hung simply on his lean frame. His face was a copy of Hansu's.

Sunja opened the car door and stepped out.

"Noa!" she cried, and rushed toward him.

He turned around and stared at his mother, who stood not ten paces from him.

"*Umma*," he murmured. Noa moved close to her and touched her arm. He had not seen his mother cry since Isak's funeral. She was not the sort to cry easily, and he felt bad for her. He had imagined that this day would come and had prepared for it, but now that she was here, he was surprised by his own sense of relief.

"There's no need to be upset. We should go inside my office," he said. "How did you get here?"

Sunja couldn't speak because she was heaving. She took a deep breath. "Koh Hansu brought me here. He found you, and he brought me here because I wanted to see you. He's in the car."

"I see," he said. "Well, he can stay there."

Upon his return to the office, his employees bowed, and Sunja followed behind. He offered her a seat in his office and closed the door.

"You look well, *umma*," Noa said.

"It has been such a long time, Noa. I've worried so much about you."

Seeing his hurt expression, she stopped herself. "But I'm glad you wrote to me. I have saved all the money you sent. It was very thoughtful of you to do that."

Noa nodded.

"Hansu told me that you're married and you have children."

Noa smiled. "I have one boy and three girls. They are very good kids. All of them study except for my son, who is a good baseball player. He is my wife's favorite. He looks like Mozasu and acts like him, too."

"I know Mozasu would like to see you. When can you come to see us?"

"I don't know. I don't know if I can."

"Haven't we wasted enough time? All these years. Noa, have mercy.

Have mercy, please. *Umma* was a girl when I met Hansu. I didn't know he was married, and when I found out, I refused to be his mistress. Then your father married me so you could have a proper name. All my life, I was faithful to your father, Baek Isak, who was a great man. Even after he died, I have been true to his—"

"I understand what you did. However, my blood father is Koh Hansu. That cannot change," Noa said flatly.

"Yes."

"I'm a Korean working in this filthy business. I suppose having yakuza in your blood is something that controls you. I can never be clean of him." He laughed. "This is my curse."

"But you're not a yakuza," she protested. "Are you? Mozasu owns pachinko parlors and he's very honest. He's always saying how it is possible to be a good employer and to avoid the bad people as long as you—"

Noa shook his head.

"*Umma*, I am honest, but there are people you cannot avoid in this business. I run a very large company, and I do what I have to do." He made a face like he'd tasted something sour.

"You're a good boy, Noa. I know you are—" she said, then felt foolish for having called him a child. "I mean, I'm sure you're a good business-man. And honest."

The two sat quietly. Noa covered his mouth with his right hand. His mother looked like an old exhausted woman.

"Do you want some tea?" he asked. Over the years, Noa had imagined his mother or brother coming to his house, discovering him there rather than in his white, sun-filled office. She'd made it easier for him by coming here instead. Would Hansu come to his office next? he wondered. It had taken longer for Hansu to find him than he'd expected.

"Would you like something to eat? I can order something—"

Sunja shook her head. "You should come home."

He laughed. "This is my home. I am not a boy."

"I'm not sorry to have had you. You are a treasure to me. I won't leave—"

"No one knows I'm Korean. Not one person."

"I won't tell anyone. I understand. I'll do whatever—"

"My wife doesn't know. Her mother would never tolerate it. My own children don't know, and I will not tell them. My boss would fire me. He doesn't employ foreigners. *Umma*, no one can know—"

"Is it so terrible to be Korean?"

"It is terrible to be me."

Sunja nodded and stared at her folded hands.

"I have prayed for you, Noa. I have prayed that God would protect you. It is all a mother can do. I'm glad you are well." Each morning, she went to the dawn service and prayed for her children and grandson. She had prayed for this moment.

"The children, what are their names?"

"What does it matter?"

"Noa, I'm so sorry. Your father brought us to Japan, and then, you know, we couldn't leave because of the war here and then the war there. There was no life for us back home, and now it's too late. Even for me."

"I went back," he said.

"What do you mean?"

"I'm a Japanese citizen now, and I can travel. I went to South Korea to visit. To see my supposed motherland."

"You're a Japanese citizen? How? Really?"

"It's possible. It is always possible."

"And did you go to Busan?"

"Yes, and I visited Yeongdo. It was tiny but beautiful," he said.

Sunja's eyes filled with tears.

"*Umma*, I have a meeting now. I'm sorry, but why don't we see each other next week? I'll come by. I want to see Mozasu again. I have to take care of some urgent things now."

"Really? You'll come?" Sunja smiled. "Oh, thank you, Noa. I'm so glad. You're such a good—"

"It's best if you leave now. I'll phone you later tonight when you get home."

Sunja got up quickly from her seat, and Noa walked her back to the spot where they met. He would not look into Hansu's car.

"We'll talk later," he said, and crossed the street toward his building.

*　　*　　*

Sunja watched her son enter his office building, then tapped the passenger door of Hansu's car. The driver came out and held the door open for her.

Hansu nodded.

Sunja smiled, feeling light and hopeful.

Hansu looked at her face carefully and frowned.

"You should not have seen him."

"It went well. He'll come to Yokohama next week. Mozasu will be so happy."

Hansu told the driver to go. He listened to her talk about their meeting.

That evening, when Noa did not call her, she realized that she had not given him her home number in Yokohama. In the morning, Hansu phoned her. Noa had shot himself a few minutes after she'd left his office.

9

Yokohama, 1979

Etsuko Nagatomi loved all three of her children, but she did not love them all the same. Being a mother had taught her that this kind of emotional injustice was perhaps inevitable.

By midmorning, Etsuko had finished everything she had to get done for Solomon's party and was sitting in her office in the back of the airy, birch-paneled restaurant. She was forty-two years old, a native of Hokkaido who'd moved to Yokohama following her divorce six years before. She had maintained a youthful prettiness that she felt was important to being a restaurant owner. Etsuko wore her jet-colored hair in a chignon style to set off her lively, egg-shaped face. From afar she could appear stern, but up close her face was animated, and her small, friendly eyes missed nothing. She applied her makeup expertly, having worn rouge and powder since middle school, and the red wool Saint Laurent suit that Mozasu had bought her flattered her reedy figure.

Though Etsuko would normally have been pleased with herself for being so ahead of schedule, today she was not. She continued to stare at the phone message from her high school–aged daughter, Hana, with an unfamiliar Tokyo number. How did Hana get there from Hokkaido? Calls with her daughter could take five minutes or an hour, depending, and Mozasu was coming to pick her up soon. Her boyfriend was a patient man about many things, but he liked her to be punctual. Etsuko dialed anyway, and Hana picked up on the first ring.

"I've been waiting."

"I'm sorry. I just got the message." Etsuko was afraid of her fifteen-year-old daughter, but she had been trying to sound more firm, the way she was with her staff.

"Where are you?"

"I'm four months pregnant."

"*Nani?*"

Etsuko could almost see her daughter's large, unblinking eyes. Hana resembled the girls in comic books with her cute lollipop head and small, girlish body. She dressed to get attention—short skirts, sheer blouses, and high-heeled boots—and accordingly, she received that attention from all kinds of men. This was her *unmei*, Etsuko thought; her ex-husband used to dismiss this idea of fate as a lazy explanation for the bad choices people made. Regardless, life had only confirmed her belief that there was indeed a pattern to it all. To Etsuko, this had to happen, because as a girl she had been no different. When she was seventeen, she had been pregnant with Tatsuo, Hana's oldest brother.

Etsuko and Hana remained silent on the line, but the poor phone reception crackled like a campfire.

"I'm in Tokyo at a friend's."

"Who?"

"It's just some friend's cousin who lives here. Listen, I want to come to your place right away."

"Why?"

"What do you think? You have to help me with this."

"Does your father know?"

"Are you stupid?"

"Hana—"

"I know how to get to you. I have the money. I'll call you when I arrive." Hana hung up.

Two years after the divorce, when Hana was eleven, she'd asked Etsuko if they could talk to each other like friends rather than mother and child, and Etsuko had agreed because she was grateful that her daughter continued to talk to her at all. Also, Etsuko agreed because when she'd been a girl, she had lied to her mother and father about everything. But Etsuko found that being detached as a mother had its own burdens. She wasn't allowed to ask any prying questions, and if she sounded too concerned (something Hana hated), her daughter hung up the phone and wouldn't call for weeks.

Etsuko had many regrets about her life in Hokkaido, but what she was most sorry about was what her reputation had done to her children. Her grown sons still refused to talk to her. And she had only worsened matters by continuing to see Mozasu. Her sister Mari and her mother urged her to end it. The pinball business was dirty, they said; pachinko gave off a strong odor of poverty and criminality. But she couldn't give him up. Mozasu had changed her life. He was the only man she had never cheated on—something Etsuko had never believed could be possible.

The spring before her thirty-sixth birthday, when she was still married and living in Hokkaido, Etsuko had seduced another one of her high school boyfriends. She had been having a series of affairs for almost three years with various men from her adolescence. What amazed her was how difficult it was the first time but how effortless it was to have all the others that followed. Married men wanted invitations from married women. It was no trouble to phone a man she had slept with twenty years ago and invite him to her house for lunch when her children were at school.

That spring, she began sleeping with a boyfriend from her freshman year in high school. He'd grown into a handsome, married playboy who still had the tendency to talk too much. One afternoon, in her tiny Hokkaido living room, as the playboy was getting dressed to return to his office, he bemoaned the fact that she wouldn't leave her husband, who preferred the company of his work colleagues to hers. He laid his head between her small breasts and said, "But I can leave my wife. Tell me to do it." To this, she said nothing. Etsuko had no intention of leaving Nori and the children. Her complaint about her husband was not that he was boring or that he wasn't home enough. Nori was not a bad person. It was just that she felt like she had no clear sense of him after nineteen years of marriage, and she doubted that she ever would. He didn't seem to need her except to be a wife in name and a mother to his children. For Nori, this was enough.

There was no good excuse for her behavior. She knew that. But at night, when Nori sat at the kitchen table to eat the dinner that had gotten cold because he'd come home late once again from another company gathering, she waited for something to come, some insight, some feeling. As she watched him with his eyes locked to his rice bowl, she wanted to shake him, because in all her life she had never expected this kind of loneliness. Around that time, someone had handed her a cult pamphlet as she came out of the grocery store. On the flimsy cover, a middle-aged housewife was pictured as half skeleton and half flesh. On the bottom of the page it said, "Every day you are closer to your death. You are half-dead already. Where does your identity come from?" She tossed the pamphlet away almost as soon as she got it, but the picture stayed with her for a long while.

The last time she saw the playboy, he gave her a sheaf of poems that he had written for her. As he left through the kitchen door, he confessed that he loved only her. His eyes pooled with tears as he told her that she was his heart. For the rest of the day, she ignored the housework and read and reread the maudlin and erotic poems. She couldn't say if they were good or not, but she was pleased by them. Etsuko privately marveled at the effort they must have taken, and she reasoned that in his showy way, he did love her. Finally, this one affair had given her what she had wanted from all the others—an assurance that whatever she had handed out so freely in her youth had neither died nor disappeared.

That night, when her family was sleeping, Etsuko soaked in the wooden tub and glowed in what felt to her like a victory. After her bath, she dressed in her blue-and-white *yukata* and headed toward her bedroom, where her innocent husband was snoring gently. One sad thing seemed clear to her: If she needed all the men who had ever loved her to continue loving her, she would always be divided. She would always cheat, and she'd never be a good person. It dawned on her then that being a good person was something she had not given up on completely after all. Would she die living this way? In the morning, she told the playboy not to call her anymore, and he didn't. He just moved on to the next pretty housewife in town.

But a few months later, Nori found the poems that she should have destroyed, and he beat her for the first time in their marriage. Her sons tried to stop him, and Hana, just nine years old then, screamed and screamed. That evening, Nori threw her out, and she made her way to her sister's house. Later, the lawyer said it would be pointless for her to try to get custody of the children since she had no job and no skills. He coughed in what seemed like politeness or discomfort and said it would also be pointless because of what she had done. Etsuko nodded and decided to give up her children, thinking that she would not trouble them anymore. Then, following a want ad for a restaurant hostess, Etsuko moved to Yokohama, where she knew no one.

Etsuko wanted to believe that being with Mozasu was changing her. That she was sexually faithful to him, she took as proof. She had once tried to explain this to her sister, and Mari had replied, "A snake that sheds its skin is still a snake." And her mother, on hearing that Mozasu wanted to marry her, said, "*Honto*? To a pachinko Korean? Haven't you done enough to your poor children? Why not just kill them?"

The penalties incurred for the mistakes you made had to be paid out in full to the members of your family. But she didn't believe that she could ever discharge these sums.

At noon, Mozasu came to get her. They were going to pick up Solomon at his school to take him to get his alien registration card. Koreans born in Japan after 1952 had to report to their local ward office on their fourteenth birthday to request permission to stay in Japan. Every three years, Solomon would have to do this again unless he left Japan for good.

As soon as she got in the car, Mozasu reminded her to put on her seat belt. Etsuko was still thinking about Hana. Before she'd left, she had phoned the doctor, and the procedure was scheduled for the end of the week.

Mozasu took her hand. Etsuko thought his face had strength to it; there was power in his straight neck. She hadn't known many Koreans before

him, but she imagined that his squared-off facial features were tradition-
ally Korean—his wide jawbone, straight white teeth, thick black hair, and
the shallow-set, narrow, smiling eyes. He had a lean, slack body that reminded her of metal. When he made love to her, he was serious, almost
as if he was angry, and she found that this gave her intense pleasure.
His physical movements were deliberate and forceful, and she wanted
to surrender to them. Whenever she read about something or someone
Korean, she wondered what Korea was like. Mozasu's deceased father, a
Christian minister, was from the North, and his mother, who'd had a confection business, had come from the South. His plainspoken mother was
so humble in her manner and dress that she could be mistaken for a modest housekeeper rather than the mother of a millionaire pachinko parlor
owner.

Mozasu was holding a wrapped present, the size of a block of tofu. She
recognized the silver foil paper from his favorite jewelry store.

"Is that for Solomon?"

"No. It's for you."

"*Ehh*? Why?"

It was a gold-and-diamond watch nestled in a dark red velvet box.

"It's a mistress watch. I bought it last week, and I showed it to Kuboda-
san, the new night floor manager, and he said that these fancy watches are
what you give to your mistress because they cost the same as a diamond
ring but you can't give a ring to your mistress since you're already married."

He raised his eyebrows with amusement.

Etsuko checked to see if the glass partition separating them from the
driver was closed all the way; it was. Her skin flushed with heat.

"Make him stop the car."

"What's the matter?"

Etsuko pulled her hand away. She wanted to say that she wasn't his
mistress, but instead, she burst into tears.

"Why? Why are you crying? Every year for the past three years, I bring
you a diamond ring—each one bigger than the one before it—and you say
no to me. I go back to the jeweler, and he and I have to get drunk. Nothing

has changed for me." He sighed. "You are the one who says no. Refuses the pachinko yakuza."

"You're not yakuza."

"I am not yakuza. But everyone thinks Koreans are gangsters."

"None of that matters to me. It's my family."

Mozasu looked out the window, and when he spotted his son, Mozasu waved at him.

The car stopped, and Solomon got in the front passenger seat. The glass partition opened, and he stuck his head through to say hi. Etsuko reached over to straighten the rumpled collar of his white dress shirt.

"*Arigato* very much," he said. They often mixed up words in different languages as a joke. He dropped back into his seat and closed the glass partition so he could talk with the driver, Yamamoto-san, about the previous night's Tigers game. The Tigers had an American manager this year, and Solomon was hopeful for the season. Yamamoto was not so optimistic.

Mozasu picked up her left wrist gently and clasped the watch on it.

"You're a funny woman. I bought you a gift. Just say thanks. I never meant that you were a—"

The bridge of her nose hurt, and she thought she would start crying again.

"Hana called. She's coming to Yokohama. Today."

"Is she okay?" He looked surprised.

Etsuko went to Hokkaido twice yearly to see her children. Mozasu had never met them.

"Maybe she can go to Solomon's party. See the famous singer," Mozasu said.

"I don't know if she likes Hiromi-san," she replied. Etsuko had no idea if Hana liked pop music. As a child, she hadn't been the kind who sang or danced. Etsuko stared at the back of the driver's gray-streaked head. The driver nodded thoughtfully while Solomon talked to him, and their quiet gestures appeared intimate. She wished she had something like baseball that she could talk about with her daughter—a safe subject they could visit without subtext or aggression.

Etsuko told Mozasu that Hana had an appointment with a doctor in Yokohama. When he asked if she was sick, she shook her head no.

This was how life had turned out. Her oldest, Tatsuo, was twenty-five years old, and it was taking him eight years to graduate from a fourth-rate college. Her second son, Tari, a withdrawn nineteen-year-old, had failed his college entrance exams and was working as a ticket collector at a movie theater. She had no right to expect her children to hold the aspirations of other middle-class people—to graduate from Tokyo University, to get a desk job at the Industrial Bank of Japan, to marry into a nice family. She had made them into village outcasts, and there was no way for them to be acceptable anymore.

Etsuko unclasped the watch and put it back in the velvet case. She laid it down in the space between them on the white, starched doily covering the black leather seats. He handed it back to her.

"It's not a ring. Save me a trip to the jeweler."

Etsuko held the watch case in her hands and wondered how they'd stayed together with him not giving up and her not giving in.

The Yokohama ward office was a giant gray box with an obscure sign. The first clerk they saw was a tall man with a narrow face and a shock of black hair buzzed off at the sides. He stared at Etsuko shamelessly, his eyes darting across her breasts, hips, and jeweled fingers. She was over-dressed compared to Mozasu and Solomon, who wore white dress shirts, dark slacks, and black dress shoes. They looked like the gentle Mormon missionaries who used to glide through her village on their bicycles when she was a girl.

"Your name—" The clerk squinted his eyes at the form Solomon was filling out. "So-ro-mo-n. What kind of name is that?"

"It's from the Bible. He was a king. The son of King David. A man of great wisdom. My great-uncle named me." The boy smiled at the clerk as if he was sharing a secret. He was a polite boy, but because he had gone to school with Americans and other kinds of foreigners at his inter-national schools, he sometimes said things that a Japanese person would never have said.

"So-ro-mo-n, a king. Great wisdom." The clerk smirked. "Koreans don't have kings anymore."

"What did you say?" Etsuko asked.

Quickly, Mozasu pulled her back.

She glanced at Mozasu. His temper was far worse than hers. Once, when a restaurant guest had tried to make her sit with him, Mozasu, who happened to be there that night, walked over, picked him up bodily, and threw him outside the restaurant, breaking the man's ribs. She was expecting no less of a reaction now, but Mozasu averted his eyes from the clerk and stared at Solomon's right hand.

Mozasu smiled.

"Excuse me, sir," he said with no trace of irritation or anger. "We're in a hurry to return home, because it's the boy's birthday. Is there anything else we should do?" Mozasu folded his hands behind him. "Thank you very much for understanding."

Confused, Solomon turned to Etsuko, and she flashed him a warning look.

The clerk pointed to the back of the room and told Mozasu and Etsuko to sit. Solomon remained standing opposite the clerk. In the long, rectangular room, shaped like a train car, with bank teller windows running parallel along opposite walls, half a dozen people sat on benches, reading their newspapers or manga. Etsuko wondered if they were Korean. From their seats, Etsuko and Mozasu could see Solomon talking to the clerk, but they couldn't hear anything.

Mozasu sat down, then got up again. He asked if she wanted a can of tea from the vending machine, and she nodded yes. She felt like slapping the clerk's face. In middle school, she had once slapped a bossy girl, and it had been satisfying.

When Mozasu returned with their tea, she thanked him.

"You must have known—" She paused. "You must have warned him. I mean, you told him that today would not be so easy?" She didn't mean to be critical, but after the words came from her mouth, they sounded harsh, and she was sorry.

"No. I didn't say anything to him." He opened and closed his fists rhythmically. "I came here with my mother and brother, Noa, for my first registration papers. The clerk was normal. Nice even. So I asked you to come. I thought maybe having a woman by him might help." He exhaled through his nostrils. "It was stupid to wish for kindness."

"No. No. You couldn't have warned him. I shouldn't have said it like that."

"It is hopeless. I cannot change his fate. He is Korean. He has to get those papers, and he has to follow all the steps of the law perfectly. Once, at a ward office, a clerk told me that I was a guest in his country."

"You and Solomon were born here."

"Yes, my brother, Noa, was born here, too. And now he is dead." Mozasu covered his face with his hands.

Etsuko sighed.

"Anyway, the clerk was not wrong. And this is something Solomon must understand. We can be deported. We have no motherland. Life is full of things he cannot control so he must adapt. My boy has to survive."

Solomon returned to them. Next he had his photograph taken, and afterward, he had to go to another room to get fingerprinted. Then they could go home. The last clerk was a plump woman; her light green uniform flattened her large breasts and round shoulders. She took Solomon's left index finger and gently dipped it into the pot filled with thick black ink. Solomon depressed his finger onto a white card as if he were a child painting. Mozasu looked away and sighed audibly. The clerk smiled at the boy and told him to pick up the registration card in the next room.

"Let's get your dog tags," Mozasu said.

Solomon faced his father. "Hmm?"

"It's what we dogs must have."

The clerk looked furious suddenly.

"The fingerprints and registration cards are vitally important for government records. There's no need to feel insulted by this. It is an immigration regulation required for foreign—"

Etsuko stepped forward. "But you don't make your children get fingerprinted on their birthday, do you?"

The clerk's neck reddened.

"My son is dead."

Etsuko bit her lip. She didn't want to feel anything for the woman, but she knew what it was like to lose your children—it was like you were cursed and nothing would ever restore the desolation of your life.

"Koreans do lots of good for this country," Etsuko said. "They do the difficult jobs Japanese don't want to do; they pay taxes, obey laws, raise good families, and create jobs—"

The clerk nodded sympathetically.

"You Koreans always tell me that."

Solomon blurted out, "She's not Korean."

Etsuko touched his arm, and the three of them walked out of the airless room. She wanted to crawl out of the gray box and see the light of outdoors again. She longed for the white mountains of Hokkaido. And though she had never done so in her childhood, she wanted to walk in the cold, snowy forests beneath the flanks of dark, leafless trees. In life, there was so much insult and injury, and she had no choice but to collect what was hers. But now she wished to take Solomon's shame, too, and add it to her pile, though she was already overwhelmed.

10

One of her mother's waitresses had brought her a Coke, and Hana was sitting at a table near the bar, playing with the straw. No longer permed, her hair was straight and its natural color, a reddish black. It was cut in one even length and splayed across her small shoulders. She wore a neatly ironed, white cotton blouse and a dark pleated skirt coming to her knees, with gray wool stockings and flat schoolgirl shoes. She hadn't dressed like this since she was in primary school. Her stomach was flat, but her bud-like breasts looked fuller; otherwise, there was no way of knowing that she was pregnant.

Closed for a private event, the restaurant dining room was set up for the party. White linen cloths covered a dozen round tables, and in the middle of each sat an elegant floral arrangement and candlesticks. A busboy stood at the edge of the room, blowing up one red balloon after another with a helium tank. He let them all float up to the ceiling.

Etsuko and Solomon entered the restaurant quietly. He had insisted on coming by the restaurant to say hello to her daughter before heading home to change. At first, his mouth opened in surprise at the decorations and the dramatic transformation of the room. Then, seeing the girl at the empty table, he asked, "Is that her?"

"Yes."

Hana smiled shyly at them.

Solomon and Hana greeted each other formally. Their mutual curiosity was obvious. Hana pointed to the balloons hiding the ceiling, and before Etsuko had a chance, Solomon replied quickly in Japanese, "It's my birthday. Why don't you come to the party? There's going be an American dinner here tonight, and then we're going to a real disco."

Hana answered, "If you wish. I might."

Etsuko frowned. She had to speak to the chef about the menu, but she was reluctant to leave them alone. A few minutes later, when she returned from the kitchen, they were whispering like a pair of young lovers. Etsuko checked her watch and urged Solomon to get home. At the door, he shouted, "Hey, I'll see you at the party," and Hana smiled like a courtesan as she waved good-bye.

"Why did you make him go? I was having fun."

"Because he has to get dressed."

"I looked in them." Hana glanced at the bags near the entrance. There were a hundred party bags in four long rows that had to be transported to the disco—each bag filled with tapes, a Sony Walkman cassette player, imported teen magazines, and boxed chocolates.

"I wish my dad was a yakuza."

"Hana, he's not—" Etsuko looked around to see if anyone could hear them.

"Your boyfriend's son doesn't seem like a brat."

"He doesn't have it easy."

"Not easy? American private schools, millions in the bank, and a chauffeur. Get some perspective, Mother."

"Today, he had to go to the ward office to request permission to stay in Japan for another three years. If he was denied, he could have been deported. He has to carry around an alien registration card and—"

"Oh, really? But he wasn't deported, right? Now he gets a fancy party that's nicer than most weddings."

"He was born in this country, and he had to be fingerprinted today on his birthday like he was a criminal. He's just a child. He didn't do anything wrong."

"We're all criminals. Liars, thieves, whores—that's who we are." The girl's carbon-colored eyes looked hard and ancient. "No one is innocent here."

"Why must you be so hard-hearted?"

"I'm the only one who still talks to you."

"I've said I'm sorry enough times." Etsuko tried to control her voice, but the waitresses heard everything, and suddenly it didn't matter anymore.

"I made the appointment."

Hana looked up.

"The day after tomorrow, we'll take care of your problem." Etsuko looked straight at her daughter's pale, angry face. "You shouldn't be a mother. You have no idea how hard it is to have children."

The steady line of Hana's lips crumpled, and she covered her manga-pretty face with her hands and began to cry.

Etsuko didn't know if she should say something. Instead, she put her hand on her daughter's head. Hana winced, but Etsuko didn't immediately pull her hand back. It had been so long since she had touched her daughter's satiny hair.

When Etsuko lived in the cramped, three-bedroom house in Hokkaido with its leaky roof and tiny kitchen, certain labors had sustained her. At this moment, with a kind of pinprick pain, Etsuko recalled watching her sons devour the shrimp that she had fried for dinner, piled high on paper-lined plates. Even in the middle of July, it had been worth it to stand in front of a hot tempura pan, dropping battered shrimp into bubbling peanut oil, because to her sons, Mama's shrimp was better than candy, they'd said. And it came to her like a tall and dark wave how much she'd loved combing Hana's freshly washed hair when her cheeks were still pink from the steamy bathwater.

"I know you didn't want us. My brothers told me, and I told them they were wrong even though I knew they weren't. I clung to you because I wasn't going to let you just leave what you started. How can you tell me how hard it is to have children? You haven't even tried to be a mother. What right do you have? What makes you a mother?"

Etsuko grew silent, utterly transfixed by the realization that how she saw herself was actually how her children saw her, too. They thought she was a monster.

"How can you think that I didn't want the three of you?" She recalled all the letters, gifts, and money she'd sent, which the boys had returned. And worse, the phone calls to the house to check on them when her husband wouldn't say anything beyond *moshi-moshi*, then would hand the phone to Hana because she was the only one who would take the receiver. Etsuko wanted to justify herself—her numerous and repeated attempts—to offer proof. Being a mother was what defined her more than any other thing—more than being a daughter, wife, divorced woman, girlfriend, or restaurant owner. She hadn't done it well, but it was who she was, and it was what had changed her inside forever. From the moment Tatsuo was born, she had been filled with grief and self-doubt because she was never good enough. Even though she had failed, being a mother was eternal; a part of her life wouldn't end with her death.

"But, but, I didn't marry Mozasu. I don't even live with him. So I wouldn't make things worse for you and your brothers."

Hana tilted her head back and laughed.

"Am I supposed to thank you for this great sacrifice? So you didn't marry a Korean gangster, and you want me to congratulate you for this? You didn't marry him because you didn't want to suffer. You're the most selfish person I know. If you want to sleep with him and take his money to set up a fancy place and not marry him, that's your self-serving choice. You didn't do it for me or my brothers." Hana dried her face with her shirt sleeve. "You don't want to be judged. That's why you haven't married him. That's why you left Hokkaido to hide out in the big city. You think you're such a victim, but you're not. You left because you're afraid, and you slept with all those men because you were afraid of getting old. You're weak and pathetic. Don't tell me about sacrifices, because I don't believe in such crap."

Hana started to cry again.

Etsuko slumped in her chair. If she married Mozasu, it would prove to everyone in Hokkaido that no decent Japanese man would touch a woman like her. She would be called a yakuza wife. If she married him, she'd no longer be considered the tasteful owner of a successful restaurant in the best part of Yokohama—an image she only half believed herself. Mozasu must have thought that she was a better person than she actually was, but Hana wasn't fooled. Etsuko picked up Hana's travel bag next to her chair and nudged her daughter to stand up to go.

Etsuko's apartment was in a luxury building four blocks from the restaurant. On the way there, Hana said she didn't want to go to the party anymore. She wanted to be left alone so she could sleep until morning. Etsuko unlocked the front door to her apartment and led Hana to her bedroom. She would sleep on the sofa tonight.

Hana lay across the futon, and Etsuko pulled a light comforter over her thin young body and turned out the light. Hana curled into herself; her eyes were still open, and she said nothing. Etsuko didn't want to leave her. Despite everything, it struck her that what she was feeling was a kind of contentedness. They were together again. Hana had come to her for care. Etsuko sat down on the edge of the bed and stroked her daughter's hair.

"You have this scent," Hana said quietly, "I used to think it was your perfume. Joy, *nee*?"

"I still wear that."

"I know," Hana said, and Etsuko resisted the urge to sniff her own wrists.

"It's not just the perfume, though, it's all the other creams and things that you wear, and it makes up this smell. I used to walk around department stores wondering what it was. The smell of *mama*."

Etsuko wanted to say many things, but above all that she would try not to make any more mistakes. "Hanako—"

"I want to go to sleep now. Go to that boy's party. Leave me alone." Hana's voice was flat but more tender this time.

Etsuko offered to stay, but Hana waved her away. Etsuko mentioned then that her schedule was open the next day. Maybe they could go and buy a bed and a dresser. "Then you can always come back and visit me. I can make up a room for you," Etsuko said.

Hana sighed, but her expression was blank.

Etsuko couldn't tell what her daughter wanted. "I'm not saying you have to go. Especially after—" Etsuko put her fingertips across her lips, then quickly removed them. "You can stay. Start school here even."

Hana shifted her head on her pillow and inhaled, still saying nothing.

"I can call your father. To ask."

Hana pulled the blanket up to her chin. "If you want."

Etsuko had to go back to the restaurant, but she settled on the sofa for a few minutes. When she had been a young mother there used to be only one time in her waking hours when she'd felt a kind of peace, and that was always after her children went to bed for the night. She longed to see her sons as they were back then: their legs chubby and white, their mushroom haircuts misshapen because they could never sit still at the barber. She wished she could take back the times she had scolded her children just because she was tired. There were so many errors. If life allowed revisions, she would let them stay in their bath a little longer, read them one more story before bed, and fix them another plate of shrimp.

II

The children invited to Solomon's party were the sons and daughters of diplomats, bankers, and wealthy expatriates from America and Europe. Everyone spoke English rather than Japanese. Mozasu had chosen the international school in Yokohama because he liked the idea of Westerners. He had specific ambitions for his son: Solomon should speak perfect English as well as perfect Japanese; he should grow up among worldly, upper-class people; and ultimately, he should work for an American company in Tokyo or New York—a city Mozasu had never been to but imagined as a place where everyone was given a fair shot. He wanted his son to be an international man of the world.

A line of black limousines snaked along the street. As the children left the restaurant, they thanked Mozasu and Etsuko for the fine dinner they'd eaten. Mozasu lined up the children in front of the restaurant and instructed, "Ladies first," a saying he had picked up from watching American movies. The girls trooped into the gleaming cars in sixes and drove away. Then the boys followed. Solomon rode in the last car with his best friends, Nigel, the son of an English banker, and Ajay, the son of an Indian shipping company executive.

The disco was dimly lit and glamorous. From the high ceiling, twenty or so mirrored balls hung at different heights, flooding the large room with tiny panes of light that flashed and swayed with the movements of the balls. They had the effect of making anyone who walked across the floor shimmer like a fish underwater. After everyone arrived and sat down at the lounge tables, the manager, a handsome Filipino, got up on the elevated stage. He had a beautiful, round voice.

"Dear friends of Solomon Baek! Welcome to Ringo's!" He paused for the children's cheers. "For Solomon's birthday fiesta, Ringo's presents the hottest star in Japan—one day the world: Ken Hiromi and the Seven Gentlemen!"

The children didn't seem to believe him. The curtain rose to reveal the seven-piece rock band, and the singer emerged from the back. Hiromi looked utterly normal, almost disappointingly so. He dressed like a businessman who'd forgotten his necktie and wore thick-framed eyeglasses just like the ones on his album covers. His hair was impeccably combed. He couldn't have been more than thirty.

Solomon kept shaking his head, bewildered and delighted. The band was loud, and the kids rushed to the stage to dance wildly. When the long set ended, the emcee asked everyone to gather around the stage, and Ichiro, the cook, wheeled a spectacular ice cream cake shaped like a baseball diamond toward Solomon. Tall thin candles lit the large surface of the cake. A girl shouted, "Don't forget to make a wish, baby!"

In one huff, Solomon blew out the candles, and everyone clapped and hollered.

Etsuko handed him the beribboned knife so he could cut the first slice. A spotlight shone on him as he poised the long, serrated blade over the cake.

"Do you need help?" she asked.

"I think I got it," he said, using both hands to make a straight cut.

"Oh," she uttered, seeing the ink under his nails. He'd washed off most of it, but a shadow of the stain remained on his fingertips.

Solomon looked up from what he was doing and smiled.

Etsuko guided his arm lightly to return him to his task. After the first slice, Solomon gave the knife back to her, and she cut the remaining pieces. Waiters passed out the cake, and Hiromi, who was sitting by himself, accepted a piece. Mozasu gave Solomon a fat blue envelope filled with yen notes and told him to give it to the singer. Ken Hiromi motioned to Solomon to sit down. In this light, Etsuko thought, no one else would notice the ink.

The band played another set, then a DJ played popular songs for the kids. As the party wound down, Etsuko felt pleasantly exhausted—the way she did after the restaurant closed. Mozasu was sitting in a booth drinking champagne by himself, and she sat down beside him. Mozasu refilled his glass and handed it to her, and she drank it in two gulps. She laughed. He said she did a good job for Solomon, and Etsuko shook her head. "*Iie.*"

Without thinking, she said, "I think she would have been pleased."

Mozasu looked confused. A moment later, he nodded. "Yes, she would have been so happy for him."

"What was she like?" Etsuko shifted her body to see his face. Little squares of light danced across his sharp features.

"I've told you before. She was a nice lady. Like you." It was difficult to say any more than that about Yumi.

"No, tell me something specific about her." Etsuko wanted to know how they were different, not how they were the same. "I want to know more."

"Why? She is dead." Mozasu looked hurt after saying this. He noticed that Solomon was now dancing with a tall Chinese girl with short hair. His forehead glistened with sweat as he followed the girl's elegant moves. Etsuko stared into her empty champagne glass.

"She wanted to name him Sejong," he said. "But it's tradition for the husband's father to name the grandson. My father's dead so my Uncle Yoseb named him Solomon." He paused. "Sejong was a king in Korea. He invented the Korean alphabet. Uncle Yoseb gave him the name of a king from the Bible instead. I think he did it because my father was a minister." He smiled.

"Why are you smiling?"

"Because Yumi"—Mozasu said her name out loud, and it surprised him to hear the sound of the two syllables—"was so proud of him. Her

411

son. She wanted to give him the life of a king. She was like my father and uncle, I think. Proud. She was proud of me and my work. It was nice. But now that I'm older, I wonder why." Mozasu sounded wistful. "What do we Koreans have to be so proud of?"

"It's good to be proud of your children." She smoothed down her skirt. When her children had been born, what she had felt was amazement at their physical perfection. She had marveled at their miniature human form and their good health. But not once did she consider a name taken from history—the name of a king. She had never been proud of her family or her country; if anything, she was ashamed.

"One of those girls came up to me today and said Solomon looked like his mother." He pointed to a cluster of girls in the corner of the room. They wore bandeau tops and jersey skirts clinging to their thin hips.

"How could she know that?"

"She meant you."

"Oh." Etsuko nodded. "I wish I was his mother."

"No. No, you don't." Mozasu said this calmly, and she felt like she deserved that.

"I'm no better than that woman clerk this afternoon, *nee*?"

Mozasu shook his head and placed his hand over hers.

Why did her family think pachinko was so terrible? Her father, a traveling salesman, had sold expensive life insurance policies to isolated housewives who couldn't afford them, and Mozasu created spaces where grown men and women could play pinball for money. Both men had made money from chance and fear and loneliness. Every morning, Mozasu and his men tinkered with the machines to fix the outcomes—there could only be a few winners and a lot of losers. And yet we played on, because we had hope that we might be the lucky ones. How could you get angry at the ones who wanted to be in the game? Etsuko had failed in this important way—she had not taught her children to hope, to believe in the perhaps-absurd possibility that they might win. Pachinko was a foolish game, but life was not.

Etsuko removed her new watch and put it in his hand. "It's not that I don't want a ring—"

Mozasu didn't look at her, but he put the watch in his pocket.

"It's late. Almost midnight," he said gently. "The children have to get home."

Etsuko rose from the table and went to hand out the party bags.

Not wanting the evening to end, Solomon claimed that he was hungry, so the three of them returned to her restaurant. The place was clean again and looked open for business.

"A little bit of everything," he said when she asked him what he wanted to eat. He looked so happy, and it pleased her to see him like this. She could count on him to be a happy person. Maybe that was what Solomon was for her and Mozasu.

At the very back of the dining room, Mozasu sat down at a table for four and opened his evening-edition newspaper. He looked like a middle-aged man waiting calmly for his train to arrive. Etsuko headed for the kitchen with Solomon trailing her.

She put down three white plates on the prep counter. From the refrigerator, she pulled out the tray of fried chicken and the bowl of potato salad—dishes that Ichiro had made following an American cookbook.

"Why didn't Hana come? Is she sick?"

"No." Etsuko didn't like to lie to a direct question.

"She's pretty, you know."

"Too pretty. That's her problem." Her own mother had once said this about her when a family friend had complimented Etsuko.

"Did you have fun tonight?" she asked.

"Yeah. I still can't believe it. Hiromi-san talked to me."

"What did he say?" She put two large pieces of chicken on Mozasu's and Solomon's plates and a small drumstick on hers. "Was he nice?"

"Very nice and cool. He said his best friends are Korean. He told me to be good to my parents."

Solomon hadn't denied her as his mother, and though this should have been a nice thing, it only made her feel more anxious.

"Your father told me tonight that your mother was proud of you. From the moment you were born."

Solomon said nothing.

She didn't think that he should need a mother anymore; he was already grown up, and he was doing better than most kids she knew who had mothers who were alive. He was almost a man.

"Come to the sink. Hold out your left hand."

"A present?"

She laughed and put his left hand over the sink basin and turned on the faucet. "There's still ink left."

"Can they make me leave? Really deport me?"

"Everything went well today," she replied, and softly scrubbed the pads of his fingers and nails with a dishwashing brush. "There's no need to worry, Solomon-chan."

He seemed satisfied with her answer.

"Hana told me she came to Yokohama to get rid of her little problem. Is she pregnant? Nigel got his girlfriend pregnant, and she had to get an abortion."

"Your friend Nigel?" She remembered the blond-haired boy who played Atari with him on the weekends. He was only a year older than Solomon.

He nodded. "Yup. Hana seems great."

"My children hate me."

Solomon picked at the ink beneath his fingernails. "Your kids hate you because you're gone." His face grew serious. "They can't help it. They miss you."

Etsuko bit the inside of her lower lip. She could feel the small muscles inside her mouth, and she stopped herself from drawing blood. She was afraid to look at his face, and though she had tried to restrain herself, she burst into tears.

"Why? Why are you crying?" he asked. "I'm sorry." Solomon's eyes welled up.

She inhaled to calm her breathing.

"When Hana was born, the nurses put her footprints on a card. They washed the ink off, but not very well, so when I went home I had to get it off. I don't think she could see anything really, because she was just born, but I felt like she was looking at me like I was hurting her, and she just cried and cried—"

"Etsuko-chan, Hana will be okay. Nigel's girlfriend is fine. They might get married after college. That's what he said—"

"No, no. It's not that. I'm just so sorry that you might have thought that I didn't want to be your mother." She clutched her stomach, and she tried to regulate her breath. "I've hurt so many people. And you're such a good boy, Solomon. I wish I could take credit for you."

His dark, straight hair clung to the sides of his face, and he didn't brush it away. His eyes strained with worry.

"But I was born today, and isn't it funny how no one gets to remember that moment and who was there? It's all what's told to you. You're here now. You are a mother to me."

Etsuko covered her mouth with her open palm and let his words go through her. Somewhere after being sorry, there had to be another day, and even after a conviction, there could be good in the judgment. At last, Etsuko shut off the water and put down the swollen yellow sponge in the sink. The curved brass spout let go its last few drops, and the kitchen grew silent. Etsuko reached over to hold the child on his birthday.

12

Osaka, 1979

Sunja had left her son and grandson Solomon in Yokohama and returned to Osaka when she learned that her mother, Yangjin, had stomach cancer. Through fall and winter, Sunja slept at the foot of her mother's pallet to relieve her exhausted sister-in-law, Kyunghee, who had been nursing Yangjin faithfully after her own husband, Yoseb, finally died.

Yangjin lived on her thick cotton pallet, more or less immobile, in the front room, which had effectively become her bedroom. The largest room in the house smelled of eucalyptus and tangerines. The floor had been lined recently with fresh tatami mats, and a double row of greenery in ceramic pots flourished by the two sparkling windows. The large basket by the pallet, filled to the brim with Kyushu tangerines—a costly gift from fellow parishioners at the Korean church in Osaka—released a glorious scent. The new Sony color television was on, its volume low, as the three women waited to watch Yangjin's favorite program, *Other Lands*.

Sunja sat on the floor beside her mother, who was sitting up as well as she could, and Kyunghee remained at her usual place on the other side of the pallet by Yangjin's head. Both Sunja and Kyunghee were knitting sections of a navy woolen sweater for Solomon.

Strangely, as Yangjin's limbs and joints quit, one after the other, and as her muscles softened into jelly, her mind felt clearer and more free. She could imagine leaving her body to run swiftly like a deer. Yet in life, she could hardly move at all; she could barely eat anything recognizable as food. Nevertheless, the unexpected dividend of this illness was that for the first time in her life, perhaps since the moment she was able to walk and perform any chores, Yangjin felt no compulsion to labor. It was no longer possible to cook meals, wash dishes, sweep the floors, sew clothing, scrub toilets, tend to the children, do laundry, make food to sell, or do whatever else needed doing. Her job was to rest before dying. All she had to do was nothing at all. At best, she had a few days left.

Yangjin wasn't sure what happened after this was over—but she felt she would go home either to all those who had died before or to *Yesu Kuristo* and his kingdom. She wanted to see her husband, Hoonie, again; once, in church, she'd heard a sermon that said that in heaven, the lame could walk and the blind could see. Her husband had opposed the idea of God, but she hoped that if there was a God, He would understand that Hoonie was a good man who had endured enough with the restrictions of his body and deserved to be well. Whenever Yangjin tried to talk about dying, Kyunghee and Sunja would change the subject.

"So did you send the money to Solomon?" Yangjin asked. "I wanted you to send crisp, new bills from the bank."

"Yes, I sent it yesterday," Sunja replied, adjusting her mother's pillow so she could see the monitor better.

"When will he get it? I haven't heard from him."

"*Umma*, he'll get the card tonight or tomorrow."

Solomon hadn't phoned to speak to his great-grandmother this week, but that was understandable. He had just had a big birthday party, and Sunja was the one who would have reminded him to write a letter or to phone someone to say thank you or just to check in on them. "He's probably busy with school. I'll phone later."

"So is the singer really a famous talent?" Yangjin asked. Mozasu had furnished the house and provided for their upkeep ever since the women closed their confection business; it was still difficult for Yangjin to grasp that her grandson Mozasu could have so much money that he could hire pop stars for his son's birthday party.

"That must be so expensive! Is he really a celebrity?"

"Well, that's what Etsuko said." Sunja was also curious as to how

Solomon was faring; he would have had to get his identification card for the first time. She had been worried about that.

The show came on, and Kyunghee bolted up to adjust the antenna. The picture improved. The familiar Japanese folk music for the program drifted into the room.

"Where will Higuchi-san go today?" Yangjin smiled broadly.

In *Other Lands*, the interviewer Higuchi-san, a spry, ageless woman with dyed black hair, traveled all over the globe and interviewed Japanese people who had immigrated to other lands. The interviewer was no ordinary woman of her generation; she was unmarried, childless, and a skilled world-traveling journalist who could ask any intimate question. She was reputed to have Korean blood, and the rumor alone was enough for Yangjin and Kyunghee to find Higuchi-san's pluck and wanderlust relatable. They were devoted to her. When the women still ran their little confection shop, they'd rush straight home as soon as they closed to avoid missing even a minute of the program. Sunja had never been interested in the show, but now she sat through it for her mother's sake.

"Pillows!" Yangjin cried, and Sunja fixed them.

Kyunghee clapped her hands as the opening credits rolled. Despite all the restrictions, she had always hoped that Higuchi-san could somehow go to North Korea. Koh Hansu had told her husband that her parents and in-laws were dead, yet she still yearned to hear news of home. Also, she wanted to know if Kim Changho was safe. No matter how many sad stories she heard from the others whose family members had gone back, she could not imagine that the handsome young man with the thick eyeglasses had died.

As the opening music faded, a disembodied male voice announced that today, Higuchi-san was in Medellín to meet an impressive farming family who now owned the largest chicken farm in Colombia. Higuchi-san, wearing a light-colored raincoat and her famous green *boshi*, marveled how the Wakamura family had decided to migrate to Latin America at the end of the nineteenth century and how well they had raised their children to be good Japanese in the world. "*Minna nihongo hanase-masu!*" Higuchi-san's voice was full of wonder and admiration.

The camera zoomed in on Señora Wakamura, the surviving matriarch, a tiny, wrinkled woman who looked far older than her actual age of sixty-seven. Her large, sloping eyes, buried beneath layers of crepey, folded skin, appeared wise and thoughtful. Like her siblings, she was born in Medellín.

"Things were very difficult for my parents, of course. They didn't speak Spanish and didn't know anything about chickens. Father died of a heart attack when I was six, then Mother raised us by herself. My oldest brother stayed here with our mother, but our other two brothers went to study in Montreal, then returned. My sisters and I worked on the farm."

"That must have been difficult, difficult work," Higuchi-san exclaimed breathlessly.

"A woman's lot is to suffer," Señora Wakamura said.

"*Soo, soo.*"

The camera panned to show the interior of the cavernous farm, a moving sea of white feathers comprised of tens of thousands of fluffy chickens; brilliant red combs streaked the pale, fluttering mass.

At Higuchi-san's behest, Señora Wakamura listed the number of chores that she'd had since she was tall enough to sprinkle chicken feed and avoid getting pecked.

"How very hard all this must have been," Higuchi-san repeated, trying not to wince from the noxious odors.

Señora Wakamura shrugged. Her stoicism was undeniable as she showed all the moving parts of a working chicken farm, including lifting heavy machinery while trudging through muddy fields.

At the end of the thirty-minute program, Higuchi-san asked Señora Wakamura to say something to the viewers in Japanese.

The woman farmer with the ancient face turned to the camera shyly, then looked away like she was thinking.

"I have never been to Japan"—she frowned—"but I hope that wherever I am in life and whatever I do, I can be a good Japanese. I hope to never bring shame to my people."

Higuchi-san grew teary and signed off. As the closing credits rolled, the announcer said that Higuchi-san was now heading to the airport to reach the next destination of *Other Lands*. "Till we countrymen meet again!" the announcer said brightly.

Sunja got up and turned off the television. She wanted to head to the kitchen to boil some water for tea.

"*Go-saeng*," Yangjin said out loud. "A woman's lot is to suffer."

"Yes, *go-saeng*." Kyunghee nodded, repeating the word for suffering.

All her life, Sunja had heard this sentiment from other women, that they must suffer—suffer as a girl, suffer as a wife, suffer as a mother—die suffering. *Go-saeng*—the word made her sick. What else was there besides this? She had suffered to create a better life for Noa, and yet it was not enough. Should she have taught her son to suffer the humiliation that she'd drunk like water? In the end, he had refused to suffer the conditions of his birth. Did mothers fail by not telling their sons that suffering would come?

"You're upset about Noa," Yangjin said, "I know. He's all that you ever think about. First it was Koh Hansu, and now it's Noa. You're suffering because you wanted that terrible man. A woman can't make a mistake like that."

"What else should I have done?" Sunja blurted out, then immediately regretted doing so.

Yangjin shrugged, almost in comic imitation of the woman farmer. "You brought shame on your child by having that man as his father. You caused your own suffering. Noa, that poor boy, came from a bad seed. You're fortunate that Isak married you. What a blessing that man was. Mozasu came from better blood. That's why he's so blessed in his work."

Sunja covered her mouth using both hands. It was said often that old women talked too much and said useless things, but it seemed like her mother had been storing these specific thoughts in reserve for her. This was like some sort of mean inheritance her mother had been planning to give her. Sunja couldn't fight her. What was the point?

Yangjin pursed her lips, then inhaled deeply through her nostrils.

"That man was bad."

"*Umma*, he brought you here. If he hadn't brought you—"

"That's true that he brought me here, but he was still awful. You can't change that. That poor boy didn't have a chance," Yangjin said.

"If Noa didn't have a chance, then why did I suffer? Why should I have even tried? If I'm so foolish, if I made such unforgivable mistakes, is that your fault?" Sunja asked. "I don't, I don't ... I won't blame you."

Kyunghee looked at Yangjin imploringly, but the old woman seemed oblivious to her silent pleas.

"Sister," Kyunghee said gently. "May I get you something? To drink?"

"No." Yangjin turned to Sunja, pointing to Kyunghee. "She's been better to me than my own family. She cares more about me than you do. You just care about Noa and Mozasu. You only came back when you learned that I was going to die. You don't care about me. You don't care about anyone else except your children." Yangjin bawled.

Kyunghee touched Yangjin's arm gently.

"Sister, this is not what you mean. Sunja had to take care of Solomon. You know that. You said it yourself so many times. And Mozasu needed his mother's help after Yumi died," she said quietly. "Sunja has suffered so much. Especially after Noa—" Kyunghee could barely say Noa's name. "And you, you have had whatever you needed here, right?" She tried to sound as soothing as possible.

"Yes, yes, you have always done your best for me. I wish Kim Changho could have stayed in Japan. Then he could have married you after your husband died. I worry that after I die who will take care of you. Sunja-ya, you must take care of Kyunghee. She can't stay here by herself. *Aigoo*, if only Kim Changho hadn't rushed off to the North and probably gotten himself killed. *Aigoo*. The poor man probably died for nothing."

Kyunghee crumpled visibly.

"*Umma*, your medicine is making you say crazy things," Sunja said.

"Kim Changho only went to Korea because he couldn't marry our Kyunghee, and he couldn't suffer any more waiting," Yangjin said, having stopped crying. It was like watching a toddler whose tears could stop at will. "He was much nicer than Yoseb. After his accident, Yoseb was a drunk, but Kim Changho was a real man. He would've made our wonderful Kyunghee happy, but he's dead. Poor Kim Changho. Poor Kyunghee."

Seeing Kyunghee's shocked expression, Sunja said firmly, "*Umma*, you should go to sleep. We're going to leave you to rest. You must be tired. Come on, let's go to the back room and finish the knitting," Sunja said, helping Kyunghee up. At the door, Sunja turned out the light.

"I'm not tired! You're going to leave again, are you? When things get difficult, it's easy to leave. Fine. I'll die now, then you won't have to stay here, and you can rush back to your precious Mozasu! I never created a burden for you one single day of my life. Until I couldn't move, every minute I have been here, I have worked to support myself. I never took a yen above what I needed to eat and to put a roof over our heads. I always held up my share, you know. I raised you when your kindhearted father died—" At the mention of her husband, Yangjin began to cry again, and Kyunghee rushed to her, unable to watch her being so miserable.

Sunja watched Kyunghee pat her mother gently until she quieted down. Her mother was unrecognizable to her; it would have been easy to say that the illness had changed her, but it wasn't so simple, was it? Illness and dying had revealed her mother's truer thoughts, the ones her mother had been protecting her from. Sunja had made a mistake; however, she didn't believe that her son came from a bad seed. The Japanese said that Koreans had too much anger and heat in their blood. Seeds, blood. How could you fight such hopeless ideas? Noa had been a sensitive child who had believed that if he followed all the rules and was the best, then somehow the hostile world would change its mind. His death may have been her fault for having allowed him to believe in such cruel ideals.

Sunja knelt at her mother's pallet.

"I'm sorry, *umma*. I'm sorry. I'm sorry I was away. I'm sorry about everything."

The old woman looked weakly at her only child, hating herself suddenly. Yangjin wanted to say she was sorry, too, but strength passed from her body, forcing her to close her eyes.

13

"You're not a Christian, are you?" Hana asked Solomon. She was sitting next to him in the pew. The minister had just finished eulogizing his great-grandmother, and the organist began to play "What a Friend We Have in Jesus." The funeral service would end after the song and a closing prayer.

Solomon tried to shush Hana politely, but as ever, she was persistent.

"It's like a cult, *nee*? But you don't do anything interesting like get naked outdoors in a group or sacrifice babies? I read that people in America do things like that if they are serious Christians. But you don't seem like one of those. You probably have to give lots of your money away since you're rich, right?"

Hana was whispering to him in Japanese with her lips close to his ear, and Solomon made a serious face like he was trying to concentrate. He could smell her strawberry lip gloss.

He didn't know how to reply. Some Japanese did believe that Christianity was a cult. His friends at school who were foreigners didn't see it this way, but he didn't know many Japanese who were Christians.

Hana poked him in the ribs with her left pinkie finger while looking straight ahead at the choir.

The choir was singing his great-grandmother's favorite hymn. She used to hum it often.

Like everyone in his family, Solomon was a Christian. His paternal grandfather, Baek Isak, had been one of the early Presbyterian ministers in Osaka. When Solomon was growing up, people at church referred to his grandfather as a martyr because he had been jailed for his faith and had died upon his release. Sunja, Mozasu, and Solomon went to service each Sunday.

"It's almost over, *nee*? I need a beer, Solomon. Let's go? I've been a good girl, and I sat through the whole thing."

"Hana, she was my great-grandmother," he said at last. Solomon remembered her as a gentle old woman who smelled like orange oil and biscuits. She didn't speak much Japanese but always had treats and coins for him in her dark blue vest pockets.

"We should be more respectful."

"Great-granny is now in heaven. Isn't that what Christians say?" Hana mimicked a peaceful face.

"Still, she's dead."

"Well, you don't seem very upset. Your grandmother Sunja doesn't seem very sad," she whispered. "Anyway, you're a Christian, right?"

"Yeah, I am a Christian. Why do you care so much?"

"I want to know what happens after you die. What happens to babies that die?"

Solomon didn't know what to say.

After her abortion, Hana had moved in with her mother. She'd refused to go back to Hokkaido and spent her days hanging out at Etsuko's restaurant, bored and irritated by everything. She couldn't handle the English at Solomon's school, and she hated kids her own age and refused to go to the local high school. Etsuko was trying to figure out what Hana should do, but in the meantime, Hana had decided that Solomon was her project and followed him around at every opportunity.

Like everyone else, Solomon thought that Hana was exceptionally pretty, but Etsuko warned him that her daughter was a troublemaker and that he should befriend girls from his school.

"Finally! The prayer is over. Come on, we can get out now before the exits clog up." Hana elbowed him gently, then pulled him out of his chair, and he let her lead him out of the building.

*   *   *

In the brightly lit alley behind the church, Hana leaned backward with one foot remaining on the ground and the other leg bent against the wall. She was smoking a cigarette. Again, she asked him why they couldn't get beers.

There were kids at his school who drank, but Solomon didn't like the taste much, and his friends invariably got in trouble when drunk. His father wouldn't have gotten mad at him for stuff like that, and in a way, Solomon felt free to say no to his friends at parties because it wasn't a big deal. But it was difficult to say no to Hana, because she was relentless when it came to what she wanted. Hana already thought he was too square.

Hana inhaled her cigarette deeply, making a lovely pout as she exhaled.

"No beer. Respects his great-grandmother's funeral. Never angry at his father. Oh, Solomon, maybe you can be a minister."

She clasped her hands in prayer and closed her eyes.

"I'm not going to be a minister. But what should I do when I grow up?" he asked.

An older boy at school had told a bunch of guys that all women are whores and all men are killers; girls cared about your future job because they wanted to marry rich guys.

"I don't know, Minister Pachinko." She laughed. "Hey, Christians aren't supposed to fuck before marriage, right?"

Solomon buttoned his suit jacket. It felt chilly outside, and his coat was still hanging in the hall closet upstairs.

"You're still a virgin," she said, smiling. "I know. That's okay. You're only fourteen. Do you want to?"

"What?"

"With me? I can, you know." She sucked on her cigarette again, even more suggestively. "I've done it. A lot. I know what you'll like." Hana held the necktie his father had tied for him that morning by the knot, then released her grasp slowly.

Solomon refused to look at her face.

The back door of the church opened slowly. Etsuko waved to them from the threshold.

"It's cold. Why don't you come inside? Solomon, you should be with your dad to greet the guests, right?"

Solomon could hear the anxiety in Etsuko's voice. Hana tossed her cigarette and followed him inside.

At the reception, Hana continued to trail after Solomon. She asked him to guess her bra size. Solomon had no idea, but he was now thinking of her breasts.

The guests, mostly old people, left them alone, so the two milled around the reception.

"Let's get beer at the 7-Eleven. We can go to my house to drink it. Or we can go to the park."

"I don't feel like beer."

"Maybe you feel like having some pussy."

"Hana!"

"Oh, shut up. You like me. I know you do."

"Why do you have to talk like that?"

"Because I'm not a nice girl, and you don't want to fuck a nice girl. Especially for your first time. Nobody does. I don't want to marry you, Solomon. I don't need your money."

"What are you talking about?"

"Fuck you," Hana said, and walked away from him.

Solomon caught up with her and grabbed her arm.

Hana gave him a chilly smile. It was as if she'd become someone else. She was wearing a dark blue wool dress with a white Peter Pan collar that made her look younger than him.

His grandmother Sunja appeared.

"*Halmoni*," Solomon said, relieved to see her. He felt excited around Hana, but she also made him nervous and afraid. In her presence, it felt safer to have an adult around. Just yesterday, he caught her stealing a packet of chocolate wafers at the *conbini*. When she left the shop, Solomon had lingered to give the clerk the money for the wafers, worried that the clerk might get in trouble. In his dad's business, if items were missing, clerks were fired immediately.

Sunja smiled at them. She touched Solomon's upper arm as if to calm him. He looked flustered.

"You look very handsome in your suit."

"This is Hana," Solomon said, and Hana bowed to her formally.

Sunja nodded. The girl was very beautiful, but she had a defiant chin.

Sunja was on her way to talk with Mozasu but felt funny leaving Solomon with the beautiful girl.

"I'll see you at home afterwards?" she asked.

Solomon nodded.

As soon as Sunja turned in the other direction, the girl led him outside the building.

Koh Hansu was walking with a cane. When he spotted Sunja walking diagonally across the reception room, he called out to her.

Sunja heard his voice; this was too much.

"Your mother was a tough woman. I always thought she was tougher than you."

Sunja stared at him. In the moments before her death, her mother had said that this man had ruined her life, but had he? He had given her Noa; unless she had been pregnant, she wouldn't have married Isak, and without Isak, she wouldn't have had Mozasu and now her grandson Solomon. She didn't want to hate him anymore. What did Joseph say to his brothers who had sold him into slavery when he saw them again? "You intended to harm me, but God intended it for good to accomplish what is now being done, the saving of many lives." This was something Isak had taught her when she'd asked him about the evil of this world.

"I came by to see if you were okay. If you needed anything."

"Thank you."

"My wife died."

"I'm sorry to hear that."

"I could never divorce her because her father was my boss. He had adopted me."

A while back, Mozasu had explained to her that after Hansu's father-in-law retired, Hansu became the top man in the second most powerful yakuza family in all of Kansai.

"You don't have to explain anything to me. We don't have anything to talk about, you and I. Thank you for coming today."

"Why do you have to be so cold? I thought you'd marry me now."

"What? This is my mother's funeral. Why are you still alive and my Noa gone? I couldn't even go to my own child's—"

"He was my only—"

"No, no, no. He was my son. Mine."

Sunja marched to the kitchen, leaving him leaning on his cane. She could not stop sobbing, and when the women in the kitchen saw her, they embraced her. A woman she did not know rubbed her back gently. They thought she was grieving for her mother.

14

Yokohama, 1980

It was too exciting, and Solomon had never been with anyone. Hana knew a lot, so she taught him to think about other things, to close his eyes if he got too excited, because it was important for him to wait until she was done. Girls would not want to fuck again if he came in a minute, she said. Solomon did everything Hana told him to do, not just because he was in awe of her, but because he wanted to make her happy. He would have done almost anything to make her laugh, because even though she was smart, too lovely to bear almost, and thrilling, she was also sad and restless. She could not be still; she could not bear not to drink every day. It was also important for her to have sex, so for six months she made him her ideal lover, even though he was not yet fifteen. She was almost seventeen.

It started after Yangjin's funeral. Hana bought beer, and they went to Etsuko's apartment. She removed her dress and blouse, then she took off his clothes. She pulled him to her bed, put a rubber on his cock, and showed him what to do. He was amazed at her body, and she was amused by his happiness. Hana was not angry that he came right away—she had expected this—but after he did, she started her lessons.

Almost every day, they met at Etsuko's place and made love several times. Etsuko was never home, and Solomon told his grandmother that he was with friends. He went home for dinner, because his father expected him at the table, and usually she went to Etsuko's restaurant for her meal.

After being with her, Solomon felt different; he felt older and more serious about life. He was still a boy; he knew that, but he started to think
about how he could be with her all the time, not just after school and during breaks. When he was at school, he did as much work as possible so
he could see her without thinking about schoolwork. His father expected
good grades, and Solomon was a strong student. When he wasn't with
her, he wondered what she did when she went out. Often, he worried
about losing her to an older boy, but she said there was nothing to worry
about.

Etsuko and Mozasu did not know they were having sex, and Hana told
Solomon that they must never know. She told him, "I'm your secret girl,
and you are my secret boy, *nee?*"

One afternoon, about four months in, Solomon came over to the apartment and found Hana waiting for him wearing flesh-colored lingerie and
high heels. She looked like a petite-sized centerfold in *Playboy*.

"Do you have any money, Solomon?" she asked.

"Yeah, sure. Why?"

"I want some. I have to buy things to turn you on. Like this. Pretty,
nee?"

Solomon tried to embrace her, but she pushed her left hand out gently.

"Money, please."

Solomon pulled out his billfold and took out a thousand-yen note.

"What do you need it for?" he asked.

"I just do. Do you have any more?"

"Uh, sure." Solomon pulled out the emergency five-thousand-yen note
that he kept folded in a square behind the wallet-sized photograph of his
mother. His father told him he always had to have some money just in case
something important came up.

"Give it to Hana-chan, please."

Solomon handed it to her, and Hana put it on the table with the
thousand-yen note.

Hana walked slowly to the shelf where Etsuko kept a radio and fiddled
with the channels until she found a pop song she liked. She bent over and
started swaying her hips in time to the music, making sure that he was

watching her. Solomon went to her, and she turned around and unbuttoned his jeans. Without saying a word, she pushed him into the armchair
near her and got on her knees. Solomon never knew what she was going
to do.

Hana slid the straps of her lace-trimmed brassiere over her shoulders
and pulled out her breasts over the small cups so he could see her nipples.
He tried to touch them, but she swatted him away. With her hands
cradling his bottom, she started to suck him.

When he was done, he saw that she was crying.

"Hana-chan, what's the matter?"

"Go home, Solomon."

"What?"

"You're finished."

"I came to see you. What's this all about?"

"Go home, Solomon! You're just this little boy who wants to fuck. I
need money, and this isn't enough. What am I going to do?"

"What are you talking about?"

"Go home and do your homework. Go have dinner with your daddy
and granny! You're all the same. I'm just a kid with divorced parents. You
think I'm nothing. You think I'm a loser because my mother was the town
whore."

"What are you talking about? Why are you mad at me? I don't think
that, Hana. I could never think that. You can come over, too. I thought
you were going to your mother's restaurant after I left."

Hana covered her breasts and went to the bathroom to get her robe.
She returned, wearing a red *yukata*. She got really quiet, then told him to
get more money and come back the next day.

"Hana, we are friends, *nee*? I love you. All the money I have, you can
have. I have cash at home from my birthday presents, but my grandmother keeps it for me in her bureau. I can't take it out all at once. What
do you need it for?"

"I have to go, Solomon. I can't stay here anymore. I have to be independent."

"Why? No. You can't go."

Every day and night, he had been thinking of what he could do for work so they could live together. They were too young to marry, but he thought that after he graduated from high school, he could get a job and he could take care of her. He would marry her. Once, she had said that if she married, she would never divorce, because she could never do that to her children. Her brothers and she had been treated worse than lepers after her mother left, she'd said. But Solomon's father wanted him to go to college in America. How could he leave her behind? He wondered if she would come with him. They could marry after he finished college.

"Solomon, I'm going to go to Tokyo and get a real life. I'm not going to stay in this apartment and wait for a fifteen-year-old to come and fuck me."

"What?"

"I have to do something with my life. Yokohama is stupid, and I'd rather be dead than return to Hokkaido."

"How about that school your mom found?"

"I can't go to school. I'm not smart like you. I want to be on television, like those girls in the dramas, but I don't know how to act. I can't sing, either. I have a terrible voice."

"Maybe you can learn how to act and sing. Aren't there schools for that? Can't we ask your mom to find you a school?"

Hana brightened for a moment, then looked disappointed again.

"She'd just think it's foolish. She wouldn't help me. Not for that. Besides, I can't read well, and you have to be able to read your lines and memorize them. I saw this really good actress interviewed on TV, and she said that she works really hard at reading and memorizing. I'm not good at anything—except sex. But what do I do when I'm not pretty anymore?"

"You'll always be beautiful, Hana."

She laughed.

"No, dummy. Women lose their looks fast. My mother is looking old. She better keep your dad. She's not going to do any better."

"Can you work for your mom?"

"No, I'd rather die. I hate the smell of shoyu and oil in my hair. It's disgusting. I can't imagine bowing all day to lazy, fat customers who complain about nothing. She hates the customers, too. She's a hypocrite."

"Etsuko is not like that."

"That's because you don't know her."

Solomon stroked her hair, and Hana opened her robe and slipped off her panties.

"Can you do it now? Again?" she asked. "I need that thing inside me, you know? It's always better the second time, because it lasts longer."

Solomon touched her, and he could.

Every day, she asked for money, and every day he gave her some of his birthday money from the bureau until there was no more left. Whenever he came over, she wanted to try things, even when it hurt her a lot, because she told him that she needed to master this. Even if he didn't like a certain method, she made him practice it and play certain roles. She learned how to make sounds and to talk the way girls talked in sex movies. A week after the money ran out, Solomon found a note she had hidden in his pencil case: "One day, you will find a really good girl, not someone like me. I promise. But it was fun, *nee*? I am your dirty flower, Soro-chan." That afternoon, Solomon ran to Etsuko's apartment, and he learned that she was gone. He didn't see her again until three years later when she met him at a famous *unagiya* in Tokyo to give him a sweater before he went to college in New York.

15

New York, 1985

Where are you?" Solomon asked in Japanese. "Your mom doesn't know where you are. Everyone's worried."

"I don't want to talk about her," Hana replied. "So you have a girlfriend-o now?"

"Yes," Solomon answered without thinking. "Hana, are you okay?" No matter how many drinks she'd had, she tended to sound sober.

"Tell me about her. Is she Japanese?"

"No." Solomon wanted to keep her on the line. About five years before, after she moved out of Etsuko's apartment, she took a long string of hostessing jobs in Tokyo, refusing to tell anyone where she lived. Etsuko didn't know what to do anymore; she'd hired an investigator but had little luck tracking her down. "Hana, tell me where you are, and please call your mother—"

"Shut up, college boy. Or else I'll hang up."

"Oh, Hana. Why?" He had to smile, having missed even her petulance. "Why are you so difficult, Hana-chan?"

"And why are you so far away?"

Hana poured herself a smaller glass of wine, and Solomon heard the *glug* of the liquid hitting the glass. It was morning in Tokyo, and she was sitting on the bare floor of her tiny apartment in Roppongi, which she shared with three other hostesses. Two were sleeping off the whiskey tea from the night before, and the third hadn't returned home from a date.

"I miss you, Solomon. I miss my old friend. You were my only friend. You know that?"

"You're drinking. Are you okay?"

"I like to drink. Drinking makes me happy. I'm very good at drinking." She laughed and swallowed a thimbleful of wine. She wanted to make the bottle last. "I'm good at drinking and fucking. *Soo desu nee.*"

"Can you please tell me where you are?"

"I'm in Tokyo."

"Still working in a club in Roppongi?"

"Yes, but at another club. You don't know which one." She had been fired two nights ago, but she knew she could get another job. "I am an excellent hostess."

"I'm sure you would be excellent at whatever you decide to do."

"You do not approve of my work, but I do not care. I am not a prostitute. I pour drinks and make conversation with incredibly boring men and make them feel fascinating."

"I didn't say that I didn't approve."

"You lie."

"Hana-chan, why don't you go to school? I think you would like college. You're smarter than most of the kids here. Maybe you can study in America; learn English first, then apply to a college here. Your mom and my dad would pay for it. You know that."

"Why don't I finish high school first?" Hana replied tartly. "Hang on, is your girlfriend with you now?"

"No, but I have to meet her soon."

"No, you will not meet her, Solomon. You will talk to me. Because you are my old friend, and I want to talk to my old friend tonight. Can you cancel? And I will call you back."

"I'll call you. Yes, I'll cancel, then I'll call you back."

"I am not giving you my number. You cancel with girlfriend-o, and I will call you in five minutes."

"Are you okay, Hana?"

"Why don't you say you miss me, too, Solomon? You used to miss me desperately. Don't you remember?"

"Yes, I remember everything."

When they met for lunch after being apart for three years, she gave him a crimson-colored cashmere sweater from Burberry as a graduation present. "It's cold in Manhattan, *nee*? The sweater is bloodred and hot like our burning love." During the meal, however, she would not come close to him. She wouldn't even touch his arm. She had smelled wonderful, like jasmine and sandalwood.

"How could I forget you?" Solomon said quietly. Phoebe would be coming by in a few minutes. She had the key to his room.

"Ah, there. There is my Solomon. I can tell when you are hungry for me."

Solomon closed his eyes. She was right; this felt like hunger. It had been nothing short of physical pain when she had left him, and he'd had no words to describe her departure. He loved Phoebe, but it wasn't what he'd felt for Hana.

"Hana-chan. I have to go now, but may I please phone you later? May I please have your number?"

"No, Solomon. You may not have my number. I call you when I want to speak to you. You do not call me. Nobody calls me."

"And you get to leave when you want to leave," he said.

"Yes, I do get to leave, but Solomon, you will never tire of me, because I will never ask anything of you. Except for today. I want you to talk to me so I can go to sleep. I cannot sleep anymore, Solomon. I do not know why, but I cannot sleep anymore. Hana-chan is so tired."

"Why won't you let your mother help you? I'm in New York. You won't even tell me your number. How can I help—"

"I know, I know, you are studying and becoming an international businessman of the world! This is what your rich papa wants, and Solomon is a good boy and he will make his pachinko papa proud!"

"Hana, you have to be careful with the drinking, *nee*?" He tried to sound calm. She would disappear if he sounded cross.

The door opened, and it was Phoebe, looking happy at first, then puzzled because he was on the phone. Solomon smiled and gestured for her to sit down beside him. The dorm room had only a narrow bed and a serviceable desk, but he was lucky to have a single. He put his finger to his lips, and Phoebe mouthed to ask if she should go. He paused, then shook his head no.

"Will you cancel with your girlfriend-o and help me sleep?" Hana asked. "If you were here, you'd fuck me, and I would sleep in your arms. We never got a chance to sleep in the same bed, because you were still a boy. Now you are twenty. I want to suck on your man cock."

"What do you want me to do, Hana? How can I help you?"

"So-lo-mon-Ul-tra-man. You should sing. You should sing to me. You know, the song about sunshine. I like that baby song about sunshine."

"I will sing if you will give me your phone number."

"You have to promise me that you will not give it to my mother."

"Okay. What is it?" Solomon wrote down the numbers on the backflap of his macroeconomics textbook. "I'm going to hang up, and then I will call you in a few seconds, okay?"

"Okay," she said weakly. She had finished the second bottle already. She felt awake but heavy, like her limbs were soaked through. "I'll hang up now. Call me. I want to hear you sing."

When he hung up, Phoebe asked, "Hey, what's going on?"

"One minute. Just one minute. I'll explain."

He dialed his father, and Mozasu picked up.

"Papa, this is Hana's number. I think she's really sick. Can you find out where she is just from this number? Can you ask Haruki or Etsuko's investigator? I better go. I have to call her back now. She sounds like she's drunk or drugged out."

Solomon dialed the number. It was for a Chinese restaurant in Roppongi.

Phoebe took off her overcoat and stripped down and got into bed. Her dark hair hung loosely around her pale collarbone.

"Who was that?"

"Hana. My stepmother's daughter."

"Which makes her your stepsister? The one who's working as a hooker."

"She's not a hooker. She's a hostess."

"They have sex for money, right?"

"No. Not always. Sometimes. Depends."

"Well, gosh, that's a major distinction. Once again, you've enlightened me on the finer points of Japanese culture. Thank you."

The phone rang, and Solomon rushed to pick up. It was Etsuko this time.

"Solomon. The number. It was for a Chinese restaurant."

"Yes, I'm sorry. But I did speak to her, Etsuko. She was very drunk. She said she's working at a different club now. Didn't her former mama-san say anything about where she is now?"

"We couldn't find anything. She'd been fired from two other places. Every time we get closer, she gets fired for drinking too much."

"If I hear anything, I'll let you know right away, okay?"

"It is night there, *nee*?"

"*Hai*. Hana said she couldn't sleep. I was worried she was taking speed while drinking. I heard girls do that at clubs."

"You should go to sleep, Solomon. Mozasu said you're doing well in school. We're proud of you," she said. "Night-night, Solomon-chan."

Phoebe smiled.

"So you lost your cherry to your hooker half sister, and now she's in trouble."

"Compassionate of you."

"Quite liberal and tolerant of me not to be upset that your ex is calling you drunk when she's a professional sex worker. Either I'm confident in my value, or I'm confident in our relationship, or I'm just ignorant of the fact that you're going to hurt my feelings when you return to a troubled young damsel whom I know you're interested in rescuing."

"I can't rescue her."

"You just tried and failed, because she does not want your help. She wants to die."

"What?"

"Yes, Solomon. This young woman wants to die." She pushed back his forelocks and looked at him kindly. She kissed him on the mouth. "There are a lot of troubled young women in this world. We can't save them all."

Hana didn't phone him again. Months later, Etsuko learned that she was working in a Kabukicho *toruko-buro* where she bathed men for money. The investigator told her what time Hana would finish her shift, and Etsuko waited outside the building. Several girls came out, and Hana was the last to leave. Etsuko couldn't believe how much she'd aged. The investigator had explained that Etsuko might not recognize her because she would look much older. Hana's face was withered and dry. She wore no makeup, and her clothes didn't look clean.

"Hana," Etsuko said.

Hana saw her, then walked in the other direction.

"Leave me alone."

"Hana, oh, please, Hana."

"Go away."

"Hana, we can forget all this. Start again. I shouldn't have tried to make you go to school. I'm sorry."

"No."

"You don't have to work here. I have money."

"I don't want your money. I don't want the pachinko man's money. I can earn my own."

"Where do you live? Can we go to your place to talk?"

"No."

"I'm not going to go away."

"Yes, yes, you will. You're selfish."

Etsuko stood there, believing that if she could just listen and suffer, then maybe her daughter could be saved.

"I am terrible. *Soo desu.* Forgive me, Hana. Anything but this."

Hana dropped her large tote bag from her shoulder, and the two wine bottles wrapped in a towel made a muffled clinking sound on the pavement. She wept openly, her arms hanging by her side, and Etsuko knelt on the ground and held her daughter's knees, refusing to let her go.

16

Tokyo, 1989

Solomon was glad to be back home. The job at Travis Brothers was turning out better than expected. The pay was more than he deserved for a job a year out of college, and he enjoyed the numerous benefits of being hired as an expat rather than as a local. The HR people at Travis got him a fancy rental broker who found him a decent one-bedroom in Minami-Azabu, which Phoebe didn't think was too awful. As his corporate employer, Travis was named guarantor on the lease, since Solomon was legally a foreigner in Japan. Solomon, who had grown up in Yokohama in his father's house, had never rented an apartment before. For non-Japanese renters, requiring a guarantor was common practice, which, of course, incensed Phoebe.

After some cajoling, Phoebe had decided to follow him to Tokyo. They were thinking of getting married, and moving together to Japan was the first step. Now that she was here, he felt bad for her. Solomon was employed at the Japanese subsidiary of a British investment bank, so he worked alongside Brits, Americans, Aussies, Kiwis, and the occasional South African among the Western-educated locals, who were less parochial than the natives. As a Korean Japanese educated in the States, Solomon was both a local and a foreigner, with the useful knowledge of the native and the financial privileges of an expatriate. Phoebe, however, did not enjoy his status and privileges. Rather, she spent her days at home reading or wandering around Tokyo, not sure why she was here at all since Solomon was rarely home. It was impossible for her to get a work visa, as they weren't married; she was thinking of teaching English, but she didn't know how to get a tutoring job. Now and then, when a Japanese person asked her an innocent question like if she was South Korean, Phoebe tended to overreact.

"In America, there is no such thing as a *Kankokujin* or *Chosenjin*. Why the hell would I be a South Korean or a North Korean? That makes no sense! I was born in Seattle, and my parents came to the States when there was only one Korea," she'd shout, relating one of the bigotry anecdotes of her day. "Why does Japan still distinguish the two countries for its Korean residents who've been here for four fucking generations? You were born here. You're not a foreigner! That's insane. Your father was born here. Why are you two carrying South Korean passports? It's bizarre."

She knew as well as he did that after the peninsula was divided, the Koreans in Japan ended up choosing sides, often more than once, affecting their residency status. It was still hard for a Korean to become a Japanese citizen, and there were many who considered such a thing shameful—for a Korean to try to become a citizen of its former oppressor. When she told her friends in New York about this curious historical anomaly and the pervasive ethnic bias, they were incredulous at the thought that the friendly, well-mannered Japanese they knew could ever think she was somehow criminal, lazy, filthy, or aggressive—the negative stereotypical traits of Koreans in Japan. "Well, everyone knows that the Koreans don't get along with the Japanese," her friends would say innocently, as if all things were equal. Soon, Phoebe stopped talking about it with her friends back home.

Solomon found it peculiar that Phoebe got so angry about the history of Koreans in Japan. After three months of living in Tokyo and reading a few history books, she'd concluded that the Japanese would never change. "The government still refuses to acknowledge its war crimes!" Strangely, in these conversations, Solomon found himself defending the Japanese.

They planned on visiting Seoul together for a week when the deal season ended and work slowed down. He hoped Seoul would be some sort of neutral territory for them—a place to feel normal since they were both Korean immigrants of a kind. And it didn't hurt that Phoebe spoke very good Korean; his Korean was pathetic at best. He had visited South Korea with his father several times, and everyone there always treated them like they were Japanese. It was no homecoming; however, it was great to visit. After a while, it had been easier just to play along as Japanese tourists who had come to enjoy the good barbecue rather than to try to explain to the chest-beating, self-righteous Koreans why their first language was Japanese.

Solomon was in love with Phoebe. They had been together since sophomore year. He couldn't imagine life without her, and yet, seeing her discomfort here made him realize how different they were. They were both ethnically Korean and had grown up outside Korea, but they weren't the same. Back home, on the ground in Japan, their differences seemed that much more pronounced. They hadn't had sex in two weeks. Would it be that way when they married? Would it get worse? Solomon thought about these things as he headed to the game.

Tonight was his fourth poker night with the guys at work. Solomon and one other junior associate, Louis, a *hapa* M & A guy from Paris, had been asked to join; the rest of the players were managing directors and executive directors. The cast changed a little, but there were usually six or seven guys. Never any girls. Solomon was a brilliant poker player. In the first game, he had played it easy and come out neutral; in the second game, when he felt more comfortable, he came second, and after the third game, Solomon walked out with most of the 350,000-yen pot. The others were annoyed, but he thought it was worth making a point—when he wanted to win, he could.

This evening, he planned to pay up a little. The guys were a good bunch—no sore losers; Solomon hoped to keep playing with them. No doubt, they had invited him thinking he was more or less a fish; they didn't know that he was an econ major at Columbia who had double minored in poker and pool.

They played Anaconda, also called "Pass the Trash" because you could get rid of your bad cards to the guy on your left—first three cards, then two cards, and then one more, betting all the while. A moron could have won the game, because there was so much luck involved, but what Solomon enjoyed was the betting. He liked watching others bet or go out.

The players met in the paneled basement of a no-name *izakaya* in Roppongi. The owner was a friend of Kazu-san, Solomon's boss and the most senior managing director at Travis, and he let them use the room once a month as long as they drank enough and ordered plenty of food. Each month, one guy hosted and picked up the tab. Initially, the managing directors thought it wasn't fair to make the associates pay, since they earned much less, but after Solomon won on the third game, enough of them said "The kid can buy dinner." Solomon was hosting this one.

Six guys were playing, and the pot was 300,000 yen. Three hands in, Solomon kept it safe: He won nothing and lost nothing.

"Hey, Solly," Kazu said, "what's going on? Did luck leave you, buddy?"

His boss, Kazu, was a Japanese national who was educated in California and Texas, and despite his bespoke suits and elegant Tokyo dialect, his English speech pattern was pure American frat boy. His family tree was filled with dukes and counts who had been stripped of their titles after the war, and his mother's side came from connected branches of shogun families. At Travis, Kazu made lots of rain. Five of the six most important banking deals last year took place because Kazu had made them happen. It was also Kazu who had brought Solomon into the game. The older guys grumbled about losing to the kid, but Kazu shut them up, saying that competition was good for everyone.

Solomon liked his boss; everyone did. He was lucky to be one of Kazu's boys and to be invited to the famous monthly poker games. There were guys in Kazu's team who had worked for Travis for ten years and had never been asked. Whenever Phoebe said Japanese people were racist, Solomon would bring up Etsuko and Kazu as personal evidence for his argument to the contrary. Etsuko was the obvious example of a Japanese person who was kindhearted and ethnically unbiased, but Phoebe barely understood her, since Etsuko's English was terrible. Kazu was Japanese, and he had been far kinder to Solomon than most Koreans in Japan, who had occasionally eyed him with suspicion as a wealthy man's son or as competition at school. Yes, some Japanese thought Koreans were scum, but some Koreans were scum, he told Phoebe. Some Japanese were scum, too. There was no need to keep rehashing the past; he hoped Phoebe would get over it eventually.

It was time to discard, take new cards, and place bets. Solomon threw away a useless nine of diamonds and a two of hearts, then picked up the jack and a three he needed for a full house. Luck had never left him. Whenever Solomon played cards, he felt strong and smooth, like he couldn't lose; he wondered if he felt this way because he didn't care about the money. He liked being at the table; he liked the bullshit guy talk. With this hand, he had a solid chance at the current pot, which was easily over a hundred thousand yen. Solomon bet thirty thousand. Louis and Yamada-san, the Japanese Aussie, folded, leaving Solomon, Ono, Giancarlo, and Kazu. Ono's face was blank and Giancarlo scratched his ear.

Ono bet another twenty thousand, and immediately, Kazu and Giancarlo folded. Giancarlo said, laughing, "You two are assholes." He took a long sip of his whiskey. "Are there any more of those chicken things on sticks?"

"*Yakitori*," Kazu said, "You live in Japan; dude, learn what to call chicken on a stick."

Giancarlo gave him the finger, smiling and revealing his short, even teeth.

Kazu signaled to the waiter and ordered for everyone.

It was time to show hands, and Ono only had two pairs. He'd been bluffing.

Solomon fanned out his cards.

"You son of a bitch," Ono said.

"Sorry, sir," Solomon said, sweeping the money toward him in an easy, practiced manner.

"Never apologize for winning, Solly," Kazu said.

"He can apologize a little for taking my money," Giancarlo retorted, and the others laughed.

"Man, I can't wait until I put you on one of my deals. You will be hanging out with boxes of due diligence all fucking weekend, and I will make sure you only get ugly girls to work with," Ono said. He had a doctorate in economics from MIT and was on his fourth marriage. Each successive wife was even more gorgeous than the prior one. As a very senior electronics banker during the Japan boom, he had made obscene money and still worked without stopping. Ono said that the purpose of hard work was simple: Sex with pretty women was worth whatever it took.

"I will find the worst deal with the maximum diligence. Just for you, my little friend." Ono rubbed his hands together.

"He's taller than you," Giancarlo said.

"Status trumps size," Ono replied.

"*Gomen nasai*, Ono-san, *gomen nasai*." Solomon bowed theatrically.

"Don't worry about it, Solly," Kazu said. "Ono's got a heart of gold."

"Not true. I'm capable of holding a grudge and taking vengeance at the most opportune moment," Ono said.

Solomon raised his eyebrows and shivered. "I'm just a boy, sir," he pleaded. "Have mercy." He proceeded to make neat stacks of cash in front of him. "A rich boy who deserves some mercy."

"I heard you were filthy rich," Giancarlo said. "Your dad's a pachinko guy, right?"

Solomon nodded, not sure how he knew.

"I used to date a hot Japanese *hapa* who played a lot of pachinko. She was an expensive habit. Figures you know how to gamble. It must be that clever Korean blood," Giancarlo said. "Man, that girl used to go on and on about the tricky and smart Koreans who owned all the parlors and made fools out of the Japanese—but, man, she used to do this crazy thing with her tits when—"

"Impossible," Kazu said. "You never dated a hot girl."

"Yeah, you got me, *sensei*. I dated your wife, and she's not very hot. She's just a real—"

Kazu laughed. "Hey, how 'bout if we play poker?" He poured soda into his whiskey, lightening the color considerably. "Solly won fair and square."

"I'm not saying anything bad. It's a compliment. The Koreans here are smart and rich. Just like our boy Solomon. It wasn't like I was calling him a yakuza! You're not going to get me killed, are you, Solly?" Giancarlo asked.

Solomon smiled tentatively. It wasn't the first time he'd heard these things, but it had been a very long while since anyone had mentioned his father's business. In America, no one even knew what pachinko was. It was his father who'd been confident that there would be less bigotry at the offices of a Western bank and had encouraged him to take this job. Giancarlo wasn't saying anything different from what other middle-class Japanese people thought or whispered; it was just strange to hear such a thing coming from a white Italian who had lived in Japan for twenty years.

Louis cut the cards, and Kazu shuffled and dealt the guys a fresh hand.

Solomon had three kings, but he discarded them one by one in three consecutive rounds, then folded, losing about ten thousand yen. At the end of the night, he paid the tab. Kazu said he wanted to talk to him, so they walked out to the street to hail a taxi.

17

Y ou lost on purpose. The three kings came from you," Kazu said to Solomon. They were standing outside the *izakaya* building. Kazu lit a Marlboro Light.

Solomon shrugged.

"That was dumb. Giancarlo is a social retard. He's one of those white guys who has to live in Asia because the white people back home don't want him. He's been in Japan for so long that he thinks when Japanese people suck up to him, it's because he's so special. What a fucking fantasy. That said, not a bad guy overall. Effective. Gets shit done. You gotta know this by now, that people here, even the non-Japanese, say the dumbest things about Koreans, but you gotta forget it. When I was in the States, people used to say stupid-ass crap about Asians, like we all spoke Chinese and ate sushi for breakfast. When it came to teaching US history, they'd forget the internment and Hiroshima. Whatever, right?"

"That stuff doesn't get to me," Solomon replied, scanning the dark streets for a taxi. The trains had stopped running half an hour before. "I'm good."

"Okay, tough guy," Kazu said. "Listen, there is a tax, you know, on success."

"Huh?"

"If you do well at anything, you gotta pay up to all the people who did worse. On the other hand, if you do badly, life makes you pay a shit tax, too. Everybody pays something."

Kazu looked at him soberly.

"Of course, the worst one is the tax on the mediocre. Now, that one's a bitch." Kazu tossed his cigarette and crossed his arms. "Pay attention: The ones who pay the shit tax are mostly people who were born in the wrong place and the wrong time and are hanging on to the planet by their broken fingernails. They don't even know the fucking rules of the game. You can't even get mad at 'em when they lose. Life just fucks and fucks and fucks bastards like that." Kazu wrinkled his brow in resignation, like he was somewhat concerned about life's inequities but not very. He took a deep breath. "So, those losers have to climb Mount Everest to get out of hell, and maybe one or two in five hundred thousand break out, but the rest pay the shit tax all their lives, then they die. If God exists and if He's fair, then it makes sense that in the afterlife, those guys should get the better seats."

Solomon nodded, not understanding where this was going.

Kazu's stare remained unbroken. "But all those able-bodied middle-class people who are scared of their shadows, well, they pay the mediocre tax in regular quarterly installments with compounding interest. When you play it safe, that's what happens, my friend. So if I were you, I wouldn't throw any games. I'd use every fucking advantage. Beat anyone who fucks with you to a fucking pulp. Show no mercy to chumps, especially if they don't deserve it. Make the pussies cry."

"So then the success tax comes from envy, and the shit tax comes from exploitation. Okay." Solomon nodded like he was starting to get it. "Then what's the mediocre tax? How can it be wrong to—?"

"Good question, young Jedi. The tax for being mediocre comes from you and everyone else knowing that you are mediocre. It's a heavier tax than you'd think."

Solomon had never thought of such a thing before. It wasn't like he saw himself as terribly special, but he'd never seen himself as mediocre, either. Perhaps it was unspoken, even to himself, but he did want to be good at something.

"Jedi, understand this: There's nothing fucking worse than knowing that you're just like everybody else. What a messed-up, lousy existence. And in this great country of Japan—the birthplace of all my fancy ancestors—everyone, everyone wants to be like everyone else. That's why it is such a safe place to live, but it's also a dinosaur village. It's extinct, pal. Carve up your piece and invest your spoils elsewhere. You're a young man, and someone should tell you the real truth about this country. Japan is not fucked because it lost the war or did bad things. Japan is fucked because there is no more war, and in peacetime everyone actually wants to be mediocre and is terrified of being different. The other thing is that the elite Japanese want to be English and white. That's pathetic, delusional, and merits another discussion entirely."

Solomon thought some of this made sense. Everyone he knew who was really Japanese did think he was middle-class even when he wasn't. Rich kids at his high school whose fathers owned several country-club memberships worth millions and millions thought of themselves as middle-class. His uncle Noa, whom he'd never met, had apparently killed himself because he wanted to be Japanese and normal.

An empty taxi approached them, but Solomon didn't notice, and Kazu smiled.

"So, yeah, idiots are going to get on your case and notice that your dad owns pachinko parlors. And how do people know this?"

"I never talk about it."

"Everyone knows, Solomon. In Japan, you're either a rich Korean or a poor Korean, and if you are a rich Korean, there's a pachinko parlor in your background somewhere."

"My dad is a great guy. He's incredibly honest."

"I'm sure he is." Kazu faced him squarely, his arms still crossed against his chest.

Solomon hesitated but said it anyway: "He's not some gangster. He doesn't do bad things. He's an ordinary businessman. He pays all his taxes and does everything by the book. There are some shady guys in the business, but my dad is incredibly precise and moral. He owns three parlors. It's not like—"

Kazu nodded reassuringly.

"My father's never taken anything that wasn't his; he doesn't even care about money. He gives away so much of it—"

Etsuko had told him that Mozasu paid the nursing home bills for several of his employees.

"Solly, Solly. No, man, there's no need to explain. It's not like Koreans had a lot of choices in regular professions. I'm sure he chose pachinko because there wasn't much else. He's probably an excellent businessman. You think your poker skills came out of a vacuum? Maybe your dad could have worked for Fuji or Sony, but it wasn't like they were going to hire a Korean, right? I doubt they'd hire you now, Mr. Columbia University. Japan still doesn't hire Koreans to be teachers, cops, and nurses in lots of places. You couldn't even rent your own apartment in Tokyo, and you make good money. It's fucking 1989! Anyway, you can be polite about it, but that's fucked up. I'm Japanese but I'm not stupid. I lived in America and Europe for a long time; it's crazy what the Japanese have done to the Koreans and the Chinese who were born here. It's fucking bonkers; you people should have a revolution. You don't protest enough. You and your dad were born here, right?"

Solomon nodded, not understanding why Kazu was getting so worked up about this.

"Even if your dad was a hit man, I wouldn't give a shit. And I wouldn't turn him in."

"But he's not."

"No, kid, of course he's not," Kazu said, smiling. "Go home to your girlfriend. I heard she's a looker and smart. That's good. Because in the end, brains matter more than you think," he said, laughing.

Kazu hailed a taxi and told Solomon to take it before him. Everyone said that Kazu wasn't like regular bosses, and it was true.

A week later, he put Solomon on the new real estate deal, and Solomon was the youngest one on the team. This was the cool transaction that all the guys in the office wanted. One of Travis's heavyweight banking clients wanted to purchase land in Yokohama to build a world-class golf course.

Nearly all the details had been worked out; they needed to get three of the remaining landowners to sign on. Two were not impossible, just expensive, but the third was a headache—the old woman had no interest in money and could not be bought out. Her lot was where the eleventh hole would be. At the morning meeting, with the client present, two of the banking directors gave a strong presentation about the beneficial ways of structuring the mortgage, and Solomon took careful notes. Right before the meeting broke up, Kazu mentioned casually that the old woman was still holding up progress. The client smiled at Kazu and said, "No doubt, you will be able to handle the matter. We are confident."

Kazu smiled politely.

The client left quickly, and everyone else scattered out of the conference room shortly thereafter. Kazu stopped Solomon before he had a chance to return to his desk.

"What are you doing for lunch, Solly?"

"I was going to grab something from downstairs. Why? What's up?"

"Let's go for a drive."

The chauffeur took them to the old woman's lot in Yokohama. The gray concrete building was in decent condition, and the front yard was well maintained. No one seemed to be home. An ancient pine tree cast a triangular shade across the facade of the square structure, and a thin brook gurgled from the back of the house. It was a former fabric-dyeing factory and now the private residence of the woman. Her children were dead, and there were no obvious heirs.

"So how do you get a person to do what you want when she doesn't want to?" Kazu asked.

"I don't know," Solomon said. He'd figured that this was a kind of field trip for Kazu, and his boss wanted the company. Rarely did Kazu go anywhere alone.

The car was parked in the wide, dusty street opposite the old woman's lot. If she was home, she would have noticed the black town car idling not ten yards from her house. But no one came outside or stirred within.

Kazu stared at the house.

"So this is where Sonoko Matsuda lives. The client is confident that I can get Matsuda-san to sell."

"Can you?" Solomon asked.

"I think so, but I don't know how," Kazu said.

"This will sound stupid, but how can you get her to sign if you don't know how?" Solomon asked.

"I'm making a wish, Solly. I'm making a wish. Sometimes, that's how it starts."

Kazu asked the chauffeur to take them to an *unagi* restaurant not far from there.

18

Yokohama, 1989

On Sunday morning, after church services, Solomon and Phoebe took the train to Yokohama for lunch with his family.

As usual, the front door of the house was closed but unlocked, so they let themselves in. A designer friend of Etsuko's had recently renovated it, and the house was unrecognizable from the one of Solomon's childhood filled with dark American furniture. The designer had removed most of the original interior walls and knocked out the small back windows, replacing them with thick sheets of glass. Now it was possible to see the rock garden from the front of the house. Pale-colored furniture, white oak floors, and sculptural paper lamps filled the vast quadrant near the woodburning stove, leaving the large, square-shaped living room light and uncluttered. In the opposite corner of the room, tall branches of forsythia bloomed in an enormous celadon-colored ceramic jar on the floor. The house looked like a glamorous Buddhist temple.

Mozasu came out from the den to greet them.

"You're here!" he said to Phoebe in Korean. When she spent time with Solomon's family, the group spoke three languages. Phoebe spoke Korean with the elders and English with Solomon, while Solomon spoke mostly in Japanese to the elders and English to Phoebe; with everyone translating in bits, they made it work somehow.

Mozasu opened the shoe closet by the door and offered them house slippers.

"My mother and aunt have been cooking all week. I hope you're hungry."

"Something smells wonderful," she said. "Is everyone in the kitchen?"

Phoebe smoothed her navy pleated skirt.

"Yes. I mean, sorry, no. Etsuko couldn't be here today. She's very sad to miss you. She asked me to apologize."

Phoebe nodded, glancing briefly at Solomon. It seemed impolite for her to ask where Etsuko was, but she couldn't understand why Solomon didn't ask his father where she was. Phoebe was curious about Etsuko. She was the only person Phoebe couldn't speak to directly, because neither woman spoke the other's language. Also, she wanted to meet Hana, who was never around.

Solomon grabbed Phoebe's hand and led her to the kitchen. Around his family, he felt younger than usual, almost giddy. The scents of all his favorite dishes filled the wide hallway connecting the front of the house with the kitchen.

"Solomon is here!" he shouted, no different than when he'd come home from school as a boy.

Kyunghee and Sunja stopped their work immediately and looked up, beaming. Mozasu smiled, seeing their happiness.

"Phoebe is here, too, Solomon!" Kyunghee said. She wiped her hands on her apron, then came out from behind the thick marble counter to embrace him.

Sunja followed her and put her arm around Phoebe's waist. Sunja was a head shorter than Phoebe.

"This is for both of you." Phoebe gave her a box of candy from the Tokyo branch of an exclusive French chocolate shop.

Sunja smiled. "Thank you."

Kyunghee untied the ribbon to take a peek. It was a large box of glazed fruits dipped in chocolate. Delighted, she said, "This looks expensive. You kids should be saving money at your age. But the candies look so delicious! Thank you."

She inhaled the chocolate aroma dramatically.

"It's so good to have you here," Sunja said in Korean, folding Phoebe's slender shoulders into her thick embrace.

Phoebe loved being with Solomon's family. It was much smaller than her own, but everyone seemed closer, as if each member were organically attached to one seamless body, whereas her enormous extended family felt like cheerfully mismatched Lego bricks in a large bucket. Phoebe's parents had at least five or six siblings each, and she had grown up with well over a dozen cousins just in California. There were relatives in New York, New Jersey, DC, Washington State, and Toronto. She had dated a couple of Korean American guys and had met their families, but Solomon's family was different. Solomon's family was warm but far more muted and intensely watchful. None of them seemed to miss anything.

"Is that for *pajeon*?" Phoebe asked. The mixing bowl was filled with creamy pancake batter flecked with thin slices of scallion and chunks of scallops.

"You like *pajeon*? So does Solomon! How does your *umma* make it?" Kyunghee asked; her tone was casual, though she held strong opinions about the ratio of scallions to shellfish.

"My mother doesn't cook," Phoebe said, looking only a little embarrassed.

"What?" Kyunghee gasped in horror and turned to Sunja, who raised her eyebrows, sharing her sister-in-law's surprise.

Phoebe laughed.

"I grew up eating pizza and hamburgers. And lots of Kentucky Fried Chicken. I love the KFC corn on the cob." She smiled. "Mom worked in my dad's medical office as his office manager and was never home before eight o'clock."

The women nodded, trying to understanding this.

"Mom was always working. She did all the medical paperwork at the dining table next to us kids while we did our homework. I don't think she ever went to bed until midnight—"

"But you didn't eat any Korean food?"

Kyunghee couldn't comprehend this.

"On the weekends we ate it. At a restaurant."

The women understood that the mother was busy and hardworking, but it seemed inconceivable to them that a Korean mother didn't cook for her family. What would Solomon eat if he married this girl? What would their children eat?

"She didn't have time. That makes sense, but does your mother know how to cook?" Kyunghee asked tentatively.

"She never learned. And none of her sisters cook Korean food, either."

Phoebe laughed, because the fact that none of them cooked Korean food was a point of pride. Her mother and her sisters tended to look down at women who cooked a lot and constantly tried to make you eat. The four of them were very thin. Like Phoebe, they were the kind of women who were constantly moving around and seemed uninterested in eating because they were so absorbed in their work. "My favorite aunt cooks only on the weekends and only for dinner parties. She usually makes Italian food. Our family always meets at restaurants."

Phoebe found it amusing to see their continuing shock and disbelief at such a mundane detail of her childhood. What was the big deal? Why did women have to cook, anyway? she wondered. Her mother was her favorite person in the world. "My brother and sisters don't even like kimchi. My mother won't even keep it in the refrigerator because of the smell."

"*Waaah*," Sunja sighed. "You really are American. Are your aunts married to Americans?"

"My aunts and uncles are married to non-Koreans. My brother and sisters married ethnically Korean people, but they're Americans like me. My older brother-in-law, the lawyer, speaks fluent Portuguese but no Korean; he grew up in Brazil. America is full of people like that."

"Really?" Kyunghee exclaimed.

"Who are your aunts married to?"

"I have aunts and uncles by marriage who are white, black, Dutch, Jewish, Filipino, Mexican, Chinese, Puerto Rican, and, let's see, there's one Korean American uncle and three Korean American aunts. I have a lot of cousins. Everyone's mixed," she added, smiling at the older women wearing spotless white aprons, who were paying such careful attention to what she was saying that it looked as if their minds were taking notes.

"When we get together, like on Thanksgiving and Christmas, it's really fun."

"I've met several of them," Solomon said, worried that his grandmother and great-aunt wouldn't approve of her family, although he could tell they were more curious than reproachful. Neither of them had ever said that he had to marry a Korean person, but he knew his father's relationship with Etsuko made them uncomfortable.

When the frying pan was hot enough, Sunja poured a scant cup of the scallion pancake batter into it. She checked the edges and lowered the heat. Phoebe was lively and good for the boy, she thought. Her mother used to say a woman's life was suffering, but that was the last thing she wanted for this sweet girl who had a quick, warm smile for everyone. If she didn't cook, then so what? If she took good care of Solomon, then nothing else should matter, though she hoped that Phoebe wanted children. Lately, Sunja wanted to hold babies. How wonderful it would be not to have to worry about a war or having enough food to eat, or finding shelter. Solomon and Phoebe wouldn't have to labor the way she and Kyunghee had, but could just enjoy their children.

"When are you going to marry Solomon?" Sunja asked, without shifting her focus from the frying pan. An older woman had a right to ask this sort of thing, though she was still a little afraid to do it.

"Yes, when are you two getting married? What are you waiting for? My sister and I have nothing to do—we'll move to Tokyo if you want help with the babies and the cooking!" Kyunghee giggled.

Solomon shook his head and smiled at the three women.

"And this is when I go to the den and talk man stuff with Dad."

"Thanks a lot, Solomon," Phoebe said. She didn't actually mind their questions, since she had been wondering about this, too.

Mozasu smiled, and the men left them in the kitchen.

Father and son sat down in the armchairs in the center of the large room. Baskets of fruits and bowls of nuts topped the glass and stainless-steel coffee table opposite the long low-back sofa. A stack of today's Korean and Japanese newspapers remained half-read.

Mozasu turned on the television and lowered the volume on the news; he was scanning the ticker running across the screen with stock prices. The two often talked with the television on.

"How's work?" Mozasu asked.

"Much easier than school. The boss is really great—a Japanese guy, but he went to college and business school in California."

"California? Your mother would've liked that," Mozasu said quietly. The boy resembled her so much, especially around the brow and nose.

"Where's Etsuko?" Solomon stared at the blue background of the news screen. The newscasters were talking about a flood in Bangkok. "Is it Hana? She okay?"

Mozasu sighed. "Etsuko will fill you in. Give her a call."

Solomon wanted to know more, but his father didn't know about what had happened between the two of them. Mozasu never liked to talk about Hana, because she upset Etsuko so much.

"Your grandmother and great-aunt like Phoebe. They want you to get married."

"Yes, I heard that. Five minutes ago."

Mozasu faced his son. "Does Phoebe want to live in Japan?"

"Not sure. She hates that she doesn't know Japanese."

"She can learn."

Solomon looked doubtful. "She wants to work. It's not easy to get your career going straight out of college in Japan. And she doesn't have the language skills. Staying home is not good for Phoebe."

Mozasu nodded. Solomon's mother had been the same way.

"You okay with money?"

"Yes, Dad," he replied, almost amused by his father's concern, "I have a good job now. Hey, Dad, do you know an older lady named Sonoko Matsuda? She owns an old textile factory in Yokohama. Not far from Goro-san's place."

"No." Mozasu shook his head. "Why?"

"Kazu, my boss, is trying to finalize this real estate transaction, and the lady, Matsuda-san, won't sell her property. It's holding up the deal.

I thought maybe you might know someone. You know a lot of people in Yokohama, I mean."

"I don't know her, but sure, I can find out. That's not hard," he said. "Your boss wants the lady to sell?"

"Yeah. Her lot is the last important piece for the golf course development."

"Huh, okay. That sort of thing does happen. I'll ask Goro-san or Haruki. One of them will know. Goro just sold his last pachinko parlor. Now he's only doing demolition, construction, and real estate. He wants me to go in with him, but I'm too busy. It's too late for me to start something new. I don't understand his business as well as pachinko."

"Why don't you sell the shops, too, Dad? Retire maybe. You're set, right? Pachinko is a lot of work."

"What? Quit the business? Pachinko put food on the table and sent you to school. I'm too young to retire!"

He shrugged.

"And what would happen if I sell my stores? They might fire my workers. And where would my older workers go? And we give work to the people who make the machines. Pachinko's a bigger business in Japan than car manufacturing."

Mozasu stopped talking and raised the volume on the news. The newscasters were now talking about the value of the yen.

Solomon nodded and stared at the screen, trying to pay attention to the currency news. His father didn't seem the least bit embarrassed by what he did for a living.

Mozasu caught a glimpse of his son's darkened expression.

"I'll call Goro tonight and ask about the lady. Your boss wants her to sell, right?"

"That would be great. Thanks, Dad."

On Monday afternoon, Mozasu called Solomon at the office. He had spoken to Goro-san. The old lady was Korean—an old-school Chongryon type whose children had returned to Pyongyang and died there; Matsuda was her *tsumei*. She didn't want to sell the property to the Japanese. Goro-san thought the old lady was being stubborn; he said he could buy the property from the lady, because she said he'd sell it to her. Then he'd sell it to Kazu's client for the same price.

After Solomon got off the phone, he rushed to Kazu's office to tell him the good news.

Kazu listened carefully, then folded his hands together and smiled.

"Excellent work, Jedi. I can always spot a winner."

19

Tokyo, 1989

Even in her condition, Hana could not keep from flirting.

"You shouldn't have come," she said. "I look ugly. I wanted to be beautiful when you saw me again."

"I wanted to see you," Solomon replied. "And you are lovely, Hana. That will never change." He smiled, suppressing his shock at her altered appearance. Etsuko had warned him, but still, it was difficult to recognize her original features beneath the reddish scabs and sparse hair. The skeleton of her body made a distinct impression through the thin blue hospital sheet.

"Mama said you brought the girlfriend-o all the way to Tokyo," Hana said. Only her voice had not changed. It was difficult to know if she was teasing or not. "And I thought you were coming back to me. You will marry her, *nee*? Of course, I will try to forgive you because I know you loved me first."

With the curtain drawn, the ceiling lamp off, and only the light coming from the low-wattage electric bulb by her bedside, the room at the clinic was dark like night even though it was sunny outside.

"When are you going to get better?" he asked.

"Come here, Solomon." Hana raised her right arm, stick thin and chalky. She waved it like an elegant wand of death. "I have missed you so much. If I'd never left you that summer...Well, I would have made you marry me. I would have ruined you, though—I ruin everything. I ruin everything."

Solomon sat on the hard chair by her bed. None of the medications was working, Etsuko had told him. The doctors said there were only a few weeks or perhaps two months left at best. Dark lesions covered her neck and shoulders. Her left hand was unblemished, but her right was dry like her face. Her physical beauty had once been so extraordinary that it seemed to him that her current state was particularly cruel.

"Hana-chan, why can't you go to America to see the doctors there? There have been so many advances in the States. I know things are much better there for this—" He didn't want to play this stupid game where they wouldn't talk about what was real. Just hearing her voice and sitting in her room where she couldn't float away from him reminded him of everything magical and shining about her. He had been in her thrall, and oddly, even now, he felt so many things. He could not imagine her dying. He wanted to pick her up and spirit her away to New York. In America, everything seemed fixable, and in Japan, difficult problems were to be endured. *Sho ga nai, sho ga nai.* How many times had he heard these words? *It cannot be helped.* His mother had apparently hated that expression, and suddenly he understood her rage against this cultural resignation that violated her beliefs and wishes.

"Oh, Solomon. I don't want to go to America." Hana exhaled loudly. "I don't want to live. I'm ready to die. You know? Do you ever want to die, Solomon? I've wanted to die for so many years, but I was too cowardly to say it or to do anything to make my wish come true. Maybe you could have saved me, but you know, even wonderful you, even you, my Solomon, I don't think so. Everyone wants to die sometimes, *nee*?"

"That spring. When you left. I wanted to die." Solomon grew quiet, never having admitted this to anyone. Sometimes he'd forget about that time, but being with her made the memory sharp and mean.

Hana frowned and began to cry.

"If I had stayed, we would've loved each other too much, and I felt certain that I would hurt you. You see, I'm not a good person, and you are a good person. You shouldn't be with me. It's simple. Mama said you got tested in America for your life insurance and that you are okay. I'm grateful for this. You're the only person I have never ever wanted to hurt. And Mama told me that your girlfriend-o is a nice girl and educated like you. I don't want to know if she is pretty. Tell me she's hideous but has a good soul. I do know that she is a Korean girl. *Tsugoi*, Solomon. How amazing. You should marry her. Maybe people should marry from the same background. Maybe life is easier then. I am going to imagine you having three or four beautiful Korean children—with lovely Korean skin and hair. You have such wonderful hair, Solomon. I would have liked to have met your mother. Name one of your little girls after me, *nee*? Because you see, I will not have any. Promise me you will love little Hana, and you will think of me."

"Shut up," he said quietly, knowing she'd never listen. "Please, please shut up."

"You know that you're the one I loved. *Hatsukoi* was such a stupid idea to me until I met you. I've been with so many men, Solomon, and they were disgusting. All the filthy things I let them do. I'm so sorry for all of it. You, I loved, because you are good."

"Hana, you are good."

She shook her head, but for a moment she looked peaceful.

"I did bad things with boys after Mama left. That's why I came to Tokyo. I was so angry when I met you, then when I was with you, I stopped being so upset. But I couldn't handle it so I left and started hostessing. I didn't want to love anybody. Then you went to America, and I was, I was—" Hana paused. "When I was drinking a lot, I thought you would look for me. Like in that American movie. I thought you would find where I lived, climb on a ladder up to the window, and carry me away. I used to tell all the girls that you would get me. All the girls wanted you to come for me."

Solomon stared at her mouth as she spoke. She had the prettiest mouth.

"It's disgusting, isn't it?"

"What?" He felt like someone had slapped him.

"This." She pointed to the lesions on her chin.

"No. I wasn't looking at that."

She didn't believe him. Her eyes fluttered lightly, and Hana leaned back into the pillow.

"I want to rest now, Solomon. Will you come back soon?"

"Yes, I'll come back," he said, rising from the chair.

When he returned to his desk, Solomon could not stop thinking about her. Why hadn't Etsuko helped her? Something inside him hurt, and the ache felt familiar. He could not read the documents in front of him. He was supposed to run through some projections for the golf club project, but it was as if he had forgotten how to use Excel. What would have happened if she had not left him that summer? Would he have been able to go to New York and stay away for so long?

Phoebe wanted to marry him now; he knew this, but she never brought it up because she was a proud person and wanted to be asked. When he heard Kazu's voice in the hallway, Solomon looked up to see his boss standing before him. Solomon's office mates were out; Kazu closed the door behind him, walked over to the credenza near Solomon's desk, and stood in the space between the credenza and the enormous window.

"She's dead," Kazu said.

"What? I just saw her."

"Who?"

"Hana. Did my father call you?"

"I don't know who that is, man, but Matsuda-san, the old lady, is dead, and it doesn't look good. When the client wanted the property, he didn't expect that the holdout seller would die a few days afterwards."

"What?" Solomon blinked. "The seller is dead?"

"Yes. She sold the property to your father's friend Goro-san, then our client bought the property from him. Our client is not in trouble, but it smells bad. Do you know what I mean?" Kazu said this in a flat, calm voice while staring at Solomon's face thoughtfully. He picked up the Hanshin Tigers baseball on the credenza, tossed it up and caught it.

"How did she die?"

"Not sure. It could have been a heart attack or a stroke. They don't know. There are two nieces apparently. I don't know if they're going to make a fuss or what the police might do."

"She could have died of natural causes. Wasn't she old?"

"Yes, I expect that could be true; however, our client has canceled this transaction for now because the news could affect their public offering next spring."

"What public offering?"

"Never mind that." Kazu sighed. "Listen, man, I have to let you go. I am sorry, Solomon. I really am."

"What? What did I do?"

"We have to do this. There's no other way. I think your father's friend responded a bit too enthusiastically about the land sale, *nee*?"

"But you have no proof, and you are accusing my father's friend of something impossible. Goro would never ever do anything to hurt—"

"I'm not accusing your father's friend of anything. But the facts remain that there is a dead woman who didn't want to sell her property. Everyone knew she wouldn't sell, and moments after she sold, she died."

"But Goro paid a lot of money for that property; it was fair market value; and he's Korean. She didn't mind selling it to a Korean. I thought that's how we were supposed to get around her refusal. He wouldn't have killed an old woman for something like this. All his life, he's helped all these poor people. What are you saying? Goro did this as a favor for my father and me—"

Kazu held the ball between his hands and looked down at the carpet.

"Solly, don't tell me anything more. Do you understand? The investigators are going to want to know what happened. They may not make a big deal of it, but the client is very spooked, dude. The client wanted to develop a country club; they weren't looking for a run-in with the yaks. Do you know what kind of hell they can raise in shareholder meetings?"

"Yaks? Goro is not yakuza."

Kazu nodded and tossed the ball again and caught it.

"The transaction is unfortunately contaminated, so it will be put on hold. This comes at a great financial cost to the client, and it looks poorly for us as a premiere banking company. My reputation—"

"But the client got the property."

"Yes, but no one was supposed to die. I didn't wish for that." Kazu made a face like he was tasting something sour.

Solomon shook his head. All he could think of were the innumerable times he had spent in Goro's presence listening to his hilarious stories about his many girlfriends and his constant encouragements for Solomon's future. Goro had this remarkable clarity about the world. A great man, his father always said about Goro—a noble man—a true *bushi* who understood sacrifice and leadership. It had been Goro alone who had built up Haruki Totoyama's mother's uniform business from nothing, and all because he'd felt bad for a single mother raising two boys. His father said that Goro was always doing good things for poor people quietly. It was absurd to consider that Goro could have been responsible for the lady's death. The woman would have sold the property to Goro because he was known as a good Korean businessman. Everyone knew this.

"Human Resources is waiting outside. Solomon, you don't know how it works, I don't think, because this is your first job at a bank, but when you're terminated from an investment bank, you have to leave the building immediately for internal security reasons. I'm sorry."

"But what did I do?"

"The transaction is postponed for now, and we will not need such a large team. I'm pleased to give you a reference. You can put me down for whatever you want. I would never mention this to your future employers."

Solomon leaned back in his chair and stared at Kazu's hardened jaw. He paused before speaking:

"You brought me in on purpose. Because you wanted me to get the Korean lady to sell. You knew—"

Kazu put down the baseball and moved to the door.

"Brother, I gave you a job, and you were fortunate to have it."

Solomon covered his mouth with his hands.

"You're a nice boy, Solomon, and you will have a future in finance, but not here. If you are trying to imply that you were being discriminated against, something that Koreans tend to believe, that would be incorrect and unfair to me. If anything, you have been preferred over the natives. I like working with Koreans. Everyone knows this about me. The whole department thought that you were my pet associate. I didn't want to fire you. I just don't agree with your father's tactics."

"My father? He had nothing to do with this."

"Yes, of course. It was this man, Goro," Kazu said. "I believe you. I do. Good luck, Solomon."

Kazu opened the office door and let the two women from Human Resources in before heading to his next meeting.

The speech from HR passed quickly, sounding like radio static in Solomon's head. They asked him for his identification card, and he gave it to them automatically. His mind kept returning to Hana, though he felt like he should call Phoebe to explain. He needed air. He threw things in the white banker's box but left the baseball on the credenza.

The HR women escorted him to the elevator and offered to send his box to his apartment by messenger, but Solomon refused. Through the glass-walled conference room, he saw the guys from the poker game but no Kazu. Giancarlo spotted him holding the white box against his chest, and he half smiled at him, then returned to what he was doing. On the street, Solomon got into a taxi and asked the driver to drive him all the way to Yokohama. He didn't think he could walk to the train station.

20

Yokohama, 1989

Empire Cafe was an old-style Japanese curry restaurant near China-town—a place Solomon used to go with his father on Saturday afternoons when he was a boy. Mozasu still ate there on Wednesdays with Goro and Totoyama. Empire served five different kinds of curries, only one kind of draft beer, and as much tea and pickles as you wanted. The cook, who was always in a bad mood, had a deft hand with the seasonings, and his curries were unrivaled in the city.

Late in the afternoon and long past lunch hour, the café was nearly empty except for the three old friends sitting at the corner table near the kitchen. Goro was telling one of his funny stories while making clown-ish faces and dramatic hand gestures. Mozasu and Totoyama took bites of their hot curry and sipped beer. All the while, they nodded and smiled at Goro, encouraging him to continue.

When Solomon pushed open the perpetually swollen front door, the cheap sleigh bells attached to the door jingled.

Scarcely bothering to turn from clearing the tables, the diminutive wait-ress bellowed, "*Irasshai!*"

Mozasu was surprised to see his son. Solomon bowed in the direction of the men.

"You skipping work?" Mozasu asked. The edge of his eyes crinkled deeply when he smiled.

"Good, good. Skip work," Goro interrupted. He was delighted to see the boy. "I hear you go to the office on the weekends, too. That's no way to be for a handsome boy like you. You should be busy chasing skirt. If I had your height and your diploma, you'd feel sorry for all the women of Japan. I'd be breaking hearts at a rate that would shock a gentle boy like you."

Goro rubbed his hands together.

Totoyama said nothing; he was staring at the lower half of Solomon's face, which seemed fixed; the boy's lips made a thin, crumpled line above his chin. Totoyama's own face was flushed, since it took only half a small beer to redden his ears, nose, and cheeks.

"Solomon, sit down," Totoyama said. "You okay?"

He lifted his briefcase resting on the empty chair and set it down on the linoleum floor.

"I—" Solomon tried to speak, then gasped.

Mozasu asked his son, "You hungry? Did Etsuko tell you that you'd find us here gossiping like old women?"

He shook his head no.

Mozasu laid his hand on the boy's forearm. He'd bought the dark blue suit Solomon was wearing now from Brooks Brothers the time he'd visited Solomon in New York. It had been a nice feeling to be able to buy his son however many interview suits and whatever else he needed at such a nice American store. That was the whole point of money, wasn't it, to be able to get your kid whatever he needed?

"Have some curry," Mozasu said.

Solomon shook his head.

Goro frowned and waved the waitress over.

"Kyoko-chan, give the boy some tea, please."

Solomon looked up and stared at his father's former boss.

"I don't know what to say, Goro-san."

"Sure, you do. Just talk."

"My boss, Kazu, said that the lady, you know, the seller, she died. Is that right?"

"That's so. I went to the funeral," Goro said. "She was ancient. Died of a heart attack. She had two nieces who inherited all that money. Pleasant girls. One married and one divorced. Beautiful skin. Nice, open brows. Real Korean faces. They reminded me of my mother and aunt."

The waitress brought his tea, and Solomon held the brown, squat mug between his hands. These were the same mugs that Empire had used ever since he could remember.

Totoyama patted the boy's shoulder gently as if to wake him.

"Who? Who died?"

"The lady. The Korean lady who sold the property to Goro-san. My boss's client wanted this property, and the lady wouldn't sell to a Japanese, so Goro-san bought it and sold it to the client, but the lady is dead now, and the boss's client won't touch the deal. Something about having a clean public offering and possible investigations."

Totoyama glanced at Mozasu, who looked equally puzzled.

"She died? Is that so?" Mozasu glanced at Goro, who nodded calmly.

"She was ninety-three years old, and she died a couple of days after she sold her property to me. What does that have to do with anything?" Goro shrugged. He winked at the waitress and tapped the edge of his mug for another beer. When he pointed to the empty beer mugs of Mozasu and Totoyama, the men shook their heads. Totoyama covered the top of his beer mug with his hand.

"What did you pay for the property?" Mozasu asked.

"A very good price, but not crazy. Then I sold it to that client for exactly what I paid for it. I sent Solomon's boss the copies of the contract. I didn't make a single yen. This was Solomon's first deal, and—"

Mozasu and Totoyama nodded. It was unthinkable that Goro would ever seek to profit from Solomon's career.

"The client bought it for less than what he would have if he'd bought it himself," Solomon said slowly, as if Kazu were in the room.

"The client got a piece of property that he would never have gotten because he's Japanese, and she had refused on several occasions to sell to him. He got it cheap." Goro grunted in disbelief. "So now the client is saying he won't build the country club? Bullshit."

"Kazu said the project will be on hold because they didn't want the bad news contaminating the public offering."

"What bad news? The old lady died in peace. Though it might take time to wash away that dirty Korean smell," Goro said. "I'm sick of this."

Totoyama frowned. "If there had been something questionable about her death, I would know. There's been no complaint."

"Listen, the deal's done. If this little prick wants to cheat you out of your cut, fine. I didn't expect him to give you a fair bonus, but remember this: That bastard will not profit from you again. I will watch that motherfucker until the day I die." Goro inhaled, then calmly smiled at the boy.

"Now, Solomon, you should eat some curry and tell me about this American girl, Phoebe. I've always wanted to go to America to meet the women there. So beautiful, so beautiful." He smacked his lips. "I want a blonde American girlfriend with a big ass!"

The men smiled but they didn't laugh as they would have before. Solomon appeared unconsoled.

The waitress brought Goro a small beer and returned to the kitchen; Goro watched her walk away.

"Too skinny," he said, smoothing back his dyed black pompadour with his brown hands.

"I was fired," Solomon said.

"*Nani?*" the three men said at once. "For what?"

"Kazu said that the client is holding off on the deal. They don't need me anymore. He said that if there was an investigation because of—" Solomon stopped himself before saying the word "yakuza," because suddenly, he wasn't sure. His father wouldn't have associated with criminals. Should he be speaking like this in front of Totoyama? He was Japanese and a high-ranking detective with the Yokohama police; he wouldn't be friends with criminals. The suggestion alone would have hurt all the men deeply.

Goro studied Solomon's face and nodded almost imperceptibly, because he understood the boy's silence.

"Was she cremated?" Totoyama asked.

"Probably, but some Koreans get buried back home," Mozasu said.

"*Soo nee,*" Totoyama said.

"Solomon, the lady died of natural causes. The niece said it was the heart. She was ninety-three years old. I had nothing to do with her death. Listen, your boss doesn't actually think I killed the old lady. If he did, he'd be too scared to fire you. What would keep me from killing him? This is crazy stuff from television. He used your connections, then he fired you by making up some excuse. The client just wanted the Korean shit to go away."

"You'll get a better job in finance. I'm sure of it," Mozasu said.

Goro was visibly irritated, however. "You should never work for a dirty bank again."

"*Iie*. Solomon majored in economics. He studied in America to work in an American bank."

"Travis is a British bank," Solomon said.

"Well, maybe that was the problem. Maybe you should work in an American bank. There are a lot of American investment banks, *nee*?" Mozasu said.

Solomon felt awful. The men at this table had raised him. He could see how upset they were.

"Don't worry about me. I'll get another job. I have savings, too. I better go now." Solomon stood up from his seat. "Papa, I left a box at your office. Can you send it to me in Tokyo? Nothing important."

Mozasu nodded.

"Here, why don't I take you home? We can take a drive to Tokyo."

"No, it's okay. I'll catch the train. It's faster. Phoebe is probably wondering about me."

When she didn't answer the phone, Solomon returned to the hospital. Hana was awake. Pop music played on the radio. The room was still dark, but the dance hit made the room feel lively, like a nightclub.

"You came back already? You must have really missed me, Solomon."

He told her everything, and she listened without interrupting him.

"You should take over your father's business."

"Pachinko?"

"Yes, pachinko. Why not? All these idiots who say bad things about it are jealous. Your father is an honest person. He could be richer if he was crooked, but he's rich enough. Goro is a good guy, too. He might be a yak, but who cares? I don't. And if he isn't, I'm sure he knows them all. It's a filthy world, Solomon. No one is clean. Living makes you dirty. I've met plenty of fancy people from IBJ and the BOJ who are from the best families, and they like to do some sick shit in bed. A lot of them do very bad things in business, but they don't get caught. Most of the ones I've fucked would steal if they had the chance. They're too scared to have any real ambition. Listen, Solomon, nothing will ever change here. Do you see that?"

"What do you mean?"

"You're a fool," she said, laughing, "but you are my fool."

Her teasing made him feel sad. He missed her already. Solomon couldn't remember ever feeling this lonesome before.

"Japan will never change. It will never ever integrate gaijin, and my darling, here you will always be a gaijin and never Japanese. *Nee?* The *zainichi* can't leave, *nee?* But it's not just you. Japan will never take people like my mother back into society again; it will never take back people like me. And we're Japanese! I'm diseased. I got this from some Japanese guy who owned an old trading company. He's dead now. But nobody cares. The doctors here, even, they just want me to go away. So listen, Solomon, you should stay here and not go back to the States, and you should take over your papa's business. Become so rich that you can do whatever you want. But, my beautiful Solomon, they're never going to think we're okay. Do you know what I mean?" Hana stared at him. "Do what I tell you to do."

"My own father doesn't want that. Even Goro-san sold his parlors and is doing real estate now. Papa wanted me to work in an American investment bank."

"What, so you can be like Kazu? I know a thousand Kazus. They're not fit to wipe your father's ass."

"There are good people in the banks, too."

"And there are good people in pachinko, too. Like your father."

"I didn't know you liked Papa."

"You know, after I got here, he visited me every Sunday when Mama needed a break. Sometimes, when I was pretending to be asleep, I'd catch him praying for me in that chair. I don't believe in God, but I guess that doesn't matter. I never had someone pray for me before, Solomon."

Solomon closed his eyes and nodded.

"Your grandmother Sunja and great-aunt Kyunghee visit me on Saturdays. Did you know that? They pray for me, too. I don't understand the Jesus stuff, but it's something holy to have people touch you when you're sick. The nurses here are afraid to touch me. Your grandmother Sunja holds my hands, and your great-aunt Kyunghee puts cool towels on my head when I get too hot. They're kind to me, though I'm a bad person—"

"You're not bad. That's not true."

"I've done terrible things," she said drily. "Solomon, when I was a hostess, I sold drugs to one girl who ended up overdosing. I stole money from a lot of men. I've told so many lies."

Solomon said nothing.

"I deserve this."

"No. It's a virus. Everybody gets sick."

Solomon smoothed her brow and kissed it.

"That's okay, Solomon. I'm not doing bad things anymore. I've had time to think about my stupid life."

"Hana—"

"I know, Solomon. *Otomodachi, nee?*"

She pretended to bow formally as she was lying down, and she picked up the corner of her blanket as if she were holding a fold of her skirt to curtsey. The trace of flirtation remained in her still-lithe movements. He wanted to remember this little thing forever.

"Go home, Solomon."

"Okay," he said, and he did not see her again.

21

Tokyo, 1989

I never liked him," Phoebe said. "Too smooth."

"Well, I'm obviously an idiot, because I did," Solomon said. "Besides, how in the world did you get that impression of Kazu in the little time you had? You met him for about two minutes when we ran into him at Mitsukoshi. And you've never mentioned this before."

Slumped in the rented leather armchair, Solomon could barely face Phoebe. He wasn't sure what kind of reaction he'd expected from her, but he was surprised by how unruffled she was by the news. She seemed almost pleased. Phoebe sat on the bench near the window with her folded knees to her chest.

"I actually liked him," he said.

"Solomon, that guy screwed you."

Solomon glanced up at her placid profile, then dropped his head back again on the back of the armchair.

"He's a dick."

"I feel much better now."

"I'm on your team."

Phoebe didn't know if she should get up and sit by him. She didn't want him to think that she felt sorry for him. Her older sister used to say that men hated pity; rather, they wanted sympathy and admiration—not an easy combination.

"He was a phony. He talked to you like you were his little buddy. Like he's some big man on campus and you're one of his 'boys.' Does that system still even exist? I hate that frat-boy brother shit." Phoebe rolled her eyes.

Solomon was dumbstruck. She had managed to encapsulate his entire relationship with Kazu from that brief, almost nonexistent encounter at the food court of the Mitsukoshi department store. How had she done this?

Phoebe hugged her knees, lacing her fingers together.

"You don't like him because he's Japanese."

"Don't get mad at me. It's not that I distrust the Japanese, but I don't know if I trust them entirely. You're going to say that I've been reading too much about the Pacific War. I know, I know, I sound a little bigoted."

"A little? The Japanese have suffered, too. Nagasaki? Hiroshima? And in America, the Japanese Americans were sent to internment camps, but the German Americans weren't. How do you explain that?"

"Solomon, I've been here long enough. Can we please go home? You can get a dozen terrific jobs back in New York. You're good at everything. No one interviews better than you."

"I don't have a visa to work in the States."

"There are other ways to get citizenship." She smiled.

Solomon's family had hinted on innumerable occasions that he wanted to marry her and that he should marry her; the only person who hadn't said so explicitly was the man himself.

Solomon's head lay immobile on the back of the armchair. Phoebe could see that he was staring at the ceiling. She got up from the bench and walked to the front hall closet. She opened the closet doors and pulled out both of her suitcases. The suitcase wheels rolled loudly across the wooden floor, and Solomon looked up.

"Hey, what are you doing?"

"I'm going home," she said.

"Don't be like that."

"Well, it occurs to me that I lost my life when I came here with you, and you're not worth it."

"Why are you being like this?"

Solomon rose from his chair and was now standing where she'd been only a moment ago. Phoebe dragged the suitcases behind her into the bedroom and shut the door quietly.

What could he say? He wouldn't marry her. He had known it almost as soon as they'd landed in Narita. Her confidence and self-possession had mesmerized him in college. Her equanimity, which had seemed so important in the States, seemed like aloofness and arrogance in Tokyo. She had lost her life here, this was true, but marrying her didn't seem like a solution.

Then the whole Japan-is-evil stuff. Sure, there were assholes in Japan, but there were assholes everywhere, *nee?* Ever since they got here, either she had changed or his feelings for her had changed. Hadn't he been leaning toward asking her to marry him? Yet now, when she put forward the idea of marrying for citizenship, he realized that he didn't want to become an American. It made sense for him to do so; it would have made his father happy. Was it better to be an American than a Japanese? He knew Koreans who had become naturalized Japanese, and it made sense to do so, but he didn't want to do that now, either. Maybe one day. She was right; it was weird that he was born in Japan and had a South Korean passport. He couldn't rule out getting naturalized. Maybe another Korean wouldn't understand that, but he didn't care anymore.

Kazu was a shit, but so what? He was one bad guy, and he was Japanese. Perhaps that was what going to school in America had taught him. Even if there were a hundred bad Japanese, if there was one good one, he refused to make a blanket statement. Etsuko was like a mother to him; his first love was Hana; and Totoyama was like an uncle, too. They were Japanese, and they were very good. She hadn't known them the way he had; how could he expect her to understand?

In a way, Solomon was Japanese, too, even if the Japanese didn't think so. Phoebe couldn't see this. There was more to being something than just blood. The space between Phoebe and him could not close, and if he was decent, he had to let her go home.

Solomon went to the kitchen and made coffee. He poured two cups and approached the bedroom door.

"Phoebe, may I come in?"

"The door's open."

The suitcases on the floor were brimming with clothes folded and rolled like canisters. The closets were nearly empty. Solomon's five dark suits and half a dozen white dress shirts hung on the long rod with a yard of hanging space left. Her neat rows of shoes still took up most of the closet floor. Phoebe's shoes were black or brown leather; a pair of pink espadrilles, which had once given her terrible blisters, stood out from the others like a girlish mistake. During their junior year, they'd gone to a party, and she'd had to walk back to the dorm barefoot from 111th Street and Broadway because the pink espadrilles had been too narrow.

"Why do you still have those shoes?"

"Shut up, Solomon." Phoebe started to cry.

"What did I say?"

"I have never felt so stupid in my life. Why am I here?" She took a deep breath.

Solomon stared at her, not knowing how to comfort her. He was afraid of her; perhaps he had always been afraid of her—her joy, anger, sadness, excitement—she had so many extreme feelings. The nearly empty room with the solitary rented bed and floor lamp seemed to highlight her vividness. Back in New York, she had been spirited and wonderful. Here, Phoebe was almost too stark, awkward.

"I'm sorry," he said.

"No. You're not."

Solomon sat down on the carpeted floor cross-legged, leaning his long back against the narrow wall. The freshly painted walls were still bare. They hadn't hung anything on them because the landlord would have fined them for each nail hole.

"I'm sorry," he repeated.

Phoebe picked up her espadrilles and threw them into the overflowing waste basket.

"I think I'm going to work for my dad," he said.

"Pachinko?"

"Yeah." Solomon nodded to himself. It felt strange to say this out loud.

"He asked you?"

"No. I don't think he wants me to."

She shook her head.

"Maybe I can take over the business."

"You're kidding, right?"

"No."

Without saying a word, Phoebe continued to pack. She was willfully ignoring him, and he continued to look at her. She was more cute than pretty, more pretty than beautiful. He liked her long torso, slender neck, bobbed hair, and intelligent eyes. When she laughed at a joke, her laughter was whole. Nothing seemed to scare her—she thought anything was possible. Could he change her mind? Could he change his? Maybe the packing was just a dramatic gesture. What did he know about women? He'd known only two girls really.

She rolled up another sweater and dropped it on the growing pile.

"Pachinko. Well, that makes it easier then," she said finally. "I can't live here, Solomon. Even if you wanted to marry me, I can't live here. I can't breathe here."

"That first night we arrived, when you couldn't read the instructions on the aspirin bottle, and you started to cry. I should have known then."

Phoebe picked up another sweater and just stared at it like she didn't know what to do with it.

"You have to dump me," he said.

"Yes, I do."

She left in the morning. It was like Phoebe to make a clean exit. Solomon took her to the airport by train, and even though they were pleasant, she had changed literally overnight. She didn't seem sad or angry; she was cordial. If anything, she seemed stronger than before. She let him hug her good-bye, but they agreed not to talk for a long time.

"It would be better," she said, and Solomon felt powerless against her decision.

Solomon took the train to Yokohama.

His father's modest office was lined with gray metal shelves, and stacks of files rested on the credenzas along the walls. Three safes holding papers and the day's receipts were located below the high windows. Mozasu sat behind the same battered oak table that he'd used as a desk for over thirty years. Noa had studied for his Waseda exams at this table, and when he moved to Tokyo, he'd left it for Mozasu.

"Papa."

"Solomon," Mozasu exclaimed. "Is everything okay?"

"Phoebe went back."

Saying it to his father made it real. Solomon sat down on the empty chair.

"What? Why? Because you lost your job?"

"No. I can't marry her. And I told her that I'd rather live in Japan. Work in pachinko."

"What? Pachinko? No, no." Mozasu shook his head. "You'll get another job in banking. That's why you went to Columbia, *nee*?"

Mozasu touched his brow, genuinely confused by this announcement.

"She's a nice girl. I thought you'd get married."

Mozasu walked around from his desk and handed his son a packet of tissues.

"Pachinko? *Honto*?"

"Yeah, why not?" Solomon blew his nose.

"You don't want to do this. You don't know what people say."

"None of that stuff is true. You're an honest business person. I know you pay your taxes and get all your licenses, and—"

"Yes, yes, I do. But people will always say things. They will always say terrible things, no matter what. It's normal for me. I'm nobody. There's no need for you to do this work. I wasn't smart at school like my brother. I was good at running around and fixing things. I was good at making money. I've always kept my business clean and stayed away from the bad things. Goro-san taught me that it's not worth it to get involved with the bad guys. But Solomon, this business is not easy, *nee*? It's not just tinkering with machines and ordering new ones and hiring people to work on the floor. There are so many things that can go wrong. We know lots of people who went belly-up, *nee*?"

"Why don't you want me to do this?"

"I sent you to those American schools so that no one would—" Mozasu paused. "No one is going to look down at my son."

"Papa, it doesn't matter. None of it matters, *nee*?" Solomon had never seen his father like this before.

"I worked and made money because I thought it would make me a man. I thought people would respect me if I was rich."

Solomon looked at him and nodded. His father rarely spent on himself, but he had paid for weddings and funerals for employees and sent tuition for their children.

Mozasu's face brightened suddenly.

"You can change your mind, Solomon. You can call Phoebe when she gets home and say you're sorry. Your mother was a lot like Phoebe—strong-willed and smart."

"I want to live here," Solomon said. "She will not."

"*Soo nee.*"

Solomon picked up the ledger from his father's table.

"Explain this to me, Papa."

Mozasu paused, then he opened the book.

It was the first of the month, and Sunja had woken up upset. She had dreamed of Hansu again. Lately, he had been appearing in her dreams, looking the way he did when she was a girl, wearing his white linen suit and white leather shoes. He always said the same thing: "You are my girl; you are my dear girl." Sunja would wake and feel ashamed. She should have forgotten him by now.

After breakfast, she would go the cemetery to clean Isak's grave. As usual, Kyunghee offered to come with her, but Sunja said it was okay.

Neither woman performed the *jesa*. As Christians, they weren't supposed to believe in ancestor worship. Nevertheless, both widows still wanted to talk to their husband and elders, appeal to them, seek their counsel. They missed their old rituals, so she went to the cemetery regularly. It was curious, but Sunja felt close to Isak in a way that she hadn't when he was alive. Then she had been in awe of him and his goodness. Dead, he seemed more approachable to her.

When the train from Yokohama reached Osaka Station, Sunja bought ivory-colored chrysanthemums from the old Korean woman's stall. She had been there for years. The way Isak had explained it, when it was time to be with the Lord, your real body would be in heaven, so what happened to your remains didn't matter. It made no sense to bring a buried body favorite foods or incense or flowers. There was no need for bowing, since we were all equal in the eyes of the Lord, he'd said. And yet Sunja couldn't help wanting to bring something lovely to the grave. In life, he had asked for so little from her, and when she thought of him now, she remembered her husband as someone who had praised the beauty that God had made.

She was glad that Isak had not been cremated. She had wanted a place for the boys to visit their father. Mozasu visited the grave often, and before Noa disappeared, he had come with her, too. Had they talked to him, too? she wondered. It had never occurred to her to ask them this, and now it was too late.

Lately, every time she went to the cemetery, she wondered what Isak would have thought of Noa's death. Isak would have understood Noa's suffering. He would have known what to say to him. Noa had been cremated by his wife, so there was no grave to visit. Sunja talked to Noa when she was alone. Sometimes, something very simple like a delicious piece of pumpkin taffy would make her sorry that now that she had money, she couldn't buy him something that he had loved as a child. *Sorry, Noa, sorry.* It had been eleven years since he'd died; the pain didn't go away, but its sharp edge had dulled and softened like sea glass.

Sunja hadn't gone to Noa's funeral. He hadn't wanted his wife and children to know about her, and she had done enough already. If she hadn't visited him the way she had, maybe he might still be alive. Hansu had not gone to the funeral, either. Noa would've been fifty-six years old.

In her dream last night, Sunja had been happy that Hansu had come to see her again. They met at the beach near her old home in Yeongdo to talk, and recalling the dream was like watching another person's life. How was it possible that Isak and Noa were gone but Hansu was still alive? How was this fair? Hansu was living somewhere in Tokyo in a hospital bed under the watchful gaze of round-the-clock nurses and his daughters. She never saw him anymore and had no wish to. In her dreams, he was as vibrant as he had been when she was a girl. It was not Hansu that she missed, or even Isak. What she was seeing again in her dreams was her youth, her beginning, and her wishes—so this was how she became a woman. Without Hansu and Isak and Noa, there wouldn't have been this pilgrimage to this land. Beyond the dailiness, there had been moments of shimmering beauty and some glory, too, even in this *ajumma*'s life. Even if no one knew, it was true.

There was consolation: The people you loved, they were always there with you, she had learned. Sometimes, she could be in front of a train kiosk or the window of a bookstore, and she could feel Noa's small hand when he was a boy, and she would close her eyes and think of his sweet, grassy smell and remember that he had always tried his best. At those moments, it was good to be alone to hold on to him.

She took the taxi from the train station to the cemetery, then walked the many rows to Isak's well-maintained grave. There was no need to clean anything, but she liked to wipe down the marble tombstone before she spoke to him. Sunja fell to her knees and cleaned the flat, square tombstone with the towels she'd brought for the purpose. Isak's name was carved in Japanese and Korean. 1907–1944. The white marble was clean now and warm from the sun.

He had been such an elegant and beautiful man. Sunja could recall how the servant girls back home had admired him; Bokhee and Dokhee had never seen such a handsome man before. Mozasu took after her more and had her plain face, but he had his father's straight carriage and steady stride.

"*Yobo*," she said, "Mozasu is well. Last week, he called me, because Solomon lost his job with that foreign bank, and now he wants to work with his father. Imagine that? I wonder what you'd make of this."

The silence encouraged her.

"I wonder how you are—" She stopped speaking when she saw Uchida-san, the groundskeeper. Sunja was sitting on the ground in her black woolen pants suit. She glanced at her handbag on the ground. It was an expensive designer bag that Etsuko had bought for her seventieth birthday.

The groundskeeper stopped before her and bowed, and she returned the bow.

Sunja smiled at the polite young man, who must have been about forty or forty-five. Uchida-san looked younger than Mozasu. How did she look to him? Her skin was deeply grooved from the years of sun, and her short hair was bright white. No matter—seventy-three did not feel very old to her. Had the groundskeeper heard her mumbling in Korean? Ever since she'd stopped working at the confectionery, her limited Japanese had deteriorated further. It was not terrible, but lately she felt shy around native speakers. Uchida-san picked up his rake and walked away.

Sunja put both hands on the white marble, as if she could touch Isak from where she was.

"I wish you could tell me what will happen to us. I wish. I wish I knew that Noa was with you."

Several rows from her, the groundskeeper cleared wet leaves from stone markers. Now and then he would glance up at her, and Sunja felt embarrassed to be seen talking to a grave. She wanted to stay a little longer. Wanting to look like she was busy, Sunja opened her canvas bag to put away the dirty towels. In the bottom of her bag, she found her house keys on the key ring with thumbnail-sized photographs of Noa and Mozasu in a sealed acrylic frame.

Sunja started to weep, and she could not help her crying.

"Boku-san."

"*Hai*?" Sunja looked up at the groundskeeper.

"May I get you something to drink? I have a thermos of tea in the cottage. It is not very fine tea, but it is warm."

"No, no. Thank you. All time, you see people cry," she said in broken Japanese.

"No, actually, very few people come here, but your family visits regularly. You have two sons and a grandson, Solomon. Mozasu-sama visits every month or two. I haven't seen Noa-sama in eleven years, but he used to come on the last Thursday of each month. You could set a watch to him. How is Noa-sama? He was a very kind man."

"Noa come here? Come before 1978?"

"*Hai.*"

"From 1963 to 1978?" She mentioned the years he would have been in Nagano. She said the dates again, hoping that her Japanese was correct. Sunja pointed to Noa's photograph on the key ring. "He visit here?"

The groundskeeper nodded with conviction at the photograph, then looked up in the sky like he was trying to see some sort of calendar in his mind.

"*Hai, hai.* He came in those years and before, too. Noa-sama told me to go to school and even offered to send me if I wished."

"Really?"

"Yes, but I told him I have an empty gourd for a head, and that it would have been pointless to send me to school. Besides, I like it here. It's quiet. Everybody who comes to visit is very kind. He asked me never to mention his visits, but I have not seen him in over a decade, and I'd wondered if he moved away to England. He told me to read good books and brought me translations of the great British author Charles Dickens."

"Noa, my son, is dead."

The groundskeeper opened his mouth slightly.

"My son, my son," Sunja said quietly.

"I am very sad to hear that, Boku-san. Truly, I am," the groundskeeper said, looking forlorn. "I'd been hoping to tell him that after I finished all the books he'd brought me, I bought more of my own. I have read through all of Mr. Dickens's books in translations, but my favorite is the first one he gave me, *David Copperfield.* I admire David."

"Noa loved to read. The best. He loved to read."

"Have you read Mr. Dickens?"

"I don't know how," she said. "To read."

"*Maji?* If you are Noa's mother, you are very smart, too. Perhaps you can go to night school for adults. That is what Noa-sama told me to do."

Sunja smiled at the groundskeeper, who seemed hopeful about sending an old woman to school. She remembered Noa cajoling Mozasu to persevere with his studies.

The groundskeeper looked at his rake. He bowed deeply, then excused himself to return to his tasks.

When he was out of sight, Sunja dug a hole at the base of the tombstone about a foot deep with her hands and dropped the key ring photograph inside. She covered the hole with dirt and grass, then did what she could to clean her hands with her handkerchief, but dirt remained beneath her nails. Sunja tamped down the earth, then brushed the grass with her fingers.

She picked up her bags. Kyunghee would be waiting for her at home.

Acknowledgments

I got the idea for the story in 1989.

I was a junior in college, and I didn't know what I'd do after graduation. Rather than ponder my future, I sought distractions. One afternoon, I attended what was then called a Master's Tea, a guest lecture series at Yale. I'd never been to one before. An American missionary based in Japan was giving a talk about the *"Zainichi,"* a term used often to describe Korean Japanese people who were either migrants from the colonial era or their descendants. Some Koreans in Japan do not wish to be called *Zainichi* Korean because the term means literally "foreign resident staying in Japan," which makes no sense since there are often third, fourth, and fifth surviving generations of Koreans in Japan. There are many ethnic Koreans who are now Japanese citizens, although this option to naturalize is not an easy one. There are also many who have intermarried with the Japanese or who have partial Korean heritage. Sadly, there is a long and troubled history of legal and social discrimination against the Koreans in Japan and those who have partial ethnic Korean backgrounds. There are some who never disclose their Korean heritage, although their ethnic identity may be traced to their identification papers and government records.

The missionary talked about this history and relayed a story of a middle school boy who was bullied in his yearbook because of his Korean background. The boy jumped off a building and died. I would not forget this.

I graduated college in 1990 with a degree in history. I went to law school and practiced law for two years. After quitting the law, I decided to write as early as 1996 about the Koreans in Japan. I wrote many stories and novel drafts, which were never published. I was despondent. Then in 2002, *The Missouri Review* published the story "Motherland," which is about a Korean Japanese boy who gets fingerprinted and receives a foreigner's identity card on his birthday, and later it won the Peden Prize. Also, I'd submitted a fictionalized account of the story I'd heard in college and received a New York Foundation for the Arts fellowship. With that grant money, I took classes and paid for a babysitter so I could write. This early recognition was critical, because it took me so long to publish anything at all. Moreover, the NYFA fellowship confirmed my stubborn belief that the stories of Koreans in Japan should be told somehow when so much of their lives had been despised, denied, and erased.

I wanted very much to get this story right; however, I felt that I didn't have all the knowledge or skills to do this properly. In my anxiety, I did an enormous amount of research and wrote a draft of a novel about the Korean Japanese community. Still, it did not feel right. Then in 2007, my husband got a job offer in Tokyo, and we moved there in August. On the ground, I had the chance to interview dozens of Koreans in Japan and learned that I'd gotten the story wrong. The Korean Japanese may have been historical victims, but when I met them in person, none of them were as simple as that. I was so humbled by the breadth and complexity of the people I met in Japan that I put aside my old draft and started to write the book again in 2008, and I continued to write it and revise it until its publication.

I have had this story with me for almost thirty years. Consequently, there are many people to thank.

Speer Morgan and Evelyn Somers of *The Missouri Review* believed in this story first. The NYFA gave me a fiction fellowship when I wanted to give up. Thank you.

When I lived in Tokyo, a great number of individuals agreed to sit with me and answer my many questions about the Koreans in Japan as well as about expatriate life, international finance, the yakuza, the history of colonial Christianity, police work, immigration, Kabukicho, poker, Osaka, Tokyo real estate deals, leadership in Wall Street, *mizu shobai*, and of course, the pachinko industry. When we could not meet in person, many spoke to me on the phone or answered my questions via e-mail. I am in debt to the following generous individuals: Susan Menadue Chun,

Jongmoon Chun, Ji Soo Chun, Haeng-ja Chung, Kangja Chung, the Reverend Yean Won Chung, Scott Callon, Emma Fujibayashi, Stephanie and Greg Guyett, Mary Hauet, Danny Hegglin, Gen Hidemori, Tim Hornyak, Linda Rhee Kim, Myeong Gu Kim, Alexander Kinmont, Tamie Matsunaga, Naoki Miyamoto, Rika Nakajima, Sohee Park, Alberto Tamura, Peter Tasker, Jane and Kevin Quinn, Hyang Yang, Paul Yang, Simon Yoo, and Chongran Yun.

I have to note here that this book could not have been written without the significant scholarship of the following authors: David Chapman, Haeng-ja Chung, Haruko Taya Cook, Theodore F. Cook, Erin Chung, George De Vos, Yasunori Fukuoka, Haeyoung Han, Hildi Kang, Sangjun Kang, Sarah Sakhae Kashani, Jackie J. Kim, Changsoo Lee, Soo im Lee, John Lie, Richard Lloyd Parry, Samuel Perry, Sonia Ryang, Tessa Morris-Suzuki, Stephen Murphy-Shigematsu, and Mary Kimoto Tomita. Although I relied heavily on their scholarship, any errors of fact are my own.

I want to thank my friends and family in Japan, South Korea, and the United States for their love, faith, and kindness. Without them, it would have been impossible to write, revise, and rewrite this book: the Reverend Harry Adams, Lynn Ahrens, Harold Augenbraum, Karen Grigsby Bates, Dionne Bennett, Stephana Bottom, Robert Boynton, Kitty Burke, Janel Anderberg Callon, Scott Callon, Lauren Cerand, Ken Chen, Andrea King Collier, Jay Cosgrove, Elizabeth Cuthrell, Junot Díaz, Charles Duffy, David L. Eng, Shelley Fisher Fishkin, Roxanne Fraser, Elizabeth Gillies, Rosita Grandison, Lois Perelson Gross, Susan Guerrero, Greg and Stephanie Guyett, Shinhee Han, Mary Fish Hardin, the Reverend Matthew Hardin, Robin Marantz Henig, Deva Hirsch, David Henry Hwang, Mihoko Iida, Matthew Jacobson, Masa and Michan Kabayama, Henry Kellerman, Robin F. Kelly, Clara Kim, Leslie Kim, Erika Kingetsu, Alex and Reiko Kinmont, Jean Hanff Korelitz, Kate Krader, Lauren Kunkler Tang, the Reverend Kate Latimer, Wendy Lamb, Hali Lee, Connie Mazella, Christopher W. Mansfield, Kathy Matsui, Jesper Koll, Nancy Miller, Geraldine Moriba Meadows, Tony and Suzanne O'Connor, Bob Ouimette, Asha Pai-Sethi, Kyoungsoo Paik, Jeff Pine, Cliff and Jennifer

Park, Sunny Park, Tim Piper, Sally Gifford Piper, Sharon Pomerantz, Gwen Robinson, Catherine Salisbury, Jeannette Watson Sanger, Linda Roberts Singh, Tai C. Terry, Henry Tricks, Erica Wagner, Abigail Walch, Nahoko Wada, Lindsay Whipp, Kamy Wicoff, Neil and Donna Wilcox, and Hanya Yanagihara.

My early readers Dionne Bennett, Benedict Cosgrove, Elizabeth Cuthrell, Junot Díaz, Christopher Duffy, Tom Jenks, Myung J. Lee, Sang J. Lee, and Erica Wagner gave me their invaluable time, keen insights, and the necessary courage to persevere. Thank you.

In 2006, I met my agent Suzanne Gluck, and I remain deeply grateful for her friendship, wisdom, and goodness. I want to thank Elizabeth Sheinkman, Cathryn Summerhayes, Raffaella De Angelis, and Alicia Gordon for their brilliant work and generous faith. I am thankful to Clio Seraphim for her thoughtful support.

Here I declare my profound gratitude to my amazing editor Deb Futter, whose clear-eyed vision, superb intelligence, and exceptional care shaped this book. Thank you, Deb. My brilliant publisher Jamie Raab has supported my writing from the very beginning, and I am thankful to call Jamie my friend. I want to acknowledge the very talented people at Grand Central Publishing and the Hachette Book Group: Matthew Ballast, Andrew Duncan, Jimmy Franco, Elizabeth Kulhanek, Brian McClendon, Mari Okuda, Michael Pietsch, Jordan Rubinstein, Karen Torres, and Anne Twomey. I am very grateful to Chris Murphy, Dave Epstein, Judy DeBerry, Roger Saginario, Lauren Roy, Tom McIntyre, and the excellent salespeople of HBG. Also, many thanks to my fantastic copy editor Rick Ball. As ever, many thanks to the wonderful Andy Dodds, whose passion and excellence inspire me. I thank the exquisite Lauren Cerand.

Here, I want very much to thank these tremendous individuals at my UK publishing house for their faith and support: Neil Belton, Madeleine O'Shea, and Suzanna Sangster. Thank you.

Mom, Dad, Myung, and Sang: thank you for your love. Christopher and Sam: You fill my life with wonder and grace. Thank you for being my family.

MJL

About the Author

Min Jin Lee is the national bestselling author of *Free Food for Millionaires*, and has received the New York Foundation for the Arts fellowship for Fiction, the Peden Prize for Best Story, and the Narrative Prize for New and Emerging Writer. She has written for the *New York Times*, *Condé Nast Traveler*, the London *Times*, *Vogue*, the *Wall Street Journal*, and *Food & Wine*, among others. For more information, please visit MinJinLee.com.